Other Books In This Series

Tesseracts 1
edited by
Judith Merril

Tesseracts 2
edited by
Phyllis Gotlieb & Douglas Barbour

Tesseracts 3
edited by
Candas Jane Dorsey & Gerry Truscott

Tesseracts 4
edited by
Lorna Toolis & Michael Skeet

Tesseracts 5
edited by Robert Runté & Yves Maynard

Tesseracts 6
edited by
Robert J. Sawyer & Carolyn Clink

Tesseracts 7
edited by
Paula Johanson & Jean-Louis Trudel

Tesseracts 8
edited by
John Clute & Candas Jane Dorsey

Tesseracts Nine
edited by
Nalo Hopkinson and Geoff Ryman

Tesseracts Ten
edited by
Robert Charles Wilson and Edo van Belkom

Tesseracts Eleven
edited by
Cory Doctorow and Holy Phillips

TesseractsQ
edited by
Élisabeth Vonarburg & Jane Brierley

New Novellas of Canadian Fantastic Fiction
Tesseracts Twelve

Foreword by Brett Alexander Savory

Edited by Claude Lalumière

EDGE

EDGE SCIENCE FICTION AND FANTASY PUBLISHING
AN IMPRINT OF HADES PUBLICATIONS, INC.
CALGARY

Copyright © 2008

All individual contributions copyright
by their respective authors

This is a work of fiction. Names, characters, places, and incidents are the products of the author's imagination or are used fictitiously and are not to be construed as real. Any resemblance to actual events, locales, organizations, or persons, living or dead, is entirely coincidental.

EDGE

Edge Science Fiction and Fantasy Publishing
An Imprint of Hades Publications Inc.
P.O. Box 1714, Calgary, Alberta, T2P 2L7, Canada

In-house editing by Brian Hades
Interior design by Brian Hades
Cover Illustration by Michael Oswald
ISBN-13: 978-1-894063-15-9

All rights reserved. No part of this book may be reproduced, scanned, or distributed in any printed or electronic form without written permission. Please do not participate in or encourage piracy of copyrighted materials in violation of the author's rights. Purchase only authorized editions.

EDGE Science Fiction and Fantasy Publishing and Hades Publications, Inc. acknowledges the ongoing support of the Canada Council for the Arts and the Alberta Foundation for the Arts for our publishing programme.

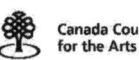

Alberta Foundation for the Arts   Canada Council for the Arts   Conseil des Arts du Canada

FIRST EDITION
(i-20080914)
Printed in Canada
www.edgewebsite.com

Contents

Foreword
    Brett Alexander Savory 1

Ancients of the Earth
    Derryl Murphy 3

Beneath the Skin
    Michael Skeet & Jill Snider Lum 31

Intersections
    Grace Seybold 79

The Story of the Woman and Her Dog
    E. L. Chen 110

Ringing the Changes in Okotoks, Alberta
    Randy McCharles 141

Wonjjang and the Madman of Pyongyang
    Gord Sellar 176

Wylde's Kingdom
    David Nickle 233

Afterword
    Claude Lalumière 281

Biographies 283

Foreword

I'm a writer, so I have a lot of friends who read. I'm also a Canadian, so I have a lot of friends who are Canadian. In these many Canadian readers'/writers' homes, the series of anthologies that each of them has at least one of is *Tesseracts*. It is the only currently running series of spec-fic anthologies that focuses entirely on Canadian writers. And, for that, we should be thankful. We all know that there should be more. But the publishing business hangs on to the idea that anthologies don't sell particularly well — which sucks for those of us who love short stories.

I've been publishing short fiction at my webzine, *ChiZine: Treatments of Light and Shade in Words,* since 1997, and I was lucky to secure a sponsorship deal that enabled me to just buy the stories and concentrate on the editorial side of things. Most webzines — and print zines, for that matter — aren't so lucky. Unlike anthology editors, I don't need to worry about "the bottom line." So long as I can show that people are coming to the site, my sponsors are happy. Subscriber bases for print zine editors and "numbers of copies" sold for anthology editors are less nebulous markers that make it incredibly difficult for editors to convince publishers to take a chance on short stories. Novels are potentially the big money-makers, and novels are fine, but the short story gets short shrift, so we lovers of the form have to embrace it wherever it thrives.

And it thrives in the *Tesseracts* series.

I won't go into the star-studded cast of past volumes' editors because, if you're reading this, you probably already know all the names. And, excuse my French, but adding Claude Lalumière to that list is a great idea.

When Claude asked me to do the foreword to this year's volume, I was taken aback. I mean, *Tesseracts* is science fiction, isn't it? Or, okay, maybe it's SF and fantasy, and here's me with my dark, weird, surreal, disturbing back catalogue of dare-I-say-it *horror* short stories and novels. So, despite being incredibly honoured and flattered to have been asked, I was also a bit confused. But then I thought about it and realized that the genre lines in the series aren't nearly so clear cut — and I knew they would be even less so in Claude's hands. If anyone was going to buy fiction that blurred those lines, it would be Claude.

Okay, so Claude and *Tesseracts* are helping keep the battle-fatigued arena of short fiction alive for one more year. Wonderful. I couldn't be happier. But then I find out Claude's going one step further — he's going to put together an anthology of *novellas*. If there's one kind of fiction that's even harder to market than short-story anthologies, it's novellas. Publishers reading this right now are crossing themselves and shuddering violently just seeing the word in print. A dirtier word I do not think they know. So I'm not sure what kind of black magic Claude used on the publishers of *Tesseracts* to get them to agree to this, but I'm certainly glad it worked. The world needs more novellas. Some tales don't fit into short stories, nor do they need to languidly spread out into novels. For some story arcs, the novella is the baby bear of lengths.

The novellas on offer here are strange and fascinating tales, each one stamped with its author's specific brand of storytelling. These — as with all other *Tesseracts* stories over the past 20+ years — are not stories that could have been written by anyone else. They belong in *this* book, edited by *this* editor, told at *this* length, and read by *this* audience: you, the ones who have enabled this series to continue to flourish as it has — and hopefully will for many years to come.

As a Canadian writer and reader, I couldn't be prouder of this series, nor more thankful to Claude, who has assembled an incredibly varied and remarkable bunch of novellas that, hopefully, will encourage more publishers to take a chance on this length of fiction. But, even if none ever do, we have this one.

Strip away the names of the publisher, the editor, and the authors and forget about the word count — we'll *still* have these stories.

And it is for that which I am most thankful.

Brett Alexander Savory
Toronto, March 2008

Ancients of the Earth
Derryl Murphy

Through the frozen streets of Dawson, Samuel runs from two cavemen.

They're well-dressed, these cavemen, one of them even in tie and tails. But their hair is long and scraggly, and Samuel would almost swear that their brows protrude slightly; aside from the already out-of-place fancy dress, they're a neanderthalian version of your typical northerner, not at all worried about the niceties of polite society, here at the ass end of the nineteenth century.

Except that most northerners, even trappers and prospectors who spend almost all of their time alone in the bush, can speak in more than grunts and gibberish, and Samuel doubts even the most ruthless of them would be so keen to smash in his skull.

It is late in the evening, and the temperature is most certainly below minus twenty. Samuel rounds a corner, skidding on packed snow and patches of ice, but he retains his balance. Down an alley to his right he catches a glimpse of two more, one a cavewoman, resplendent in a glittering evening gown, which is up around her waist as the male apparently has his way with her from behind. They both yell inarticulately as Samuel passes them by but do not break off their primeval assignation.

Another yell tells him the first two cavemen are back on his trail.

He rounds another corner, and the door to a dilapidated cabin swings open. From the blackness within a voice quietly calls to him. "Quickly! Inside!"

Samuel does as he is bid, and the door closes behind him. It is darker inside than out; he can see nothing, but outside, over the pounding of the blood in his temples, he hears the footsteps of the two cavemen going past and strains to listen as they fade into the distance.

He hears his rescuer stand and shuffle over to the window. In the sliver of light allowed in from outside, he can see now who it is. "How'd you get here?" he asks.

She puts a finger to her lips and holds up her other hand, and pretty soon two more sets of footsteps go running by, accompanied by words in a guttural, prehistoric tongue. When they're gone she sits on the floor beside him. "They saw me when they first arrived, but I don't think they're after me. Still, I came here to stay safe until they're gone."

Samuel frowns. "How do you get to be so lucky? The moment they saw me I could see they wanted to get all over me like sled dogs on a bone."

She takes his hand and feels at the makeshift bandage he still has wrapped there. "I think you know."

TWENTY-TWO DAYS EARLIER

Two miners managed to melt and dig their way through a patch of ice and permafrost at the bottom of a stub of a cliff, and there they found the remains of a strange and large creature. News spread round the town, and soon a gaggle of onlookers stood in the mud surrounding the site, watching as the still-frozen remains were dug up.

Once the creature was finally completely disinterred from its grave of ice and soil, several of the bystanders allowed that they thought it looked something like an elephant. Perhaps a circus had come through town, one time long before anyone there could remember, and one of the beasts had passed on and been taken out into the bush and pitched over the edge of the cliff and then had somehow been missed by the wolves and crows until it had finally been swallowed by the frozen earth.

No, by consensus that didn't seem at all likely.

Standing in the cold wind, staring down at the remains of an alien creature that looked as if it could have died just yesterday, one of the miners had the idea to fetch Samuel. He was book smart, was Samuel, a former schoolteacher who'd come north to make his fortune in a fashion that involved as few personal ties and relationships as possible.

Unlike the miners who had discovered the creature, when the gold rush had petered out Samuel had given up on his stake and settled into his one-room cabin, writing the odd dispatch for the local rag and tutoring ill-lettered prospectors in exchange for flakes of gold dust or odd fossils that they felt had no value. Once Fanny Alice had even given him a molar from what Samuel assumed was a mammoth, one that she'd been given by a customer, and that tooth — larger than his fist, yellowed and dirty and well-worn from an apparently long life of grinding down vegetation — held a special place of pride in his small collection. She had told him that it had special "properties," but he had dismissed that as exaggeration.

It so happened that Samuel was just bidding farewell to one of his students — scraggly and unkempt, smelling of tallow and burnt caribou flesh, as they all did — when a small crowd seemed to spontaneously form on the icy patch of road beside his sagging grey front stoop. He blinked in surprise at the sight of so many people, wondering if perhaps he'd drunkenly promised a group lesson the other night while consuming his self-assigned monthly allotment of alcohol.

"We need you to come see somethin', Samuel," said a trapper named Ozark who had a line not too far from town and who would come into town for drinks himself. "Mick and Temple come up with some strange creature while they was diggin' at their claim, and we figure you're the man who can tell us what the hell it is."

Samuel scratched his head. "A creature, you say. How do you mean, like a bear or something?"

"Nope," said Fanny Alice, who was out pretty early in the day considering the line of work she was in. "Bigger than that. Looks somethin' like a smaller version of Jumbo the elephant."

It turned out to not be an elephant. At least, not exactly. The creature was still young, that much was apparent. Not just the fact that it was only about five feet tall at the shoulder, but also that there was something ineffably youthful about its appearance, like how a puppy could easily be distinguished from an adult dog. Excepting, of course, that this creature was not actually a dog.

It had a trunk, just like an elephant, but its ears were small and its tusks were still just ivory nubs, and it was covered with thick reddish-brown fur. It lay on its side in the partially frozen mud, and Samuel could see that a puddle was beginning to form below its belly as it thawed in the weak mid-day sun, which was soon to disappear behind the small overhang immediately behind Samuel.

After a moment or two of searching, Samuel found his voice. "That's no elephant," he said, and he jumped down into the mud beside the beast. "It's a woolly mammoth." He grinned up at Fanny Alice. "A young one probably of the same type as the one that tooth you gave me last year came from."

"A woolly what?" asked one of the miners.

"Mammoth," said Samuel. "Probably an ancestor or distant cousin of the elephant, from many — many — thousands of years ago." He looked back down at the animal's corpse. "Maybe even longer."

"An antediluvian beast somehow washed up on our frozen and landlocked shores," said Pete Marliss, pushing his way to the front of the crowd. Pete was a town councilman, a large and florid man with a full thatch of white hair and an equally white and bristly beard. He was also a local hotelier as well as a lapsed Presbyterian minister who still sometimes exhibited signs of that faith. "Certainly anything older than the time of Noah is, of course, impossible. It seems obvious to me that this poor unfortunate beast was unlucky enough to step off the edge of the ark one unfortunate night, perhaps as the result of a stumble when the vessel bumped up against an iceberg. Its poor mate likely spent the rest of its days alone and despondent, aware that she was the last of her kind."

Samuel glared at Pete for a moment, astonished by his delusional line of reasoning, but after searching for the right words he finally shrugged in response. He knew from tired experience that there was no sense in stepping into an argument with Pete. Instead, he turned his attention back to the baby mammoth and put his hand on its shaggy coat and instantly felt the shock of ages drift past and run up through his arm and through his body, grappling with his memories all the way. For a fraction of a second he saw and smelled a different world, enormous stretches of gleaming white punctuated by small oases of green, and then he felt himself stumble as a dreadful pain lanced into his right side.

He snatched his hand away and sat down hard on the mud beside the creature, rubbing his ribs until the ghost pain died away. When he finally thought to once again pay attention to his surroundings, he saw that Fanny Alice was bending over and had her hands on his face, trying to get his attention.

"I'm with you," he said, and gingerly he stood again. "Sorry about that. I don't know what happened there."

Now, it was widely accepted that Fanny Alice was not the best-looking woman ever to practice her trade, but it was also well known that she had some conjuring skills and that some of those skills involved activities in the non-marital bed. But other skills of hers had nothing to do with physical bliss, and she was often useful that way, seeing the magic in life when others might have completely missed it.

This, Samuel was sorry to realize, appeared to be one of those times.

"Somethin's reached out and touched you," she said, and she herself reached out and put a hand on his side, where he'd felt the sharp pain. "I don't know that I recognize it, but I can tell you that I don't like it. It looked like very old magic, and very powerful as well. Certainly different than the magic in that tooth I gave you."

Samuel's own experiences with magic had been low-key and usually from a great remove. He was disinclined to think that this had been anything other than sheer imagination, him working himself into a state of great agitation and excitement over such a discovery. At worst, though, it could only have been an echo of something from thousands of years before, long dead and forgotten but still hanging in the fabric of the world, like ripples at the edge of a large pond long after the rock had been dropped. So he smiled and shook his head in disagreement. "I'm just fine, Fanny Alice, and you can be assured that there was no magic involved. Only me being overwhelmed by the idea of reaching across millennia and touching flesh that could as easily have been alive only days before." He walked away from her and from the corpse of the mammoth, stepping gingerly even though the pain had long since faded. "I'll tell Ed he should get down here and take a picture for the paper. And maybe we should consider getting word out to some scientists somewhere." Suddenly completely and mind-numbingly exhausted, Samuel raised his hand to bid them all farewell and shuffled back to town and to his cabin, fighting the urge the whole way to look back over his shoulder in case he was being followed.

No, not followed. Stalked.

※┉┋┉┋┉※

The herd is in a panic, spread out across the open land, any hope of working together defensively gone, scattered to the cold winds as effectively as each member of the herd. He runs, terror crushing his heart and his breathing ragged and punctuated by desperate pleas to his mother, to any of the aunties, but none of them answer.

He risks a turn of his head and sees that the two-legs are still after him, coming up the side of the hill. They raise their sticks, and some are thrown at him. He feels a horrible pain in his side and stumbles and bleats in fear and pain but regains his feet and continues running. But then one of the aunties comes to his rescue and heads off the creatures running hard on his heels. A toss of her head sends several of them flying through the air, and he is free of them, still running, still feeling that agonizing pain in his side but unwilling to stop while fear remains.

The ground gives way, and he first stumbles and then falls and falls some more. Pain returns, but after a few moments that fades away, as does everything else.

❖❖❖

Weird dreams plagued Samuel's night, and he awoke with the pain in his right side renewed. He lay there for a spell, unwilling to jump from his warm cocoon of a bed and dash for the stove to rekindle the fire before having to make an even madder and colder dash to the corner to piss in his bucket. Staring at the ceiling, though, all he could think of was that dead animal and the fact that he was likely the only one in town who knew just how significant and important it was.

Having an interest in things prehistoric, Samuel fancied himself knowledgeable about fossils and such. But he thought it pretty obvious that you didn't need to have even a marginal interest to know that a find such as the frozen body of the baby mammoth would be of vital importance to scientists and to newsmen. *Pretty obvious* often didn't cut through the fat up here, though, since you could never tell just how capable any one person was at recognizing what was required of them in a social situation.

And so with a strangled cry he threw back the covers and jumped out of bed, the cold floor clawing at him even through his woollen socks, the air working quickly to find its way to his skin through his undergarments. The embers were low, but some dry kindling and a few choice gusts from his lungs got the flames hopping again, and after adding a small log he ran to the corner and did his morning business, desperately happy to tuck things in when he was done and run back to the stove to put on a pot of two-day-old coffee and feel the tenuous curtain of heat reach slowly outward from the fire and find its way to the farthest corners of the cabin.

Once his fingers were warm enough and the jolt of tar-like coffee had re-ignited his brain, he gave the juvenile mammoth more thought. Obvious as it was to him, he knew he couldn't rely on anyone else from town to do the right thing about the animal. He'd told Ed to go down and get a picture, but wasn't sure if that would translate itself to an attempt to get the news out to the world at large. If anything, he feared that instead it would result in someone contacting some two-bit circus impresario, and there would go any chance for any true science to be done. Or worse, someone with magical powers, either real or imagined, would make some wild and bizarre claim about the creature that would lead to some freakish hoodoo rites being performed as its body was burned at a makeshift altar.

He had a quick breakfast and then got dressed, all the while working through his mind how he could word a telegram to make the most impact, convince people to come here at this time of year rather than them asking for the corpse to be packed in a railroad car full of blocks of ice and shipping it on to Skagway and then south by boat to California. An hour later he found himself at the telegraph office, pen and paper in hand, dashing off a note to his sister's husband in Toronto. The fellow was a teacher and was smart enough to know whom to approach and how to do so.

Unfortunately, Fanny Alice's words kept drifting back into his head every time he made to write his message, and several fits and starts were only able to produce sad attempts such as "Mystical find of great value, send help" and "Dead baby mammoth. Frozen. Of interest to someone warmer" and "Frozen mammoth body dug up nearby, how did it die?" This last was moderately conversational but not at all useful in getting across the main point, which was of course that someone with a modicum of expertise needed to come north forthwith and be here to supervise any investigations into the former life of this extinct creature.

He shook his head to clear it of all of Fanny Alice's nonsense about magic. Finally, he decided he needed to splurge for a few extra words, and soon enough the message was sent. "Frzn baby mammoth found whole. Get news out. None here qualified. Hurry." Satisfied, he left the office and headed over to see what Ed had for photos and how he intended to run with the story, perhaps even talk him into allowing Samuel to write something about the beast and what he knew of its former life.

Ed was at his desk wearing his shit-eating grin when Samuel walked in. "You done good telling me to go out and get a picture of that beast, Samuel!" He jumped up and ran to the darkroom and hurried out with a handful of pictures he'd taken of the mammoth, all but one with Mick and Temple, the miners who'd found the creature, posing beside the body. The exception was a picture of the baby mammoth with Pete Marliss, doing his best to look important. Even in a moderately out-of-focus photograph he managed to look like a stuffed-shirt blowhard.

"Glad it worked out for you," said Samuel. "Bet you one of these pictures ends up in a big paper down south somewhere."

Ed grinned again. "Just about guaranteed, I'd say. I sent a telegram first thing when I got back from taking the pictures yesterday. Pretty sure there'll be some newsmen coming up from Edmonton, or maybe across from Alaska. And my pictures'll be the only ones they can use!" He sounded positively gleeful at this.

Samuel scratched his head but couldn't help smiling in response to Ed's infectious good humour. "Hell, Ed," he responded, "there's no guarantee that they won't bring along their own photographer or at least send along someone who's capable of using a camera."

"Yeah, but the body won't be here by the time anybody arrives. Just bones by then, I expect."

This bit of news brought Samuel up short. "How's that again?"

"Jesus, Samuel, what've you been doin' all morning? It's practically all anyone in town has been talkin' about. You even walked right by it when you came through the door." He smiled again and puffed out his chest. "My printing press, and I did the layout for it, too."

Samuel blinked away his momentary rush of confusion and looked over to the door where Ed had waved his finger. On it was tacked a small poster with the words at top big enough, all in capitals and bold type, that he could read them from across the room: **Special Townwide Prehistoric Feast!!!**

"Holy shit, Ed, no," said Samuel in a low and worried voice, and he rushed over the read the rest of the poster.

Come celebrate the amazing mammoth discovery this Saturday night, 7pm, at the Klondiker Hall. $5/head gets you a THREE course meal INCLUDING STEW made of choice cuts from 6 THOUSAND YEAR OLD baby MAMMOTH. Don't miss this once in a lifetime opportunity! Tickets from Pete Marliss.

Without another word to Ed, Samuel ran out the door and down the road to the Klondiker, blood rushing in rage through his head, keen to find Pete and give him a piece of his mind. At the very least.

"Marliss!" shouted Samuel as he slammed through the doors into the hotel lobby. His target looked up from whatever he was working on at the front counter and smiled, but before he could say anything Samuel proceeded to tear into him. "What the blue blazes do you think you're doing, offering up that fossil for a fuckin' *banquet*?"

"I bought the body from Mick and Temple," replied Pete. "It's mine now, and I get to do with it what I like. And since it cost me money, I aim to make back that investment and then some."

Samuel was beside himself with rage, and for a moment he had trouble finding any words. This was a travesty, a crime against science and reason and humanity. Finally, unable to think of anything else but needing to say something in response to the smirk that had formed on Marliss's face, he said, "But you can't! The body should be preserved for the scientists to study."

"I'm sure they'll be happy with a complete skeleton, don't you think? I expect there will be plenty of museums willing to pay for one. And maybe a different one to pay for the hide, too."

Samuel's hands bunched into fists, but before he could take a step toward Marliss the man had calmly placed a shotgun on the counter. Still smiling, he said, "Now, Samuel, you stay calm with me, and I just might have a present to give you." Seeing where Samuel's eyes were looking, he chuckled and said, "No, not a rear full of buckshot."

"Then what? What the hell do you have that I could possibly want?"

Marliss reached under the counter and came up with something small that he tossed across the room to Samuel. It looked like a stone, but just before he caught it he saw that it was a spear point. As his hand closed over it the sharp edge bit into his palm, and for a brief second he could feel his blood spill over the artefact.

And then everything faded away.

⊷⊹•⊹•⊹⊶

There are precisely a hand of them able to hunt, not enough to hold off starvation much longer. This will be their last attempt before they again have to run from the ice and snow, and the shaman knows that the magic for this hunt has to be especially strong.

He starts with a dance that represents their prey, one of the hairy long noses that are still in the valley, eating the last of the green before they also escape the oncoming wall of ice. The five hunters sway in time to his chants, skins and furs dangling loose from scrawny bodies. Outside of the small circle, the women and children and elders watch and wait for him to finish, only the oldest of them able to conceal the desperation and hunger that crosses the faces of the others.

Or the anger. He knows that a ruined hunt this time might indeed do worse than damage his reputation as the holder of the magic, that failure would, at best, result in banishment from the tribe, at worst bring about a demand for his sacrifice, either to feed the tribe through the strong magic that would come from his death or by a more direct and hideous route.

Once done with the dance, but still chanting, he grabs the spear from their strongest hunter and slashes his palm, then takes the hand of each hunter in turn and does the same, intermingling the blood of each of them. He then takes the spear to the outer circle and cuts in turn the palm of each tribe member, until that one spear is imbued with the power of the blood of the shaman's entire tribe, now truly glowing with the strength of their unity of purpose and desire. His words grow stronger, calling down all the magic he knows and much more than that, magic he can sense and see but magic whose full capabilities he is unaware of. Everything in or nothing out. He repeats this ritual with four other spears, although only with his own blood and that of the other hunters, and then presses his bloody hand to the ground beneath his feet, feeds some of his life to the life that surrounds them, an offering in return for the life that he and his tribe plan to take.

It is all he can do. All five spears stand high above the heads of the hunters, sharpened edges crusted over with their blood, power shining from each and every one of them. After a short nod to his young assistant, he shouts the finality of the ritual to the tribe and to the sun and the earth, and they go. The hunters casually wave aside all the calls of goodbye and the imprecations and pleadings, stern and strong and anxious to prove that they can still provide for the tribe, and yet cautious not to show any break in their masks, for fear that they might be seen as weak or afraid.

Normally the shaman would not go with them, but he needs to keep these five in sight and in earshot, make sure that they are not conspiring against him. Certainly these are lean times, but he has kept them all alive through worse than this, and he is not yet ready to hand it all over to his apprentice. He knows that his apprentice does not feel he is ready, either, and so the shaman feels safe leaving him behind with the weaker members of the tribe.

The walk to where the long noses are supposed to be is almost a half a day, leading them away from the running water and over fields and small hills, places mostly still green and alive but increasingly covered in white as snow falls and refuses to melt under the gaze of the weakened sun. As they approach the bottom of the hill that leads to the overlook where their prey should be, the shaman feels relief wash through him, powerful enough to weaken his knees for a moment, when he hears the sounds of the creatures in the distance.

He has the hunters lean their spears inward one last time, all of the points touching, and chants and prays some more, adding strength and luck at this final stage. Then he separates from them, goes to find a safe place from which he can watch the hunt.

The long noses have been tracked by the tribe as they walked their path over this plateau, finding their way through the green and away from the ice. But almost everywhere they've been it has been impossible for the hunters to get close enough to make a kill. So the hunters scouted ahead, and the shaman consulted his secrets, and together they came to an agreement that, on this day at this time, the long noses would be here, in a place where they could be more readily and more safely hunted.

He makes it to the top of the hill and settles in behind some rocks, watches as the hunters flow down the hill, almost invisible even to him. He sees even before they single it out that their target will be a young one, off grazing far from its mother and in the right direction as well.

The hunters jump as one then, screaming and slashing the air with their spears, the magic in the points amplifying everything, noise as well as numbers, and the long noses go wild with fear and scatter in all directions, the young one ever further separated from its mother and the rest of its family. It runs up the hill opposite the shaman — a mistake — as it stumbles on the loose rocks there, and it realizes this mistake and turns to come back down but instead sees what it thinks might be an opening and is running across the side of the hill, somehow managing the increased steepness.

All of the hunters still chase it, and two, including the strongest, raise their arms and hurl their spears. The shaman speaks words to the air to aid the flight of the spears. The words connect, and one spear flies true, stabbing into the side of the young long nose; it stumbles and bleats in agony. He is so sure of the kill to come that he doesn't pay attention, doesn't see the adult long nose rush up the hill until it is already in the midst of the hunters, throwing them angrily through the air with its tusks and crushing them with its huge stamping feet. He is then so intent on watching the future of his tribe die before him that he doesn't see the young long nose lose its footing and fall.

All he can see is that none of the hunters are getting up, or even moving. As the snow begins to fall, heavier and heavier with each passing moment, he searches for and finds one last incantation of magic that he pulls deep from the earth and sends toward the animal that had so indiscriminately killed the hunters of his tribe, the adult long nose... and toward the rest of its herd. The magic is invoked in a fit of anger that the beasts probably do not deserve, but this act of vengeance makes him feel slightly better — for a brief moment. And then he picks his way back down the hill and tries to retrace his path back to his people, all the while worrying at the scab on the palm of his hand.

⋙⋅⊹⋅⊹⋅⊹⋅⋘

Samuel woke up on a chair in Smitty's Barbershop, across the street from the Klondiker. Fanny Alice was there, leaning over him and looking with no small amount of concern into his eyes. "You still in there?" she asked.

He tried to talk, but his mouth was too dry. A moment taken to reinvigorate it with spit, and then Samuel croaked, "I'm fine. How..." He paused, found more spit. "What the hell am I doing here?"

"Ed was worried about you," she replied. "Once he saw you running over to the 'Diker, he came and found some folks who could get you out of there before you went and did somethin' stupid."

"Stupid." Samuel looked down to his hand, saw that it was still balled into a fist, blood crusted underneath his nails and even down to his wrist. He opened it and stared at the spear point, stained with blood both ancient and new. "They tried to kill that mammoth, wanted to eat it." He looked up, saw that Fanny Alice was not the only one in Smitty's, that perhaps a dozen people were there, all watching him with worried eyes. But in Fanny Alice he could see something else, a spark of some sort of recognition.

Smitty himself stepped forward. "Hell, Samuel, ain't nobody coulda killed that mammoth. It was deader than a doorknob when Mick and Temple found it. You know that." He rubbed his hands anxiously, probably worried that with Samuel taking up a seat and everyone in here just standing around he had no chance of getting any business.

Samuel stood up and pocketed the spear point, then with a nod of encouragement from Smitty dipped his hand into a basin of ice-cold water. He spoke as he scrubbed away the dried blood. "It's wrong what Marliss is doing, you know." Nobody interrupted, nobody argued, so he continued on, now drying his hands on his jacket and looking around for a clean cloth he could wrap around the wound on his hand, which he had reopened. "That creature is an amazing find, a find that should be dedicated to science, not to some base desire to consume so precious a rarity."

Looking somewhat aghast at the blood dripping onto the floor, something that shouldn't have bothered him considering his reputation with a razor, Smitty tore off a strip from a relatively clean white towel and handed it to Samuel, then said, "He bought it fair and square, Pete did. I don't see how anybody can stop him from doin' this."

"Besides," interjected Loudon McRae, a trapper who had been one of Samuel's students and had likely come into town to trade some pelts for supplies, "there's plenty of folks who've bought tickets already. I expect if he doesn't watch how many he sells he may have trouble feeding everyone. Just about the whole damn town wants to go, although mostly only the business folk can afford it."

Samuel tapped the pocket where the spear point rested, some small part of him aware that his behaviour was scaring the rest of them. And so instead of carrying on in front of them, with the slightest of nods to Smitty and to Fanny Alice and then the rest, he stalked out the door and headed back home.

The scent of defeat and loss followed along behind him, whether from the here and now or from his prehistoric hallucinations he couldn't be sure. Certainly there was enough to go around.

◆•I••I••I•◆

As the night of the banquet approached, Samuel noticed more and more that the people of Dawson were avoiding him, giving him wide berth wherever he went, and not visiting him for lessons or company when he was home in his cabin. His one attempt to go out for drinks — not at the Klondiker, never again at the Klondiker — was a sour and shortened evening at the Northern Light, a bar poorly populated as most carousers that night were already off celebrating with Pete Marliss, even though the banquet was still a day away. Even the patrons at this bar, though, were unwilling to come near him, lest he harangue them about the atrocities being visited on science and knowledge and their complicity in them.

The day of the banquet he had been out for another unhappy walk, and when he returned to the cabin he saw that two pieces of paper were nailed to his door. The first was a telegram, from a fellow at the Museum of Natural History, all the way down in New York City: *Sending team from Edmonton to preserve/ship mammoth. Pls keep frozen. Advise of any problems.*

He crumpled the telegram into a tight little ball and stuffed it into his pocket as he leaned back against the doorframe. Even if some miracle brought the team into town today, he could be sure the bones had mostly been picked clean by now, what with the banquet only hours away. He thought for a moment about heading back to the telegraph office and sending off a message telling the museum director to recall his team, but then he thought that they could at least recover the skeleton. He left it for the time being, figuring he could spare at least a day before he had to make a hard and fast decision.

The other piece of paper was a yellowed envelope. He opened it carefully and then blew into it to open it wide. Inside were a note and two small chits with numbers on them. He read the note first: *Samule, I know you dont want ta go, but i got theese tikets from a customer and need some one to go with. We dont have to eat the thing, but I figure we shold be there so you can no about it and tell about it. FA.*

Samuel sat down on the porch, heedless of the cold wind blowing up the deserted street. Should he go? He knew that everyone important in town was going to be there and that most of them would be dressing up in their Sunday finest, or even nicer if they had it. He had no nice clothes to speak of, and Fanny Alice had known well enough to suggest that they needn't eat the primeval stew. He sat there and turned things over and over again in his head, trying to find one good reason to go, and then, after finding that, searching for one good reason to turn down the invitation. By the time Fanny Alice came to collect him, he had come up with at least a dozen good reasons in either direction, the last being that it would at least be warm in the banquet hall of the Klondiker after all those hours spent sitting out in the wind.

She helped him pick an outfit that would at least not peg him as a grubstaker just in from the bush, and then they walked on to face the desecration of the past, her hand resting gently on his elbow. In another situation the looks he got when he presented the two tickets would have perhaps made it all worthwhile, but there was no way in hell he was going to grant anyone satisfaction out of this evening, especially himself. He allowed that he would be good company for Fanny Alice and that he needn't harass each diner this evening — his presence here was scold enough, he felt — but that would be the outer limit of whatever good nature he normally had.

It turned out that Marliss had known, or at least hoped, that he was coming and had arranged for Samuel and Fanny Alice to sit at a special table up front, along with Mick and Temple as well as Marliss, his wife (who was decidedly uncomfortable in the presence of Fanny Alice), and the mayor. Upon hearing this Samuel had started to beg off and insist that he would sit in the back, but one look from Fanny Alice had quashed that attempt. She had a way of bringing out the meek in him, he realized.

Drinks weren't a part of the price of the evening, but there was very little grumbling over that situation as pretty much everyone in town knew what Pete Marliss was like and had expected nothing more. But Marliss did buy a round of drinks for the VIP table, and once they arrived he stood on his chair and waited for the crowd of diners, some sixty strong, to quiet down.

"You all know," he started, looking what Samuel thought was pretty damned smug, "that our friends Michael Callahan and Roger Templeton recently found the whole remains of a supposedly ancient baby mammoth—" Someone at another table raised a hand, and Marliss paused, obviously trying very hard to not get angry at being interrupted so early in his speech. "What?"

"Um. *Who* found the mammoth?"

Marliss rolled his eyes and then looked down and gestured to Mick and Temple to stand. When they did, he said, "These guys," which was followed by a lot of muttering and nods as people who had never in their lives heard Mick and Temple's proper names finally understood. Applause followed, and Marliss had to wait even longer, and finally he pointed at their chairs; the two miners, both somewhat red-faced, sat back down.

"As I was saying, Mick and Temple discovered the body, and our friend Samuel Denicola was the one who identified it." More polite applause, although Samuel could see by the looks on the faces of most of those nearby that they were indeed worried that he was here. Marliss carried on. "Now, as you are no doubt aware, there has been some controversy over the final disposition of the body of this creature that Mick and Temple found, but I am here to tell you that I have no doubt more bodies will be found as more of the north is opened up and explored, and I also have no doubt that some of those creatures will be sacrificed on the altar of science rather than the altar of community and business. But with Ed Mortensen here to take a photograph..." Here he paused and gestured at Ed, who was busy setting up his camera on the stage to take a picture of everyone as they tucked into the meal. Again, everyone applauded, and Ed took a second to wave in response. "As I was saying, with Ed here to take a photograph and to write about this historic event, we can be assured of plenty of attention from the outside world. Why, all that coupled with some good and honest hard work, and we may be able to recreate some of the action that we all remember from the peak times of the gold rush. And wouldn't that be something!"

There were cheers and huzzahs at this, and soon enough most people in the room were standing as they applauded. There were few trappers and prospectors who would say they wanted more people coming back to Dawson, but most of the folk in the room that evening were businessmen, people whose livelihoods depended on as much custom as possible. Store owners, bar owners, hotel owners, restaurant owners, now that Samuel was paying attention he could see that most attendees held those occupations; as he'd been told in the barbershop, others from town couldn't afford the tickets, or perhaps had been too late to buy them. At that moment he understood why his hope that the mammoth should have gone to science would have never panned out: too many people in town had a stake in the success of this evening. He sat back in his chair, finally feeling the complete acceptance of defeat.

Marliss sat back down, and the people around Samuel made small talk as they waited for the food. Samuel brooded, idly playing with his silverware and waiting for the first course to arrive. Fanny Alice stirred in her chair, looking increasingly uncomfortable whenever Samuel glanced up at her, but she didn't seem to want to make eye contact with him, so he left her alone.

Waiters finally came out of the kitchen, and Samuel saw that almost all of them were prospectors that Marliss must have hired for the occasion. Each table got a large plate of sourdough bread and a bowl of thin soup, which Marliss stood and announced was the course before the stew and contained nothing from the mammoth. There were more mutterings at this, although Samuel imagined they were likely in relief that this meagre offering wasn't what everyone had come for.

Happy that there was at least something he could eat without feeling guilty, Samuel served Fanny Alice some soup and then spooned some into his own bowl. Then he cut off two slices of bread, saving the heel for himself. For the next ten minutes or so there was little sound aside from the slurping of soup and the clanking of spoons against the sides of bowls. Almost everyone seemed to be rushing through this course, most probably hoping to speed up the main offering of the night.

Knowing he wouldn't be eating the stew Samuel procured himself a second bowl of the soup and another chunk of bread in order to mop up its remnants. Thin though it was, it wasn't at all bad — although the fact that it was free had predisposed him in its favour early on. But soon enough he was done, and the waiter was there to take his dirty dishes away, likely to clean them for reuse with the stew.

There was time then for talk as they waited for the next round. Marliss sat back in his chair and eyeballed Samuel for a moment, a big grin on his face. "Glad to see you're no longer of a mind to harass or attack me, my friend."

Samuel shrugged. "What's done is done. But I don't think you've figured this whole thing out so well."

Marliss cocked an eyebrow. "How so?"

Samuel looked up at the stage where Ed was ready now, waiting to take the photograph once everyone had received their main course. "Any pictures or stories that go out about this, no matter how pretty they dress things up, are going to make us look like a bunch of illiterate, ill-mannered troglodytes. You'll attract few people, and the ones you do get will just be more of the same. Buffoons who have no respect for nature or for history, who are only out to make a fast buck, no matter the cost."

Marliss frowned and leaned forward across the table, glass of whiskey in his right hand. The rest of the hall was dead silent, waiting to hear what came next. "Your *opinion* in this matter is certainly of interest to me, Samuel, but the fact that I am a successful businessman and you are... not, tells me I can value it only so much. I'm sorry that you feel this event will reflect on us so poorly, but that is in fact only one man's opinion, and it must be weighed against the greater good."

Samuel rolled his eyes. "Greater good?" He was about to say more, once again feeling free to rant about money and greed and superstition, but the kitchen doors swung open with a crash and in came the waiters bearing bowls of mammoth stew. The hall erupted in applause and cheers, and while Samuel sat back in his chair with his arms folded, knowing that he looked for all the world like a petulant child who was refusing his supper, bowls of piping hot stew filled with carrots and potatoes and small chunks of extinct mammoth were delivered to all the diners.

A bowl was set in front of Fanny Alice and another was almost given to Samuel, but a glare from him had the waiter beating a hasty retreat. Fanny Alice leaned forward and smelled the stew and immediately her face turned white. "Are you alright?" he asked.

She shook her head. "I don't know. I don't think so." She stood, and so did all the other men at the table — Mrs. Marliss was again discomforted and irritated by this attention to a woman such as Fanny Alice — and then Fanny Alice walked away, out the doors to the lobby. Samuel made to follow her, but the others sat back down, then everyone else in the hall was now digging into their stew, and on the stage Ed decided that that was just the moment to take his photograph. Flash powder went off, a noise that was almost immediately followed by a few grunts and then some strange sort of gibberish.

His eyes momentarily blinded by the powerful explosion of light, Samuel stood there, listening as the sounds around him grew increasingly strange and frightening. When the spots cleared from his eyes he saw that a strange sort of miasma had risen up from the tables, like a greenish-yellow fog, and he was worried for a moment that the flash powder had done serious and permanent damage to his eyes.

But then he heard a grunt from the table to his right, and saw that the fog was rising from the bowls of stew and that it was surrounding and seemingly permeating the people who were eating. They were all making similar, strange noises, not simple grunts of pleasure derived from a meal well enjoyed, but primitive, angry rumbles and groans, accompanied by what he thought were words but that were beyond his comprehension.

Samuel then heard a gasp from the doors where Fanny Alice had exited, but before he could turn that way one of the diners looked up at him, and he saw that this was no longer a citizen of his town, or even a citizen of his time. This was a primitive man of some sort, complete with hair and beard and a furious, equally primitive look that announced that Samuel was no longer safe in this room.

On the other side of the tables, Ed gave a strangled cry and fell back on his rear, and for a moment the attention of the primitive man turned that way, but then his eyes were back full bore on Samuel and with a cry and a stream of gibberish he jumped to his feet and pointed. Around him, other cavemen — Samuel knew full well they had nothing to do with caves, but this was still the term that came to his appalled and frightened mind — jumped to their feet and did the same, and then they launched themselves at him, fighting with each other to get around tables and chairs while struggling with unfamiliar clothing, all of which gave Samuel the slimmest of head starts.

Which is how he found himself running down a darkened, frozen street, being chased by primitive men from another time, beings somehow brought to life by feeding on a stew that also, at least partly, dated from their time.

⊹•✣•✣•⊹

"They think you're the baby mammoth," whispers Fanny Alice in the darkness of the dilapidated cabin.

Samuel nods. "They do."

"Something must have transferred over to you when you touched the body. Some life force, still strong after centuries and centuries."

"But why me?" He does his best to keep his voice low, although his fear and aggravation over the situation threatens to raise it to unsafe levels. "Mick and Temple must have touched the beast digging it out, and I didn't see *them* getting singled out."

"I don't know. What makes you different?"

Samuel reaches into his pocket and pulls out the spear point, fiddles with it while he thinks. "Don't know," he finally answers. "As far as I know, I'm just an ordinary guy. I never claimed to have any special powers or to be able to see any spirits or ghosts or any such nonsense. But then there was the mammoth, and after that there was this."

"That's right, there *is* that." Fanny Alice reaches out and takes the spear point, turns it over in her hands. "What happened to you when you touched the mammoth?"

"I— I became it, I was inside its body while it was running from the hunters."

"And what happened?"

"I — um, no — *it* managed to get away, but then it slipped and fell, and I expect that was when it died."

"Alright, so what about when you touched the spear point?"

"Well, I wonder if it wasn't so much that I touched it as it was that I cut the palm of my hand with it. Then I was in the body of the, uh, the shaman, the medicine man for this tribe that was hunting the mammoth. He did something special, some sort of big magic, with the spears of all the hunters." He closes his eyes for a moment, trying to remember what it was he'd experienced. "But things didn't work out so well. They thought they had the baby, one of them managed to stick it with his spear, but then a big adult mammoth came in with tusks and trunk and feet all going in different directions, attacking all of the hunters, and I'm pretty sure all of them were killed."

Fanny Alice is silent for a moment, and then she says, "We have to get back to your cabin."

Samuel doesn't like the sound of that. Where they are feels as safe as he will ever be, and that's good enough for him. "Why? They've gone running on past, I'm sure things will be just fine when morning comes around."

"They won't, I'm afraid. If the rest of them jumped forward in time to hunt for the baby mammoth, for *you*, then I would think the medicine man did as well. Whatever magic he works, I don't doubt that they'll soon turn to him and ask him to lead them to you."

"Son of a bitch. If you'll pardon me for saying so." Samuel leans his head back against the wall and closes his eyes, feeling completely helpless and hopeless right now. "So how does going to my cabin make this any better for me? Or is it just so I can die in my own home instead of some stranger's place?"

She squeezes his hand. "I never touched that frozen body, Samuel, but I'll bet you that if I had I'd be the one being hunted right now instead of you. There's one other piece of ancient magic that somehow came out of this, something that ties it all together. Can you think of what it might be?"

Samuel casts his mind back, looking through the memories of his current life and memories from his two experiences back in time, once as the baby mammoth, the other time as the shaman. And then he remembers the molar sitting on the shelf beside his wood stove in his cabin. The mammoth molar. "I'll be damned," he whispers. "That tooth. The shaman, he cast a final spell as he left after all the hunters died, something that was meant for the adult mammoth that killed them all. Do you suppose the tooth is from that very animal?"

"I think it's likely. At least, as likely as any of this has been. That last spell he did must have tied everything together, and whatever is happening now it's the remnants of that spell and of any others he cast playing themselves out, all these thousands of years later."

Samuel starts to stand, then catches himself. "Wait," he says. "What the hell do we do when we get the tooth? Do we just bash them over the head with it? Don't know how many I could hit before they got a hold of me and I was skinned to feed the remainder of the tribe, of course."

Fanny Alice stands and then takes Samuel's hand and pulls him fully to his feet. "What's on that spear point that Pete Marliss gave you?"

He strokes the edge gently with his thumb. "Blood," he answers. "My blood, and the blood of the shaman..."

At first he doesn't know what the feeling is, having never

sensed it before, but suddenly he knows how this could work, how everything over the eons connects to this one point of time and space. His voice quavers with wonder as he finishes his sentence, the pieces all slowly coming together: "And of the entire tribe."

"And?"

"And..." He tightens his grip on the artefact. "Blood from the baby mammoth!" He leans forward and looks out the window, happily sees no sign of the cavemen. "So what do we do with the tooth when we get there?"

"I'm not really sure," she answers. "All we can do is hope an idea reveals itself to us."

Samuel shrugs and grunts.

One last check out the window, and then the door is open, and they are running.

⁕⁘⁕⁘⁕

The run to Samuel's cabin is remarkable only in the fact that so much of it is rather unremarkable. Every noise and every shifting of shadow sends his heart jumping and his mind racing off into new and frightening territory, but for almost the whole distance there is no sign at all of his Paleolithic pursuers. He begins to think that this might be his lucky day, but then he notices that Fanny Alice, whose hand he is holding, is chanting something as she runs, and he realizes that she is using what magic she has, probably to keep them off his trail.

Then they round the final corner, and he can see his cabin down the street, but Fanny Alice slips on the ice. As she falls to the street, she loses her grip on him and stops her steady stream of incantations. Just like that, the protection or charm or whatever it is has been broken, and he hears the shouts and cries of the prehistoric hunting party as they suddenly appear behind him. Samuel reaches down and hauls Fanny Alice to her feet, and they are running again, luckily avoiding the oncoming spears — spears? where did they get spears? — that clatter to the road on either side of them. And then he is inside his cabin and reaching up onto the shelf to pull down the mammoth tooth.

Fanny Alice has for some unknown reason stayed outside, and he tries to pull her in with him, but she pulls harder, and he finds himself standing on the porch, spear point and molar from a long-dead mammoth in his right hand, a lady of the night at his side, and an advancing horde of primitive men and women coming down the street, prepared to kill him and probably to eat him as well. He giggles, prompted by the absurdity of the situation and by a feeling of absolute mental and physical exhaustion.

Fanny Alice stares at him for a second, then takes the molar and puts it down on the street. Then, with the cavemen less than one hundred feet away and their spears quite obviously being prepared for more deadly throws, she grabs Samuel's hand and pulls him until he is standing over top of the tooth. She takes the spear point from him and once again cuts his hand with it, then shakes the resulting blood over top of the tooth. The blood that misses it stains the snow and ice it sits upon.

Samuel hears a strangled cry from the oncoming tribe, and although he never saw his face in his vision, he knows that this must be the shaman, and he also knows that the shaman is aware that what Fanny Alice is doing will have its desired effect. An effect the shaman probably doesn't want, judging by what little Samuel can see of the look on his face and by the tone of his voice.

The others in the tribe react almost instantaneously, arms up and ready to throw their spears to finish this once and forever, but before they can do so the tooth is suddenly gone and Samuel realizes he can no longer see the cavemen. Instead, the only thing he can see is the large, smelly, hairy rear end of a very large mammoth.

No, scratch that. Several very large mammoths. Lots and lots of very large mammoths.

He jumps backward and would have fallen if not for tumbling right into the arms of Fanny Alice. The mammoths, every one of them, recognize the smell of the creatures who took away their young one all those millennia ago, and with trumpeting and a cataclysmic stamping of feet launch themselves toward them, bent on retribution. Samuel can't see them, but he assumes that the entire tribe of cavemen turn and run. By the time the mammoths have disappeared from view, the streets are completely empty.

Samuel looks at Fanny Alice, and he can tell by the look on her face that she feels every bit as bewildered as he does. One, maybe, but an entire herd...! A question comes to his lips even as he knows she wonders the same thing: "What do we do now?"

EIGHT WEEKS LATER

Springtime in the north. Things still green up slower here than they do anywhere civilized, but Samuel wouldn't have it any other way. The team sent from Edmonton arrived at the same time as the reporter from the *Globe*, having taken a train from Skagway after discovering that they needed to go through Vancouver. Time was wasted by both parties because of this, but knowledge of geography this far north is not the strong suit of most people who live in more temperate climes.

Of course they were all angry, even furious, when they arrived to discover what had been done to the body of the baby mammoth. The men who had been sent by the museum were especially furious at such a waste, while the reporter had gotten over his initial displeasure when he realized that there was a new and very different story in all this.

But moods changed when Samuel told them all that there was now a herd of woolly mammoths currently living only a few miles out of town, followed for the moment in their circuit by a freshly minted Paleolithic tribe of undetermined origin, some fifty strong. Very quickly more telegrams were sent out, and word came back that scientists and reporters were coming from all over the world, as well as Canadian Government officials who needed to deal with the situation of all these refugees from another time.

As for Samuel, he hopes that, once the caribou come through, the cavemen will abandon their attachment to the mammoths and move on to follow those much more plentiful and easy-to-kill animals. And then there's their obsession with Samuel: twice now they've stalked him through the streets of Dawson, and twice now one of the woolly mammoth aunties has come to his rescue, all of this to the consternation of the other citizens of Dawson.

It's not the attempts to kill him with spears that he minds so much as it is the smell of the mammoths that lingers on his clothes and in his hair.

Beneath the Skin

Michael Skeet & Jill Snider Lum

Hirota Satoshi rolled over, became aware of the green smell of new tatami, and was, for a moment, completely lost. *Where's the blood?* he thought. It had been all over his fingers, but when he tried lifting his hands something held them.

Then he smelled sandalwood and the delightful pulse-quickening tang of a woman, and the bad dream receded into shadows and was forgotten.

He felt his mouth curve up. Forcing an eye open, he confirmed that the sun had not yet risen. The futon was soft and warm. So: he still had no idea where he was, but it was a good place; that much was certain. He rolled onto his back again. His leg brushed against silk.

"Hirota-san?" The woman's voice was low and flowed sensually over the syllables of his name. The sound brought memory — and desire — back to him in a wonderful rush.

"Good morning," he said, reaching for her, questing through layers of silk and — what *was* she wearing? — until he was stroking soft skin. "Dawn isn't here yet, Akemi."

"Then we don't have to get out of bed yet," she said. "It isn't as though I need to be back in the women's quarters before dawn. Or ever again."

The pleasure in her voice made his heart beat even faster. "Prince Isao was a fool to give you away," he said. "What could he have been thinking?"

"I like the way he thinks, Hirota-san," said Akemi. "And I definitely like—"

"I can think of several ways to finish that sentence, none of which involve the prince." Satoshi slid his hand along the curves and planes of her as best he could through the maze of fabric, until his searching hand encountered a breast. "So why not let me do the thinking for us both, for at least a while longer?" He brushed the tip of a finger across her nipple.

"As you wish, my lord." He could hear her smile as she reached for him.

※❖※❖※

"Why are you still here?" Masa glared down at Satoshi, shifting in the saddle as if insulted by the fact that he couldn't pace while on horseback. "You are supposed to be meeting Prince Isao this morning."

"The old man won't be awake yet, Masa. They do things differently in the capital, Elder Brother."

"My name is Masahiro," Masa said. "I am the head of the family and your sworn lord. You will treat me with respect, Satoshi. How many times do I have to remind you?" He glared, his face reddening. "My patience with you will not last forever."

When will you learn that I'm still on your side? Satoshi thought. He didn't want to fight, though, especially not after such a lovely night. So instead he bowed his head, saying, "I'm sorry, Masahiro — Hirota-san. I'll go and wake the prince. You have a safe journey back to Ikewara. I'll send messengers to let you know how Hideki and I are doing."

"You should have left him in Ikewara. Hideki is a disgrace to his family, to his swords, and to our clan. To say nothing of the negative influence he has on you."

Satoshi pulled his kimono tighter around him. It was cool this morning; he wanted tea — or, better still, warm sake. "I was always under the impression," he said, "that I was the bad influence on him. That's what his mother says, anyway."

"She does? I will have her punished for the insult to the family."

Satoshi sighed. "Masahiro, I was joking. You don't have to punish anybody. Arai-san has the utmost respect for you, as does her son. We all respect you." *Even when you're a fool — which is more and more often, these days.* Satoshi bowed his head again, hoping he looked appropriately cowed and respectful.

He was saved further annoyance and embarrassment by the arrival of Masa's escort: a dozen mounted samurai, all armoured, and their bearers. Satoshi knew that some thought it in poor taste to wear armour on the road, or indeed anywhere other than a battlefield, but the roads weren't safe — in his twenty years he had never known a single month in which there hadn't been fighting somewhere as the clans struggled for ascendancy — and the roads around the capital were especially bad.

"You see?" he said. "Now you can set out for home without delay." Satoshi smiled.

"Very well. Now get yourself to the prince and earn that gift he sent you yesterday. Find out why he's complaining and why the taxes he owes aren't being paid. Resolve the situation so you can get back to Ikewara as soon as possible. This isn't a holiday." Masahiro scowled — at Satoshi, at the cold, at the entirety of creation, perhaps — as he kicked his horse into motion.

"A *holiday*?" Satoshi looked beyond the guesthouse, to the capital huddled below these hills, and tried to count the burned-out shells of temples and homes destroyed during the latest round of fighting. "He thinks I'm going to enjoy this?"

"Your brother is an unhappy man, I think."

Satoshi turned. Akemi had appeared behind him. She had come so quietly he hadn't even heard the sound of her wooden sandals on the frozen earth. "Masahiro has a lot to think about, perhaps too many responsibilities," he said, resenting a little the uncontrollable urge to defend his brother. "The role of daimyo is a difficult one."

"All true," she said, her voice soft and low, pitched for him alone, "but he should still show you more respect than he does. Command and leadership are more effectively exercised without arrogance."

He stepped back from her. "Akemi," he said, "my brother is evidently not the only unhappy person this morning. Is something bothering you?" Then he realized what might be upsetting her. *Why can't life ever be simple?* he asked himself. "Is it something to do with the prince? Is there something I need to know about?" It was ridiculous to be so infatuated so quickly.

"No, there is nothing to do with the prince," she said. "It's interesting, though, that you thought I might be unhappy. Most men don't notice their women. I think I would be wise to keep my thoughts to myself, if I'm to continue being your concubine." She smiled, but something in the way she showed her teeth made Satoshi shiver with more than the morning's cold. Looking down, he realized that he'd crossed his arms to protect his belly.

"Oh, Hirota-san," she said, laughing. "You don't have to fear me. I'm not spying for Prince Isao; and any way, nobles like him have no power, not over samurai. Remember — your brother called *Isao-sama* to account, not the other way around."

"All true," he said, liking the boldness in her that would have bothered some men. "And yet, I still have the strongest sense that I should keep some parts of myself safe from those lovely, sharp little teeth."

She laughed again, and this time her smile was of such genuine delight that he was soon laughing with her. "Will you accompany me to the prince's mansion this morning?" he asked. She wore multiple kimonos, but she wasn't really dressed for travel. He hoped she wouldn't make him wait too long.

"No, I would only be in the way. I will be of more use to you getting this house into suitable condition, should you wish to entertain or should a second meeting with the prince be necessary." Satoshi grinned, pleased that she had anticipated his wishes — well, his brother's orders. Left to his own desires, Satoshi would have been happier meeting the prince in a warm, cozy tavern beside the river or on the Philosopher's Path. But Masa had insisted on a demonstration of the family's prestige and power — such as they were. Hence his moving into the shogun's guesthouse, scarcely used in the years of the shogun's retirement from earthly concerns. This being the case, though, who better to have as a mistress of the guesthouse — in all senses of the word — than this beautiful former possession of a prince of ancient lineage? How lucky had he been that Isao had sent her to him the day before — presumably as soon as the older man had learned it was Satoshi, and not Masa, he'd be dealing with — and, even more, that she had been so taken with him? *I wonder what he sent Masa.*

"I have to agree with you," he said. "Not that you would be in my way, but that someone does have to take this place in hand." He checked the sun's height. "And I have my own challenge. I have to wake Arai-san."

"No need. Arai-san is here, and with sustenance." Satoshi turned from Akemi to find Hideki standing in an open doorway, a flask of steaming sake in one large hand. "I bought this on Philosopher's Path," he said. "It's better than what was here. I had to sign your name for it—" he waved the paper he held in his other hand "—but I'm good for it." He tucked the paper back inside his kimono; when his hand emerged again it held two cups. "We want to be fortified for our day's work, brother." Stepping down from the house, he filled a cup and handed it to Satoshi. Then he filled the second cup. "To your good health, brother."

"And yours." Satoshi drained his cup. "An auspicious start to our journey."

"Please don't make it too auspicious." Akemi's expression was not friendly, and for a moment Satoshi was concerned. Then he relaxed, realizing that Hideki was the object of her displeasure. Hideki prompted that response in many people, especially women. Sometimes people — Masa, for instance — responded that way even though they knew Hideki well, knew of his loyalty, his cleverness, his tenacity. "Prince Isao may not have much power," Akemi said when she saw Satoshi looking at her, "but he prides himself on his manners. You will not impress him if you arrive at his mansion drunk before mid-morning."

"Never fear, my lady disdain," Hideki said with a conspiratorial grin. "It takes much, *much* more than the contents of this tiny thing—" he waved the flask "—to get me drunk. This is just a little something to warm our journey."

"Speaking of which," said, Satoshi, "it's time we began it."

◈⊹┼⊹┼⊹◈

"It's prettier in the hills," Hideki muttered. "We should have made the prince come to us. Better still, we should have stayed in Ikewara. The sake there is so much better than this slop. I wouldn't feed this to fish." He drained his cup.

"There are plenty of burned temples and homes in the hills, too," Satoshi said. He called on Amida Buddha as they passed a giant bird's nest of blackened posts and timbers. A ragged old peasant picked over the ruins. "I wish the shogun was stronger."

"The way your brother is strong?" Hideki flicked his reins, evidently anxious to put the ruined temple behind them. "If you think your life is busy now, Satoshi, imagine what it would be like with a bigger Masahiro passing judgment over every aspect of it. Chaos may be bad for some people, but it makes it a lot easier for those like us to enjoy ourselves undisturbed."

Mention of his brother brought something to the fore of Satoshi's mind. "Tell me," he said, "has anything struck you as unusual or odd about this tax problem of the prince's? Taxes are paid in rice, and while we don't know the prince at all I'm pretty sure he—"

He didn't finish. The capital and its early morning quiet vanished; Satoshi found himself, sweaty and bloodied, standing in a field of golden rice. A man knelt before him, head lowered. The man's right arm ended at the wrist in a dripping, dirt-encrusted stump. Satoshi tasted blood; a katana flashed — his own, he realized — and the stranger's head fell among the rice stalks. Satoshi reached down, grabbed the blood-spattered hair...

"Hey, brother! You've cut yourself!"

Satoshi found himself back in Heian-kyo. On the ground. Hideki was looking down at him; so was his horse, and the latter wore an expression suggesting amusement.

"Did the horse throw me?" That would be deeply embarrassing.

"No," said Hideki, lifting him up — when had his friend become so strong? — "nothing so entertaining. You just slumped forward, then slid off the saddle. Must have hit the stirrup on your way down." That explained the blood, at least. Satoshi touched his forehead. The wound, just above his left eye, felt enormous, which meant it was probably no bigger than a grain of rice. "I think you were under a spell there," Hideki said.

"It was my nightmare," Satoshi said. "I woke suddenly, before dawn, but by the time I was awake I couldn't remember what it was that had frightened me. But this was it." He shook his head. "I know it."

"What did you see?" Hideki helped him back onto his horse, looking at him very closely.

"I don't want to talk about it. What I want to do is go back to the guesthouse and get cleaned up."

→•┃•┃•┃•←

Late as they were in arriving at the decaying mansion Prince Isao called home, Satoshi and Hideki still had to wait an insultingly long time, sipping weak tea, while the prince had himself dressed to receive them. Masahiro would have barged in on the old man after the first cup of tea, Satoshi knew. *I can afford to wait,* he thought.

He was on the verge of changing his mind about waiting when he and Hideki were finally ushered into Prince Isao's presence. The prince wore the full regalia of a member of the kuge, the hereditary nobility that had ruled the empire hundreds of years ago. If the prince thought overmuch of how he and his class depended utterly on the samurai who had displaced them, he showed no sign of it as he gestured his visitors to sit.

However impressive the prince may have looked, the instant he opened his mouth he demolished any sense of awe his costume might have built up. He cut into Satoshi's formal thanks for the gift of Akemi in a way hardly consistent with pride in good manners. "It is most unfair," the prince said, and his voice was the shrill screech of some insignificant small bird, "that my house is accused of malingering. It is not that we refuse to pay taxes. We are unable to."

"The harvest in Yamanokage has utterly failed, has it?" The comment was meant as a sour joke, so it was with some shock that Satoshi saw the prince solemnly nod his head, as though the dead rice had been his personal possession. Satoshi found himself looking more closely at the prince. He didn't much enjoy being ordered about by his brother as if he were some household servant, but he found himself enjoying this old man even less. "The nôshi you are wearing," he said, "looks rather new for a loyal servant who claims to be unable to pay a single koku in taxes."

"The peasants in Yamanokage are starving. Is that not suffering enough?" The prince sniffed and ate a tiny rice ball — having offered nothing to his guests.

"Perhaps it isn't," Satoshi said. "Tell me more about your problem with the rice harvest."

"I'm not a *farmer*," the prince said, pronouncing the word as if naming a species of pest. "I can't tell you anything other than that rice does not come in."

Satoshi looked away from the prince. Hideki was rolling his eyes, not even trying to disguise his contempt. "Allow me to remind you," Satoshi said, still not looking at the prince, "that farmers feed us. They may not be as favoured by heaven, but they still deserve our — your — respect." He got to his feet. "Please excuse us," he said, using words and intonation that were as far from respectful as it was possible to be, "but it is time for us to be going."

Hideki got up, taking care to knock over his teacup as he rose.

"You should have told him to enjoy his new nôshi," Hideki said as they walked away from the prince. "It's likely to be the last he can afford for a long time."

"I'd rather leave him wondering what I'm going to do," Satoshi said. "Gives me more options."

"My lord," Prince Isao whined from behind them, "I wish you will hurry up and get this problem solved. It reflects so badly on me. The headman and the villagers haven't given me any answers at all about the crop failure."

Satoshi turned around; the prince was clearly upset — it showed in his face as well as in the way he'd used an honorific in addressing Satoshi. *Nothing at all?* he wondered. *That's odd.* Aloud he said, "I cannot imagine why they would be so reluctant."

"But how am I to feed my household?"

"Live more frugally," Satoshi said. More quietly, he said to Hideki, "We have to go to Yamanokage and see what's going on."

↦⊹⊹⊹↤

"This is not my idea of a good time," Hideki said after his horse had slipped for a third time on the muddy turf that some dared call a road into the hills. "So of course your brother would call this a vacation."

After looking over his shoulder to ensure that Akemi was safe and the pack animals and servants still moving well, Satoshi turned to grin at his friend. "You could have it a lot worse, you know. Masa could have come with us."

Hideki choked in theatrical fashion. "I take your point."

"At least this way there's a chance you and I can get a bit of drinking in while we work." Satoshi looked ahead. The road, or what he could see of it, was getting worse the further they got from Lake Biwa. "How much farther do we have to go, do you think?" This was their second day out from Heian-kyo, and nearly the end of that day, too. Last night's accommodation had been primitive enough; if the condition of the road was any indication, tonight might find them sleeping in the open.

"We'll have to stop soon no matter where we are," Hideki said. "Sun's going down soon." He kicked his horse into a canter. "I'll see what's beyond this hill," he said as he passed Satoshi.

Hideki disappeared into the trees that loomed over the road like the beams of some enormous roof. For a moment Satoshi just sat, listening as the sound of the horse's footfalls were swallowed up by the forest. Then he nudged his own horse back into movement, waving the others forward after him.

He rejoined Hideki at the crest of the hill, from which the trees had largely been cut down. "We're here, I think," Hideki said. He pointed down the hill, to a town — more a village, really — wreathed in smoke and drowsy with autumn stillness. "Nikawa, right?"

Satoshi reined in his horse and looked a moment. The late afternoon sun turned the red-and-gold trees to lanterns and glinted on the two rivers that gave the town its name. Overlooking the rivers' confluence at the outskirts was an old castle, not a grand residence but a businesslike fortification that had fallen greatly into disrepair and looked only fitfully maintained. Farther along the river lay the graceful building that Satoshi thought the town's best feature: a tavern, locally famous for the high quality of its shochu.

"Yes," he said to Hideki. "This is Nikawa." He sighed. "I'd much rather we just stopped there at the River House. Wonder if I'd make a good tavern keeper?"

Hideki grinned, his good humour evidently restored by the end of the journey. "They have to work awfully hard, brother," he said. "It's not a job that appeals to *me*."

Satoshi made a disgusted sound and was about to reply when something fell on his head. He brushed it off; it was a plum pit. He looked up, then pointed for his companions to look as well. Balanced on a tree branch above them, a fat raccoon dog was eating late plums, not very neatly.

"He's getting ready for his winter sleep," said Akemi. "Lucky fellow, to have found his own plum tree."

"I think I was born into the wrong species," said Satoshi. "I'd have made a great tanuki."

Hideki's laugh, Satoshi thought, had a nervous edge to it. *Maybe he thinks I'm losing my mind.* "You want to be a raccoon dog?" said Hideki. "You want to eat seeds and frogs, and live in a hole?"

"No, not that kind of tanuki. A youkai tanuki. You know — the shape-changing kind. The ones who spend their time pretending to be humans: lying around, drinking sake, playing tricks on people. They enjoy life. What's wrong with that?"

Hideki was frowning now. "I really can't see you as a trickster," he said. "You have too much regard for other people's feelings. Not to mention their well-being."

Satoshi snorted. "Well, now that we're here let's get on with it. If I don't resolve this tax-shortfall business, Masa's going to put *my* well-being in a sling."

"I think perhaps we could ride a trifle more quickly, Hirota-san," said Akemi, with a faint smile.

"You ride out in front, then, my lady," said Satoshi, amused. "No doubt you'll be a more welcome sight than the rest of us."

Akemi cocked an eyebrow at him. "I am sometimes dangerous, when I have free reign," she said. "You should be careful." She urged her horse to motion, setting a brisk pace along the road. Watching her, Satoshi found himself shifting in his saddle. He bit his lower lip.

"What's Masahiro's problem, anyway?" asked Hideki in an undertone, as the two men urged their horses along the road behind Akemi. "I mean, no disrespect intended or anything, but why's your brother always riding you?"

Satoshi was silent for a moment, running a few memories through his mind. "It's himself Masa's riding, I think," he said, quietly. "Our father's shoes were pretty big. And he let Masa know that he expected them filled."

"Not easy to deal with," said Hideki. "Not easy at all." But he was only contemplative for a moment or two, and then Satoshi saw him grin again. "Your brother needs to drink more sake, you know. Then he'd relax more. It's healthy."

Satoshi forced a chuckle. "You suggest it to him, then. If I tried, he'd take my head off." And then he fell silent, remembering his dream.

They caught up with Akemi and rode briskly the rest of the way. The three tethered their horses in front of the village headman's spacious residence. Bunya Yukio was lowly as samurai went — not much more than a farmer himself. But he understood duty: aware of their arrival, he was waiting for them with refreshments — hot tea and a few little round mochi cakes filled with sweet bean paste, served in a pretty tatami room that Satoshi guessed was reserved for visiting officials. After bows and introductions and courtesies had been exchanged and Akemi had been shown to another guest room, Satoshi brought the subject round to the problem at hand. "Is it really the harvest, Bunya-san? Or do you think someone's hoarding?"

Bunya shook his round head; Satoshi sensed that only the man's innate good manners kept him from scratching it. "It's a mystery, Hirota-sama," Bunya said. "But it's not hoarding, that I know for certain. Last winter I thought as you have asked, because harvests here have always been good. But I checked and found no hoards. Even Nikawa's rice merchant had next to nothing put away when he died. His sons are suffering now, same as the rest of us."

Bunya took a slow sip of tea. "The farmers in this district have good land, and they know what they're doing. They can't understand what's wrong any more than I can. They've been setting the rice plants just as usual, the soil absorbs the fertilizer quickly, irrigation is fine — but the crop yields have been just terrible again this year. They've tried using more fertilizer, and even that didn't help. I'm sorry that the prince has been troubled with this matter, but it's lean times. Believe me, Hirota-sama, we haven't been holding back the daimyo's due. We just don't have it. We aren't really able to feed ourselves now."

Hideki paused in the act of reaching for a mochi cake, then drew back his hand. Smiling at his friend, Satoshi turned and studied the headman. Bunya blinked at him.

"Bunya-san," said Satoshi, softly, "there's something else, isn't there?"

He was aware of Hideki's eyes on him, as Bunya lowered his gaze.

"I don't know," he said. "No-one does. I expect that is why you and Arai-san have been called here, to find out."

What are you hiding from me? Satoshi thought. *Or are you so unsure of your own suspicions that you don't want to risk telling me?* He pursed his lips but said nothing.

"Now then," said Bunya, "I've made ready a guest room for you and your concubine, and another one for you, Araisan. Be pleased to relax there and get settled for a bit, while my wife prepares dinner, and then we'll have a meal together. I'll show you over the fields first thing next morning. You can talk with the farmers then if you wish."

Satoshi nodded, rising to his feet. "Thank you for your hospitality, Bunya-san," he said. "I trust we shall be able to discover what is troubling your town."

"Oh, I am sure you will, gentlemen," said Bunya, with a polite smile; but Satoshi could see that the headman doubted it.

Hideki waited until the shoji door closed and Bunya's footsteps faded. "I have to tell you, it's going to take more than a *little* drinking to make this even remotely enjoyable."

"To tell you the truth, Hideki," Satoshi said, "I'm already enjoying myself. This is turning into so much more than the boring delivery-boy task I thought I'd been given. This is becoming a challenge." He watched the delightful sway as Akemi walked ahead of him. "Crops that fail for no obvious reason. Uncomfortable silences. Tell me this doesn't intrigue you, my friend."

"You forgot to mention the nightmare and the vision that you won't describe to me," Hideki said. "That, I confess, intrigues me."

Satoshi looked back to find Hideki looking at him in a way that seemed almost feral. "No, I'm still not ready to talk about it." He gestured ahead, to where Akemi had disappeared into their bedroom. "Why can't you be more like her? She doesn't press me for details of my dreams. Even when she knows they're about her." He smiled, but Hideki didn't return the smile. After a moment, Satoshi sighed. "Later, Hideki."

It's just a bad dream, Satoshi told himself. *It's not worth fighting with a friend over.* Then he wondered, *So why is Hideki so interested?*

"I wonder, is Bunya-san telling the truth?" Satoshi whispered to the ceiling, but Akemi, evidently not asleep after all, rolled over to face him.

"Of course he isn't," she said. "Your real question, Hirota-san, is 'What is his lie hiding?'"

"I'm sorry if I woke you," he said, tracing her cheek with a finger. "You make a good point, though. What is happening here, that Bunya-san feels compelled to lie about it? Nobody seems to be hoarding rice: the only logical suspect would be the local rice merchant, and he's dead and his sons wouldn't dare: they're still new at managing the business. I can't see Bunya-san secretly hoarding rice either. He doesn't look that stupid."

"No, he looks like a good man who is confused and maybe even frightened," she said. "What is happening here may well be beyond his ability or wisdom."

"If so, he may not be the only one. Masahiro—" Satoshi swallowed the rest of the sentence. After a moment he felt a soft, smooth hand brush against his arm. "What?" he said.

"You've got the futon in a death grip, Hirota-san," Akemi said. "Let it go and relax."

Satoshi looked down. His hand was bunched around the fabric; now that his focus had been broken he could feel how tightly he'd been clenching his fists. He let go, expelling his breath in a rush. "I'm never going to get to sleep if I stay like this."

"I can help you with that," Akemi said. She should have laughed — her laughter was wicked, her voice deep and thick with desire, when they were in bed or talking of sex — but tonight she sounded distressingly matter-of-fact. Like a monk prescribing sutras, he realized.

"You have to help me help you, though," she added. "You are unhappy with your brother. I understand, my lord: it is unfair of him, even cruel, to ask you to do something he likely could not do himself. But if you dwell on that injustice you will be awake all night, and nothing I can do will help you."

"I'm not angry with my brother," he said. "It's just that I—" He took a deep breath, unable to finish the sentence. *Am I angry? I'm not. I just want Masa to appreciate what I do for him. That's not anger, and it's not disrespect. So why can't I say this to Akemi?*

"You would have to be a fool, my lord, not to see that the wrong Hirota is head of the family." Akemi's finger moved unerringly in between the folds of his sleep kimono. "And you are no fool." The finger drew a delicate, tickling line over his belly. "But your karma is to be your brother's loyal vassal, my lord. So please try — for me if not for any other reason — to not think of what has been done to you. Think instead of what I can do for you." Her finger found its target, and he felt her hand wrapping around him. Her strength was a pleasant surprise.

"I will try, Akemi," he said, unable to resist a smile. "It's the least I can do for you, given all you're trying to do for me."

⇸⊹⊹⊹⇷

Satoshi stood in the field. The golden stalks of rice, ripe for harvest, blew in the wind all around him. An odd creature, red-haired and naked and bloated, caught the corner of his eye. He noticed it bend down to pick something up from between the rows of grain, like some famished peasant gleaning another's land.

His attention was distracted by the figure kneeling before him, head bent. It wore the armour of a high-ranking Samurai, and Satoshi thought the colours looked familiar, but he couldn't place them. It was on the tip of his tongue to ask the man who he was, what was his family name; but instead he lashed out with the blade in his hand, cleaving the man's head cleanly from his shoulders. Blood fountained from the neck stump as the body fell limp to the ground, staining the rice bright red.

Satoshi picked up the head by its hair — red spattered on black, suggesting the silk cords that tied the black-lacquered armour together — and turned it, trembling, to look into the face of the man he had just murdered.

As his mind flew to wakefulness, a cry of horror on his lips, he carried with him the coherent thought of how greatly he had feared to see that face — so greatly that he had awakened himself rather than look.

"Hirota-san?"

He could barely see her outlines in the pale, new dawn. "Akemi," he said, and saw that he was clutching at her. "I — I am sorry. I had a nightmare—"

"Again? This is not natural, my lord. Should I call for a priest?"

He heard genuine concern in her voice, and swallowed. "It's alright," he said. "It's nothing."

"Tell me."

I don't dare. Something evil has hold of me, Akemi. I will not — I cannot — put you at risk by exposing you to whatever it is. Hideki had thought it might be a spell; perhaps he was right. Whether it was a spell, or karma suddenly gone wrong, keeping Akemi safe had somehow become important.

Still, he ought to tell her something. Could he make up some sort of story that would persuade?

You don't have to make up anything. There was one thing about this dream you can tell anyone.

He smiled at her, hoping she would see it as indulgence rather than the relief he felt. "There was a horrible little creature in a field," he said. Now that he was thinking about it, in at least one way that creature was the worst part of the dream. Cruel though they were, battle and killing were natural parts of a samurai's life; something this grotesque, even trapped in a dream, was vile. "It had red hair and a hideous face. And it looked like it was starving. Do demons starve? Is there anyone in this han who isn't short of food?" It came to him that he ought to feel vulnerable, or even unmanned, to be pouring out his fears to his concubine in the dark; but he didn't.

"It sounds like a dreadful dream," said Akemi, in a matter-of-fact voice. "What do you think it means?"

Satoshi folded her in his arms; it made him feel better, somehow. "I don't know." An idea occurred to him. *It was starving?* "It seems pretty clear to me, now that we're talking about it, that it has something to do with the rice problem here. But what? Are demons cursing the crops? Surely exorcisms have been performed."

"Perhaps you have to have this dream again, in order to understand it."

"I do not want to see that creature again."

She kissed his neck, gently. "You may have to, eventually," she said. "To make the dream go away."

He felt his body stirring with the soft touch of her lips. "I can think of much nicer ways to make bad dreams go away," he said. "You're a dream yourself, Akemi." He slid a fingertip slowly down the centre of her nightrobe, parting it to expose her pale skin. "Tell me, my concubine, do you miss Prince Isao?"

Akemi stretched, wriggling sensuously as his finger traced her further. "Prince Isao?" she said. He heard her smiling, wickedly. "Do you really think I was anything but a decorative bed-warmer to Prince Isao?"

He couldn't think of an answer. "I didn't know," he said, finally.

"I was relieved to be nothing more than a bed-warmer," said Akemi. "That whiny, arrogant voice of his, and those whiny, arrogant thoughts... the idea of lying with him turned my stomach. I only went to him because my family is involved in a dispute with a daimyo, and I thought Prince Isao might help them. But I don't want to be an old man's bed-warmer, Hirota-san. I need more than that, and he knew it. I was so glad when he gave me to you."

"And you — you are pleased to belong to me, Akemi?"

"Oh, yes," she said, and he heard her smile again. "Very pleased."

"But is that not what a concubine always says?"

She rose up on one elbow. He could feel her looking down at him.

"Not this one," she said.

Satoshi grinned widely in the half-dark. "Good," he said. "Now let me give you what you need." And he heard her groan of pleasure as he spread her robe with both hands.

⇥⊷⊶⊷⊷⊷⇤

Have I ever seen anything, Satoshi wondered, *quite as depressing as these fields?* He crouched down to pick up a brittle, splintering stalk whose head was so atrophied not even the birds had wanted it. On the far side of the field, Hideki — already bored, evidently — threw a stone at a crow. "I hope you were able to salvage at least something from this, Bunya-san."

"We got a few koku," the samurai said, "but for the most part we've all been eating millet and burdock for two years now."

"Four harvests." Satoshi stood, regretting every bite he'd taken since arriving in Nikawa. He looked closely at Bunya, seeing more clearly now the lines furrowing a face made thin by hunger. "I'm sorry it has taken so long for us to address this."

"Please don't apologize, Hirota-san. This is our fault. I only wish—"

"Yes, I know exactly what you mean." Satoshi stared at the dead rice, willing it to reveal the secret of its demise. "I wish it hadn't come to this, too. For your sake as much as mine." He crumbled the stalk and let it fall. "This isn't getting us anywhere. If the solution to this problem was in your fields, you'd have found it by now." He scuffed the soil with his boot. "What do your farmers tell you about this soil? It seems unusually dry to me, even for this time of year." It looked pale and grey; the soil in his dream had been almost black — rich and moist and full of life even in the midst of death and blood.

"They say the soil seems to be dying, my lord. But that makes no sense. Farmers are a suspicious lot, and we can't always take what they say at face value. How could the soil be dying?"

"I don't know about the soil, but I'm dying for a drink," Hideki said, more loudly than was necessary. "I'm freezing my balls off out here!"

"Try looking for useful information instead of fighting with birds. You'll never win against a crow." Satoshi bit back the further insult that had been forming in his mind — *Why am I so angry with everyone?* — and turned back to Bunya. "I don't know anything about farming, I'm afraid. But soil is alive, isn't it? Soil has kami in it or around it, or what are farmers making offerings to? So perhaps they're right. Maybe something is killing the soil." He remembered the weird, starving man-thing from his dream. Could that have been a rice-field kami?

"Or is it that the soil is starving," he said, "the same way people here are starving? Perhaps Nikawa is under some sort of curse."

"They've read the sutras!" Hideki shouted from across the field. "They've done the exorcisms! If it was a curse we'd know about it! Now can we *please* go someplace warm?"

"We are not finished here yet!" Satoshi kicked at the dirt, sending rice straw flying. "Damn it, Hideki," he said to himself.

"I am sorry that this is so displeasing to you and your friend," Bunya began.

"No, don't." Waving away the headman's apology, Satoshi found he was smiling in spite of himself. "The truth is, I envy Hideki-san. He's not even supposed to be here; only his loyalty to me keeps him in my company, much less out in the fields on a cold morning. If I had my way, Bunya-san, I'd be hunkered down someplace warm. I just don't have the courage to say so, the way Hideki-san does."

"You two are clearly good friends," Bunya said, but his smile was uncertain.

"And it's your bad karma, Bunya-san, to have to put up with us." Satoshi looked down at sickly soil and dead straw. "Let's check the edges of the field. If someone's been poisoning your soil, there might be some evidence of it on the verges."

When he looked up again after a few minutes of fruitless examination, Hideki was gone.

"I don't suppose he was being much help anyway," Satoshi said. "But did you see him leaving, Bunya-san?"

"I did not, lord. I'm pretty sure I know where he went, though."

"Oh? Are you blessed with second sight?"

"No, but I do know that the River House is only a few minutes' walk through those trees."

Satoshi laughed. "Is the shochu really as good as the reports have it?"

"Oh, better than that, my lord." Bunya smiled. For a change Satoshi saw neither uncertainty nor fatigue in it, saw only the sort of pride that proved his devotion to this han and this town.

"Perhaps we have, then, earned ourselves a bit of a rest and a warming drink." Satoshi pointed to the woods. "Take me to your shochu, Headman Bunya."

⁘⋅⊦⋅⊦⋅⊰

The River House, up close, was a building whose pleasant proportions would have been improved by a new roof and a little paint; but inside it was warm, and the somewhat shabby interior took nothing away from the congenial atmosphere. A group of travellers, pausing on their way from one town to the next, had apparently broken their journey and were catching a quick cup before heading back out on the road, chatting with one or two local farmers who were seeking refreshment. The farmers, Satoshi noticed, looked dispirited — and thin.

Satoshi saw Hideki, who was at a table in the corner with a flask of shochu and two cups before him. "There you are, brother," Hideki said, raising a hand. "I figured you'd be here before too long, so I took the liberty of claiming a cup for you. Oh, and Bunya-san, I'll get one for you, too. It's much more pleasant in here than out in that chilly field; though a few women about the place would make the interior much more attractive, don't you think?"

Satoshi wasn't certain whether Bunya was amused at Hideki, or annoyed by him. *Probably both.* "Have you started on that flask already?" he asked, as he and Bunya joined Hideki at the table.

"Just unsealed it," said Hideki, making a gesture to the tavern keeper about the addition of a third cup. "Haven't had the chance to taste it yet. You've come in good time."

The third cup arrived. "I'll do the honours," said Hideki, pouring a good measure of shochu for each of them.

"Kanpai," said Satoshi. They raised their cups and drank. Satoshi was impressed. The shochu was smooth, yet bright in flavour, not too sweet, and slightly stronger than the standard. "Delicious," he said. "No wonder your district is known for this."

"Oh, yes, this is good stuff," said Hideki. "Much, much better than the slop I've had in the capital. Good kick, too."

Bunya smiled. "I am glad you're enjoying it," he said, looking pleased. A moment later, he seemed to sag. "I hope we'll continue to be famous for shochu. Hope we'll be able to."

"You will, Bunya-san," said Satoshi, with a confidence he didn't feel. "I'm sure we'll be able to solve your problem, with enough investigation."

Bunya sipped at his shochu, as though it had lost its flavour. "I — I appreciate your confidence, and your help," he said, sounding careful, "but I will certainly understand if you can't resolve this situation, Hirota-san. It may be beyond anyone's power to change it."

Satoshi felt his jaw tighten up. "I refuse to believe that," he said. "Between the three of us, we'll fix this. There's no reason why we can't."

Bunya nodded. By his face, he was still doubtful, but grateful for Satoshi's optimism. He looked as though he had none of his own left.

"And if we can't," Hideki added, cheerfully tossing off the rest of his shochu, "we'll at least have enough for a couple of good drunken weeks, before the alcohol runs out."

Satoshi saw Bunya's expression fall. He felt a sharp stab of anger. "Oh, Hideki, for the love of Buddha, shut up, will you?" he said. "If you can't provide us with anything but cheap jokes, you might as well stay here and soak yourself in sake."

Hideki grinned. "My purpose is accomplished," he said. "I don't suppose you could front me some cash? I seem to have left my purse back at your house, Bunya-san."

Satoshi sighed. "Here," he said, fishing a handful of coins out of the bag he carried as he and Bunya rose. "Have fun."

"Why, thank you, brother," said Hideki, receiving the coins with a bow so correct that he seemed like a caricature of himself. "Join me later, why don't you? Shame to work so hard, on such a beautiful day."

"How would you know?" said Satoshi, sharply. "You haven't worked at all since we started this exercise."

Hideki waved a hand. Satoshi turned away and strode the length of the tavern to the back door. To his horror, he caught himself wondering why he'd brought Hideki along. *Great*, he thought. *I'm turning into my brother. May as well open my belly right now.*

Bunya followed him out. "If you'll excuse me, my lord," he began. He looked very uncomfortable. "I have administrative work I must do. These men" — he gestured at a trio of farmers standing just beyond the tavern's privy — "are at your disposal."

Satoshi spent only a quarter hour with Bunya's men, discovering nothing in the rice fields but an increasing sense of futility. "I am going back to speak with your master," he said, eventually. "I think a few questions may be in order. We're learning nothing here."

The tallest man looked at him, too polite to come right out and say, Of course we're not, you idiot, what did you expect?

"Well, I have to investigate," Satoshi said, answering the unspoken comment. "If I don't check everything out thoroughly, I might miss something obvious. Which I suppose I might be doing anyway. Let's go, shall we? I'm sure you don't want to spend the whole day out here; I know I don't."

"Yes, Hirota-sama," said the tall man, more agreeable now. "That is very sensible, I think."

The sun was midway between noon and setting when they got back to Bunya's house. The headman was there to greet them, offering Satoshi green tea and a few tiny salted fish. Satoshi ate one to be polite, feeling guilty; he knew that Bunya, like the other villagers, hadn't any food to spare.

"And may I be allowed to ask how you have progressed, Hirota-sama?" Bunya asked, after they had made a little mannerly conversation.

Satoshi looked at Bunya over his teacup. "So far," he said, "I haven't found anything useful at all. I suspect, however, that this is not news to you."

Bunya sighed. "Well, it doesn't surprise me, if that's what you mean," he said. "We haven't found anything, either."

Satoshi sipped his tea, and thought for a moment. "What have you done so far, then?" he asked. "In terms of trying to solve the problem, I mean."

Bunya eyed him closely. "As I told you, we put extra fertilizer on the crops," the headman said. "And it didn't work. So we assumed that likely the trouble was with spirits. As a village, we made extra offerings to our ancestral kami. We performed all the seasonal rituals on the most auspicious days. We went through all the procedures for invoking spirits to help the crops... we prayed to our lord Buddha, and to all the kami we could think of. We even performed ritual exorcisms and atonements, in case it was an evil spirit in the soil, or some villager's bad deed coming back to curse us all. Nothing has worked, Hirota-san. Nothing we've thought of, nothing we've done. I tell you, we are about ready to give up."

Satoshi fingered his chin, wondering how he was supposed to solve a problem that an entire village couldn't fathom. Bunya seemed to have thought of every possible solution. And Bunya didn't strike Satoshi as a man who gave up easily.

Hideki doesn't, either, Satoshi thought. *Not usually.* He felt a deep frown form on his face, and he deliberately removed it.

The sun had set by the time the rest of the pleasantries were over. Satoshi took his leave of Bunya for the evening, promising to be back later that night, and stopped in briefly to greet Akemi as she chatted with Bunya's wife. He noticed concern in her eyes, behind her polite smile and conventional courtesies. He smiled back at her, trying to look reassuring, then let himself out into the early dark.

He found the path to the river easily enough in the remains of the sunset and let his feet move him along it. Hideki would still be at the River House, three parts drunk and beyond all responsibility. Satoshi realized that the irritation of the afternoon still mingled with envy for his friend's freedom. Bunya's last words to him had been, "Why don't you get a little tipsy tonight, Hirota-san? I think you deserve it; and maybe it'll inspire you to think of something we haven't considered."

A little tipsy is as drunk as I dare get, Satoshi thought, disgusted. It was alright for Hideki. Hideki didn't have Masa on his back, ready to slice his head off at the slightest provocation. Hideki wasn't forever having to walk on eggs around a brother who was so afraid of failure that he made everyone in the vicinity afraid of *him*.

Satoshi pulled his jacket closer around him, hearing his boots crunch on dead leaves as he walked. It hadn't occurred to him before, but that really was Masa's problem: not just that he felt pressure to fill his father's shoes but that he was afraid he wasn't up to the task. And that poisoned all Masa's efforts to do the job, put him at odds with everyone who didn't share his purpose of the moment. He couldn't be flexible, because in his fear he equated flexibility with weakness, and he was terrified of appearing weak.

The River House's privy had seen better days. The makeshift door stuck as he slid it aside, and the smell was worse than he'd expected. Satoshi held the lamp up, prepared for something less than pleasant.

He froze. The creature from his nightmare was squatting over the toilet hole, reaching down it with one hand and stuffing feces into its mouth with the other. Its wizened genitals swung beneath its bloated belly as it moved. Its neck looked too scrawny for anything to pass through; but as Satoshi stared in horror, the creature swallowed, and the lump slid visibly down its emaciated throat. It turned its head and looked at Satoshi with huge, hungry eyes, and he realized that it had once been human.

Satoshi shrieked, backing away. The reflex of a lifetime spent in wooden buildings kept the lamp clamped in his grip, but it hit the ground anyway when he stumbled and fell backward.

The lamp guttered out. Satoshi sat up, feeling his throat close with fear at the sight of the odd, sickly glow leaking through the open privy door. He scrambled to his feet, and caught a brief glimpse of the creature. Then the glow faded and was gone.

He turned and hurled himself toward the back door of the tavern, his only thought to get away from whatever that thing was in the privy.

He stumbled into the tavern from the rear and made straight for Hideki, who sat at a small table in a corner, working on his third flask of sake and eyeing a lovely young woman across the room. Satoshi landed, more than sat, at the table.

Hideki looked at him over the rim of his sake cup. "Great heavens, brother," he said, "you look as if you've seen a ghost."

Satoshi realized his hands were shaking. "I've certainly seen something," he said. "Something horrible, in the privy out back."

Hideki giggled. "Well, they don't clean it very often."

"Not like that," said Satoshi. "Pour me some sake. I need it."

Hideki's thick brows knit with concern as he filled his sake cup. "What happened?" he asked, handing the cup to his friend.

Satoshi tossed it off in a single swallow. "More," he said, passing the cup back to Hideki and watching him fill it.

"I saw this... thing in the privy," said Satoshi, sipping the second cup more slowly. "It had horrible red hair sticking out on its head, and it was thin and bloated, and naked, with wizened-up privates and a skinny neck like a crane, and it was eating shit. It... it *glowed*, Hideki. And I was so scared I fell over backward, and the lantern went out, and I could see the glow coming from the privy, and then it just disappeared. I dreamed about something like this monster a couple of nights ago. But — this was real, Hide-kun, as real as you. Either that, or you're not real either, and I'm somewhere in a bed with people watching over me to make sure I don't do myself an injury. Do *you* have any ideas about what the hell that thing was?"

Hideki's eyes, Satoshi thought, were remarkably steady and sober. "Eating shit? It was a gaki," said Hideki. "A hungry ghost. Must be wandering from gaki-do for some specific reason; maybe it was someone who lived around here and has unfinished business. When they don't eat shit, they eat corpses. It's a kind of curse. They were so greedy and single-minded in life that they get condemned to be always hungry after they die, and to seek after foul things, and never realize what's nourishing, and never be satisfied. The object of their life's greed is perverted into a craving for something foul. It's strange, though: people usually don't see them. I guess you must be... favoured."

Satoshi realized he was rubbing his forehead, and stopped. "I had the impression it didn't know I was there at first," he said. "I don't think it appeared to me. More like I caught it in the act."

"Weird," said Hideki. "I wonder *why* you're so favoured, though. It's not as if you're a very good Buddhist or anything."

"How do you know all this, brother?" Satoshi asked. "You're not much of a Buddhist either. Have you seen a gaki before?"

"Once or twice," said Hideki, and Satoshi thought there was something studied in his casual voice. "I've had an odd life, you know, before coming into your service. Things have happened to me that even my honoured mother doesn't know about." He signalled for a waiter to bring another cup and flask, then filled both cups when the man had gone. "Well, now, you've had your fright for the year," Hideki said, more amused than before. "Whenever Masahiro starts getting on your nerves, just think of this gaki fellow and you'll be glad to be where you are. It's not worth it, wanting things too much, getting all knotted up when you don't get them. Just live your life happy, brother, and you won't end up eating shit from outhouses for all eternity!"

An odd mental picture flashed through Satoshi's mind — his brother, crouched beside a privy pit, scooping feces out of the hole. He closed his eyes for a moment, shaking his head, to banish the vision.

Then he opened his eyes wide. "Oh."

Hideki paused in the act of raising his sake cup. "What?"

"My dream," said Satoshi, leaning forward suddenly. "Bunya-san was right — this *is* a problem with spirits! This gaki thing I saw in my dream wasn't in an outhouse; it was in a rice field. Bending over and picking something up." He rested his chin on his hands, feeling a little more smug than shaken. "Do you see what I'm driving at?"

Hideki stared at him a moment, then nodded. "Of course," he said, his face lighting up in a rather goofy-looking smile. "Well done, Satoshi! They fertilize the crops with night soil here. The gaki, which is condemned to eat shit for all eternity, eats it all before it can get into the soil and be fertilizer. So of course the crops fail! It makes perfect sense."

"Remember, Bunya-san said they put extra fertilizer on, and it didn't help?" said Satoshi, smiling himself. "It was just an extra treat for the gaki." He thought a moment more, then felt his face droop. "The thing is, though," he said, "what are we going to do about it? How do you get rid of a gaki?"

Hideki cocked his head. "My guess is, the rituals they've done to exorcise evil spirits haven't worked, but the villagers know something strange is going on," he said. "Didn't you think Bunya was holding something back, that day when we first got here and he was explaining the problem to us? I'll bet they know something's here, even if they don't realize what it is, or that it's eating all their fertilizer. And every summer they'll have held their segaki ceremony at the O-bon festival, to get rid of hungry ghosts. It obviously doesn't work with this one."

Satoshi made a face and drank more sake. "Bunya-san said they'd tried every prayer and exorcism they could think of," he said. "So we'll have to do something else. Wish I knew what."

Hideki poured more into his friend's empty cup. "Have a drink, brother," he said. "Have a drink."

⋆•⊱•⊰•⋆

The blood sprayed, bright lacquer-red in the late-afternoon sun. The head bounced once when it hit the black soil. Red drops began wobbling down rice stalks; the too-rich smell of shit filled Satoshi's nostrils as dying men voided their bowels onto the hungry fields. There was surprisingly little noise. Good samurai died silently, making a final statement about their bravery, even as the victors took the losers' heads to prove their own courage.

And I am too afraid to look at the man I just killed. Satoshi was aware of a strange sensation: he seemed to be floating above himself. *I am dreaming,* he realized.

And I know that I am dreaming.

Satoshi's dream-self appeared to freeze. *Bend down,* Satoshi thought, and his dream-self shifted the heavy, lacquered armour up his chest and bent from the waist. *I am not going to frighten myself awake tonight,* he thought.

At his command, his dream-self gripped the hair on the back of the head and lifted. And this time he forced himself to look as he turned the head around, willed himself to not just see the dead face but to remember it.

Masahiro.

The world went dark, and Satoshi found himself awake. His face was cold, but sticky with sweat. This dream's previous visits had left him with a thudding heart, but that didn't afflict him now. A sickness in the base of his stomach was the only physical reminder, beside the cold sweat, that he had just dreamed of usurping his brother.

And there was no doubt in his mind that this was what the dream had been about. Masahiro had been dead because murder was the only way Satoshi was going to replace Masa at the head of the clan.

Satoshi sat up. Beside him, Akemi shifted slightly, murmuring something muffled by the comforter that covered nearly her entire face. *No,* he thought. *Not this time. Let her sleep, and face yourself by yourself.*

He got to his feet. There was just enough light coming from the flickering charcoal in the brazier that he could find his riding boots and his coat; picking them up, he walked to the inner shoji screen and let himself into the main part of the big farmhouse. Down the hall was another shoji, opening to the outside. Wrapping himself up and putting on his boots, Satoshi sat on the step, feet on the frozen mud, and tried to decide whether the dream had been warning or invitation.

⇥•⊹•⊹•⇤

"You probably ought to spend a little less time tumbling your new concubine," Hideki said as the two of them picked their way down the path from Bunya's house to the centre of the village. "You are obviously not getting enough sleep, brother: you look like hell." He popped a pickled plum into his mouth, spitting out the pit with a happy face.

"Good morning to you, too." Satoshi thought about eating and his stomach flipped. *A drink would be good, though.* "In this case you're wrong, though." Hideki arched an eyebrow. "I only made love to Akemi once last night, right after we went to bed."

"Too much shochu last night, brother?"

"What do you mean? First you think I'm too much in her, now you're complaining that it's not enough because I was drunk last night? Consistency, Hide-kun, please."

"I'm not required to be consistent. I'm only required to give you a hard time, to remind you that you're mortal and only the younger brother of the daimyo."

Satoshi felt his jaw clench. A vision of the blood-spattered head jumped into his mind.

"Oh," Hideki said after a moment. "That seems to have gone beneath the skin. What's the matter, brother?"

"I had that dream again, Hideki. Last night. Couldn't get to sleep after." Satoshi found his hand straying to the hilt of his katana, and pulled back.

"The dream you won't tell me about. Except that I see it seems to have something to do with your brother. Well, that's easily understood; I have nightmares about Hirota-san myself." He paused to eat another pickled plum; then, with the pit still in his mouth he said, "We could always do this another day, you know. Give you a chance to get some sleep. I'm not saying we have anything to be worried about — that gaki is a shit-eater and he doesn't seem violent — but, just in case, it might be better if you were sharp and alert." He spat the pit down the path. Something in the tall grass scrambled away, the better to hide.

"No," Satoshi said. "I don't see any point in delaying this. You tell me that gaki are seeking after something."

"Something they wanted, or craved, in life. Yes."

"A greedy ghost. The leftover of a greedy life."

"And this has what to do with Nikawa village?"

"Who are the greediest people we know of, Hideki?"

Hideki grinned broadly. "I assume you aren't including Prince Isao in your assessment."

"Yes, but only because he's not dead. Yet." Satoshi found himself smiling, too. That was the best thing about Hideki; it was almost impossible to stay gloomy in his company — even when he behaved as badly as he'd been behaving this week. "So what people besides princes are mostly greedy?"

"Merchants," Hideki said. Then, after a pause: "Oh."

"Exactly. The rice merchant, Kentaro. Dead just over two years — about as long as the harvests have been failing here."

"But surely if it was that obvious, Bunya would have figured it out already. And, if he has, why is the gaki still here?"

Satoshi jostled his friend lightly as they reached the small wooden bridge and crossed over the river into the village proper. "It can't have been all that obvious, Hideki, because you didn't figure it out." Hideki glowered at him, but it was a poor impression of anger. "I don't think Bunya-san *had* figured out that part. I guessed, the first night, that he was hiding something. But I don't think he knows enough about gaki — or the spirit world in general — to know anything more than that something very strange is happening here."

Ahead of them was a building nearly as large as Bunya's house, albeit without any sense of refinement to its design, and no shoji at all to let in light without also allowing the prying eyes of passersby. "What I haven't been able to guess, Hideki, is what it was the gaki was trying to find. And I think that until we know that, we won't be able to exorcise the ghost."

"And you're going to find it out."

"Yes. If I have to put Kentaro's sons to the torture, I'm going to find out what it is that his ghost is searching for."

Torture, it developed, wasn't necessary. Satoshi and Hideki had no sooner announced the reason for their interrogation than his two adult sons and their wives were all prostrate on the floor in front of Satoshi, begging for his forgiveness and his help. "If our father is a ghost we know what he's looking for. But we don't know where it is," the eldest pleaded, "and that's the truth, lord."

"And what is it he's looking for?" Satoshi was so pleased at having guessed the identity of the ghost that he had to remind himself to look angry with these merchants. Merchants were the lowest form of human life in the world — in fact, some argued, plausibly, that merchants were a different species entirely from the samurai.

"Silver, lord," the eldest said. "And we are starving because the miserable old wretch wouldn't tell us where he'd hidden his hoard."

"Oh, that makes sense," Hideki said, pitched so that only Satoshi could hear. "Misers often become gaki. It's a sort of punishment for their greed."

"In this case, it would appear that Kentaro isn't the only one being punished." To the sons he said, "You do realize that I could have the lot of you executed for keeping the truth about this silver hidden from me." The women wailed at that and beat their foreheads against the floor.

"Are you serious?" Hideki whispered in his ear. "Are you really going to cut down your best potential sources of information?"

"Of course not. I'm not interested in killing anyone." The words came easily enough; the realization of their absolute truth came as a shock. *What's the dream about, then?*

"But I'm not going to let them know that. I want them on edge, Hideki. They think they don't know anything, but whatever hold the gaki has on them might slip if they're frightened enough." To the rice merchants he said, "Get up. I want you to show me every place in this house and the grounds that you've searched. And we're going to dig up your privy."

Two hours later Satoshi wondered if his proud self-confidence had been misplaced. The rice warehouse turned out to have a multitude of secret hiding places, but every one of them was empty. The privy, which the family had not even thought of searching, proved to be a messy, smelly frustration. Whatever else was down those pits, there was no silver.

"Your father," Satoshi said, "was a nasty, vile man."

"Agreed," said Hideki. "I want a drink. A big one."

And we didn't even shovel, thought Satoshi.

"At least one man is going to benefit from this, then," the rice merchant said. "Goro be damned, anyway."

"Damned?" Goro was the proprietor of the River House. "Why begrudge his success?"

"Because it should be ours." The merchant looked sullen, a petulant child. *No wonder they're despised.*

"That seems a selfish attitude," Hideki said. Bits of sticky rice flew from his mouth: somehow he had got hold of a rice ball. "You people don't own everything, you know."

"We *did*. Or at least we should have. Father and Goro were partners; Goro built the River House with money Father provided. Title to that tavern was supposed to come to us."

Hideki said, "You've made a serious accusation against an honest man." *Are you really concerned for Goro, or is it for the fact that he doesn't charge you for the sake and shochu you drink, Hideki?* Satoshi asked silently.

"Bunya-san told us that Father had stated, in his presence, that on his death the title to the tavern was to go to Goro. But that doesn't make sense!"

It suddenly did to Satoshi. "Come on," he told Hideki.

❖❖❖❖

Hideki didn't arrive at the River House until the last of the silver bars had been washed clean and placed on the small but very valuable stack in front of the tavern's privy. Satoshi's hands were still clean, though he'd been so sure of himself he would gladly have done all the digging, no matter how foul. As it had developed, his enthusiastic haste had pulled the merchant's family behind him, and they had in turn attracted others, so that, by the time Satoshi had explained to Goro what had to be done, there was no shortage of people ready to do the work.

"You've been drinking and eating too much, brother," Satoshi said, laughing, when his friend finally strolled around to the back of the tavern. "You've missed all the fun." He pointed to the stack of slender bars; they resembled nothing so much as miniature grave markers.

"It stopped being fun," Hideki said, "as soon as you solved the mystery. I didn't see the point of rushing up here when I already knew what you'd find."

That was rude, Satoshi thought. *Or incredibly selfish.* "And how did you know I'd turn out to be right? I wasn't sure myself."

"Yes, you were," Hideki said. "You just didn't want to admit it to yourself. I'm not Masahiro, Satoshi. I recognize how intelligent you are. As soon as I saw the expression on your face when you heard about the River House, I knew you'd solved it. The only real question was, where up here would the silver end up having been buried?"

"You mean you didn't guess that it would be under the shit in the privy?" Satoshi cocked his head, grinning. "Why do you think I insisted on searching the privy at Kentaro's?"

Hideki frowned. "I still don't understand."

"Let's go back to the beginning. You're the one, Hideki, who told me that gaki ate disgusting things as a substitute for what they'd craved in life. Either shit or corpses." He walked over to the silver and picked up a bar. "At first, I guessed that the gaki had eaten the shit from the fields, which had caused the crop failure. Then I realized Kentaro was the gaki — he was a greedy man, and he had died at the right time. So the question was, what had Kentaro craved in life, that his curse had perverted into a craving for shit? I didn't know, but Kentaro's sons told me: silver. So it only remained to tie the two things together. Why did the gaki, searching for the silver, turn to eating shit, and not corpses? Because he hid the silver somewhere near shit."

He turned to Kentaro's sons. "You have my sympathies. He could not have been an easy man to live with." Satoshi saw Masahiro's glowering face, heard his bitter, snarling voice. *I know something of that, I think.*

"Thank you, lord," the eldest said. "We are very grateful to you for all that you've done." The man's eyes, Satoshi saw, were not on him at all, but rather stared at the silver. *That's a very unpleasant expression to go with such a supplicant tone.*

"I think that perhaps you have misunderstood me here," Satoshi said. "The silver is not staying in Nikawa."

"What?" Several people said the word simultaneously. Hideki, Satoshi noted, was not among them.

"You want to be rid of the gaki, don't you?" Satoshi pointed to the fields across the river. "You'll never get another good crop if you don't, and that will mean the daimyo will remove you from this land."

He turned to Kentaro's sons. "The fact that your father didn't tell you where the silver was stored meant that he didn't want you finding it — apparently not even when he was no longer alive. So he hid it away from his house, and then took steps to keep the River House — and the silver — forever even from you, his children."

He walked over and picked up another bar of silver. "Remove this, and you remove the thing that draws him. He'll be pulled back to gaki-do, and your crops and livelihoods will be saved. Leave the silver here, and you'll never be free of him."

He put the bars back on the pile. "And this silver will pay all of your back taxes, and possibly even buy you exemption for a year or two, so that you can all set some of your next harvests aside, to carry you over in the event of another poor harvest. Ah, Bunya-san," he said, seeing the headman approaching. "I believe your harvest problems are over."

"Yep," Hideki said. "There he goes."

"There who goes?" Bunya said.

"Where?" Satoshi turned from Bunya to Hideki. His friend looked almost squat, leaning against a post from the disassembled privy. *He really has put on weight,* Satoshi thought. Hideki was looking out into the fields across the river from the tavern; when Satoshi followed his friend's gaze, he caught a brief glimpse of something red, fading into the mid-day haze. He had, he realized, seen stringy red hair as it disappeared from the world of men. "That was him," he said. "The gaki. Returning to gaki-do?"

"Yes." Hideki sighed. "A pity. I was beginning to like it here."

"Thank heavens it was only a gaki." Bunya turned to Satoshi, a look of relief on his face. Then he realized the full import of what he had said. Falling to the ground he said, "Please accept my apology, lord. I did not mean to withhold information from you. And I should have guessed that what was haunting us was a hungry ghost. I am — unworthy of your trust. I know what I must do."

"You will not." Satoshi gestured to him to get up. "You are forbidden to take your life. You have not in any way failed to serve your lord, Bunya. Suicide is out of the question." Satoshi pointed to the silver. "You do have one more service to perform, though. This silver now belongs to Hirota Masahiro, in payment of this han's outstanding taxes. Please see that it is all securely packed. When we leave you will arrange it on our draft animals. Until then, you are responsible for its safety."

"Yes, lord!" Bunya scrambled to his feet, the scabbards of his two swords knocking together as he rose. "Thank you, lord!" He began grabbing silver, handing bars to a farmer until the man staggered under the weight, then moving to the next man, until all of the silver was on its way to his house.

"I wonder," said Goro as the last of the farmers left the yard behind his shop, "which of us was supposed to get that silver."

"None of you," Hideki said. "Misers don't think that way. They truly believe that they'll be able to take it with them. The man intended the silver for himself, and himself alone."

"At least he did us some good, in the end," Goro said. "Lords, my stock is entirely at your disposal. I have sake warming already, and shochu if you want more immediate warmth."

"A farewell drink sounds like an excellent idea," Hideki said. "One that starts now and ends when the sun comes up tomorrow and we take our leave of this fine place. You are a splendid man, Goro."

We're not ready to go, Satoshi thought. *I'm not, at any rate. I have a dream to finish.*

⁂

Satoshi turned, feeling grass give under the weight of his shoulder. *Am I lying on a battlefield? Or am I feeling the grass of the tatami? Or am I dreaming, but aware again that I am dreaming?*

He got to his feet, feeling the weight of the armour on his shoulders as he stood. *I am in the dream. But I know that I am in the dream. That's good.* He had been lying in wait, it seemed, along with what looked like an army. Ahead of him, as he stood, Masahiro and his men stopped abruptly, surprised by Satoshi's sudden appearance. The battle began; Satoshi resisted it.

This is not where I wanted to start. Tell me why *we are fighting! I know how this ends; how does it begin?*

Cold rushed in on him, and he was alone in the dark. "Damn," he said softly, raising himself on one elbow. *I will not do what you want,* he told himself, *until I know why you want it. And, for that matter, until I know who* you *are.*

A faint sound of snoring reached his ears, but he couldn't tell if it was Hideki or Bunya. He hoped it was the latter; the headman had told Satoshi he expected to sleep well tonight for the first time in a year. The sound he didn't hear was Akemi's soft breathing. Much as it pained him to do so, he had banished her tonight to another room. She hadn't asked him why he was doing it, and he hadn't told her. *You don't know why you did it,* he told himself. *But love might have something to do with it, don't you think?*

He sat up. This wasn't helping. On the other hand, what he needed was to get back into the dream. At this hour, sex with Akemi would probably make for a very pleasant passage back to sleep. His right hand twitched, and for a moment he enjoyed the thought that his hand couldn't decide what it wanted to grip, Akemi or a sword. She might be nothing more than a concubine, but she seemed to know him better than any other woman — something especially impressive given how recently they'd met. And the way she responded to him — he had never encountered anyone like this before.

No. He would stay in this room and leave Akemi in hers. The way this dream had been progressing, until he knew what the end of the dream would be, it was safer to sleep apart.

He fussed with the bedding, then lay back down and tried to will himself to sleep. He turned — one side, then the other. "Amida Buddha," he muttered. "This is ridiculous."

The head came off the neck, cleanly. The blood sprayed for the same brief moment, before the body collapsed into the rice stalks. Satoshi saw his hand reach for the hair.

How did this happen? I don't remember falling asleep. He fought against picking up the head; his fingers wrapped around the hair anyway and began to lift. Satoshi relaxed — he didn't seem to be in control this time anyway — and waited to see what would happen once he'd looked at his brother's dead face.

What happened was that his hand dropped the head beside the body. He looked to his left, out across the field, to where the battle continued. Then he turned to his right — and saw another army approaching. The mon on the banners was unfamiliar, and the colours of the armour were, he somehow knew, none he'd seen before, anywhere. The lacquer shone like the rainbow one saw on spilled oil.

The army didn't move — the samurai simply stood under waving banners — but somehow they were beside Satoshi anyway, and then they were in the midst of what remained of Masahiro's men, fighting alongside Satoshi's band.

Then Akemi was beside him, saying, "Thank you, my lord, for avenging this wrong against my family." She kissed him, and when she stepped back he saw blood on her mouth.

My blood? Masa's blood? Does it really matter, now? She kissed him again, and this time he pushed her away. She reached for him—

Satoshi sat up, knowing that he wouldn't be going back to sleep now. What had Masa done to her family? It could have been anything; in a temper Masa was capable of anything if he thought his dignity had been insulted. *Why is his death the only solution?*

You would have to be a fool, my lord, not to see that the wrong Hirota is head of the family. Akemi had said that to him not too many nights ago. *I would make a good daimyo,* he told himself. He had never allowed the thought to fully form before. But it would explain his constant chafing against Masa's orders, his arbitrariness. *I am on your side,* he remembered not quite telling Masa the day he'd been ordered to begin this investigation.

What if he wasn't?

He lay back down, shifted onto his left side. *Akemi is a concubine. She has no right to ask you for anything,* he told himself. Ah, but had she? No: she had only mentioned that her family was involved in some sort of dispute with a daimyo. It was his dream that had linked her family with his.

And it is my own desire for power, he thought, *that makes me dream of killing my brother and his son* — the son and his mother would have to die, of course, before Satoshi could ascend to the leadership of the clan.

What do I do? He tried to imagine life without Akemi, and couldn't. It was too easy to imagine battling his brother — he was bred to fight, after all — and even to imagine winning. But it was equally easy to imagine Masa continuing to lead the clan.

I am dreaming my own death.

He opened his eyes. There were his swords, curved and silent, waiting in the lacquered rack that travelled with him. Something else Akemi had told him came to him, then: it was his karma to be his brother's support and vassal. To dream so frequently — so clearly — of usurping his brother wasn't just dangerous, it was treason. Better to dream of overthrowing the shogun than to wish to usurp his daimyo.

If I cannot stop this dream, I must end it.

Satoshi felt a chill that implied winter's arrival. He pulled the comforter up to his chin. *If I have the dream again, knowing what it means, my honour leaves me only one way out.*

※※※

When Satoshi finally slept it was close to sunrise, so he stayed late in bed. Shortly before noon he rose, grumpy and depressed, to be greeted by the enthusiastic congratulations of the villagers. Akemi spoke words of polite congratulation with the others, and then, when no-one was looking, wound her arms around his neck. Her spontaneous affection sent a thrill and a warmth all through him, but he found it hard not to be reminded of his dream.

Even Goro from the River House came by after the noon meal to offer Satoshi formal thanks and a large cask of his finest shochu, which Hideki promptly confiscated. "Celebration!" Hideki said, smiling widely. "It's too late to start back for the capital anyway. And this cask is far too heavy to carry back with us, brother, given all that silver we're taking. Surely you must agree."

Satoshi nodded, not really caring. "By all means," he said, making his face look cheery. "Let's get drunk."

He didn't drink much, though. Bunya's wife did; she clearly had no head for alcohol and excused herself after the first hour, looking woozy. Bunya's men each took a ration of the shochu and then retired to a private party of their own, no doubt with their own stock of beverages. Eventually, after a couple of hours, Bunya was called away because Kentaro's two sons were fighting, so seriously that observers had decided only the village headman could break them up. After that there were only Satoshi, Hideki, and Akemi left in Bunya's tatami room.

From his curiously detached position, sipping slowly at his shochu, Satoshi saw that Akemi had quite a head for alcohol; but Hideki could outdrink even her. Today,

Hideki could apparently outdrink all the fish in the sea. It occurred to Satoshi to wonder why. Bunya's noon meal had been the best he could manage, but it had still been obvious that the region was just one step away from famine. More than half the cask of shochu on a poorly filled stomach should have sent Hideki reeling into a corner. All it seemed to do was make him more mischievous instead.

"Akemi-san," Hideki said, with that vast amount of shochu coursing through his veins, "I'll wager you're not a very good dancer."

"Why do you say that, Arai-san?" She sent him a look that was not entirely friendly.

"Because of the way you arrange your hair," Hideki said, in tones that showed he knew he was being outrageous. "It's obvious that you can't be a good dancer. Not with that hairstyle."

Akemi looked down her nose at Hideki. "You don't make any sense," she said. "What's my hair got to do with the way I dance?"

Hideki shook his head. "I have never seen a girl with her hair done like that who was able to dance. It's characteristic. You have the hopelessly-dreadful-dancers' hair arrangement. And what's more, I'll bet your feet are flat."

"Be quiet, Hideki," said Satoshi. He realized his hands were curling into fists. "I'll thank you not to insult a member of my household."

Hideki giggled. "You sound like your brother," he said. "He can't take a joke, either."

"You're drunk, Arai-san," said Akemi, and hiccupped.

"No, I'm not." Hideki grinned and tossed off his cup of shochu. "But you are, Akemi-san. No use pretending otherwise."

A slow smile spread across Akemi's face. "I'm not too drunk to dance," she said. "And my feet aren't flat. Are they, Hirota-san?"

"No," said Satoshi. "They're not."

If they were any more sober, he knew, they would be looking at him, curious about the tone of his voice. He felt the air thick with hidden meanings he could not interpret, and he sat, watching.

"Observe," said Akemi. She stood up, listing a little to one side. "Hirota-san, you have never seen me dance, and so I will do it now; not to refute the idiotic notions of this gentleman of your acquaintance—" Hideki giggled "—but to show my new master what a fine dancer I am."

"But where is the music to come from?" said Satoshi, feeling it was expected of him.

"Arai-san will provide the music," said Akemi, with a wicked little smile. "Although I am quite certain he cannot sing."

"I certainly can sing," said Hideki, perking up, and still looking excessively pleased about something. "And I know lots of different melodies. What tune do you wish to dance to, my lady Akemi?"

She lifted a delicate eyebrow. "'Gagaku.'"

Hideki choked on his shochu. Satoshi felt himself smile slightly.

"I can't sing 'Gagaku'!" said Hideki, getting his breath back. "What do you think I am, an orchestra?"

"I think you cannot sing, Arai-san. Or else you would surely make the attempt. You have been at a daimyo's court, have you not? Surely you must have heard 'Gagaku' at least once."

Hideki sighed, rising to his feet as though he hadn't been drinking at all. "Alright," he said. "But it's going to sound weird."

Akemi arranged herself into a position for beginning a dance. It would have been more graceful had she been less intoxicated. Hideki took a deep breath and began an odd, wheezing drone, interspersed with peculiar intervals. It sounded to Satoshi like a musical instrument being savaged by a water buffalo. He vaguely wondered why he wasn't laughing.

Akemi began her dance. Still watching as though outside himself, Satoshi knew she would have been the most graceful dancer he had ever seen, had she not been drunk to the point of recklessness. As it was, the tempo of 'Gagaku' was hard enough to follow even for a sober person, when it was performed on actual instruments. Akemi lost the rhythm, tried to catch up, and confused her movements even as she made them. Hideki, as though to purposely make things worse, moved closer to her and began a sober-faced dance of his own, completely at odds with hers and totally unrelated to the tempo of what he was singing.

Akemi noticed him. Laughing, she threw herself into her dance with renewed vigour, as though determined not to let him sabotage her efforts. And it was at the point where she was attempting a poised, bent-knee manoeuvre that Hideki stepped behind her, drew a bronze hand-mirror from the folds of his clothing, held it up so that it reflected the back hem of Akemi's kimono, and pointed it out for Satoshi with a flourish and a smile.

Satoshi stared at the image in the mirror.

Akemi had a tail.

He felt his mouth open. The tail in the mirror swished gently, out of time with the impossible music. He wondered, insanely, whether the orange hairs were getting caught in the straw-weave of the tatami. And the next minute, he wondered how she could have tricked him this way.

"Stop!"

He heard himself shout, felt his detachment suddenly abandon him as he scrambled to his feet.

"Hideki," he said, not looking at his friend, "get out of this room."

Hideki giggled. Satoshi would have slapped him, but his friend was gone too quickly. The next moment it didn't matter, because Satoshi had hold of Akemi's delicate shoulders, shaking her. It took an act of will to stop before he snapped her neck.

"You're a fox-spirit!" He didn't trouble to speak quietly. "You're a kitsune, and you took advantage of my trust! How could you, Akemi? I — how *could* you?"

She looked up at him, her eyes wide. He wondered whether he could trust that the regret in her eyes was real.

"I did it for my family," she said. "I had to. One of my cousins thought it would be fun to possess the body of a maid in the residence of your brother the daimyo. She... caused some trouble. Your brother was furious; he threatened to put all the foxes to death. It was only a harmless prank, Hirota-san, and my cousin is a foolish young thing; we would have disciplined her, made sure it wouldn't happen again. But Hirota Masahiro-san was so hostile and provoking, it upset the heads of my clan badly and they took it as an act of war."

Satoshi stared at her, trying to reconcile Akemi — his Akemi — with this new, mad situation. She still looked like his Akemi, sounded like her, smelled and felt delightfully the same. And yet she had lied to him, and — he stared at her, knowing in full now what she had done.

"And you decided that I would be more... pliable?... than my brother, so you filled my head with dreams of power and drew me toward killing my brother — just so that I would help you? Help kitsune against my own family?" He shook her slightly. "Why didn't you just tell me? I'd have found a way to persuade my brother to cease his hostilities toward your — toward you foxes. As it is—" He thought about his swords, about his intent to die before the day was out.

She looked like she was going to cry. "I know that, now," she said. "But at the time I had no choice but to go along with my family's wishes. They thought if I got close to you, became your concubine, I could influence your dreams with fox-magic, and persuade you to depose your brother. So I cast a spell on Prince Isao, to make him give me to you."

"But why—"

"I wanted to just tell you, Hirota-san. But my family assumed you would be as hostile toward us as your brother is. People usually are hostile toward fox-spirits; it's the reaction we're most accustomed to. So I did what they wanted. Did my duty." She bit her lip. "Do you always like doing your duty, Hirota-san?"

Satoshi clenched his teeth. "I am sorry," he said, in a voice of ice, "that you found me such an *unpleasant* duty to perform. But you will no longer have to do it. I release you from your contract, Akemi. You are no longer my concubine."

"No!" She grasped his arms, and he felt her strong fingers, clutching. "Hirota-san, please—"

"Oh, don't worry, fox-woman. I'll make certain my brother doesn't make war on your clan. It's the least I can do. You've given me a few good nights, after all."

"No," she said again, and he saw that she was in tears. "No, it was more than that. I meant it was my duty to cast spells on you, Hirota-san. I didn't mean it about—"

"You can say anything you like. It doesn't matter now." Satoshi managed not to show how her tears moved him, though the restraint was physically painful. "I thought you were... well, you can't be, can you? You aren't even human, and you didn't tell me, so you obviously didn't care whether I trusted you or not. And now, I cannot."

To his horror, she knelt before him, clasping his hand and crying. "Please, Hirota-san. Please... Satoshi. Don't send me away!"

He felt his stomach lurch, with the effort not to cry himself. "You're just like my brother," he said. "You both use me for your own ends. It's not right for him to do that, and it's even worse for you. Go."

She released his hand, stood up, and left the room.

Satoshi strode out the other door to the next room, where he knew Hideki was waiting. His friend — Satoshi felt sickened by the word now — was seated on a cushion, finishing off the rest of the shochu. Satoshi hadn't even been aware that Hideki had taken it with him.

He looked up as Satoshi came into the room. "What news, brother?" he said, as though he hadn't heard everything that had gone on in the room next door.

Satoshi glared at him and pointed a finger.

"You," he said. "Let me make a few observations about you."

Hideki smiled, his usual carefree smile. "Go ahead."

Satoshi's lips tightened. "You like to drink," he said. "A lot. And you don't like to do any work."

Hideki grinned. "That's why we're brothers," he said.

"True." Satoshi nodded, feeling an odd new dimension to the anger already coursing through him. "But *you* like to drink and lie around to the exclusion of everything else."

"And I'm proud of it," said Hideki, "of course."

Satoshi grabbed him by the shoulders as he had Akemi. It occurred to him that he would rather have grabbed him by the throat. "My friend Hideki, indolent though he is, is extremely loyal to the people he cares about. And when some task or problem does come immediately before him, especially when it's something that will help a friend, he will worry away at it and won't give up until he's solved it. You, on the other hand, left me to swing in the breeze through this entire crop-failure crisis. You couldn't even keep yourself interested enough to spend an afternoon in a rice field with me, let alone help me solve this problem, even though if it wasn't solved Masa would have probably had the whole village beheaded and ordered my balls cut off."

Hideki was no longer smiling. Satoshi felt his own fingers digging into the man's shoulders — and dug harder.

"Add to that," Satoshi said, "the fact that you've suddenly developed a hellraising streak that makes all your previous efforts at trick-playing seem mild, and that you suddenly know a hell of a lot about gaki, and — and fox-spirits, and supernatural matters you never gave a damn about before, and things start looking just a little bit unnatural. So, Hideki, or whatever your damned name is — exactly what kind of shape-shifter are *you*?"

Hideki stared at him a moment. Then he chuckled, as one unable to help himself. In another moment he was laughing so hard that he rocked back and forth.

Satoshi had actually drawn back a hand to strike him, when Hideki smothered his laughter and wiped a hand across his face. His eyes danced; but they weren't Hideki's. "Oh, well done, brother," he said, unable to suppress a giggle. "You said a few days ago that you wanted to be one of us. Remember?"

Satoshi gripped the table behind him, hardly aware that he was doing it. Hideki was changing. The old, familiar shape of his friend was sliding away before his eyes, distorting like a blob of paint stirred into another colour. Satoshi felt dizzy, nauseated, his mind rebelling against what he saw; but he could not bring himself to look away.

When it was over, the colours and outlines had settled into the squat form of an animal, but much larger than the one found in nature — a short, sharp snout, a pair of rounded ears high on the head, thick limbs and a big solid belly, and a huge pair of testicles, like hairy rice sacks; and the eyes, big and round and curious, good-natured enough, but entirely without concern or generosity.

"Tanuki," said Satoshi, his voice just a breath. "You're a tanuki."

"Sure am," said the creature — Satoshi could no longer think of it as *Hideki*, and the fact that he had once done so made him feel soiled. The tanuki's voice had a husky twang, and the creature smiled as it continued. "Your friend Hideki has finished up his eight-day drunk, and now he's holed up in a backroom in Ikewara, working on an eight-day hangover. I think his mother's afraid he'll go straight to hell when he dies, but who needs hell when you've got an eight-day hangover?"

"And so, you... stole his life."

The tanuki snorted. "Don't be so judgemental. I just copied his appearance. Hey, it's what tanuki do, isn't it? I figured he had the temperament for me to replace him easily enough, for a while anyway — he's kind of like a tanuki, himself. I was curious about his life. And there was the matter of sake, of course. Figured a daimyo's brother'd understand about the need for sake."

"Did you really?" said Satoshi. He was surprised, even in his anger, to hear how his voice resembled his brother's.

The tanuki raised its hands, which were more like paws. "Hey, hey, don't be angry," it said, with a genial kind of worry. "I didn't mean any harm, after all. And I didn't do any, did I?"

Satoshi felt the urge to blink hard; instead he frowned to suppress it. "You know what you did," he said, through his teeth. "You betrayed me. You posed as my friend and you betrayed my trust and you — you ruined something I cared about. A lot." He concentrated deliberately on his anger; it seemed best just then. "And none of that matters to you, does it? All that's important to you is where your next drink is coming from, and who you can take advantage of next."

"But I did you a favour, too, didn't I?" Unbelievably, the tanuki winked at him. "I knew from the moment I met her that Akemi was a kitsune, and I knew she had to be stopped. So I stayed with you. You see? I stopped her."

"You stopped her because it amused you to, not because you wanted to help me!"

"Well... I had my fun showing you Akemi's tail; but I did some good, too, 'cause now you don't have to kill yourself. I could tell you were thinking that today, that you'd have to kill yourself. Made you a lot less fun, by the way. It was easy to tell that she was doing fox-magic on you: you looked so drained, and sex with a kitsune who's bewitching you takes your life force away. But now you know Akemi was giving you those dreams of treason against your brother; it's not that you were harbouring the urge to overthrow him. So you don't have to commit seppuku after all. Isn't that a good thing?"

Satoshi drew a long breath, then let it out. "I can't believe I ever mistook you for Hideki," he said. "You're disgusting."

The tanuki blinked at him, looking hurt. "I'm just what I am," it said. "We've all got to be what we are, Satoshi."

It picked up a straw hat that had suddenly appeared on a table nearby, and clapped the hat on the back of its head. "Anyway," it said, turning to Satoshi with a return of its impish grin, "thanks for the sake."

Hoisting its immense testicles up over one shoulder, it waddled out the door. As Satoshi watched, it made its way along the road and disappeared.

⇾⊹⇽⊹⇾⊹⇽

The morning sun hadn't reached the valley of the two rivers yet, but Satoshi trusted his horse to find the path up and out of the town. The bright scent of wood smoke mingled in Satoshi's nose with the deeper, more acrid smell of burning charcoal as the town farmers and samurai began their day. Their homes were nearly indistinguishable from the trees under which they sheltered; only the occasional dot of light from a lamp betrayed them. Behind him, nestled securely among the riders of his escort, pack animals carried his brother's silver.

Soon, the townsfolk would be performing the tasks set out for them by their places in society, just as he was doing his duty. *We've all got to be what we are,* the tanuki had told him. *That isn't right, though,* he thought. *Not for me.*

He'd been awake much of the night, wrestling with what had happened. He'd been so quick to accuse Akemi and the tanuki of betraying him, but the truth was that he'd betrayed himself. In fact, the tanuki had helped him. And the fox-magic wouldn't have been able to get its claws into him had he not harboured the envious conviction that he was more deserving of the power his brother wielded. The realization had sickened him; he had eventually slept, but only to dream of being a tanuki himself, so that he could shift from what he was.

This morning, though, he had decided that no tanuki could change in the way he had to: their shifts were all surface. He had to change what nobody could see. *I can do that,* he thought, watching the first sliver of dawn brighten the sky above the trees. *Not on the outside; but on the inside, I can change.*

Laughing, he urged his horse ahead of the others. The hooves pounded on the frozen road, and it seemed to him that the horse was sensing some of the release he felt. At the top of the hill above Nikawa he reined in the horse and turned it around. He had arrived just in time: as he watched, dawn flowed across the valley, illuminating the houses beneath the smoke plumes and glittering on frosty branches.

He heard a rustle and looked down. A few paces down the road, but well ahead of his baggage train, a fox stood in the road, looking up at him fearlessly.

Intersections
Grace Seybold

The longing hit Nadia for the third time that day as she stepped out of the sleet into the bus shelter. She wasn't sure who was drawing her; the small space was filled to capacity with heavy coats and the dreary faces of late January in Montreal. Two teenage girls in black leaned against the outside wall, passing a joint back and forth and trying not to look cold. Nadia sighed, tucking her hands into her armpits. *Here we go again.*

Three in one day was a lot; sometimes she went weeks between them. She wished this were one of those weeks; already her clothes were bloody from the first incident of the day, and despite her long coat that hid the stains she couldn't help worrying that people were staring. But the feeling here was strong, pushing at her like a railroad spike between her shoulder blades. If she turned her head a little to the left, she would see him. She did so, wondering if it was worth the bother.

Late twenties, grey coat, worn schoolbag, copy of Sartre. Caricature of a world-weary grad student. He looked preoccupied, but no more so than any of the other commuters pretending to ignore each other. He didn't look special. None of them, Nadia thought, looked special. No-one did. She focused on him, locking her eyes to his jutting wrist bones because she didn't want to look in his face, and *pushed.*

Casually, the young man took a cigarette out of his pocket and thumbed his lighter. There was a general rustle of distaste at his rudeness. Someone coughed ostentatiously.

Nadia grimaced and moved away a little. She had to help them; she didn't have to like them.

Another man, older and heavyset, abruptly turned and began to harangue the smoker in a torrent of French. Obviously not bilingual, the younger man lifted his hands placatingly, and the other's shove sent him staggering against the plastic wall. The cigarette dropped to the floor, narrowly missing Nadia's boot, and the offended man ground it out with obvious malice, his stream of invective continuing. The other occupants of the bus shelter looked uncomfortably at each other, clearly hoping someone else would do something.

The smoker stumbled out into the sleet, glaring at everyone through the clear wall, and defiantly took out another cigarette. A moment later he realized that his lighter was still on the floor inside where he had dropped it. The older man smirked.

"Here," one of the girls said, leaning over to touch the tip of her joint to his cigarette. Closest to the entrance, Nadia could hear her clearly. "That was really shitty. Some people shouldn't be allowed off leashes."

"Thanks." The young man took a long drag on his cigarette. "I'm Keith."

"Steph. Hi."

The bus came, headlights scything through the falling ice. Nadia clambered aboard, vaguely waving her pass at the driver, and watched through the window: the girl's head leaned toward the grad student's as they scurried into the bus shelter together to wait for the next bus. *She's fifteen at the most. And he's a jerk. God, this one is stupid. But they all are.*

The bus pulled away from the curb, and the longing faded from Nadia's mind. The feeling of blessed relief that followed carried her through the balancing with an unshakeable calm, as a jaywalker at the next light made a fatal dart into the path of a taxi. Horns blared at each other. The bus edged ponderously around the accident like a bull moose trying to be tactful, and the screams faded behind them. Nadia settled back in her seat and thought about dinner and sleep.

❖❖❖❖❖

Tweaking the threads of fate has consequences. Nadia Kislowicz was seventeen the first time, and the restlessness she had felt that morning might have been nothing worse than spring. She was in her second semester at Dawson College, an English major with what the teachers called a lack of application, and the classroom seemed more than usually confining. She remembered the pressure in her mind and the push, she remembered the faces of the two students who collided in the hallway. The jumper in the metro later that day still occasionally starred in her nightmares; but it was much, much later before she began to associate effect with cause.

Eleven years later, Nadia opened the door of her apartment, dropped her coat on the sofa, and flopped down after it. Her head was pounding, and the blood spots from the day's first death had probably ruined her work pants. At least she wouldn't have to see anyone else today, unless the landlord finally decided to come up and look at the sink. Even if he did, he wouldn't be the fourth; it never happened if Nadia already knew them.

Wearily she got up and went into the too-small kitchen. There were a thousand little things wrong with the apartment, but none of them were really bad enough to make it worth the hassle of moving. She filled a pot with water and turned on the stove.

I could move to a small town, she thought for the thousandth time, as she put the pasta on to boil. *Get to know everyone. Make it stop.* But there was no guarantee that it would, and there would be lost tourists, visiting relatives, people from the government — strangers would come sooner or later, no matter how remote a place she went to. She'd thought of running off and living in the woods, too. Go north, build a cabin — or buy one, really, since she had never been good with her hands. Maybe a person could avoid the whole world, at least for awhile.

Only, she had this power, and what was it meant for if not to use? She had tried to resist it at the beginning — succeeded, even, for a long while. Until one day the pressure broke through the surface like a geyser through a thin crust of clay, and she had gone to a Canadiens game at the Bell Centre and let her gaze and her blessing sweep through the stands like a searchlight, striking nearly two dozen people in a single moment of release. Later that night, as she turned her mother's car onto the off-ramp that led to her parents' house and the overpass collapsed in a shower of concrete behind her, she vowed never to do that again.

The pasta was finished, and she drained it and added oil and measured out the spices in the palm of her hand the way her mother had always done. Nadia wasn't much of a cook, but her job didn't pay enough for her to eat out very often, so it was often pasta or canned soups. It hardly mattered. Food didn't interest her all that much at the best of times.

Her plate was empty, and she put it in the sink on top of an already teetering pile — *have to do those soon, I guess, they're starting to smell* — and went into the bathroom, showered, put her pants in the sink to soak the blood out, and stumbled into sleep with her usual prayer, the only one she knew anymore. *No dreams. Please no dreams. Please.*

⇢•⊦•⊦•⊦•⇠

Morning came with grey snow swirling around the window and the warbling of the radio alarm clock. Nadia slapped it quiet and rubbed gritty salt from her eyes. She had been crying in her sleep again. She curled into a ball and debated staying there all day, but it was Friday and, once she came home from work and did the week's groceries and laundry, she wouldn't have to go outside again until Monday, so it would be tolerable.

At least she could get away with wearing jeans on Fridays, since she'd forgotten to hang up her good pants. She was a junior secretary at a company that made electrical parts, and she spent most of her time dealing with files and purchase orders rather than people, so nobody ever really got too excited about her clothing anyway.

Breakfast, toothbrush, winter coat, metro pass. She lived in Verdun, which might or might not technically be part of Montreal at the moment, it was hard to remember. Politics was another thing that didn't interest her. In any case, the geography never changed even if the borough boundaries did, so it was always thirty-five minutes by metro to the office, unless there was a shutdown and she had to take the bus instead. She left at the same time every day and always timed it so that she arrived just as the train pulled in. Her co-workers complained about their commutes, but Nadia enjoyed hers: most of the time it gave her half an hour or so to sit peacefully and read. She liked old books with leather covers that she could bring close to her face and smell, books by people who were long dead and whom she would never have to change or kill, books where people fell in love without terrible consequences.

The train came into the station in a swirl of newspapers and dust. Nadia shuffled forward with the rest of the morning crowd, and for once there was actually a seat free within reach. She sat gratefully, undoing the top of her coat, and buried her face in *Indian Love Poems of Lawrence Hope*, glad not to have to face the world just yet.

Just past Beaudry Station she felt it beginning, the first stirrings of restlessness. She sighed and put her book down. Tall black guy with a cane, reading the paper at the far end of the car, sandwiched between the window and a tiny red-haired teenager swathed in an enormous wool scarf. *Probably her*, Nadia decided. She occasionally made bets with herself who the other target would be, although she was less often right than she would have liked. She focused on him almost by rote; she was tired.

The push felt odd, as though there were an echo. It seemed to work, though, as a gust of wind from the opening doors at Papineau blew the man's paper down the car into another passenger's lap. *Not the redhead, then*, Nadia thought with a mental shrug.

She picked up her book, not wanting to see the death, though likely it wouldn't happen here anyway. She couldn't recall a time when the lovers ever saw their dead. For them the connection was always obscured; perhaps it had to be.

The words swam before Nadia's eyes. There was a prickling in the back of her skull, and with irritation she realized it was happening again already. They had never come this close together before, and her head was already pounding. She closed her book, resisting the urge to slam the covers, and looked around. The diminutive redhead, this time, whose gaze was fixed on the opposite wall with the boredom of the habitual commuter. Nadia concentrated and pushed — and, at the same time, something *pulled*.

The red-haired girl's head jerked up, and she locked eyes with Nadia, who sat stunned. The girl yanked her scarf down from her face, stalked over to Nadia's seat, and said, in tones of mingled amusement and disgust: "You have *got* to be fucking kidding me."

※※※

The metro raced away into the tunnel, a blind worm retracing its tracks into a curving burrow. Nadia and her new acquaintance stood on the Radisson Station platform, studying each other like strange cats. Nadia was the taller by 25 centimetres or more, even with her habitual stoop, and she felt awkward looking down to meet the other's gaze. The girl had taken off her scarf to reveal farmgirl braids tied with ratty scraps of denim and green eyes that glared at Nadia out of a constellation of freckles. The whole effect would have been adorable if her expression hadn't been so fierce.

"I have to get to work," Nadia said weakly at last. "I work here. I mean, near here. I'll be late." But she didn't move.

"Wren," the other said.

"Sorry?"

"My name's Wren," the girl clarified. "Wren Summerstars Duplessis. Any stupid jokes you're tempted to make, you can get them out of your system now."

"I wasn't," Nadia protested. "Sorry, I'm Nadia. Nadia Kislowicz. I'm a secretary."

"That sucks." Wren looked her up and down, taking in Nadia's worn coat and boots, the efficient ponytail that was her usual work hairstyle and the book she still clutched in one hand. "I don't get it," Wren said. "Why you?"

"Sorry?" Nadia repeated.

"You know, I *have* a girlfriend. I wasn't looking for someone. Not as such. And you're *definitely* not my type." Wren sighed. "Doesn't matter, though, does it? The mojo may not make sense, but it's never made a mistake yet that I've seen, and that means there is some reason that you and I are perfect for each other. And I can only think of one."

"You can do it, too," Nadia said. There was no real need to say it, they'd both known inside the train, but somehow she felt like the words mattered.

"Bingo." Wren glanced up and down the platform. "Well, I don't see anybody about to be run over. Shall we head up to street level before the powers-that-be start getting antsy?"

"Don't joke about that," Nadia snapped. In truth, she'd been keeping an eye out as well. It wasn't usually more than a few minutes between the meeting and the death.

"Whatever." Wren grinned suddenly, her whole face folding into a maze of laugh lines. "Hey, I'm sorry. I really am. I don't mean to come across all, you know, callous and stuff. This is just kind of a shock."

Despite herself, Nadia smiled. "Likewise."

"So do you think you can skive off work today or something?" Wren persisted. "I mean, I can skip out, I'm doing my best to get fired right now anyways, but you look kind of, you know, professional."

"How old are you?" Nadia asked suddenly.

"Nineteen. And you're, what, thirty-five?"

"Twenty-eight." Nadia thought she should be offended, but she was used to people thinking she was older, and it rarely seemed worth getting angry over. "I've been doing this maybe ten, eleven years. You?"

"Three years." Wren took Nadia's arm and pulled her a few steps toward the payphone at the end of the platform. "So, come on, call in sick. We'll go somewhere and talk."

"I really can't," Nadia said, disentangling herself. "I'm behind on this week's filing as it is, I can't just skip work for no reason—"

"Right," Wren said after a moment. "Got it." She looked so disappointed that Nadia started to apologize, but Wren waved her off. "No, seriously, I get it. You're not interested. That's cool. Listen, let me give you my coordinates, and then I'll bug off, alright? You call if you feel like calling."

"It's not that you don't seem... nice—" Nadia started to say.

"It's okay," Wren said. "Don't worry about it." She rummaged in the deep pockets of her coat and found a stub of pencil and a grocery receipt to write on. "Call if you want. Good luck."

⁂

After that there was a lull for several days, as though Nadia's powers had spent themselves in self-indulgence. No-one died. The weekend passed, and she went back to work on Monday, half wondering if she would see Wren in the train again. She didn't, and didn't really expect to. *Connections only happen once*, she thought. *Love at first sight* — but it was hardly that, now or ever. Most of the time, the people she caused to meet were friendly at best, at the beginning. They had the chance to be more, though. That was all she gave them, that chance. *So give it to yourself, Nadia, why don't you?*

It was guilt as much as anything that finally made her call. She woke up before sunrise from one of her usual nightmares, the faces of the dead blurring in and out of focus before her, and among them was someone whose image would not come clear but who she knew was the one who had died that morning in the metro. She had seen only one death that day, and she thought it must have been linked to the man with the cane; but she and Wren had met, and there should have been two. Just because she hadn't seen it didn't mean there hadn't been a death; by all her experience, there must have been. It wasn't fair to that person, whoever they were, to throw away what they'd died for. Even if it made no sense.

A male voice answered the phone. "Yeah, hi?"

"Is Wren there?" Nadia asked.

"Hang on. Hey, Brian, where's Stubby? No, cause there's somebody on the phone is all. Huh? Lemme ask. Hey, are you the cops?"

It took Nadia a moment to realize she was being addressed. "Um, no. I'm Nadia. Wren knows me."

"Oh, okay. Jesus, Brian, you're so paranoid. This is exactly why Sarah dumped you, you know that? Dumbass. *Is it the cops?* Like they'd tell you if they — no, they *don't* have to tell you, shut up. *No,* that's just on TV. Anyways, I thought you—"

"Hi?" Wren's voice broke in. "I got it, Dave."

"I thought you had a girlfriend?" Nadia asked, the first thing that came to her mind.

"Nadia! Yeah, but she doesn't live here, just these two losers. Hey, so what's up?"

"Do you want to meet?" Nadia asked all in a rush, before she lost her nerve.

"Sure. Where at? I'd ask you over, but Dave and Brian are here and it's kind of a small apartment. Where do you live?"

"Verdun," Nadia answered. "You?"

"Downtown. Here, come meet me, there's a Timmy's at Sherbrooke and University, it's a good place to chat."

All Nadia's usual instincts screamed against going outside unnecessarily, but she had to, she knew it, at least this once. Just to make it worth it. Just to make sure. She kept repeating that to herself, and the rhythm of the words carried her into the metro and out again in one breathless swoop, and she was standing just inside the door of the Tim Horton's while bundled patrons squeezed irritably past her, and all her attention was fixed on the redhead looking at her over her coffee mug with a knowing grin. "Hi," Wren said. "You came."

⇾·┆·⇆·┆·⇇

They had breakfast there and then lunch and dinner, talking as though all the words in the world would pour out of them at once, and the crowd ebbed and flowed around them, a hundred coffee-fuelled dramas in a bizarrely private public space. The air outside was bright with snow, and the last metro of the night left without them. Sometime between three and four in the morning, Wren pulled out her cellphone and broke up with her girlfriend by voicemail. Nadia watched with an eyebrow raised, a feat that raised a fit of giggles from Wren as she tried to emulate it. "That doesn't change anything, you know," Nadia said.

"Wasn't supposed to," Wren said.

Nadia shook her head. "You're something else, you know that? Do you do *everything* on the spur of the moment?"

"Of course not," Wren said haughtily. "I'm a very thoughtful person." She stretched, her shoulder blades cracking. Crumbs of toasted bagel clung to the elbows of her sweater. "But what we *are* is impulsive, you know, Nadia. We don't know any of these people—" She started to gesture around them at the crowded tables. The coffee shop was filled with students hunched over laptops, bus drivers and police officers coming off the night shift, homeless men delaying their return to the snowy streets, all of them oblivious. Nadia caught Wren's wrist.

"Don't," she said. "Don't spoil it."

"I wasn't going to," Wren protested. "I was just saying. We don't know them, we don't know anything about them, we don't know if they deserve the chances we give them—"

"Or whether the ones that die deserve to live," Nadia said softly. She picked up the empty paper cup in front of her and began absently shredding it. Her side of the table was already littered with the debris of her fidgeting.

"You can't think about that," Wren said, taking the cup from her hands and setting it firmly out of reach. "You'll go crazy."

"I have to think about it," Nadia answered. "Someone does."

"No, you *don't*," Wren insisted, leaning forward. Her braids dipped perilously close to the surface of her coffee, and she brushed them back over her shoulder. "You told me you tried to stop doing it, once. So did I, and I don't think we can, or should. So what's the good of feeling guilty? It's just self-indulgence."

"That's awfully cold," Nadia said.

Wren shrugged exaggeratedly. "People die by the dozens every day in this city. You can't bleed for all of them." But the words sounded too much like bravado, and Nadia looked at Wren with pity for the first time. She suddenly seemed so much younger than she was. *Just wait*, Nadia thought but could not say. *It grinds you down, year after year, until one day you realize you've lost any chance for a life.* And then, *But she hasn't, yet. And I never had anyone to talk to.*

It was Wren who did most of the talking, during the hours of morning until the metro opened again. They shared their life stories, but Nadia's took little time to tell: she had grown up in Montreal, graduated from Dawson College and decided against university, and worked at the same job for the past decade. "Things *happened*, obviously," Nadia said, a little defensively. "I'm not saying nothing happened. It's just — not interesting."

Wren, on the other hand, found her own life very interesting. She animatedly described the commune in the Townships where she'd grown up and her move to Montreal at fourteen after her parents' cohort of aging hippies split apart in a bitter property dispute. "I didn't really want to go to Vegas with Papa," she said, "and we don't really know where Mama went, so I moved in with this aunt of mine here. They made me go to school, though." She had coasted through high school, bright enough to skimp on classwork and still get by. Now she was in her third year at Dawson, having changed her major twice already. ("So that's one thing we've got in common," Nadia said, laughing.) Wren was in Fine Arts at the moment, but wasn't sure if she wanted to stick with it. "Besides," she added, "I figure I've got a destiny. I mean, we're special, right? So what I do in school probably won't make a difference anyway."

"Everything makes a difference," Nadia said, sipping her umpteenth coffee. "If anybody should know that, it's us."

Then the sun was rising in a square of sky between the buildings outside, glinting off the cars that nudged the curb like dolphins, friendly and inquisitive. Nadia glanced at her watch: six forty-nine. The trains would be running again, and she had her job to go to. She hadn't stayed up all night since college, and the tiredness and the coffee made her light-headed. As they walked south, everything she could see seemed edged in light.

They stood at the door of the metro, all the words of the long night suddenly gone. Wren tilted her head up, looking nervous for the first time. "Can I kiss you goodbye?" she asked. Something of Nadia's reaction must have shown in her face, because Wren gave a bright, reflexive smile. "No, that was stupid, forget I said it."

"It's just—" Nadia looked down at the ground, flustered. "It's not that — I mean, you're nice and all, I just — I don't—"

"You don't date girls," Wren supplied, looking a little amused at Nadia's floundering. The moment of vulnerability was already well buried.

Nadia shook her head. "I don't *date*," she said. "Girls or boys."

"Right," Wren said. "I get it."

That was the moment to turn away, thank Wren for a pleasant time, and go home. Nadia never remembered later which of them moved first, but she guessed it must have been her; Wren wouldn't have been so forward, not at such a time. It must have been Nadia, but being unable to remember the specifics of that moment was something that would always trouble her later.

She didn't know what she expected. Nadia had kissed three boys in her life, all in high school, and hadn't thought she had missed it. Wren's lips were rough, chapped with winter, not at all what Nadia would have expected. She could taste the toast Wren had ordered for breakfast, mixed with the bitter coffee on her own tongue. Early-morning commuters pushed past them through the pivoting doorway, brushing Nadia's coat, hands, hair, touching without impinging on her space, as though within Wren's tiny arms she was safe from all the world.

※·⁂·⁂·⁂

"You are trying *so* hard to live up to a stereotype," Nadia told her, sometime during that first long conversation. "You're such a hippie. Look at you. Look at your life."

Wren denied it, but Nadia considered herself proven right the first time Wren called her at three in the morning, high and giggling, to declare herself hopelessly in love, with her two roommates arguing about globalization at top volume in the background. The three of them were vegetarian and had a compost heap and went to protests and smoked pot in the park on the mountain. Dave played guitar in a band called Gluten Free, and Brian belonged to a bicycle collective. Between them they managed to nail every stereotype Nadia had ever heard of about activist stoner student types. Her mother, she thought, would disapprove.

It was a week before Nadia realized her nightmares had stopped, and when she noticed it she was briefly disgusted. *I'm turning into a cliché myself,* she thought. *Head over heels in love. You're nearly thirty, Nadia. Stop it.*

But that was patently impossible, and so she didn't really try. She walked through the city with an odd lightness and saw the meetings and the deaths alike with wonder instead of the stony indifference to which she'd grown accustomed. *It's because it's worth it,* she realized one afternoon, amazed, as Wren pushed and two dogs outside the window suddenly growled and lunged at each other, and the dog-walkers scolded them and apologized to each other and found they were both avid scuba divers. *If they feel what I'm feeling, if they even get the chance to, it's worth the cost.*

"Of course it is," Wren agreed blithely, when she said so aloud. "God, if anybody ever told me I'd fall in love with some forty-year-old secretary—"

"I'm twenty-eight," Nadia said indignantly, "and who said anything about love?" Across the café, a young man was half out of his seat, choking on a piece of pastry while his friends fruitlessly pounded him on the back.

"Me," Wren answered, and kissed her, and there was no good rejoinder to that. They got up and left the café, the barista frantically dialling 911 behind them. It was bright and cold outside, and a fresh snowfall had whitened the snowbanks, covering the winter filth and debris. "That's the second one today," Wren said. "Your turn next."

"Probably," Nadia agreed. They didn't always get pulled to the same people, a fact that Nadia found odd and couldn't help wondering about. Now that there was someone else to compare herself with, suddenly whole new avenues of exploration were opened up, and suddenly she found herself interested in them.

"It could be you'd met one of those two somewhere," Wren suggested when Nadia brought up the subject. "You know, old classmate, old co-worker, friend of a friend — if it *does* only work with strangers, and I've never seen anything to suggest otherwise, maybe when only one of us gets pulled to someone it's because the other knows them from someplace."

"I don't remember them," Nadia said. The dog-walkers had both been well-heeled business types, typical of downtown but not the sort of people Nadia ordinarily interacted with.

"Maybe you don't have to," Wren said with a shrug. "Maybe having met them's enough."

⸻

Without much actual discussion, Wren moved her things into Nadia's apartment one weekend in March, with the help of three casually stoned teenagers who seemed to be friends of Brian's. She set up her bedclothes on the couch, surrounded by the boxes of comic books she'd lugged up the stairs.

"I always wanted to be a superhero," she confided that evening, as they washed the dishes. Nadia's cupboard was embarrassingly bare, and dinner had ended up being packaged soup with Rice Krispies in it in place of crackers. Wren declared that she'd eaten far worse. "Ever since I was a kid, you know, like Spider-Man or something. One day I'd just wake up and be special." She laughed, standing on her tiptoes to put the bowls in the cupboard. "As superpowers go, this one's pretty crap, but I guess you take what you can get. I mean, Ant-Man talks to ants for fuck's sake. That's not exactly the grand prize in the superpower lottery."

"Ant-Man?" Nadia repeated. Wren looked at her as though she'd just admitted her ignorance of Bliss Carman or the Group of Seven. "What? I don't read comics."

...Or listen to folk music in crowded basements, or march against the war, or smoke pot on a stranger's balcony while policemen drove by below in benign indifference, or go hiking on the mountain — all of a sudden she had a life and a social circle beyond her co-workers and her landlord and her sister in Toronto. It was strange.

She mentioned this to Wren once, who had never considered it out of the ordinary, her endless parade of friends with whom she laughed and wrangled in English or French with equal fervour and fluency. She was, Nadia found out, a native bilingual, but she had no accent in English, her French heritage only perceivable in her last name and her occasional use of words like *coordinates* and *close the light*, which plenty of Anglo-Montrealers used as well.

"Well, of course you get new friends when you start dating somebody," Wren said airily. It was three weeks after she'd moved in, and five days since she'd moved from the couch to Nadia's big antique bed. That had been a surprise, but not as much of one as Nadia had expected; next to the world-shattering experience of having someone to talk to, someone with whom she didn't have to dissemble or hide, even sex paled. "I mean, you've met like fifty of my friends, and I've met — oh — well, your landlord, anyway. And that guy Jerry who delivers your pizza, you know, the one with the bolt in his knee and the suicidal girlfriend."

Nadia blinked. "*I* didn't know that. How do you know so much about the pizza guy?"

"I talked to him," Wren answered with a shrug. "He's interesting. People are always interesting, don't you think?" It was the sort of thing she said a lot. "I mean, look at you. Anyone would look at you and think, oh, boring secretary type — even your co-workers probably do. They would *not* think you're a wacky lesbian superhero. This is why I like talking to people. You find things out."

"I don't think I'm a lesbian, actually," Nadia said.

Wren giggled throatily, running her hand across the soft dark fur below Nadia's belly. "I beg to differ."

"I mean it," Nadia insisted. "I'm not attracted to women as a *group*, just — you know — just to you. I couldn't be with somebody who didn't — understand. It almost doesn't matter if you're a woman, or if you're pretty, or if—"

"Are you saying I'm not pretty?" Wren demanded with mock outrage, her lips twitching with suppressed laughter.

"You're gorgeous, and you know it. What I'm *saying* is that I'd love you no matter what, so your gender isn't a factor."

"It's a factor to *me*," Wren insisted. "We could absolutely be friends if you were a guy, but I wouldn't be dating you." She frowned. "And in that case we'd have never met. I've never known the mojo to work if people were going to be just friends. So you *have* to be a lesbian."

Nadia frowned, trying to work out this logic. "I don't see it. Just because you think like that, doesn't mean I do. You've been with girls before. I've never even wanted to. I'm not a lesbian, I'm a — a Wrensexual, how about that?"

Wren laughed delightedly at this new conceit. "Well, right now Wren is feeling very sexual indeed, and we have a good hour before either of us has to go to work." She reached for Nadia, who smiled and abandoned the attempt to explain, letting her thoughts go under and drown.

⋆⊹⋆⊹⋆

Then it was April, and a spring blizzard kept them snowbound in the apartment for three days. The power was going on and off unpredictably throughout the city, and Nadia's supervisor called from the office to tell her that there was no point coming to work. Wren took those days off from her current job (cashier at a cheese shop in the Atwater Market; their refrigerator was full of discounted cheese), and they spent the time curled up under enormous quilts in Nadia's bedroom, watching the Space Channel whenever the lights came on and ordering pizza from the one place in the neighbourhood that could be counted on to have electricity by virtue of being right next to the hospital and on their grid.

Their conversation, proceeding by fits and starts in between segments of *Mystery Science Theater*, eventually circled around to their powers. It was strange how little they discussed the subject lately. Even when one or both of them felt the pull toward some stranger in the supermarket or the downtown streets, they tended to act on it without speaking. Nadia found it comfortable to be with someone who wouldn't go into hysterics at the sight of yet another death, but, still, it was an odd habit to have fallen into.

"We can't be the only ones, you know," Nadia said. "I mean, two of us in one city and nobody anywhere else on the planet — it's pretty unlikely."

"We're probably the only ones in Montreal, though. I was looking it up on the internet—"

"Looking up *what*?" Nadia asked with a grimace. "I tried researching this back when it first started happening to me, and all I found was sappy poetry and Greek myths."

"Statistics Canada," Wren clarified. "The death rate in Montreal is about sixty people a day. Most of those are probably in hospitals and nursing homes and whatnot — Nadia, there isn't *room* for more of us here. There'd be more accidents."

"And murders," Nadia added.

Wren looked thoughtful. "I've never seen a murder yet."

"It happens sometimes. Not as common as accidents, though. I saw a guy stab the cashier at a dep once. It was pretty ugly."

"Mm." Wren hugged her, pulling the quilt tighter around both of them. "I hope the meeting was worth it."

"Couldn't tell you."

"What's the worst one you've ever done?" Wren asked lazily. "I mean, one where you just went, *aw, shit, this is a bad idea*?"

"There was one a couple of years ago, at a wedding reception," Nadia answered. "The bride and the guitarist. He broke a string, and she had a spare in her purse. When I left they were making plans to start a rock band. I don't think the groom noticed. You?"

Wren thought about it. "Car crash," she said at last.

"I don't mean deaths," Nadia said with a grimace. "I mean meetings."

"Me too," Wren said, idly rubbing her bare foot against Nadia's shin. "They met in hospital after she was paralyzed. She'll be in a wheelchair the rest of her life, but she's got her chance at true love. Who's to say whether or not she's better off?"

"Us, I guess," Nadia said with a shrug. "Who else?" Then her eyes narrowed, and she levered herself up on one elbow. "Wait a minute — how do you know about that? I mean, if you pushed the crash, and they met in hospital—"

"I followed her, of course." Wren frowned. "Don't pretend like you've never done it. I was curious, that's all. The death was the woman in the other car, and it seemed weird to have that happen *before* the meeting, so I followed the ambulance. Making sure it was all working out, you know."

Nadia shook her head. "I've never done that. Never wanted to. I just — it's bad enough I have to watch them die; I don't want to see them fuck up their chances, too. I'd feel guilty all the time."

"You mean you don't?" Wren asked wryly. "Good for you."

"That's not what I meant!" Nadia exclaimed, flustered. "Of course I — I mean — oh, stop it."

"God, I love you," Wren laughed. She always sounded a little surprised when she said it, as though she were just that moment discovering it to be true.

"How many of them *do* — you know — fuck up?" Nadia asked after a moment.

"You want to know?" Wren teased. Then she sobered. "A third, maybe. A quarter. They don't get a phone number, they say something stupid, they decide they've got better things to do — maybe a third. We only give them chances, Nadia, you and I both know that. They have to do the work themselves."

※※※

Brian's birthday was the ninth of May, and they returned to Wren's old apartment for the party. The metro was delayed half an hour by some emergency that the announcer failed to explain, and by the time they got there, the party was in full swing. Someone Nadia vaguely recognized pressed a drink into her hand. J-Pop bubbled through the stereo system while Dave and his band (currently called Cheerios of Steel) tuned up in the living room. Nadia guessed there were already more people in the apartment than the fire code allowed. Wren seemed to know them all.

"Nadia!" Brian, in a beer helmet and bedsheet and carrying a hammer, appeared at their elbows. "Hey, great, make yourselves at home. How's it going, Wren?" The doorbell rang. "It's open, just come in!" Brian shouted. Nadia winced. "Sorry. Hey, get yourselves some cake or something." He looked at them expectantly.

"He's dressed up as Thor, and he's waiting for us to compliment him on it," Wren explained to Nadia.

The doorbell rang. "It's open!" shouted half a dozen people at once. "Brian, put a fucking sign on the door saying 'Just walk in,'" Wren added.

Brian shook his head. "Nuh-uh. Then the cops can just walk in if they want to."

"Why are you always worried about the cops?" Nadia asked.

"Because they're always infringing on my fucking freedom of—"

"—stealing digital cable, yeah, we know," Wren finished. "Jesus, Brian, it isn't like it's a *secret*. Look, how about if I put up a sign saying 'Just walk in unless you're the cops?'"

"Then they'll know we're hiding something!" Brian wailed.

"Oh, for fuck's sake, Brian—"

Nadia drifted away from the conversation, over toward the buffet of cake and vegetable sticks set up in the living room. The band was arguing over microphone placement, and people were sitting in knots of conversation around the room. Nadia felt ill at ease. Three months with Wren had helped, but she was still profoundly uneasy in social situations.

She filled a paper plate with chips and vegan cookies and took up a perch on a high uncomfortable stool next to one of the couches. Two girls were excitedly detailing a road trip they were taking to Boston in July. Nadia tried to look interested.

Her attention was distracted from the group's wrangling about American youth hostels by the sound of Wren's raised voice from the back porch. "—to do with you anyway! Why can't you just fucking *leave it*?" The reply was inaudible, but it seemed to make Wren furious. "It was *never* like that!" she shouted. Nadia craned her neck, trying to see the argument, but Wren's tiny frame was hidden by the crowd. Nadia stood and started to make her way in the direction of the voices, but by the time she had made it to the living room door, Wren had pushed her way out through the partygoers and was standing in the hallway, fuming.

"Trouble?" Nadia asked mildly.

"No," Wren snapped.

"Who were you talking to?" Nadia persisted.

Wren grimaced, took her arm, and steered her back into the living room. "Nobody you want to meet. Wait here, I'm going to get another drink."

"That was Ruth," Brian said quietly at her shoulder as she watched Wren making her way to the kitchen. For someone in a toga, he managed to make himself surprisingly inconspicuous. "Stubby's ex. She's holding a grudge. Ruth, I mean. Well, maybe Stubby is, too, but Ruth's always been pretty clingy."

Uneasily Nadia thought of the all-night conversation in the coffee shop and Wren's giggling breakup phone call to her then-girlfriend. She felt guilty and was irritated at herself for it.

"Anyways, my advice is, don't get involved," Brian continued. "Nothing good comes of getting involved in shit like that. I remember this one time, Dave was seeing this girl — Shirley, Cheryl, something like that — she used to be in his band back when they were The Federal Spacewarp. And she was cheating on him with this one guy who was a lifeguard, and one night at three in the morning he calls me — Dave, I mean, not the guy — and he's all, Brian, help me out here, I'm stuck in Ottawa, and I'm like, what the fuck are you doing in Ottawa, and he's—"

Nadia kept nodding politely, certain he didn't expect any kind of response. Her fingers twitched restlessly against her plate. *Just nervous*, she told herself, but already the longing was coming over her, and she knew it for what it was. She sighed. This wasn't turning into a good night. *Just get it over with*, she told herself.

"—out of the canal, mad as hell of course, and when we finally rounded up the goats—"

"Excuse me, I need to use the washroom," Nadia interrupted, and stood and left him there, mouth open midsentence. By the time she got to the door she could hear him continuing the story for someone else's benefit.

The kitchen was crowded, a sea of faces reflected dimly in the sliding glass doors that led out to the patio. Nadia felt suddenly very warm. The tug came at her from somewhere to her left, and she pushed. The lights went out.

"You can't run the microwave and the blender at the same time," someone called. Nadia thought it was Dave. "Shit, where's the breaker box?"

Someone knocked over a chair, and someone else yelped. Apologies followed and sparked a conversation. Nadia didn't bother to listen. It was dull stuff, it always was.

"In the linen closet," Wren's voice answered from close by. There were crashing sounds all through the apartment as too many people tried to negotiate too little space. Nadia sighed and stayed put.

The lights flickered on again, revealing the same sweaty crowd as before, minus the two who had met in the dark and apparently left. Three heartbeats passed, and then the screaming started from the living room. *Here goes,* Nadia thought, and wondered whether they could still catch the tail end of the hockey game if they left now. The party was clearly going to be a bust.

"What happened?" Dave demanded. There was a general push toward the living room. Nadia peered over people's heads, more out of an attempt to blend in than because she really wanted to see. Brian and another man were kneeling on the floor beside a tall Chinese woman sprawled facedown on the carpet.

"She hit her head on the table," Brian said urgently. His face was grey. "She's not breathing. Does anyone know CPR?"

Someone did. Someone else called 911. Nadia saw Wren emerge from the hall closet, see the body, and drop to her knees. People moved back to make room. "Ruth fell," someone told her.

"Ah," Wren said. Her voice was curiously flat. "Ah, no. Nadia, no. Please."

"I'm sorry," Nadia whispered. "I didn't know."

This was her, then. Nadia looked closer at the body, its face obscured by the hair of the person trying to breathe it back to life. Ruth was tall and thin and wore a long blue dress. There was no personality in the splayed limbs and the long, still torso. As the would-be rescuer lifted his head to do the chest compressions, Nadia saw a flat nose, an eyebrow piercing, a scattering of acne across the chin, but somehow none of it resolved into a face. This woman had been part of Wren's earlier life, and now she was dead. Nadia had never known her, and she never would now. And for what? For strangers.

⇢•┼•┼•┼•⇠

They took a taxi home. After a few cheery comments about the warm night and the stars, the driver was mercifully silent. The house was dark, and it creaked and shivered around them as they crawled separately into the big bed. Nadia lay on her back, stared at the cracks in the ceiling, and wondered how long it would take for Wren to leave.

In the dead hours of the morning she woke and found herself curled on her side around Wren's smaller body, their wrists clasped in each other's hands like trapeze artists or gladiators. Wren slept, snuffling quietly as she did when she fell asleep crying. Nadia smiled, hiked the covers up higher with her feet, and went back to sleep again, convinced it would somehow be all right.

When the alarm went off, though, Ruth was still dead, and Wren went silently to school and Nadia to work with nothing between them but that.

⇥•⥁•⥁•⇤

Wren didn't come home that night, or the next night, or the next. Discreet inquiries eventually revealed that she was staying with Dave's drummer, which Nadia was vastly relieved to hear; she knew Wren was capable of staggering impulsiveness, and Nadia's first night alone — her first in months — was filled with dreams in which Wren merged with the jumper in the metro from so many years ago. Sometimes Wren was crying, sometimes angry; other times Nadia was too far away to see her face. She woke with her heart hammering behind her eyelids and was terrified to open them and see Wren still gone.

Nadia called her boss at the electrical supply company and told him she was taking the last six years' accumulated vacation time all at once. He agreed with ill grace, but she didn't care; they could fire her if they wanted to. She stayed inside as much as she could. It was the middle of May, and below the apartment window the city trees and flowerbeds were a cacophony of colour. Nadia took to sleeping rolled up in quilts on the sofa; the bed was too large, though it never had been before. A week went by, and then another.

Then Wren was home one morning, suddenly, pretending she had never been gone, but nothing was better —

it was worse. They didn't talk about it. Wren had quit her cashier job and was working as a bicycle courier, and she was out early and home late. Their conversations were filled with trivia about the groceries, the laundry, the repairs the landlord was doing on the roof, but they both steered clear of anything important. Sometimes people telephoned for Wren, and Nadia passed the phone to her without comment. She was used to not receiving calls herself.

She wanted to talk, wanted to find the words to start the conversation that they both knew they had to have, but she couldn't manage it. There was a gaping hole between the two of them, and she couldn't cross over, not now. Nothing could be said until she knew if Wren could forgive her, and she didn't think she deserved to ask.

⁂

"Do you, um—" Nadia looked up from the book she was pretending to read. Wren stood there, twisting a towel in her hands. "Could you give me a hand with the dishes?"

"Sure." Nadia got up, and they moved to the kitchen together, falling into their familiar routine.

"I had a weird one today," Wren said as the sink started to fill. "This guy in the post office accidentally stapled his hand to the desk, and when the paramedics—"

"I don't want to hear about it, okay?" Nadia said sharply, and then realized too late that this would have been a good opening, only she hadn't seen it. Wren only nodded, seeming unperturbed.

"Fine. No problem. Small talk it is. How's work?"

"I haven't been going," Nadia admitted.

Wren paused, dishtowel in hand. "You've been staying here? Every day?"

"You didn't notice," Nadia said. Even though she knew she couldn't blame Wren, that hurt.

"No. I'm sorry. Are you — I mean, why — oh, fuck." Wren grimaced, plainly frustrated by her lack of words. "It scares me when you do this," she said at last. "I know how you used to live. I thought — you know — I thought you'd gotten over it."

"Well, I haven't," Nadia said. "I just don't want to go out, that's all. I've got good reason."

"Because you're afraid!" Wren shouted. The suddenness of her fury startled Nadia, even used to her girlfriend's mercurial moods as she was. "That's all it is. All you ever do is shut yourself off. You don't go out, you don't have friends, you don't *do* anything—"

"If I go out I hurt people!" Nadia snapped back. "So do you! The more time you spend out in the city, the more strangers you see, the more—"

"So instead you run into them in the grocery store, and in the metro, and at the pharmacy — how is that better?" Wren threw the dishtowel aside in disgust. "Answer me this. How many have you done this month?"

Nadia had to think, and that took the edge off her anger. "Fourteen."

"Fourteen, sitting at home like you do. Want to know what I'm at? Twelve. And I've been going to parties, and gone hiking, and seen Dave and the Analemmas play at his brother's club, and gone to Ruth's—" She stopped.

"Ruth's funeral," Nadia said quietly.

"I don't blame you," Wren said.

"Of course you do. Why wouldn't you? I do."

"I should have been careful," Wren said. "I should have thought to introduce you. I knew it only happened with strangers, I just — I didn't think. Nadia, please. It's as much my fault as yours."

"I'm the one who killed her," Nadia said, and there it was.

She turned away from the sink, her hands still wet to the elbows and dripping on the floor, and crossed to the window.

"I didn't love her," Wren said. "I don't know if it makes a difference, but I didn't. She's not really any different than any of the others, she just — it was just a shock, that's all. Just because I knew her."

"That's the worst of it," Nadia said softly. "The others don't matter. We don't care anymore. We don't — Wren, we're monsters, and that's bad enough, but what right do we have to — to *profit* from it?"

"What are you talking about?"

"We met because we — you know, we made it happen. I've been thinking about this a lot the last few weeks. I can accept what we do if I think of it as, as a force of nature or something, as something that's just going to happen, because I can't make myself stop, not for long, but—"

"But, if you're actually happy, that makes it different," Wren finished. "Nadia, didn't you notice? Nobody died for us!"

"As far as *we* know. How do we know? They never see the deaths. Maybe there was someone, and we just didn't—"

"I can live with maybe," Wren said. "Why are you going out of your way to make yourself miserable? Everything's fine." Nadia started to speak, but Wren touched her lips. "No, it really is. I love you. That's what counts."

"It isn't enough," Nadia said. "No, let me finish. Wren, I can't do this anymore. I can't. I've tried, and I just—" Words failed her. "You have to leave," she said.

"So that's it?" Wren demanded. "Just disappear out of your life, all neat and tidy and no loose ends? Well, it's not going to be that simple. You don't get to have it that simple."

"And I don't get to be happy, either!" Nadia shouted back. "That doesn't happen to people like us!"

"I love you," Wren said again, hopelessly. Nadia heard the words, felt them drop like small stones into her, and realized with horror that they felt grotesque, outsized, like sharks in a child's wading pool, like a submarine in a bathtub. There was no longer room in her to contain them.

"If we... break up," Wren said in a small voice, clearly having to make an effort to get the words out, "are we... are we going to be strangers?"

Nadia knew what she was asking. "No, no, of course not!" The enormity of the situation hit her suddenly, viscerally, as it hadn't in all the dark hours she'd spent by herself contemplating it. "No, we'll be friends, of course we will, Wren, I need you—" She was babbling and knew it, but she couldn't stop.

"I don't need you," Wren said. "I just love you."
"I'm sorry," Nadia said. "I'm sorry."
Wren nodded and took a deep breath, as though reaching a decision. "There's something I need you to see."

※·I·※·I·※

Wren's belongings were strewn about the living room in their usual disarray of battered cardboard boxes and teetering piles, and there was what Nadia felt was an awkward silence as Wren rummaged among them. A few times Nadia made as if to speak, but then stopped: there was no way to continue the previous conversation from where it had ended, and she didn't really have anything else to say.

At last Wren emerged triumphantly with a voluminous scrapbook, the cheap kind with thick yellow paper, and handed it to Nadia without speaking. Its cover was blank. Nadia looked at her questioningly and opened it.

At first glance there was nothing to connect the various pieces of paper glued or stapled or folded into the pages: an origami crane; a ticket stub for a band called Stochastic Interference; a September bus transfer; a program for a play; a fragment of napkin on which someone had drawn a stick-figure dinosaur; several letters, and envelopes without letters; other pieces of paper that looked like they'd been fished out of the trash at random. There were photos, many of them, regular ones and Polaroids and tiny ones from photo booths, posed portraits that looked professionally done and pictures from a cellphone camera in dubious lighting that were little more than blurred shadows. Some of the people shown were friends of Wren's whom Nadia recognized from parties and protests and shows; others she had never seen before.

She flipped pages. It was all the same: a cartoon torn from the newspaper; an ad for powdered detergent; "John Halle and Christine Stettin invite you to the celebration of their marriage"; a train ticket stub from Ottawa to Belleville...

Nadia looked up. "I don't get it."

Wren took the book from her hands and turned back to the first page. "This I found in the trash," she said, touching the crane. "Andrew Lane — you've met him — made it at the Japanese culture festival a few years ago, where he met his girlfriend Aya selling food. Stochastic Interference was Dave's band, back when; that was where we first met, actually, at one of their shows. That was one that didn't work out in the long run — they were together for about four months. Then Gina's mom got cancer and she had to go back to BC, and Dave doesn't do the long-distance thing." She tapped the bus transfer. "I was never able to find out who these guys were, so I kept my transfer to remind me of them. There's a picture, too."

"You do this with everyone?" Nadia asked incredulously. It shouldn't have been shocking, but somehow it was. "I mean, you follow them?"

"Most of the time. I haven't actually been doing it as much lately; I was sort of worried you'd think it was weird. Like stalking, you know?" Wren gave a sort of sheepish smile. "I mean, when I told you about following those two to the hospital that time, you seemed kind of creeped out. And it *is* a bit weird, I guess. I just—"

"It's not," Nadia told her.

"And they're interesting, you know?" Wren went on, as though she hadn't heard. "And sometimes I get to know them, I make friends — that's how I met Dave, like I said, and Brian, and half the other people I know. I get involved, and then I just — they're interesting, and I want to meet them."

"But you can't ever tell them why," Nadia protested. "Doesn't that make you feel like — like you're playing God, or something? Changing their lives and not telling them about it?"

"A little," Wren said, and then grinned. "But once we're friends, they end up changing mine, too."

She sighed. "Look," she said. "We can't stop using this power. You've tried, I've tried — sooner or later it's too much, it breaks through. So it's going to happen. But that doesn't make it necessarily a bad thing. These," she closed the scrapbook and handed it back to Nadia, "remind me of the good side, when I need to be reminded."

"And that keeps you from feeling guilty about it?" Nadia asked wonderingly.

Wren snorted. "You know it doesn't. But it makes it bearable. I've learned to live with this, Nadia, and you've got to do the same. Maybe you can do it the same way as me, maybe you need something different, but you've got to find *something*."

"And you want to stay and help me?" Nadia asked.

"No." Wren smiled wryly, shook her head. "I actually don't. No, you need to work your shit out, and I need to let you go and do that. It's best if I leave for awhile." She smiled hesitantly. "I'll be in touch, though. If you want me to, I mean."

"Not strangers?" Nadia asked in a small voice that sounded totally unlike her.

"Never strangers," Wren promised, and abruptly stumbled forward to enfold Nadia in a hug, nearly crumpling the precious book between them. "How could I ever lose you?" She stepped back, straightening her braids. "When you get things figured out," she said, "call."

※※※

The sun beat down on the sidewalk and shimmered up from the pavement, absurdly warm for early June. The bus was late, and a dozen or so people waited below the sign with varying degrees of patience. Nadia sat on the bench, having arrived early, and tried to lose herself in a collection of Sherlock Holmes stories. With Wren's belongings out of the apartment, and the floor space no longer cluttered with comics and clothes and strange handmade art objects, she'd been able to find her own things much easier, and this had turned up while she was cleaning, one of her old favourites.

She felt the longing radiating toward her and looked around for Wren before she could stop herself. *She's not gone forever*, Nadia reminded herself. *Just for a while.* She closed her eyes and *pushed*.

"Screw this," the man next to her said. "I'm not waiting around anymore." He jammed his bus pass back into his pocket and stood up.

"Yeah, no kidding," the woman beside him agreed, doing likewise. "I can probably walk downtown faster than this bus is going to get here. Should've just taken my bike." Nadia watched the backs of their heads as they began to walk north, the way they leaned in toward each other as they spoke. *Not strangers,* she thought. They could be what she and Wren were. Every one of them could.

"I *thought* you were a cyclist," the man commented. "That tan from the bicycling gloves is as good as a badge."

The woman laughed. "Do you ever ride on the South Shore? There are some great trails there if you—" Her voice was fading; the two of them were nearly at the crosswalk by then.

For a moment Nadia thought of getting up and following them, observing how things would begin to work out — if they did. *That's what I'd do,* she could almost hear Wren saying, and Nadia thought swiftly in response, *I am not you.*

The light turned, and the couple crossed the street, disappearing out of sight over the slight rise of the road. Nadia stayed seated on the bench, calm as a cat in the warm June sun. *Any moment now*, she thought, and, sure enough, there it was, the sound of an explosion behind her and, as she turned, a sudden gout of flame from a first-floor window. The kitchen of a restaurant, it looked like, and already the fire was spreading. The others who had been at the bus stop were fleeing, panicked; one ran into the street and nearly into the path of a car. Tires squealed. Someone inside the restaurant was shouting in Greek. Nadia stood and walked quickly to a payphone on the corner, calmly gave the address to the fire department, and came back. No-one else seemed to be doing anything useful yet.

It felt strange to still be there, to be watching the aftermath for once. Ghoulish, Wren might call it. *I am not you,* Nadia thought again. Wren denied death by focusing on the lovers only; that was one way to cope, but not the only one. Someone inside the restaurant was dead, she knew it without having to see. She could do nothing for him or her, but that didn't mean there was nothing she could do.

People were pouring out of the restaurant onto the sidewalk now, patrons and waitstaff and kitchen workers with soapy hands, many of them stumbling, eyes glazed with fear or looking lost. *A first-aid course,* Nadia thought, *that would be a good idea. And carrying a cellphone.* She would have to sit down at home and make a list. Maybe she couldn't stop the deaths, but she could mitigate the damage, and maybe do more than that — at least some of the time.

Even being the one person on the scene who always stayed calm would be useful, she thought, as her gaze fell on a little boy in the crowd, about six, apparently alone. His face was streaked with white ash, and he had wet himself. He had the odd pinched expression of a child who has been told over and over not to cry but hasn't quite learned how to stop himself.

Nadia walked over and knelt on the sidewalk in front of him. The boy stared at her, bewildered. Maybe his mother or father was the one dead, or maybe he had simply gotten lost in the confusion. Either way, this was as good a place as any to begin.

"Let me help," she said.

The Story of the Woman and Her Dog
E.L. Chen

He slept in the bathtub that night.

Natasha did not know anything about dogs. She feared that he would attack her, or eat the goldfish, or piss on the bedroom carpet, or all three. When he appeared, she panicked and shooed him into the closest room, waving a towel in front of her like a toreador's cape. The towel was pale blue, the colour of his eyes. She dropped it on the bathroom floor once he was inside and shut the door.

She sprawled across the unmade bed, listening for his whine, the scrape of toenails against the bathroom door. She wondered what she would tell the neighbours if he released a torrent of desperate barking. The walls of the condo were thin; her neighbours' patience, thinner. She listened and waited because she did not know what else to do.

She heard nothing.

She had to pee but decided to hold it.

Eventually she tired of the vigil and went to bed without brushing her teeth. In the morning, it was still quiet. She wondered if she had imagined him, that he was not really a dog. She opened the bathroom door, slowly, cautiously, as if she hoped to catch him in an altered state.

She flicked on the light. The dog was still a dog. He stirred. Blinked. Yawned a doggy yawn, unrolling a long doggy tongue from between long doggy teeth. He still had not made a sound.

Natasha shut the door and went out to buy a leash and collar.

⋆⋅†⋅†⋅†⋅⋆

Six Sikhs boarded the bus. Natasha could not help but notice them, even though Toronto was a hodgepodge of ethnicities. Six robust gentlemen in their forties or fifties, with aristocratic features and neat moustaches, beards, and turbans. Yet their clothing was incongruous: shapeless nylon jackets and ill-fitting trousers in forgettable shades of khaki, olive, and tuna-grey. She imagined they were tired, displaced gods eking out a living at one of the furniture plants along the bus route. Gods from a forgotten pantheon, driving forklifts and spray-painting filing cabinets so that their children could go to medical school at U of T.

No, not gods. Princes, perhaps. Or kings. But not gods.

The men found separate seats, ignoring each other as if they were brothers or strangers. The eldest — judging from his snow-white moustache — sat beside Natasha.

"That is a beautiful dog," he said.

The dog was sitting at Natasha's feet. So faithful — even loving. Man's best friend, and this woman's bane. Natasha had just taken him to see her aunt, a veterinarian.

"I suppose," she said, sullenly. Her aunt had declared the dog to be perfectly healthy and normal. Natasha took it as a personal insult that he did not have the decency to be a little unusual. Her aunt had then asked about Paul, and Natasha had lied — hating Paul for making her lie.

"What is his — or her — name?" the man asked. His voice was gentle, cultured. From his accent, she guessed that he had been educated in England.

"His," Natasha said. "Shadow." Despite his thick white coat. She had been forced to come up with a name at her aunt's clinic, and it was the first that came to mind. A friend in grade school had owned a Siberian husky named Shadow. This dog looked a little like the husky, except that his fur was pure white, like the Sikh man's moustache.

Shadow sat bolt upright on the floor of the bus, facing Natasha. He could have easily put his head in the lap of her skirt, but she knew he would not be so bold. His fur was cool and plush against her legs, and she resented him for it. She wound the leash tighter around her hand. She touched that hand to her throat as if she were the one wearing a new collar.

"Where did you find such a magnificent creature?" The man scratched Shadow between his pointed, wolf-like ears. Shadow shook off his hand as if shaking off water.

"Sorry," Natasha said, and then wondered why she was apologizing for the dog.

The man smiled. "It is quite alright. I would not want my head touched by strangers either. Where did you find him?"

"He found me," Natasha said. She bristled at the thought that this stranger believed she had acquired Shadow of her own free will. "It's a long story. I'd rather not talk about it."

"Stories are meant to be told," he said. "That is why they are stories. How else are we to learn from our mistakes and the mistakes of others?"

Natasha snorted. "Stories are just stories. They have nothing to do with real life. They're just what people want real life to be. They're fantasies. Types and clichés strung together to form a plot."

The man sighed. "The young have no faith. They are always so angry, so sure of themselves. As I once was."

"No," Natasha said. "It's just none of your business."

He smiled. "Stubborn, are we? Not a nice trait."

"In a woman, you mean," she said, thinking of Paul and not at all of the man to whom she was speaking.

"No. In anyone. If you are not careful, your obstinacy will wrong those whom you trust." He ran his callused hands through Shadow's thick fur. This time Shadow did not shake him off.

The man's mouth smiled, but his eyes did not. "Let me tell you the story of my brothers and myself."

She glanced out the window of the bus. It would be another twenty minutes until her stop. "Alright," she said, sighing. "I'm not going anywhere. Tell me your story."

THE HISTORY OF THE SIX KINGS

I am the eldest of six brothers, the sons of a great king. As children, a marriage was arranged between myself and our cousin Nourounihar, as was the custom of my family. When our dear cousin came of age, she arrived at our kingdom to be wed. To my delight, she had become a beautiful, agreeable woman, and for our first year of marriage we had a harmonious union.

My new bride troubled me, however. At dinner, no matter how lavish the banquet, she would only consume a few grains of turmeric-stained rice and a couple of dates. She would bring them carefully to her lips with the tiny silver teaspoon she kept on a chain around her neck. Yet days and nights passed and she never exhibited signs of wasting away. When my grand vizier speculated that sorcery kept her hale, I stubbornly refused to listen to his suspicions and ordered him to be drawn and quartered.

But my faithful servant had planted the seed of doubt. A week after his execution, I stole into my wife's quarters after we had dined. Again, she had eaten little. She excused herself from the table early. Hidden in her boudoir, I watched my wife whiten her face with nightingale droppings, rouge her lips and nipples, don her filmiest veils and her brightest jewellery. When she had finished her preparations, she used the silver teaspoon around her neck to scoop a little powder out of a rough clay pot on her dressing table. She cast the powder against a wall, and a doorway appeared as if traced in smoke.

I watched as she entered the secret passage, and then I followed.

I found myself in a brilliantly jewelled cavern. Precious stones twinkled from floor to ceiling, and to either side of me brightly coloured, iridescent fish — jewels themselves — swam in shallow pools lined with gems. My wife's eager path brought her to a cloaked figure whose shadowed face was so pale, so gaunt, so wicked, he could have only been a ghoul or demon.

She flung off her veils and consorted with her unnatural lover until I could take no more of their base revelry.

Fie! I cried, springing from my hiding spot. So you will not dine with me, yet would fraternize with demons?

Foul miscreant! my wife said. I will see that you never leave this place.

She uttered a series of strange words, and I suddenly found myself thrashing underwater. She had transformed me into one of the coloured fish.

The shameless wanton married each of my brothers in turn as they inherited the throne, convincing them that it was their filial duty to provide for her. They could not resist her lustrous ink-black hair, her safflower-tinted nipples, the silky petals between her thighs that unfolded like a Chinese puzzle. Each of my poor brothers discovered her perfidy too late and joined me in the pools of the jewelled cavern.

Nourounihar ruled our kingdom with her lover by her side, and her reign was a period of terror and depravity. Often she would bring innocent men and women — already half-dead from torture — down to the cavern and push them into the water. As my brothers and I had been reduced to animals, we had no choice but to nibble away at the living flesh in order to sustain ourselves. There was nothing else for us to eat, except each other. Nourounihar enjoyed telling us whom we were devouring and the trifling reasons why she had condemned them to such a fate.

My brothers and I languished with no hope of being restored. Seven years after my transformation, however, we spotted a youth wandering through the cavern. Unlike Nourounihar's victims, he appeared whole and healthy despite his tattered clothes. The boy's pockets brimmed with jewels — no doubt plucked from the walls — but he was clearly lost.

The boy sank to his knees by our pool. He gazed hungrily at us, but we were too quick and slippery for his tired hands.

Ah! he said. What use are the finest jewels if I join the other skeletons in this cavern?

I poked my head above the water's surface and said, Young master, we know the way out.

The boy gasped and scrambled to his feet. What witchcraft is this? he asked.

None but the wicked sultana's, who keeps us imprisoned in these powerless shapes, I said. We can tell you the cavern's secrets, but we ask but one favour in return.

What would you have me do? the boy said.

I said, We require that you depose of the sultana and her degenerate consort. We were once men, and their deaths will free us from this foul enchantment.

The youth protested. I said, My five brothers and I are kings. We have a lovely sister who is sweet and well-tempered, gentle and docile. We will give you her hand in marriage, and our kingdom, if you free us.

The youth swore that he would avenge us. I directed him to the cavern's egress, and my brothers and I prayed day and night that he would deliver us from our fate. A fortnight later we awoke to discover that we were men again. We escaped the cavern to find our kingdom celebrating the death of the sultana and her consort at the brave hands of the youth.

We gave the youth our youngest sister's hand in marriage as well as our kingdom, for he had truly earned them. My brothers and I left to seek our fortunes elsewhere, and now we earn our keep with our hands and no-one knows that we were once proud, foolish kings.

⁂

"What a sexist story," Natasha said. "The women were either sluts or virgins."

The eldest brother shrugged. "It is all subjective. I am sure my youngest sister tells a different story. We cannot help our tales being influenced by who we are and what we know. How would you describe the men in your life? Are they heroes? Knaves? Villains?"

Natasha said nothing.

"Now will you tell me where you got this dog?" he asked.

She shook her head. He sighed. "Your obstinacy will be your downfall, as it was mine."

He stood up and yanked the cord. The bus halted at the next stop. The six brothers stepped off into the night. Natasha watched them through the window, turning away only when the bus continued ambling along its route. She could not talk about Shadow even if she wanted to, because she did not know where to begin.

Fortunately for her, however, the best stories start *in medias res*.

⋄⋅⋅⋅⋅⋅⋄

She woke to muffled shouts and Paul's motionless heat against her back. Something was happening in the intersection below their building. She lay quietly, listening. As the shouts grew louder, Paul stirred.

"Another goddamn parade," he groaned. "Why does every goddamn parade in Toronto have to pass through Dundas and University? Don't people have anything better to do on a Sunday morning? Like sleep in? Doesn't anyone go to church anymore?"

Natasha twisted onto her other side in order to close the distance between them in the bed. But Paul flopped onto his stomach, burying his head under a pillow. "What's this one about?" he asked.

Being a large, cosmopolitan city, Toronto was a jumble of visible minorities and special-interest groups. Every weekend there was a celebration — or a protest. Both the US consulate and the provincial government were on University Avenue, near Dundas Street, and City Hall was within marching distance.

"Who cares," Natasha said, her arm sliding across his shoulders, seeking his warmth. One of her legs scissored open over his.

He pushed her off. "Come on," he said. "You're closer to the window."

Natasha sighed and flipped over toward the edge of the mattress. Her limbs creaked and wobbled as she stood, cramped from defending her side of the bed.

She parted the blinds. Below, a procession of cement mixers and sewage trucks crept southbound on University. "It's just some construction trucks," she said.

"The white man's parade," Paul joked. Natasha punished him by not laughing.

Several spandex-clad bodies sporting large black numbers on their backs sprinted past the trucks. "There's also a marathon," she said. A few seconds later, a herd of people in shapeless white T-shirts stampeded through the intersection.

"A charity marathon," Natasha added, squinting at the logos on the participants' T-shirts. From the eleventh floor, they were indecipherable. "For breast cancer, I think. Or heart disease. Wait — wasn't there supposed to be something for juvenile diabetes this weekend?"

"That was yesterday," Paul mumbled from under his pillow. He was falling back asleep. Resentment surged from Natasha's stomach and into her chest like heartburn.

She was about to close the blinds when she noticed that there were now more women walking down University Avenue, and fewer were wearing the white T-shirts. Women of all ages, all shapes, sizes, and colours, toting makeshift signs. A pair of mounted policemen trotted behind them, ready to control the mob if necessary.

Natasha peered at the signs, unable to make out what they said. She wondered who the women were. Government employees demanding reimbursement for years of gender-biased salaries? Sex-trade workers? Mothers against drunk driving?

Furious shouts floated up from street level and buffeted the window pane. "Down with men!" the women chanted. Natasha shook her head as if to clear the cobwebs from it. Surely that could not have been what she had heard. Her frustration with Paul was warping her hearing. She glanced at Paul's side of the bed; he was snoring slightly, dead to the world. She slipped out of the bedroom and onto the balcony.

"Down with men!" the women repeated. Natasha had not imagined it. *"Down with men!"*

Natasha was shocked at their vitriol. Surely in this day and age of equality between the sexes, men were not the enemy. Yet at the same time wished she had the courage to be down there, the weight of a sign braced against her arms, the splinters from a wooden signpost digging into her hands. She wanted that pain to jolt her awake. She wanted, for once, to be angry without any fear that she was being a shrew or a bitch.

And then Natasha saw the men — men also of all ages, shapes, sizes, and colours. Men marching up University Avenue carrying similar signs. "Down with women!" they chanted. "Down with women!"

The sexes met, head-on, at Dundas Street, and then Natasha could not tell what they were shouting anymore. The occasional word bubbled to the surface of the noise and drifted up to where she stood, sounding as clear as if she had spoken the words herself.

Blame... partner... faults... vanity... understand... want... hero... goddess... equal... listen...

Hypocrite... hypocrite... hypocrite...

An arrhythmic crash of gongs and cymbals interrupted the shouting, heralding the approach of a Chinese New Year pageant. The dancing lion emerged from Dundas Street and wove around the demonstrators, prancing, blinking its long-lashed bulbous eyes in apoplectic ecstasy. It shook its shaggy head, lolled its felt tongue.

Raucous static drowned out the cymbals. A flatbed truck crawled down University, towing a Gay Pride parade float on which bare-chested men boogied under arches of rainbow-hued balloons. Smiling, sweet-faced young women marched behind the float, holding hands in twos and threes and fours. They observed the heterosexual melee with amusement.

The mounted policemen nudged their horses into the middle of the bedlam. "Move it along, please," one said from his towering perch. With no warning, a dreadlocked youth wearing a Che Guevara T-shirt leapt forward and stabbed the policeman's horse with a bowie knife.

"Fuck you, Mr. Man," he yelled.

The horse screamed and buckled. Angry young men streamed onto the street. Glass bottles and raw eggs smashed against the US consulate's barred windows.

A cohort of masked riot police swept through the crowd. Balloons popped. Men and women screamed. The Chinese lion danced away as fast as its many legs could carry it, cymbals crashing double-time.

When the smoke and tear gas cleared, a dozen upside-down clowns staggered down University, coughing and wheezing from their crotches. Eight tiny plastic reindeer bobbed behind them. Santa Claus had arrived, signifying the end of the parade. A Molotov cocktail landed in the back of his sleigh. He snuffed the flame with one of his woollen mittens and tossed the bottle back out into the crowd. Natasha marvelled at his coolness. He was a parade veteran.

She slipped back inside. "What was all that racket?" Paul asked. "You said it was a marathon."

"It was nothing," she said. Goosebumps prickled her bare arms. She climbed under the covers and curled onto her side, trying to warm up. Paul squirmed toward her and pressed himself against the small of her back. His cold fingers burrowed under her camisole. Natasha clenched her teeth, feigning sleep until he gave up and retreated to his side of the bed.

Her irritation surprised her when his snores rumbled behind the wall of her turned back. *Hypocrite.* She was not sure if she meant Paul or herself.

When did this cold war start? she asked herself. When did their bed become a tacit battlefield? Who drew the imaginary line down the centre and dug trenches on either side? When did their marriage become polarized, cleaved into silent rejection and amiable civility, divided between night and day?

She pictured Scheherazade — lying beside her husband, a near-stranger, wondering how long she could live this way before the axe would fall.

→·|·•·|·•·|·←

Natasha thought about abandoning the dog. (She refused to think of Shadow as her dog; he was simply *a* dog, *the* dog.) She thought about it all the time. She thought about the different ways she could do it: a classified ad in the paper; the doorstep of the Toronto Humane Society; the parking lot of a suburban grade school on a Sunday morning, driving a rental car away while Shadow chased butterflies outside.

The Sikh gentleman on the bus had been right. Shadow was a beautiful dog. Someone would want him. Although the fact that someone might want him more than Natasha did made her want to keep him out of spite.

Still, one day while alone in the dog park, the leash slipped from her hand. It was not intentional. Shadow was crouched beside a garbage bin. Natasha looked away, as if to be polite.

Paul had never liked using the toilet when the bathroom door was open. As she remembered this, her fingers slackened and the leather strap scraped her knuckles and dropped onto the ground. She stared at the dropped leash for a second. Shadow had not noticed.

She walked away.

She walked, and then she walked faster — and then she ran. She did not look back until she reached her building. She braced herself on the front door, panting. She dared to look behind her; Shadow was nowhere in sight. She stepped away from the door.

If she let him go now, she would never know how this would end. There would be so much left unresolved. Anyway, she was certain that he would find his way back to her, no matter where or how she abandoned him. But would he want to come back to her? Natasha was not ready to have that question answered yet.

When she returned to the park, Shadow was stretched out on the grass beside the garbage bin where she had left him. A young man bent over him, ruffling his white fur. He looked up in surprise as Shadow clambered up and trotted toward her.

"Is that your dog?" the man asked, straightening. A leash dangled from his hand. In the distance, a Dalmatian sniffed and pawed at a pile of leaves. Natasha had never seen him nor his dog at the park before. "I was about to call the Humane Society."

"He's his own dog," Natasha said. Shadow sat at her feet, waiting. She bent down and picked up his leash.

"I can see that. Got away from you, did he?" Although he smiled, there was a sadness in eyes. It intrigued her; the emotion was foreign, exotic. Lately Natasha felt only the numbness of anticipation, as if she were on a cross-country bus trip, powerless to do anything but count away the passing nights and days.

"Yes," she said. The man's dark eyes were heavy-lidded and long-lashed, and the hand that held the leash looked strong. "I haven't seen you here before."

"I am only passing through," he said. "My name is Ameer."

"Natasha," she said. "Thank you for looking after Shadow. Would you like to come back to my place for coffee?"

He blinked, and then smiled again. The sadness remained his eyes, but that was fine with Natasha. Her eyes likely betrayed something, too.

Natasha took Ameer and his Dalmatian on a tour of the condo's silent rooms, feeling a little like Bluebeard. "Do you find it lonely in this large place?" he asked.

"No," she said. "Not lonely enough, with Shadow."

The last stop in the tour was the master bedroom. The room was a war zone — barren, desolate, stripped of anything of value. Everything meaningful had been squirreled away for better times: photo frames lay face-down in drawers, jewellery rested furtively in secret compartments, the good sheets were wedged at the back of the linen closet. Only the goldfish bowl still stood on the dresser, but they would never reveal what atrocities they had witnessed, and they would never judge. Goldfish were like that — as neutral as Switzerland.

"My dog only makes me feel more alone," Ameer said.

He perched on the bed. Natasha sat next to him. She had not offered him coffee yet as she had promised. The dogs curled up at their feet: a peaceful, domestic tableau that could shatter at any moment with the right word or action. There was something comforting and alarming about this ritual, this rigmarole, this pantomime that could only end in love and — and what? Hate? Hate was too strong a word. Detachment, perhaps. Or alienation.

"In what way?" she said. *Here is someone who understands,* she thought, *who can help me understand what has happened to me.*

Ameer teased the Dalmatian's muzzle with his fingernails. The dog's tail thumped from side to side on the carpet like a metronome, timing her master's silence.

"I will tell you my story," he finally said, "and you can judge for yourself."

THE STORY OF THE HUSBAND AND THE PARROT

In hindsight it was my fault for not trusting her. But let me start at the beginning. I was young and in love, and extremely jealous. I had married a beautiful, agreeable woman, and I looked forward to spending the rest of my days in domestic harmony. But jealousy was my downfall; suspicion, my rival.

In hindsight I should have also trusted myself to be a fine husband and man enough for her. Instead I bought a parrot to spy on her, a loyal bird that told me all that occurred in my house while I worked during the day. Many times my wife was shocked that I knew the details of her daily affairs — the errands she ran, the phone calls she received, the friends and neighbours with whom she conversed.

Being a clever woman, my wife soon discovered that the parrot was betraying her. She threw a towel over its cage and ordered her maids to deceive it thus: one shone a flashlight intermittently above its head; the second sprayed water between the gilded bars; the third ran a blender beneath the cage.

I arrived home that night and consulted my feathered confidant. What news of my wife's affairs? I asked.

Ah! I could not see or hear anything but the terrible lightning, rain, and thunder, it said.

Of course, I knew this to be false; it had been a bright, temperate day. I assumed the parrot was mocking me. In a fit of rage, I seized the poor bird from its cage and dashed it to the ground, killing it. Only later did I learn from the maids of my wife's trick, and I regretted killing the one creature who had been true to me.

When I confronted my wife, she flew into a fury. What does it matter? she cried. What right have you to spy on me?

She then pronounced words that had no meaning to me until she uttered, I command you to be half-marble, half-man.

The force of her enchantment sent me flying into the nearest chair, where I found myself unable to move, as if I had been tied down. I had become marble from the waist down, and yet my head, torso, and arms were flesh.

My wife confined me to the bedroom, where for many months she took cruel pleasure in her power over me. She would lock me alone in the room for days until I begged to see another human face. She would sit on the bed and stare silently at me while I feared she was devising a new torment. Some days she would simply ignore my presence as if I were an unused armoire. If I protested, she would threaten to turn my upper body into stone as well.

She particularly enjoyed gratifying herself with my marble phallus while I sat helpless and humiliated. Sometimes she would bring home a man or a woman, or both, and I would be forced to watch their carousing — or worse, her lovers would ill-use me as well. I could still move my arms and was often tempted to strike her — but I remembered the parrot and how quickly and unnecessarily it had died.

Eventually one of my wife's maids, a clever girl who knew a little sorcery, took pity on me. One night, while my wife was out, she cured my affliction and promised to avenge me. I begged her to not punish my wife too severely; we were married, and I still loved her, despite the pain we had made the other suffer. The sorceress conceded.

When my wife returned home, she was transformed into the Dalmatian that you see now. The sorceress disappeared in a puff of smoke, and I never saw her again.

I have since realized that, although my wife wronged me, I had wronged her as well. I have been travelling from city to city for the past five years, searching for the sorceress. I wish her to change my wife back into a woman so that we can forgive each other.

❧·❧·❧·❧

Ameer named all the cities he had visited. It was a long list. Evening had fallen, limpid and languorous. His voice grew louder and clearer in the still air; night always amplifies sound and lends gravitas to feelings that would appear trivial in daylight. Natasha wondered if Scheherazade's stories would have held her husband's attention if she had told them during the day.

Finally Ameer fell silent, his downcast eyes hidden by long lashes. Natasha wished she had lashes like his, if only so she could hide behind them. A tear slid down his cheek, and she envied his ability to cry. She could not cry for fear of appearing weak or manipulative. She brushed the tear away with her thumb so that she would not have to look at it.

She slipped an arm around his shoulders. *He's lost someone, too*, she thought. Another casualty of the war between the sexes. His hand was a tentative weight on the underside of her breast. Natasha shivered, moved by his gentleness.

This is not a revenge fuck, she thought. *I am not that type of woman. I am doing this because I want to.*

They shut their dogs in the bathroom.

❧·❧·❧·❧

Shadow told the Dalmatian a story of his own. He told her how he had turned Natasha into a human. She ignored him; Dalmatians tend to be deaf. He tried to mount her but slipped off her narrow backside. She nipped him on the back of the neck. He retreated to the corner. She greedily lapped stale water from the toilet.

❧·❧·❧·❧

Drums woke Natasha the next morning. She floundered in the queen-size bed; lately she had been defiantly sleeping in the middle. She turned her face toward the bedroom window's light. A shadow flickered on the blinds. Ameer was slipping into the jeans he had discarded the previous night. Natasha feigned sleep.

He opened the bathroom door. The Dalmatian bounded out and stuck her muzzle into his hand. When Shadow followed, Ameer pushed him back into the bathroom and closed the door.

Ameer left the bedroom, his hand still on the Dalmatian's head. Oh, the shame of being dumped at dawn without even a *thank you ma'am*. Natasha covered her face with her hands as if blinding herself would make her disappear — in a puff of smoke, perhaps, like Ameer's sorceress-maid. That would have been nice — an escape from the long days and nights of uninformed anticipation.

When she heard the front door close, Natasha sat up and punched the second pillow on the bed. She was angry at herself for being hurt that Ameer had left. *She* was the one who had invited him back to her place, had let him touch her. She did not want to be a cliché — the clinging girlfriend who demands constant attention, or the gold-hearted Girl Friday who gives too much and gets hurt in return. She did not expect Prince Charming either, nor did she believe that, if she were virtuous and clever enough, she would find salvation.

But she did not know what else to do, how else to feel. She should have listened to her mother, who had scolded her for reading fairy tales as a child. Perhaps if she had read the stories her mother had wanted her to read — depressing-looking novels with Newberry Medals stamped on the front cover — she would have known what to do. But she doubted she would have learned about adult relationships from those books.

The bedroom window hummed; the drums outside were growing louder, deeper. It was late summer, so it was not Chinese New Year, St. Patrick's Day, or Christmas. Curious, Natasha climbed out of bed, threw on one of Paul's old T-shirts, and shuffled out onto the balcony.

A high-school marching band strutted down University Avenue and crossed Dundas Street. Androgynously uniformed teens clutched flutes, trumpets and glockenspiels; pudgy adolescents struggled to keep sousaphones aloft; baton-twirlers cartwheeled in flickering jailbait-short skirts. It was the start of a typical Sunday parade.

The streets were lined with people — families with children, gaggles of teenagers, curious passersby. It was as packed as if it were the Santa Claus Parade or the Gay Pride Parade. Ameer and his Dalmatian stood trapped at the intersection, unable to cross University Avenue. Natasha felt sadistic satisfaction — then checked herself. Yes, smugness was acceptable. There were no female stereotypes that were based on smugness. But she was still angry at herself for having let Ameer take advantage of her vulnerability. Even if she had been the one to ask him over. *Hypocrite*, she scolded herself.

A pair of wide-sleeved Chinese dancers traced curlicues in the air with fluid lengths of silk ribbon. Bellydancers came next, onyx-haired and almond-skinned, their arms and feet bare except for loops of fine silver chain from which hung bells — sweet-tempered, silver bells from the size of a ladybug's egg to a calf's eyeball. Their midriffs undulated in steady waves, and their serene faces did not betray the pain of dancing on hot asphalt. Natasha concluded that the parade must be a multicultural celebration.

Then — oh, a menagerie! Not a celebration after all; the parade was a tribute. A veiled woman led a camel by a leash. A ruddy-cheeked, ginger-whiskered old man steered an ostentation of peacocks. Little girls in pink dresses clutched trembling white rabbits and ferrets to their chests. A chattering capuchin monkey scampered on and off the back of a grey dappled pony. All of the animals had golden bows tied around their necks — except for the monkey, who had soiled his and stuffed it into a newspaper vending box.

Where there was a menagerie, there was a circus. A clown teetering on stilts handed down balloons to the children in the crowd. Fire-eaters belched flame from soot- and wax-coated lips. Three generations of Chinese acrobats balanced on a single bicycle. Tumblers and jugglers, dressed for a harlequinade, cavorted around a knot of body-painted contortionists.

Forty young men and women draped in white followed. Their ebony skin glowed, burnished by the sunlight reflecting off the jewelled caskets they carried. Each casket was open, and bore a jewelled egg on a red velvet cushion. Each egg bore a mechanical bird. The young men and women wound up the tiny birds and launched them into the sky. *Nubian slaves*, Natasha thought. *There are always Nubian slaves in a tribute.*

The birds soared and swooped on sapphire wings. They shat cream-coloured pearls on unattended parked cars. Their amber beaks chattered — *karak-kak-ak-ak-ak* — over the whirr of their tiny internal clockworks. When they tired, they spiralled lazily down to their eggs, where their bearers would wind them back to life.

It was a dowry fit for a sultan's daughter.

A cheer rose from the spectators. The parade's star attraction rode into view in the back of a crawling baby-blue vintage convertible. Natasha leaned over the balcony railing. She could not see his face, but she knew what he looked like. He was good-looking, but not so good-looking that you did not trust him. A charming, disarming smile. Eyes that crinkled in the corners when he laughed, and, when he laughed, he made you feel as if you were the only woman in the world who could make him happy. He had black hair, brown hair, blond hair, red hair. He had brown eyes, green eyes, blue eyes, grey eyes. He looked however you wanted him to look — your perfect picture of a perfect man. He had a battered, old-fashioned oil lamp tucked into the waistband of his pants, which he idly stroked.

A balloon escaped from a child in the crowd and drifted up to Natasha's balcony. She reached out and grabbed the dangling gold ribbon that tied it. The balloon was white and had a man's face screened on it in gold metallic ink. It was the face of the man in the convertible, most likely. He looked a little like Paul. Natasha let the balloon go. She did not watch it float away.

The air was redolent with cinnamon, rose petals, and car exhaust. "He's an impostor!" Natasha yelled down at the parade. "A liar, a thief, he'll only bring you grief!"

Her hands clutched the balcony railing, the knuckles bone-white with fury. She screamed, "He's not what he seems, he'll deceive the woman he marries! Hasn't anyone read *A Thousand and One Nights*? Or seen that Disney movie? It's the lamp, that fucking lamp!"

At eleven stories from street level, no-one could hear her save a flock of sapphire wings. The jewelled birds seized the oversize sleeves of her T-shirt in their golden talons and yanked her away from the railing. *Karak-ak-ak*, they scolded, diving off the balcony. One bird remained, however, its clockwork innards grinding to a halt. Its emerald-lidded eyes shuddered closed. Natasha caught it in the palm of her hand. She wound it up, but it disintegrated into a sandalwood-scented puff of dust and rusty springs. She brushed its remains into the geranium planter.

Shadow scratched at the bathroom door. She slipped back indoors and let him out. He padded across the room and scratched at the bedroom door. She let him out again. He navigated around the living room set to the foyer and scratched at the front door.

Natasha did not know anything about dogs and was confused by his sudden single-mindedness. By the time she realized what he wanted — and was downstairs, dressed, pacing as he squatted on the sidewalk — Ameer and his Dalmatian were gone. The asphalt was littered with flaccid balloon fragments, confetti, and animal shit. Leaflets fluttered in the gutters. Natasha read them as Shadow pissed against a concrete planter. One of the belly-dancers was offering classes at the local community centre.

⇝•⊹•⇜

The phone rang.

Natasha emerged from the bedroom with a half-full laundry basket and paused. Next to Shadow, she dreaded the phone calls the most. She was tempted to turn off the ringer, but she worried that people would come to her door instead, looking for Paul.

The closest phone was in the sitting room. Natasha set the laundry basket down by the sofa. Shadow was lounging on the rug, watching her. His mouth was open and his tongue skimmed the floor. Natasha let the phone ring three times, and then picked it up.

"Hello?" she said.

"May I speak to Paul, please?"

"He doesn't live here anymore," she said, flatly.

"Oh?" The caller paused. It was a woman, and she didn't sound as if she believed Natasha. "Can you tell me where he is now?"

"No," Natasha said, and hung up the phone.

The phone rang again. Shadow's ears perked up. Natasha told him, "It's not for you," and picked up the receiver.

"He's not here," she said.

"Who's not here?" a brusque female voice asked.

"Oh. Hi, Mom."

"So," her mother said, without even saying *hello*, and Natasha knew that she had a hard conversation ahead of her. "So. Aunt Helen says you got a dog, that you brought it to her clinic."

"Yes," Natasha said.

"What does Paul think? Isn't he allergic?"

Natasha pinched the space between her brows, anticipating the headache that conversations with her mother always sparked. She had been wondering when and how she would tell her parents. "Paul and I... Paul's not here. He left me."

"Men," her mother said, and she said it with such force that Natasha was surprised that spit didn't spray out of the phone's earpiece. "Bunch of emotional fuckwits. Just look at your father."

"I thought you loved Dad," said Natasha with surprise.

"I do."

Hypocrite, Natasha thought. Her mother was many things, but she had never known her to contradict herself, only others. Aloud, she said, "How do you and Dad do it?"

Her mother's voice was a rapid-fire machine gun. "It's not easy, hon. That's why I hated fairy tales when you were a kid. Those stories always end with a marriage. But stories don't end after you get married. They keep going. They get worse, like a good plot. That's why I let you read *A Thousand and One Nights*. Love sets you up for betrayal, unlike that happily-ever-after bullshit. And every bitch and bastard gets what's coming to them. All you can do is be careful what you wish for." She took a deep breath and reloaded. "So he left. Where did he go?"

"I don't know," Natasha lied. "It was so sudden."

"Well, go find him."

"It's more complicated than that."

"It can't be that hard these days. Use the internet. I use it to find everything now that your father's shown me how."

Anger bubbled up in Natasha's voice. "What if I don't want to find him? What if he doesn't want to be found?"

"That doesn't matter, honey. No matter how it ends, you have to see it through. Don't leave things hanging between you."

Shadow yawned. Natasha envied his peaceful, ignorant existence. It was unfair that she was the one who had to deal with the fallout, not him. "Mom, you've been happily married for almost fifty years. You're in no position to give advice."

Her mother snorted. "It wasn't always happy, hon. Remember, we almost split up before you were born."

Natasha was so flabbergasted she sank onto the sofa. Everything she knew was suddenly wrong. Again. She had always thought her parents had the perfect marriage. They were devoted to each other and never fought.

The same could have been said about you and Paul, she thought. Shadow padded over to her and put his head on her knees. She pushed him away. "You never told me that."

"Didn't I?" her mother said. "Well, let me tell you what happened."

THE STORY OF THE ENCHANTED CALF

Your father, as you know, is much older than me. I married him when I was very young, and I was not his first wife. For the first year of our marriage, we were blissfully happy. I was very much in love, and I believed that he loved me, too.

I soon discovered why his first marriage had not lasted. His first wife had not been able to bear him a child, and so your father cast her out. He then married me in the hope that I would give him children. He was worried about what would happen to his estate after he died. After a year, however, he grew increasingly disappointed as I failed to produce an heir, and he soon stopped visiting my bedroom at night.

It was at this time that we hired a new maid. She had a son of about sixteen or seventeen; a bright, handsome boy who mowed our lawn in the summer and shovelled snow in the winter. Your father took him under his wing immediately as the boy had no other men in his life.

At first I supported this act of charity, but when your father began talking about adopting him I grew fretful and jealous. Although I was his wife he acted as if he loved Amine and the boy more than he loved me, and I envisioned myself being cast out in shame as his first wife had been, with Amine taking my place.

I secretly applied myself to sorcery with the intention of ridding myself of my rival. When I had acquired some small skill, I transformed Amine and her son into a cow and calf while your father was away on business.

→·I·•·I·•·I·←

"She *was* a cow, you know," Natasha's mother said. "Hips like saddlebags. But that's beside the point."

→·I·•·I·•·I·←

I put the cow and calf in the barn, and, in my defense, they were treated well by the stablehands, likely better than they had been treated as humans.

When your father returned from his business trip, he was distraught that Amine and the boy did not greet him.
But where is Amine and her son? he asked.
Ah! I said. She quit while you were away, and I have not seen her son for some time.
Their absence upset him, but soon his attention returned to me and for a short while I was happy again.
Some months later it was nearing Christmas, and your father expressed dismay that we had nothing grand on which to dine.
There is a cow and her calf in the barn, I said. One of the local farmers gave them to us in exchange for using some of our land for grazing. The cow is strong, gentle, and healthy.
Your father agreed, and sent for the butcher. A day later, however, the butcher returned, troubled. He told your father that the cow had gazed at him so imploringly that he barely had been able to perform the deed. Tears had even fallen from her eyes. When at last he found the courage to slaughter her, he discovered her to be nothing but skin and bones.
No matter, I said. There is still a fine, fattened calf in the barn.
The next day the butcher called on us again. I cannot do it, he said in anguish. This calf is unnatural. You must see for yourself.
I tried to persuade your father that the butcher was being fanciful, but he went to the abattoir. That night he returned home with the calf.
I held the knife myself, he said, and I could not slaughter this creature. It broke free of its rope and prostrated itself at my feet, as if it were human and knew me.
I flew into a fury and was only be placated when he promised to kill the creature at next Christmas. Our family and friends arrived for dinner and were satisfied with the modest hens I had prepared, and your father was pleased.
A week later the butcher knocked on our door once more.
My daughter wishes to speak to you alone, he told your father. She claims it is important.

Your father, bemused, went with the butcher to speak with his daughter. The girl was also skilled in sorcery. After having heard her father's fantastical story about the cow and her calf, she discovered their true nature. She told your father that I was responsible for their enchantment.

The cow could not be restored, as she had been killed, but the girl could still save the calf. She only asked that Amine's son be given to her as a husband and that I be punished for my foul act. Your father readily agreed and took her back to the barn.

The girl put her hand in a bowl of water and sprinkled a little on the calf. If you were born a calf, remain a calf, she said. If you were a man, become a man.

The calf resumed the shape of Amine's son, who was delighted that the butcher's daughter wished to marry him; he had always thought her very beautiful and clever.

The girl then gave the bowl of water to your father, as well as some instructions. He found me in the kitchen and said, This is your reward for your malice, and he threw the water upon me. I changed instantly into a white mare.

Your father kept me in the same stall where I had kept Amine, but he did not treat me well. Every day he rode me hard around our pastures until I frothed and bled, and when I collapsed he would whip me until I stood again. I endured this punishment for five years, and every day I wished I were dead.

⁙

"It all worked out fine in the end," Natasha's mother said. "The butcher's daughter turned me back into a woman when she decided I had suffered enough, and your father and I forgave each other. We both grew from the experience. I learned to control my jealousy, and he learned to be less of an asshole."

"You never told me this before," Natasha said.

"There are lots of things I've never told you, and never will," her mother said. "Like how I met your father in the first place. Anyway, nine months after I became a woman again, I gave birth to you. Although I was never sure if it was actually the donkey who got me pregnant. He was a randy son of a bitch and would never take no for an answer. A lot like your father, really."

"Mom," Natasha interrupted, unable to help herself. "I didn't need to know that."

"You wanted to hear the story," her mother said. Then she laughed. "Christ. You sound like you're twelve years old again. That took me back. Now, look. I don't know what you did—"

"I didn't do anything," Natasha said.

"Right. And *I* didn't do anything either. Shush, let me finish. I don't know what you did, or what Paul did. That isn't important. There are no wrongs and rights, only miscommunications and misunderstandings, cruelties and kindnesses."

Shadow wedged his head into Natasha's lap again. This time, she let him stay there.

"Amine's son is still married to that girl. I hear they're vegetarians," her mother said, sounding as mystified as if they had become Scientologists.

"Mom, I have to go," Natasha said.

"Think about what I've said," her mother said.

"Sure. Bye."

Natasha hung up the phone. She pushed Shadow away and stood up.

※※※

"In hindsight," Natasha said, echoing Ameer's words, "It wouldn't have happened if it hadn't been night."

She sat on the bed, her feet tucked up beneath her. Shadow sprawled on the floor, his front paws stretched out in front of him. His tongue lolled out in contentment. Some would find his pleasure in little things charming. Natasha found it worrisome. Shadow's silent loyalty was a choking weight about her neck. Although she wondered whether he was really loyal or whether he merely stayed with her because he had nowhere else to go. She studied him, hating him for hiding behind that innocent, unreadable doggy face.

Was this where her story began? Did it begin with disappointment and disillusionment, with deception and devastation? Did it begin with a parade, a caravan of thieves and bandits, a clever slave girl who just happened to know a little sorcery, a mysterious bottle washed up on a beach?

Natasha's story began at the beginning, where most stories start.

"In hindsight..." she said again.

Now that she wanted to talk, there was no-one to whom to speak. She had not seen Ameer at the dog park since that day; she wondered if he had been telling the truth after all and had moved on in search of his sorceress-maid.

She hoped to find the sorceress herself and end Shadow's silence. Benevolent fairies and witches always disguised themselves as ugly hags, but no-one had revealed herself yet even though all last week Natasha had doled out spare change to panhandlers and opened doors for elderly ladies.

Evening fell, limpid and languorous. Sound increased in volume and clarity; feelings and trivialities were amplified, travelling swiftly through still, lush air. Shadow rested his head on his forepaws. Natasha thought she heard him whimper.

She acknowledged him at last. Perhaps, as with the benevolent fairies, if she showed him a small kindness, he would reveal himself.

THE STORY OF THE WOMAN AND HER DOG

In hindsight (Natasha said to Shadow), it wouldn't have happened if it hadn't been night. At night, in the dark and quiet, everything seems bigger and louder than it really is. In the daytime a closet is just a closet. At night, there's a monster inside.

I sat on the bed, reading. Paul was — I don't know where Paul was. Somewhere in the condo. Washing dishes in the kitchen, measuring out detergent in the laundry nook, puttering away in his office, watching TV. I didn't care. And yet I felt annoyed that he didn't care where I was either. *Hypocrite*, I thought. I didn't know if I meant him or myself.

The phone rang. I picked it up. A woman's breathy voice was on the other end.

...thinking about you, the voice said. It was only the last half of a sentence, thin and wispy like a mouse's tail, but it was enough.

I told you not to call me here, a man's voice said.

Paul, wherever he was, was by a phone. I slammed down the receiver.

Natasha? he called out. Where are you?

I ran the gauntlet of emotions. Hysterical, whiny, petty, jealous? Angry, vengeful, bitchy, shrewish? Weepy, desperate, clingy, needy? The options all seemed predictable.

Paul burst into the bedroom. It's not what you think, he said.

Oh? What do I think? I retorted. What should I think? Who was that?

It was Lucy, he said. You know Lucy — you met her at the office Christmas party. She's the new girl, straight out of school. You thought her skirt was too short.

Right, I said.

I did remember Lucy, but I remembered that she had worn too much makeup, not that her skirt had been too short.

It's not what you think, he repeated. I had dinner with her on our last business trip — just dinner — and now she won't stop pestering me. She comes by my desk, sends me emails all the time. I don't know how she got our home number. She calls me every day. I don't know how to get rid of her. She knows I'm married.

I said nothing, afraid that speech would set free one of the reactions I was trying to stifle. Afraid that a jealous whine would leak out, or worse — hysteria. *Maybe you're not trying hard enough to discourage her*, I wanted to say. *Yes, but does she know you're* happily *married?* I wanted to say.

Don't you trust me? he said.

I felt that, if he had to ask, I probably didn't. Or I had no reason to. We'd been married for eight years, but lately that meant nothing except civil small talk during the day and the thrust and parry of rebuffed advances at night.

For fuck's sake, he said. Why don't you ever get angry with me? Come on, yell, throw things.

Should I be throwing things? I said as calmly as I could. Do I have a good reason to?

I regretted saying that; I sounded bitchy. I remembered Lucy's too-red lips and the way she had looked me up and down, as if she were sizing me up. I remembered that she appeared to be ten years younger than me. She didn't know yet that everything she's grown up believing is wrong. She probably just saw an unhappy man with a Wife Who Doesn't Understand Him. She probably saw someone she could save with her youth and charm and cleverness. I knew because I had been that girl once.

I didn't mean it that way, he said. I mean, do whatever you feel you have to do. Cry, scream, or something. Stop bottling it up. Get it out of the way, so we can talk about this. We never talk anymore.

I wanted to cry but knew I couldn't. *I can't believe you're cheating on me*, I wanted to say. *Does our marriage mean nothing to you?* I wanted to say. But I couldn't be weepy. I hated that stereotype — the manipulative, weak-willed woman who uses tears to get her way.

Come on, talk to me, he said. Don't give me the silent treatment. That's your reaction to everything. Be reasonable.

I thought I was being perfectly reasonable. I checked myself again. Hysterical, whiny, petty, jealous? Angry, vengeful, bitchy, shrewish? Weepy, desperate, clingy, needy? No, none of those; I had smothered them. But what was left to feel?

He threw up his hands.

I don't know why I bother, he said. I don't know why I bother explaining myself. I could be having an affair with this woman, and *you don't care*. What am I supposed to make of that? You want the easy way out, don't you? You're going to make *me* say it. You want to make me the bad guy.

Stand up and fight, a voice said in the back of my head. But what was I fighting for? Those precious moments of Zen-like bliss when you're half-asleep on a Sunday morning, before the parade starts, when you can believe that the person lying next to you really understands you? It's only a fairy tale. The reality is that they're unknowable, the proverbial Other, as foreign and exotic as one of Scheherazade's stories.

Well, you know what? he said. I like it when Lucy comes by my desk to flirt. I like her emails. She's smart and funny and really hot, and, yes, I'm attracted to her. But I haven't done anything to encourage her, I swear — except maybe smile more than I should.

I couldn't remember the last time he'd smiled at me.

He said, Natasha—

I turned him into a dog.

There was no flash of smoke, no bolt of lightning from a genie's eggplant-coloured fingertips, no acrid scent of sulphur and charcoal. Just a dog. When I closed my eyes and opened them again, he was still a dog. When I begged Allah for mercy and rubbed all of my lamps and pleaded with the goldfish and said Open Sesame, he was still a dog.

I shut him in the bathroom to wait for night to pass. Things are always different at night, after all.

→•I•I•I•←

Natasha closed her mouth. She pursed her lips, waiting, watching Shadow.

The dog turned into a man.

Paul stood at the foot of the bed. "Natasha," he said. "Natasha, talk to me."

Natasha said nothing, unable to find the words to express what she felt, if only because she did not know what to feel.

Paul sighed and sat on the bed. Without thinking, Natasha tucked her legs against her body, widening the space between them. He folded his hands behind his neck and looked down in his lap. His posture admitted defeat. Natasha wondered what she had won.

"That's it," he said quietly. "I think this is it. You know it. I know it. This isn't working anymore. I don't know if it ever did. You win. I'm the bad guy. I'm leaving."

He rose slowly to his feet, as if to give Natasha time to say something. *You just want an excuse to go running to that other woman*, she wanted to say. *Don't leave me, I love you, I'll die without you*, she wanted to say. *Don't you go walking out on me, you bastard*, she wanted to say.

Instead, she remained silent. "I don't know where I'm going," he said, shuffling into the walk-in closet. She heard him tearing shirts and pants off hangers. "Ben's, if he and his wife have room. Or I'll find a hotel. I'll call you in a couple of days."

He emerged with an overnight bag. He would not look at her.

"Wait," Natasha croaked. Her voice was low, rusty. She cleared her throat and tried again. "Wait. Can I say something first?"

He stood in the doorway. He still would not look at her. His eyes were fixed off in the distance — at the front door, perhaps. He shook his head. "It's too late to talk. You're too late. I have to go. I'll call you later."

"Listen, please," she said. She clenched and twisted the bedcovers in her fingers. Her knuckles were white. "You'd want me to listen to you, wouldn't you?" He had not heard her, or was ignoring her. He walked away, his receding body framed by the door.

"Listen," she called out. "He slept in the bathtub that night. *He slept in the bathtub that night.*"

Paul stopped at last. He turned around. "What?"

"I didn't know anything about dogs," she said. "So he slept in the bathtub that night."

"What are you talking about? What dog? Was there a dog here?" he asked. He put down the bag.

"Come here," she said, "and I'll tell you the story."

He sat down at the foot of the bed. Natasha looked down at her hands. She could not look at him and speak at the same time.

She started to tell him a story about a stubborn woman and her enchanted dog. When the story didn't seem long enough to hold his attention, she added stories within the story. She told him stories of deception and betrayal, of love and lust. She told him stories of clever women, silly women, harlots and virgins and bitches, Girl Fridays and femme fatales, each one defined by how they interact with men. She told him stories about a woman who did not know what to feel or how to act because she did not want to be one of those clichés.

She threw in a couple of parades. There were always parades in these stories; they were an opportunity for the storyteller to be especially fanciful, and they made for entertaining filler. She alluded to the exotic and the erotic whenever it seemed like he was losing interest. She talked and talked, desperate to fill that long, brooding quiet between dusk and dawn, desperate to save her life.

The stories only had to last until sunrise, when everything would look different in daylight. And if they could not come to an understanding by morning, there was always another morning, and another morning after that.

Ringing the Changes in Okotoks, Alberta

Randy McCharles

The following is a true story, though if you ask the inhabitants of the township of Okotoks, Alberta, they will deny it. Small town folk are like that. They like to keep their business to themselves.

THE SUMMER SOLSTICE FLING
Litha: June 21

"Now," said Mayor Abigail Smyth-Jones in her *this is serious business* voice, "on to the Summer Fling Festival. I understand that the catering has been confirmed and that the Wild Welsh Trio has agreed to provide music and organize the Participation Dancing."

"Yes!" growled George Stromley, rising from his seat and hammering the table top. "About the Summer Fling!"

Terry Sutton looked up from the paperback novel he was reading and scrutinized George's demeanour. What he saw suggested that the next few minutes might be worth paying attention to.

George rarely showed up at Town Council meetings, and when he was pressured into coming he usually sat in a sullen huff. If George didn't own half the town he'd be dropped from the council like a rancid apple. But now here George stood in all his glory, thunder-faced and damaging the table.

"Carter Donaldson," George nodded at the stringy-haired scarecrow sitting next to him, "was friend enough to show me the festival agenda you handed out at the last meeting."

Mayor Abigail shook her head as though scolding a child. "If you had been here last week, George, you would have received your own copy."

"That's not the issue," said George, hefting Carter's agenda and blindly prodding it with a thick finger. "There's changes here from our usual festival. And, for the life of me, I can't understand them."

When no-one jumped in to explain the changes, Terry got worried. Explaining town politics to George was one of the council's favourite pastimes, but now even Mayor Abigail looked apprehensive. On impulse, Terry thumbed through his own agenda, untouched since he had received it — the festival was a no-brainer, after all. He found George's bone of contention tucked in between the BBQ and the Participation Dancing.

"A twilight run through the forest?" George shouted. "Naked?"

"It is a summer solstice tradition," Mayor Abigail explained, though without much courage. "Just a short run. More of a jog, really. Five, ten minutes tops. Through the trees by the river."

"Naked?" demanded George.

"Is this a Blackfoot tradition?" inquired Eleanor Woodhouse, who knew more about the Blackfoot Indians than anyone and should not have needed to ask.

"It's... Celtic," replied Abigail.

"Celtic," said Eleanor, her large, green eyes widening beneath short blond bangs. "Is that tribe related to the Blackfoot?"

"They're in England," offered Carter. "They have nothing to do with the Blackfoot."

"Wales, actually," said Newman Porter, the council intellectual. "And they very well could be related to the Blackfoot. It is theorized that Native Americans originally came from parts of Europe and Asia—"

George hammered the table for silence and stared Mayor Abigail down. "Naked?"

"The citizens will never go for it," asserted Carter. "Some of the high-school kids, perhaps, but I really don't think—"

"Why," demanded George, "would you even suggest that the good people of Okotoks go running naked through the woods?"

Abigail blinked. "Oh, no, George. You've got it all wrong. No-one is going to be asked to run naked."

George wiped his knuckles across his brow and lowered himself back into his chair. "That's a relief. For a while there I though you had ODed on Valium."

Mayor Abigail clenched her teeth. "Just the Town Council needs to do the run."

"Not on your life!" exclaimed Eleanor, her cheeks reddening.

"When Hell freezes over," said Carter.

"What's this all about?" asked Terry. He could think of a thousand better ways to spend a Thursday evening than imagining his co-councillors in the buff. Well, Eleanor he could imagine. "What does Okotoks care about ancient Celtic customs?"

Mayor Abigail's face turned almost as red as Eleanor's. "You'll recall during the election that I made certain campaign promises—"

"To run naked through the woods?" George objected again.

Abigail gave George the evil eye. "To do everything in my power to ensure a good harvest for the local farmers."

"Ah," said Terry, the light at last dawning. Politics, the first and foremost cause of every senseless decision. "And I gather this forest streaking business is necessary in order to ensure the harvest?"

"Our, uh, New Age advisor swears by it," said Abigail.

"I see," said Terry. "This would be Madam Peasgoody, the Irish herbalist in that four-by-six boutique across from the Teahouse?"

Mayor Abigail nodded. "Actually, Madam Peasgoody is from Wales."

"It doesn't matter where she's from," growled George. "She's nuttier than a fruitcake."

"A total loon," said Carter.

"The farmers trust her," Mayor Abigail explained in her *this is serious business* voice.

"Then let the farmers drop their drawers," suggested George. "This is the most insane thing I've ever heard. Correction. The second most insane." He shook the festival agenda at her. "After the twilight run we're to sacrifice a goat to some unnamed goddess."

"Will this be a live or a dead goat?" inquired Newman.

"What difference does it make?" said George. "I'm not sacrificing any kind of goat, especially not to some heathen goddess!"

Newman adjusted his glasses. "It makes all the difference in the world. Dead goats are virtually meaningless. Why, take the Phoenicians—"

George shook his head and buried his face in his hands. "This is why I refuse to come to council meetings."

He had a point, thought Terry, glancing at his watch. At this rate they'd be here all night. "Look," he said. "What's the worst that could happen if we don't do this nude jogging thing and conveniently forget to strangle a goat?"

Mayor Abigail pushed the current Farmer's Almanac across the table. "Drought. El Niño is going to fry the Prairies this summer."

Everyone stared at the Almanac; for most of their constituents the red and yellow weather book was holier than the Bible.

"Okay," said Terry. "And if we do as Madam Peasgoody suggests? What's the worst that could happen then?"

"We wind up looking like a collection of boneheads!" asserted George.

"Apparently," stated Mayor Abigail, "other communities have celebrated solstice with enormous success."

"I refuse to believe it. Who?" demanded George.

"Taber's been doing it for years," said Abigail. "And this year Pincher Creek is giving it a whirl."

"Bunch of loons in Taber," said Carter.

"Pincher Creek is worse," muttered Newman.

There were nods of agreement around the table.

"Well," said Terry, offering his most winsome smile. "It all sounds pretty harmless to me. I'm game."

George stared at him. "Are you crazy?"

Terry shrugged. "It's good politics. Besides, it's something to do. We could use some excitement around here."

→•I•I•I•←

Though the sun had dipped behind the Rocky Mountains there was still plenty of light along the river, most of it originating from the giant bonfire in Sheep River Park, where the town residents had been flinging it up all evening. Near the riverside, the bushes gave a quiet rustle and Terry Sutton's disembodied head poked out, his quick eyes scanning the distance to the bonfire.

Satisfied that the crowd's attention was otherwise engaged, he trotted out of the forest, naked as you please, and stopped at the gnarled mosaic known as the Sweetheart Oak for the collection of *Jimmy loves Susan*s etched into its trunk. Plucking down one of the ankle-length robes that adorned the oak's lower branches, Terry hastily dressed himself.

Eleanor had arrived only moments ahead of him and sat huddled on the nearby bench, wrapped up tight in terrycloth and breathing rapidly. "I've never been so embarrassed in my life!" She lifted her green eyes to Terry. "How did I ever let you talk me into this?"

"It's for a good cause," Terry answered cheerfully as he cinched the belt of his robe.

Eleanor's eyes widened. "Cause? What cause?"

Terry smiled. "Ours. Remaining in office. Besides, no-one got hurt."

Their conversation was interrupted by the noise of an elephant tramping out of the trees. Well, actually it was George, who snatched down one of the sweetheart oak robes and began wiping his face with it. "Did either of you see that monster deer in there?" he demanded.

"Really?" said Terry. "With all the music and dancing I can't imagine a deer sticking around."

George threw his robe onto the bench beside Eleanor and stretched his arms above his head, curling his fingers in a poor imitation of antlers. "It was a huge stag, taller than me, and its fur looked more like long, dirty hair. And its face — ugly as sin!"

"Now, George," said Terry. "Really. Sounds more like you saw Carter—"

"Saw me where?" said Carter, sidling out of the trees holding an uprooted bush in front of his essentials. He hastily traded the shrub for a robe.

George lowered his arms and pressed his fists against his hips. "It wasn't Carter, or any of the rest of you. It was a huge, butt-ugly, stag deer... or some kind of monster."

"Speaking of butts," said Terry. "You might consider putting on your robe. Poor Eleanor here is ready to faint with embarrassment."

George looked at Eleanor, at his own nakedness, then snapped up his robe and huffed off into the trees. "I'm going to find that deer. Then you'll see."

"I've seen quite enough already, thank you," murmured Eleanor.

Mayor Abigail Smyth-Jones and Newman Porter soon slipped out of the trees and clothed themselves. All the bathrobes were either yellow, green, or blue — solstice colours, according to Peasgoody. The mayor's New Age advisor had permitted no other colours for the Summer Fling. Eleanor had nearly burst into tears when she saw the neon-yellow table napkins.

Mayor Abigail did a quick head count. "All told and accounted for," she said. "Except for George — no surprise there. Has anyone seen George?"

"He went deer hunting," said Eleanor. "But he did do the run, if that's what you're worried about."

"Eleanor's telling you the naked truth," said Terry.

"Isn't that George over there with Peasgoody?" said Carter. "I thought Peasgoody was supposed to sacrifice a goat."

Next to the festival bonfire stood a mountain of hay that Peasgoody had told them was supposed to be a Wicker Man. Of course, wicker was an expensive commodity in these parts, while hay was cheap as, well, hay. Abigail had talked long and loud about budgets, and in the end Peasgoody had granted that it wasn't so important what the Man was made of, just so long as it burned. Terry had stopped trying to make sense of it all when Peasgoody insisted that the BBQ tables be decorated with lavender, daisies, and lilies — solstice flowers.

And now, here was Peasgoody again, leading George with a rope about his neck into the goat pen Terry himself had helped build inside the Hay Man.

"Has that woman got a criminal record?" asked Carter.

"Where," Newman demanded, squinting through his glasses, "is my goat? I went to a lot of trouble getting it. Have any of you the slightest idea how people react when you tell them you need a goat so that you can burn it alive at the Summer Fling? My reputation will never recover."

"Peasgoody is locking the pen!" cried Eleanor. She looked desperately at Terry. "Aren't you going to rescue George?"

Terry stared at Eleanor. "Rescue? Uh, sure, but, that Hay Man could go up any second. And hay burns like, well, hay. And this is George we're talking about."

Mayor Abigail slumped onto the bench beside Eleanor, her face ghastly white even in the poor light. She said, "I can see the headlines now: *Okotoks Mayor Commits Human Sacrifice during Public Festival. Explains She Was Trying to Make It Rain.*"

Terry looked back at the Hay Man, weighing Eleanor's favour against his personal safety. The whole idea was vaguely insane. Eleanor hated George. Following one of their frequent altercations she would gladly strike the match herself. If he did somehow manage to rescue George, Eleanor's brief admiration would soon become disdain for not letting the wretch burn.

Then, all at once, Terry's mind was made up for him as the night sky erupted with yellow light. Peasgoody, robed and wreathed, stood swaying before the blazing Hay Man, her voice raised in supplication to a goddess whose name no-one seemed to know. He imagined George screaming from what was fast becoming a funeral pyre, only he knew it was just his imagination. George's screaming, like his yelling and his fist-pounding, would be hard to miss.

"Judas Priest!" cried George, standing beside Terry. "Will you look at that hay burn!"

"George?" said Carter. "What are you doing here? You're supposed to be inside the Wicker Man."

"It's a Hay Man," corrected Newman. "And, George, if you don't tell me this instant where my goat is, I'll toss you into the fire myself."

George stared at them. "What the devil are you all talking about? I've been out looking for that stag. And you can keep your flaming goats."

"Did you find it?" asked Terry. "Your monster stag?"

George's eyes glazed over in the yellow light from the twin bonfires. "I... yes, I think so. I'm certain I did. It was... huge. Tall. And old Peasgoody was there. And a goat?"

"Aha!" said Newman. "I knew you were messing with my goat!"

In a sudden fit of compassion, or perhaps his subconscious was still hoping to impress Eleanor, Terry took George by the arm and led him toward the parking lot. "I'm going to see George home," he said. "I suggest the rest of you go home, too. We've all had a full night. I think."

"I'll see Abigail home," said Eleanor, helping the mayor to stand. Ms Smyth-Jones was still white in the face from having witnessed the supposed end of her career.

WHERE'S GEORGE?
Samhain: October 31

"The Autumn Harvest Frolic," announced Mayor Abigail Smyth-Jones in her *this is serious business* voice, "will have a few changes. It will take place a week later than usual, on October 31st."

"Samhain Night," interjected Newman, who was still looking for his goat even though two months had passed and George still rarely showed up for Town Council meetings.

Mayor Abigail continued. "After the Corn Bake and Participation Dancing, the Town Council will take the ten-minute drive out to the Big Rock, where we will bury apples in the field. Madam Peasgoody will have a large, black cauldron..."

Terry sat back in his chair and shook his head. Lighting candles in windows and burying a few apples in a field all sounded harmless enough. But this Peasgoody woman — what to make of her?

There had been rain this summer, in brazen contradiction to the Farmer's Almanac. Okotoks, Taber, and Pincher Creek had done well while drought and hail had afflicted the rest of the Prairies. The politically correct weather and George's apparent well-being had revived the mayor from her attack of despair at the close of the solstice festival.

And what about George? Terry knew what he had seen go up in flames in the Hay Man last June, and it wasn't Newman's goat. George was never quite the same again either. Not really. Oh, he still lorded over the town and bellowed and cussed and avoided council meetings. But if you mentioned goats, or stags, or nights in the forest, his eyes would glaze over and he'd start shaking like a tractor engine that had thrown a rod. Something had happened to him that night.

And now Peasgoody was insisting that the Council attend the Big Rock doings on Halloween night. The entire Town Council must be present, she had warned. Including George. Especially George.

Ah, well, it was only George, after all. Terry nodded to the mayor in favour of the Autumn Frolic changes.

※※※※

It was a quarter past ten when the headlights of George Stromley's Ford Bronco turned off the 2A Highway and bounced into the asphalt parking lot of the Big Rock, the world's largest glacial erratic, nestled in a farmer's field just eight kilometres northwest of Okotoks. It was All Hallow's Eve, and the stars were bright, with a large, gibbous moon drifting above the Rockies, not a hand's span to the west. Atop the Big Rock, the flickering glow of burning wood outlined the massive black cauldron where Madam Peasgoody worked her magic.

Terry Sutton stood at the edge of the grassy trail leading from the parking lot to the Rock. He watched the Ford Bronco roll to a stop, then cast Eleanor Woodhouse a wry grin as from the driver side door stepped a yellow, six-foot chicken with long, feathered wings and an anatomically incorrect, bobbing, three-pronged cockscomb. Before either of them could speak, the yellow chicken cried: "Has anyone got scissors? The zipper's stuck!"

"Newman?" asked Eleanor. "Is that you? Where's George?"

Newman Porter, all cluck and feathers, waddled over and grimaced at them through the shadowed opening of a giant bird's beak. "Hotter than Hades in this suit. You'd think if someone rents you a costume they'd bloody make sure the zipper works."

"A chicken?" asked Terry. "Why would you rent a chicken costume? None of the rest of us dressed up."

Newman scowled at him. "The chicken is a much maligned bird. Sacred in parts of Central America and Brazil."

"Where's George?" repeated Eleanor.

"Took my kids out trick-or-treating," Newman told her. "Of course I needed a costume."

"George took your kids trick-or-treating?" replied Eleanor. "George can't abide children."

Newman stared at her, momentarily stunned. "Of course George didn't go trick-or-treating. *I* took my kids out. Therefore the noble chicken costume. Is that a turnip?"

Terry lifted his Jack-O-Turnip to where Newman could see it. It had a carved, imp-like face with a small candle burning inside. "Traditional Celtic Jack-O-Lantern," Terry told him. "They don't have pumpkins in Wales."

"I knew that," said Newman, who claimed to know everything, pretty much on a weekly basis.

"Ah, there you are," said Carter Donaldson, shambling toward them along the path from the Rock, looking much like the scarecrow from *The Wizard of Oz*, though it wasn't a costume; he always looked like the scarecrow from *The Wizard of Oz*. "Haven't been here in years, you know. Looks different at night. No tourists." He peered into the yellow bird's beak, then stumbled backward. "You're not George!"

"You were expecting George to arrive in a chicken costume?" Eleanor asked him.

"I was expecting George to arrive in George's truck. Newman, you promised me you'd bring George."

Terry studied the Ford Bronco. "I don't see anyone else. Is George coming?"

Newman smoothed some of his feathers. Then he straightened and said: "No."

Carter wailed, his face falling into his hands. "Mayor Abigail will wring my neck. She made it my job to ensure that George showed up, and you said that you'd bring him."

Terry looked at Carter, then at Newman, then shook his head. Personally, he'd rather George didn't come to the Celtic New Year celebration at the Big Rock; the man was a royal jackass. It was only the mayor's mad devotion to Madam Peasgoody that obliged the Okotoks Town Council members to attend. Although how anyone could call one madwoman and six bureaucrats a celebration was something he had yet to figure out.

"What's happening up on the Rock?" asked Newman, his voice all business. "Is that a fire?"

"Bubble, bubble, toil and trouble," said Eleanor, smiling. "Madam Peasgoody is mixing some kind of witch's brew. I'm hoping it's root beer."

Newman glared at her from within the bowels of the bird's beak. "Root beer? This isn't a children's party. That woman is up to no good. I know. I've done research."

Terry took Eleanor's elbow and attempted to lead her away. Newman was bad enough when he knew everything, but when he resorted to looking something up there was no stopping him until he shared it with everyone.

Eleanor shook off Terry's hand. "No, I want to hear this. Just what have you discovered, Newman?"

The giant chicken beckoned them closer. Light from atop the Big Rock reflected eerily from his rubber-shrouded glasses. "Halloween is the witches' High Sabbath, when they do all manner of evil things." He paused theatrically. "With cauldrons."

"That's not all," added Carter, his expression grave. "I hear they do unmentionable things to chickens. You'd better watch out, Newman."

Newman scowled at him. "This is serious. Peasgoody is big trouble."

"You think she's a witch?" asked Eleanor.

"What do you think?" Newman demanded, pointing up at the Rock with a feathered arm.

Terry had to admit that Madam Peasgoody, dressed in a black robe and stirring her giant black cauldron atop the Big Rock in the dark of night did, in fact, look guilty as charged. Worse, there was Mayor Abigail Smyth-Jones, marching down the grass path toward them. With George absent, Peasgoody wasn't the only one guilty of something.

"Newman?" asked Abigail, peering into the chicken beak. "Yellow suits you. Where's George?"

"He's not coming," said Newman. "After what happened last summer he's not coming within ten miles of Peasgoody's sorcery."

Abigail's forehead tightened. "Nothing happened to George last summer."

"Well," admitted Terry, "we did all watch him go up in flames in Peasgoody's solstice bonfire."

"Up in flames," echoed Newman.

"That was a goat," said Abigail. "You know that, Newman. It was your goat."

"It was supposed to be my goat," asserted Newman, "but it was George that burned. I saw it with my own eyes."

"Are those police lights?" asked Eleanor.

Out on the highway a police car sped toward them, lights flashing but with no siren. It pulled up next to George's Bronco, and out stepped Sheriff Winslo and George Stromley. George marched around his truck, inspecting it for damage, then stomped up to where his fellow Town Council members stood watching.

"One of *you* stole my truck?" George's heavy face was a mix of anger and incredulity.

"The chicken did it," said Terry, only now thinking that of course Newman stole the truck. George would never let anyone borrow his Bronco.

George grabbed Newman by the neck feathers and shook him. "*You* stole my truck!"

Newman sputtered for breath. "I had to, George. It was the only way to keep you out of Peasgoody's pot. If I hadn't taken your truck you would have driven out here, and that would be the end."

"The end!" shouted George. "The only end around here is your butt. Winslo, slap him in irons! Grand theft auto."

"Wait, George," said Eleanor. "Newman was only doing you a favour. He figures Peasgoody's got it in for you and that you were better off at home."

"Judas Priest!" spat George. "For your information I had no intention of coming out here tonight. Not until my truck went missing."

"George!" Mayor Abigail crossed her arms and her forehead tightened further. "You know that as a member of the Okotoks Town Council you are required to be here."

"Why?" bellowed George, throwing his hands in the air. "To watch some mad woman stirring a pot?" He stared up at the Big Rock. "What in Judas's name is that woman doing?"

Terry turned with the rest of them. Peasgoody had ceased her stirring and was now tying a goat to a stake.

"My goat!" Newman shouted and charged up the grassy trail in his chicken suit, yellow feathers flapping in the breeze. When he reached the Big Rock, he clambered up its craggy side in a very unchickenlike fashion.

Terry turned back to the others, only to find that George's eyes had glazed over. The big man was shaking like a small earthquake, just as he always did whenever goats, stags, or nights in the forest were mentioned, even though four months had passed since his mysterious encounter with a giant stag in Sheep River Park on the night of the Summer Solstice Festival.

There was nothing you could do for George when he got like this, so Terry took Eleanor's hand and followed

Newman up the short trail to the Big Rock. Carter and Mayor Abigail came behind, leaving Sheriff Winslo to mind George.

The Rock was an easy climb — children clambered over it on a daily basis, after all — but there was always the danger of slipping in the dark. Terry set his Jack-O-Turnip on a flat surface and gave Eleanor and the mayor a hand up.

He could hear Newman railing at Peasgoody long before they reached the presumed witch where she stood with her black cauldron and her goat. Terry thought the Welsh woman's expression was bleak at the best of times, but now it carried the additional feature of astonishment. In all likelihood, Madam Peasgoody had never before been harangued by a six-foot chicken.

Terry didn't think it possible, but Newman eventually shouted himself out, at which point Peasgoody shook her head with disgust and reached past Newman to pull George, who had been standing unseen behind the bulk of Newman's chicken costume, toward the cauldron.

"George?" everyone said at once. George had stopped shaking, but his eyes were still glazed; he moved without argument at Peasgoody's direction. Terry looked back toward the parking lot and saw no sign of either George or Sheriff Winslo.

"What's going on here?" demanded Carter.

"It's animal abuse, that's what it is," said Newman. "How could anyone do such a thing to a goat?"

Terry looked back from surveying the parking lot and was so startled that he almost fell off the Big Rock. George had somehow climbed up onto the cauldron and now stood with one foot on the cauldron's rim and the other on the goat's back. George's balancing act was almost as amazing as the goat's refusal to collapse under his weight. (George was what politically correct people call *a healthy eater*.)

Peasgoody was back at her cauldron, stirring with a wooden paddle and muttering a sequence of unintelligible words that sounded vaguely Irish. Mayor Abigail watched in rapt silence, while Eleanor's silence was mostly just shock.

"Is this some kind of circus?" demanded Carter.

"I thought George was supposed to go *into* the pot, not on top of it," suggested Newman.

Peasgoody seemed to have reached some sort of denouement in her incantation. She raised her arms, and her mutterings became shouts. Then came a sudden flash of light, and George no longer stood balanced atop the cauldron and the goat. White smoke swirled where George had stood, and from within came a flapping of wings. A grey eagle, with bright startled eyes, squawked once before swooping off into the night.

"Not a circus," suggested Terry. "Perhaps a zoo."

He watched as Peasgoody, her incantation ended, collected up her things and made her way down off the Big Rock. Newman was hugging his goat, which bleated with terror at being mauled by a giant chicken, while Eleanor wandered over to the cauldron and sniffed at its contents.

Before Terry could stop her, she stuck a finger into Peasgoody's concoction and poked it into her mouth. Her large eyes widened. "It *is* root beer. And here are some Styrofoam cups!"

Terry inspected the cauldron and discovered, to his astonishment, that the waning flames beneath it weren't giving off any heat. The smoke was rising not from the fire but from a piece of dry ice floating in the root beer. From out of the darkness he thought he heard a cackling laugh.

"Where's George?" Carter asked suddenly.

Terry was about to suggest that George had flown off toward the town of Black Diamond, when he glanced back at the parking lot and saw Sheriff Winslo standing with George by the Bronco.

"We've been here the whole time," insisted Winslo when Terry and the others climbed down from the Rock and joined them. George had resumed shaking, his glazed eyes tracking Newman's goat. "What was all that fireworks up on the Rock?" Winslo demanded. "You realize that fireworks are illegal."

"I'd explain it if I could," Terry told him. "But neither of us would believe it."

Winslo frowned, then busied himself settling George into the passenger seat of the Bronco.

"I'll just stick my goat in the back," said Newman. "Then I'll drive George home."

"I'm afraid you'll be coming with me," said Winslo. "George was adamant about charges. Grand theft auto. And I'll have to add unlawful possession of a goat."

"What?" demanded Newman. "This is my goat. What do you mean unlawful? A goat is no different than a dog. They're commonly kept as pets in the Andes Mountains of Chile and Peru."

Turning a deaf ear to Newman's arguments, Sheriff Winslo stuffed the well-informed chicken and his terrified goat into the back seat of his police car then drove off down the highway, leaving Terry and the others to finish off the root beer and drive George home.

THE CHRISTMAS GOAT
Yule: December 22

Snowflakes the size of pennies fluttered to the paving stones as Terry Sutton and Eleanor Woodhouse walked hand in hand down the lane toward George Stromley's country house.

"It's not so much a house as it is a castle," Terry commented. "George adds to it every summer. It's been written up in *Distinctive Homes of Alberta* five times in the past eight years."

"Is that Newman Porter skulking around the portico?" asked Eleanor. "I thought he and George weren't speaking."

Terry nodded as he squinted into the evening gloom. "Not since Halloween, when George had Newman arrested and confiscated his goat. That's Newman alright. I'd recognize that prominent forehead anywhere."

"Hello, Newman!" called Eleanor. "Are you going to Stromley's Christmas party?"

Newman scuttled toward them down the driveway, waving his hands. "Shhh! I don't know yet. And until I do, I don't want George to know I'm here."

"You mean he invited you?" asked Terry, surprised that George would do any such thing, even if he had invited the rest of the Town Council.

"He did," said Newman. "That's what worries me. Not only that, he said I could have my goat back."

"Well, it is Christmas," suggested Eleanor. "Maybe George had a change of heart."

Terry and Newman both looked at her, and Eleanor attempted a smile. "I mean, even Scrooge had a change of heart."

Newman grimaced. "It will take more than three ghosts and a saucepan of gruel to scare George into behaving like a human being. Especially since Peasgoody's been on his case."

"Perhaps you're right," relented Eleanor. "These past few months he's been an absolute ogre. You think Peasgoody is the cause?"

"She's a witch," Newman asserted. "Like I've said all along. And not one of those New Age namby-pamby white witches either. There's something sinister about this Peasgoody woman."

"Are we going in?" asked a voice from the snow-spattered darkness. "Or is the party out here in the driveway?"

Wrapped in a whirlwind of red and green scarves, Madam Peasgoody smiled as she strutted past them on her way to the Stromleys' front door. There she rang the doorbell and was granted entrance.

→|•|•|•|←

From a dozen speakers secreted about the living room, Bing Crosby murmured something about sleigh bells and knee-deep snow. All well and good for someone who winters in a Florida orange grove, thought Terry. Obviously, the crooner had never shovelled the wretched stuff from his sidewalk November through March. And sleigh bells, or any kind of bells for that matter, rang morosely when it was forty below with gusting arctic winds and a chill factor of minus sixty.

Walking in a winter wonderland, Crosby concluded as Terry rejoined Eleanor by the Christmas tree and handed her a glass of George's high-octane eggnog.

Mayor Abigail Smyth-Jones was frowning at the tree ornaments. They included, among other oddities, fresh fruit and flowers. "It's a real tree," she said, rolling a Japanese orange in her fingers before replacing it in the pine branches next to a giant coralroot orchid. "I've never seen such a huge tree inside a house."

"I helped George bring it in," said Carter Donaldson, puffing out his chest. "We had to take out the living-room window to haul it inside, and then it wouldn't stand up until we trimmed an extra foot off the bottom."

"And it was worth all that trouble?" asked Abigail.

Carter shrugged. "It's the biggest tree in town."

"The point being?" asked Abigail.

When Carter just looked at her, Eleanor said: "I think that is the point. George invited all of us here just to show us that *his tree* is bigger than *our tree*."

"Where is George?" asked Abigail. "I haven't seen him since I arrived."

Terry coughed. "He's tending bar with his wife. Problem is, Peasgoody's there, and they're having an argument."

Newman, who had been hiding behind the Christmas tree since sneaking in the door behind Terry and Eleanor, poked his head out. "What are they arguing about? Not my goat, I hope."

Terry dropped his voice even further. "They're arguing about babies."

Eleanor, who ran a small daycare and headed up the Okotoks chapter of Child Awareness, nearly dropped her eggnog. "Babies? George hates children. What could they possibly be arguing about?"

"You've hit it exactly," said Terry. "Peasgoody is insisting that George father a child."

"What business is it of hers?" snapped Abigail. The mayor's fingers tightened into a fist, and her face grew pale. Terry could almost see the images forming in her mind: George slapping around a smaller version of himself whenever *the boy* got out of line.

"She's a witch," said Newman. "Witches make babies their business. Sometimes they eat them."

"Newman!" said Eleanor. "That's sick. Nobody eats children."

Newman folded his arms against his chest. "Tell that to Hansel and Gretel."

"Madam Peasgoody is not a witch," said Mayor Abigail. "She's a herbalist. She probably just thinks it's unnatural for a married couple not to have children."

"Unnatural?" echoed Newman. "I think Madam Peasgoody is as unnatural as they come."

Terry thrust forward his glass of eggnog to get the others' attention, then leaned in to whisper. "She, uh, wasn't exactly insisting that Mrs. Stromley be the child's mother. She said that, if Mrs. Stromley wasn't willing, any healthy woman would do."

"Is it my imagination?" suggested Abigail, sniffing the eggnog, "or is there more nog than egg in that glass?"

Just then Peasgoody marched past them. In her arms she carried one of those slow-burning Yule logs from Wal-Mart. She stopped in front of the fireplace, an enormous affair with dark slate tiles, a raised hearth, and broad oak mantle. After opening the fire screen she set the log on the cold iron grating. From her pocket she removed five bayberry candles and set them on the mantle. Then she stood back, whispered something, and the Yule log and candles ignited.

"George was," Terry admitted, "a little heavy-handed with the rum. A herbalist, you say?"

"Looks like a witch from where I'm standing," observed Newman, though his posture was closer to squatting as he huddled behind the Christmas tree, his head poking out from a cluster of mandarin oranges. "What bothers me is that she's using one of those two-hour logs. A traditional Yule log has to burn for twelve hours, or it's bad luck." He strained his head further out from behind the oranges and looked around. "It should be about time for the Yule Goat to appear."

"Yule Goat?" Carter stared at him. "There's no such thing."

"Oh, yes," Newman nodded. "The Yule Elf comes riding in on a goat and delivers presents. It's an ancient Norse tradition."

"Sounds more like something out of Charlie Brown," said Carter. "If George had half a mind to hand out presents, I'd be the first to know about it."

"I brought a present," said Eleanor. She pulled a small, fist-sized box out of her purse. It was wrapped in bright candy-cane paper and had a small pink bow on one corner. "No-one said anything about exchanging gifts, but just in case..."

"There has to be a Yule Goat," continued Newman. "Why else would George tell me to expect my goat?"

Madam Peasgoody finished her prayers or invocations or whatever in front of the fireplace and returned to the bar, where George was still arguing with his wife. Bing Crosby was just finishing "White Christmas," and Terry could hear George in the ensuing quiet: "I'm not going to have a child by another woman! I'm not going to have a child period!" Bing Crosby responded by singing "Chestnuts Roasting on an Open Fire."

⁕⁂⁕⁂⁕

The dining-room table was decked out in typical holiday fashion: Santa Claus tablecloth, matching poinsettias, bone china, silver silverware. No-one asked Peasgoody how the bayberry candles had been lit, or about the log crackling in the fireplace. Actually, no-one dared say anything. At the head of the table George fumed, his face dark, his eyes pointedly avoiding both his wife and Madam Peasgoody, who sat to either side.

When, Terry wondered, had George and Peasgoody become such good friends? More important, why? Right now they were getting along like two roosters in the same hen house.

"Could you pass the yams?" asked Mayor Abigail from behind a flowering poinsettia further down the table.

Terry obliged and followed up with the Brussels sprouts. He had already filled most of his plate with similar holiday accessories and had yet to see any sign of the turkey. It dawned on him that there possibly were no turkeys in Wales. Newman, who claimed to know everything, could probably tell him, but he was busy cringing in his seat down at the foot of the table.

"Are you comfortable, Newman?" boomed George, whose avoidance of his wife and his spiritual advisor virtually forced him to spend his time glaring across the table at Newman.

"Fine, fine," stammered Newman. "You don't happen to have a Yule Elf, do you?"

George blinked at him.

"These carrots and parsnips are delicious," said Eleanor to Mrs. Stromley. "You simply must give me the recipe."

Mrs. Stromley scowled at her. "You cut up carrots and parsnips. Then cook 'em."

"Oh," said Eleanor. "I see."

"I believe Newman should carve," growled George.

Newman about fell out of his chair.

"But..." said Mayor Abigail. "You're the host, George. Tradition—"

"Who gives a pig's fart about tradition?" snapped George.

Madam Peasgoody dropped her fork onto her plate, with more force than was really necessary. The china cracked, allowing gravy to escape and run across the tablecloth.

"George," said Mrs. Stromley. "This is a bad idea."

George rose from his seat, went into the kitchen, and returned with one of those big silver trays with the dome cover that you only ever see in posh French restaurants. He marched the length of the dining room and plunked the tray on top of Newman's plate, remashing his mashed potatoes and squirting cranberry sauce across the table. From his back pocket George produced a thick carving knife and dropped it onto the table beside the tray.

He folded his arms across his chest and glared at Newman. "I insist," he said.

"Er," said Newman, caught between fight and flight.

"If you've done what I think you've done," said Madam Peasgoody, "then you've crossed the line and there is no going back."

"As I've told you before," roared George, "your bloody lines mean nothing to me. Since simply telling you to bugger off accomplished nothing, I've had to take more desperate measures."

"Oh, George. You didn't!" said Mayor Abigail.

Eleanor slammed her hand on the table. "You're a monster!"

Terry stared hard at the silver tray, at last clueing in to what was going on. This was low, even for George.

"We're waiting," said George, nudging the knife toward Newman's hand.

Newman remained frozen. His lips trembled until at last he muttered: "Goose or pheasant?"

"Neither," said George, and he pulled the silver cover off of the tray.

There, sitting on the tray like a roast pig, sat Newman's goat, butter basted and golden brown.

Newman stared, unable to speak.

"What's the matter, Newman?" said George. "Goats are eaten all over the world. Europe, Asia, South America. I sneaked a taste in the kitchen. Yum. Yum."

"This is too much," said Mayor Abigail. "You've outdone yourself this time, George." She rose from her chair to leave.

Peasgoody was already moving. She had her coat and scarves and paused only long enough to glare at the fireplace, where the candles and the Yule log suddenly extinguished themselves.

"A plague on your house, George Stromley!" said Madam Peasgoody. "A plague of justice on your character." Then she stormed out the door.

"Humph!" said George. "If Newman isn't man enough to carve, I suppose I'll have to do it." He picked up the knife and began cutting.

Eleanor rose from her chair, and Terry quickly joined her. Newman began laughing, pointing his finger at George and giggling uncontrollably.

"Don't go hysterical on me, Newman," said George. "It's only a goat."

Newman laughed even harder. "Only a goat," he croaked.

"We'll get you another one," said the mayor.

Newman staggered out of his chair, and Eleanor handed him his coat. "Only a goat," he said, and slapped his thigh. "Just a goat."

The mayor opened the door. Outside, the snow had stopped, but clouds hid the moon and stars. There was not a breath of wind. Newman's laughter echoed into the night. In the doorway he stopped and pointed at George, who was still at the table carving the goat.

"You've been cursed by a witch," he told him. "An honest-to-God witch. A plague of justice on your character! Who could ask for anything more?"

↛╎↮╎↮╎↤

Terry and Eleanor walked hand in hand down the lane away from George Stromley's country house. Behind them, Mrs. Stromley's angry voice rained incriminations on George's head, while down a side street Newman's laughter gave no sign of abating.

"Well, that was a complete fiasco," said Terry. "George has had lousy parties in the past, but this one should win an award."

"It's not a total loss," said Eleanor. "I still have that present." She pulled the candy-cane box with the pink bow from her purse. "Let's go back to my place and open it."

"What is it?" asked Terry. After cursing witches and roast goat for dinner, he was leery of surprises.

Eleanor took his arm and pulled him closer. "A grand Christmas tradition. Mistletoe."

A WEDDING AT SHEEP RIVER
Ostara: March 21 - April 4

At first, Terry had been unsure about getting married on Easter Sunday. Though the peculiar date was at Eleanor's insistence, he couldn't quite shrug off the suspicion that Madam Peasgoody was somehow behind it, even after Newman Porter had assured him that Ostara, the witch's Easter, had come and gone two weeks earlier, so the wedding was "probably safe."

Terry was also uncomfortable with Newman's choice of words; "probably safe" was hardly an auspicious way to begin a marriage. Still, if it made Eleanor happy to get married on Easter...

"Come on, silly. We'll miss the Easter egg hunt!"

Eleanor swept toward him in a flow of white silk, very much resembling a fairy princess. Or, Terry reflected, a sun goddess. Her long, golden hair was bound with a single band of white silk that, though plain, fit her like a crown. Her throat and sleeves were rich with lace, and her gown trailed behind her like a cloud, refusing to snag on twigs or to become stained by the bright spring grass of Sheep River Park.

"I thought it was supposed to be bad luck for the groom to see his bride in her wedding gown before the wedding," Terry said, grinning to show that he wasn't disappointed with what he saw.

"No silly superstition is going to darken our wedding," said Eleanor. "Come on!" She took his hand in hers. "The egg hunt has already started."

"Lead on," said Terry. Together they bounded off toward the taller grasses along the riverbank.

A short distance away beneath the shadow of a stand of willows, a cold-eyed George Stromley watched them go.

"Do you really think this is a good idea?" asked Carter, skulking in the bushes beside him. "I mean, it's their wedding day. It's supposed to be a happy occasion."

George glared at his friend, then nudged with his foot the large basket in the grass between them. A purple and yellow banded egg rocked on top of a jumble of others all painted in a variety of colours and patterns.

"Don't be daft," said George. "Since when do weddings include an Easter egg hunt?"

"Then, what about the children? I feel bad about ruining their egg hunt."

George stared at him. "You were here this morning, just like I was. You saw. Don't tell me we're not doing the right thing."

"I'm no longer certain what I saw," admitted Carter. "So what if Madam Peasgoody started a bonfire at sunrise and danced around it ringing a bell. Madam Peasgoody does a lot of weird things."

"And after that?" prompted George.

"Well," said Carter. "Then she hid the eggs. Nothing strange about that."

"She put a curse on the eggs," said George. "I know. She put a curse on me at Christmas, and nothing has gone right since. I won't let her curse the town."

"Maybe we should ask Newman about the fire and the bells," suggested Carter. "Newman knows about curses."

"Newman is as bad as Peasgoody," said George. "Come on. Let's throw these eggs in the river." He reached down to lift the basket and was stopped by a shriek in the trees a short distance away.

"I found one!" The shrill voice that rang through the park was Newman Porter's.

"Only one?" Mayor Abigail's voice came from down by the river. "I've found three already."

"I guess we missed a few," said Carter.

From across the park a chorus of children's laughter pealed through the air. Everyone, it seemed, was finding eggs.

"More than a few, I'm thinking," grumbled George.

"I'm certain Peasgoody only had one full basket," said Carter. He lifted the basket of eggs he and George had collected that morning after Peasgoody had planted them throughout Sheep River Park. "There can't be more than a few out there."

"Eureka!" Terry's voice filled the park as he and Eleanor emerged from some bushes near the riverbank, each with an armload of coloured eggs. Eleanor set her eggs on a blanket then wiped away a smear of lipstick that had somehow found its way onto Terry's cheek.

Over by the podium and chairs, where the wedding would shortly take place, Madam Peasgoody paused from her floral arranging and turned to look into the trees where George and Carter were hiding. There was a smirk on her lips and fire in her eyes.

George plucked the purple and yellow painted egg from the top of the basket and prepared to fling it at her, but Carter caught his arm. "Not here. Not now," he said.

Peasgoody tossed her head back and resumed her work.

"She's mine," snarled George, reluctantly returning the egg to the basket. "I'll destroy her. Just you wait."

"Of course you will," said Carter. "But for now we may as well join them. I think the wedding is about to start." He hefted the heavy basket of eggs, then grinned. "You know. I think we're a shoo-in to win the egg hunt."

⋙I⋘I⋙I⋘

"Just think," said Eleanor. She and Terry stood near the pavilion, waiting for the guests to finish being seated. "It was less than two months ago, on Valentine's Day, that you proposed, and now here we are, soon to become husband and wife."

"Do you think we rushed things?" Terry asked her. "I could have waited. June or September would have been fine."

It was Peasgoody, he thought. Showing up at the oddest times. Lighting candles. Reading poems. It was Peasgoody who pushed for an early wedding, though she never came out and said it directly. That woman has power. She *encourages* things to happen. Terry couldn't think of a better word for it.

Eleanor stretched her hands up toward the sun and spun around, her white wedding gown swirling around her like river currents in a waterfall. "It's a beautiful day to get married," she said. "I wouldn't change a thing. Except, maybe I'd have someone other than George win the Easter egg hunt. I'm certain he cheated."

Terry laughed. "George? Cheat?"

Madam Peasgoody appeared just then from around the corner of the pavilion. The woman's face glowed, as if it were her own wedding about to commence.

"I would like you both to have these," she said, lifting her hands. Nestled in each palm was a tiny, elaborately decorated egg. Not chicken eggs, Terry decided. Something smaller. Robin's eggs. Or some other bird.

"Oh! They're beautiful!" Eleanor took one of the small eggs in her fingers. A thin gold chain had been affixed to the back so she could wear it around her neck.

He took up the other egg amulet and examined the painting. It had not been done with food colouring and a toy brush. It looked more like a museum piece. There were soft brown checks and bright green diamonds and tiny red runes traced into a simple yet handsome design. Earth colours.

Eleanor drew the gold chain over her head and let the egg fall to her bosom. Terry, seeing how much Eleanor welcomed the gift, did the same. "Thank you," he said. "This is very thoughtful."

Madam Peasgoody's crow-bright eyes beamed at them. "When you wear them, they will bring you luck and protection."

"Er," Terry couldn't stop himself from asking. "Protection from what, exactly?"

Madam Peasgoody gave him a solemn look. "Evil," she said. "Seen and unseen." She wagged her head toward the rear of the wedding seats where George and Carter stood over their collection of Easter eggs, arguing.

"Of course," said Terry. "Thank you."

"The ceremony is about to begin," announced Newman Porter, striding smartly toward them in his trimmed and brushed rent-a-tux from All Occasions on Main Street. Terry had asked Newman to be his best man, and Newman had strutted around town like a prize rooster ever since.

He stopped dead when he saw the amulets around Eleanor and Terry's necks. "My God! Those are pysanky eggs!" He squinted. "But they've got runes!" He stared at Peasgoody. "Can pysanky eggs have runes?"

"These ones can," said Peasgoody.

Newman opened his mouth to debate the issue, but Peasgoody stopped him by raising her hands. "I have something for you, as well."

"For me?" Newman's eyes went wide, and he took a step back.

"I feel bad," said Peasgoody, "about what George did to your goat. It was cruel and unkind."

"Well... yes," mumbled Newman. He hadn't spoken of his pet goat since George had roasted it for Christmas dinner. He hadn't spoken to George since, either.

Peasgoody reached into a sack near her feet and came back with a giant, white egg. It was larger than an ostrich egg. Newman was immediately intrigued and gladly accepted it.

"It is a gift from the Goddess," said Peasgoody. "Care for it well, and it will care for you in return."

Newman tapped at the shell with the tip of a finger. "This is too large to be real," he said. He tapped again. "Only it is. This is real eggshell."

Peasgoody smiled and walked away.

As if on cue the music for the Wedding March began. Newman gaped at Terry. "We're supposed to be at the podium!" Newman tucked the oversized egg under one arm like a football and clutched Terry's elbow with his free hand. Terry smiled at Eleanor as he allowed Newman to drag him away toward the altar.

As they approached the back ranks of folding chairs they found George and Carter still arguing, their words growing louder and their gestures more animated. Nearby guests were abandoning their seats for vacant chairs elsewhere.

"Don't do it!" pleaded Carter.

"I know what I'm doing," George insisted.

Terry pulled away from Newman's urgent tugging in order to confront the two. He noted that George had a painted egg in either hand and that Carter was trying to wrest them from him. This was childish even for George.

"Could you two take this elsewhere?" Terry suggested. "The wedding has started."

"George wants to hurl eggs at Peasgoody," complained Carter.

Terry stared at George. "At my and Eleanor's wedding?"

George raised his hands and blurted: "She's done something. Bonfires and bells!" At that moment he must have tightened his fingers, for the egg in either hand burst, splattering yellow-brown goo all over his and Carter's suit jackets. There was a stink of sulphur and ammonia.

Miraculously, none of the spoiled yolk struck Terry or Newman.

"Pee-ew," cried Carter. Stumbling backward he knocked into George who in turn tripped over the egg basket, smashing a dozen painted eggs, also rotten, and knocking himself and Carter on top of the mess. The two men squirmed in the slippery puddle of putrid egg, unable to breathe for the bad air. Eventually they stumbled to their feet and ran toward the river as fast as their legs would carry them.

Terry turned to Newman. "Eleanor invited them. Not me."

Newman sniffed at the broken eggs, then sniffed again. "Weren't these eggs rotten a moment ago? They aren't rotten now."

Terry pondered whether to inspect the broken and crushed Easter eggs or to continue on to the podium, where the minister was looking at him with impatience bordering on outrage. It was then that he noticed that the shell of the huge egg under Newman's arm had a crack in it. "Newman, I think..."

Newman staggered as enormous hunks of eggshell fell away, leaving a small, newborn animal shivering in his hands. Apart from a confusion of legs and a coat of grey fur, Terry couldn't make out what the animal was. "That's not a goat, is it?"

"No," said Newman, studying the beast. "I believe it's a grey hare." Sure enough, two long, fuzzy ears popped up and turned left then right like antennae, followed by a bewhiskered nose that twitched theatrically. Newman petted the animal's soft fur and smiled. "And now it's my grey hare."

This time it was Terry's turn to grab Newman's elbow. "Then let's get you and your hare up to the podium. I'm getting married!"

Apart from some splashing and angry shouts from the river, the ceremony went off without any further ado. Terry and Eleanor exchanged their vows and the best man's rabbit was no fuss at all.

THE RISE OF THE HOLLY KING
Beltane: May 1

Sheep River Park was turned out in carnival fashion. The Okotoks Youth Marching Band was in full swing, playing "The Happy Isle" in a crash of trumpets and drums. Children ran and shrieked in a game of tag, trailing helium-filled balloons in their wake. Young couples walked along the glades, hand-in-hand, with flowers in their hair. Near the cookhouse a group of farmers and their wives engaged in the time-honoured tradition of square dancing. Off toward the river an archery tournament was in progress.

Terry Sutton and Eleanor Woodhouse climbed out of their shiny new Toyota Matrix station wagon and surveyed their domain.

"It's a good turnout," suggested Terry.

"Yes," agreed Eleanor. "Who'd have thought the town would get so excited about celebrating so obscure a festival as May Day?"

"May Day?" said Terry. "I thought we were celebrating your election as mayor."

Eleanor laughed. "I think the only one celebrating that is Abigail. I'm sure she secretly wanted to lose."

"I don't see our ex-mayor here anywhere," said Terry. "She may be the only one not celebrating today."

"Isn't that George's Christmas tree?" asked Eleanor.

In the middle of the park a huge pine tree lay on its side. A crowd, mostly kids, stood in a loose circle around it.

"It is a tree," said Terry. "And a big one. What makes you think it's George's?"

"I don't know," said Eleanor. "Just a feeling I have. Let's go over and see what Peasgoody is up to now."

Within the circle of onlookers, Madam Peasgoody stood off to one side while Newman Porter and Sheriff Winslo hacked at branches with hand axes. Dry pine needles and shrivelled flower petals flew in all directions.

Newman straightened and wiped his hand across his forehead. "This is hot work," he said.

"George's tree?" asked Terry.

"Yup," said Newman.

"Does he know?"

"Nope." Newman went back to swinging his axe.

In short order the two men succeeded in removing all of the branches on the lower fifteen feet of the tree. Then Madam Peasgoody opened a bag and drew out several long ribbons. She tied them to the tree at the base of the remaining lowest branches, alternating red and white ribbons. Then Newman and Winslo, using a thick rope, levered the tree upright, its base sinking into a newly dug hole. When it was done, Newman pushed on the tree to straighten it while Winslo hammered shims into the hole near the tree's base for support.

When they were done Newman and Winslo stood back to appraise their work while Madam Peasgoody walked around the tree throwing flowers into the breeze. The ribbons fluttered around her like long skinny flags.

Newman whispered to Terry: "Carter Donaldson says Peasgoody was up at midnight gathering flowers by the light of the moon. Do you believe it?"

"It all looks pretty innocent to me," answered Terry. "Is it some kind of May Pole dedication?"

Newman shook his head. "I don't know."

Terry stared at him. He couldn't remember the last time Newman said he *didn't know* something.

When she was done, Peasgoody invited people to take a ribbon end and dance around the tree. Someone in the crowd pulled out a flute and began a cheery tune.

"Come on," said Eleanor, taking Terry's hand. "Let dance around the May Pole."

Peasgoody smiled when they approached, joining several others around the tree, most of them no more than ten years old.

"The red ribbons are for the boys," she said. "And white for the girls."

They were short a boy, so Newman got roped into dancing as well. He put up a fuss but in the end looked eager to give it a go.

With the flute marking a steady beat, the eight dancers kicked up their heels and pranced around the pole, their ribbons twining together, drawing them all closer to the tree with each revolution. After a dozen or so orbits, the dancers all crashed into each other and fell laughing onto the grass.

Terry was still frolicking in the grass with Eleanor when a shadow fell upon them. Terry looked up into George's frowning face. "Are you and the new mayor having fun yet?" he asked.

"Yes, we are," Eleanor answer before Terry could say anything. "You should try it, George. It might help if you loosened up."

"I am plenty loose," George said. "And I'm ready to meet Terry on the field of battle."

"What field of battle?" demanded Newman.

George swung a big stick through the air, and from Terry's perspective on the ground it looked very menacing indeed. "Softball," said George. "I challenge Terry to a game of softball."

"Er," said Newman. "Don't you need nine people on a team for softball?"

"Terry can pick his team," George said. "I already have mine." he pointed behind him to a crew of large, mean-looking men. Terry recognized a few of them from the High River YMCA. The others he didn't recognize.

The flute player stopped playing and silence descended on that corner of Sheep River Park. Terry finally decided what to say: "I guess I accept."

⁕⁕⁕

It took a while to find eight people willing to play against George and his minions. Eleanor immediately volunteered, of course. As did Newman, though he insisted he could neither throw nor catch. Carter Donaldson wasn't tough enough to play on George's team, so George appointed him umpire. The two teams drew straws, and George came up first at bat. He gave the five-pound length of white ash a few practice swings, then stood at the ready. His stance included a deep scowl and repeated spitting.

Terry stood on the pitcher's mound, squeezing the ball in his hand and flexing his arm in an attempt to limber up. He'd never been much good at baseball. As a pitcher he fairly stank. George, on the other hand, had once led the Okotoks High softball team to the regional championships. He would likely hit Terry's first throw straight to Pincher Creek.

"Batter, batter, batter, batter," Newman shouted from the catcher's position.

"No talking," said Carter, taking his role as umpire a little too seriously.

Absently, Terry lifted his free hand to touch the pysanky-egg amulet Peasgoody had given him at Easter. It was supposed to be for protection, but maybe it was a good luck charm as well. After all, Eleanor had won the election, and Terry's car dealership was booming.

"Are you going to stand there all afternoon?" George shouted.

"Batter, batter, batter, batter," Newman repeated.

George turned and waved his bat. "I'll *batter* you if you don't shut up."

"No talking," said Carter. Then louder: "Let's play ball!"

George spun back into position and made ready to slam the ball to Montana.

Terry wound back, took careful aim at Newman's glove, and pitched. He tried to watch the flight of the ball, but all he saw was George's evil grin. Terry could swear there was drool leaking out of the side of George's mouth.

From the edge of his vision, Terry saw the bat begin its swing. He anticipated the sound of the wood and the ball connecting, but, in reality, what he heard sounded somewhat softer. Then the bat flew out of George's hands, the ball fell to the plate at his feet, and George collapsed in a heap.

Carter was at his friend's side in an instant. "I think his nose is broken," he shouted.

Newman flipped up his catcher's mask and raised his right hand in a high five. "He's out!" he cried.

Carter stood and jabbed Newman in his shoulder pad. "You can't call *outs*. That's my job."

Newman just grinned at him. "Then do your job."

Carter looked down at George, lying still in the dirt, blood streaming from his nose staining home plate red. "He's out," Carter shouted, then in a softer voice, "out cold."

A cheer went up from the crowd.

⁂

As the ambulance drove off with George, Newman walked up to Terry and Eleanor. "Looks like the battle's over." He shook Terry's hand. "To the victor goes the spoils."

"There are spoils?" asked Terry.

Newman grinned. "If you ask me, sending George to the hospital is spoils enough."

"I feel kind of guilty beaning George in the head like that. I was sure my throw was over the plate."

"If it makes you feel better," suggested Newman, "you can send him a fruit basket. Anyway, you're needed over by the cookhouse. Madam Peasgoody has another May Day tradition ready for us."

"Really?" said Eleanor. "This day has been wonderful so far. I can hardly wait to see what's next."

Outside the cookhouse Madam Peasgoody had a small fire going beneath the cauldron Terry had last seen on Halloween atop the Big Rock. Then it had held dry ice and root beer. This time the flames were real flames and some kind of broth was simmering.

Terry and Eleanor watched as John Robin and his wife Mary jumped over the cauldron together.

"I know this!" said Newman. "It's supposed to be good luck. Couples who want to have children jump over the cauldron together. Nine months later they'll have a healthy baby."

"Uh," said Terry.

"I thought our romp in the woods last night was supposed to..." Eleanor began, but then fell silent.

Madam Peasgoody beckoned for them to jump over the cauldron.

"Shall we?" asked Terry.

"We shall," agreed Eleanor.

Terry took her hand, and together they jumped over the cauldron.

Everyone clapped and cheered, and then a new couple stepped up to take a turn.

"Well, if that doesn't do it I don't know what will," said Eleanor. "A roll in the hay by moonlight followed by a leap over a cauldron. That has to count for something."

"You were hay-rolling by moonlight?" asked Newman.

Terry was spared from answering by a commotion near the parking lot. They all looked and saw a crowd of people moving toward them, laughing and shouting. Carter Donaldson was in the group and ran toward them.

"You won't believe it!" he shouted.

"Believe what?" Newman called back at him.

Carter ran up to them and stopped, resting his hands on his knees to catch his breath.

"Believe what?" repeated Terry, when Carter just stood there, gasping for air.

Finally, Carter straightened up and looked at them. His eyes twinkled. "You won't believe me if I tell you. You'd best see for yourselves."

Together they all watched as the crowd neared.

Madam Peasgoody stepped up beside them and said: "My, my. This is a surprise." Her expression suggested that whatever it was, she approved.

When the crowd was almost upon them, it parted to reveal a woman with incredibly long blond hair riding a white pony. Terry realized three important things all at once. First: the hair was fake; a wig of some kind. Second: the woman was Abigail Smyth-Jones, until recently the mayor of Okotoks. And last, that beneath the cloak of false hair, Abigail was naked.

Beside him, Newman let out a long whistle.

"You know," said Eleanor. "I don't think Abigail took losing the election well at all."

"Well, said Terry. "A lot can change with the seasons. Perhaps the Goddess will be kinder to her next time around."

Wonjjang and the Madman of Pyongyang
Gord Sellar

1. WORKING HARDLY

"Then..."
—right uppercut to the chin—
"...tell me..."
—left hook to the temple—
"...the goddamned..."
—a finger in the little bastard's good eye—
"...passcode!" Wonjjang finished the sentence with a backhanded slap hard enough to break a normal man's neck.

His enemy, of course, was no normal man: though less than four feet tall, Kim Noh Wang, the Madman of Pyongyang, was North Korea's last uncaptured criminal mastermind. He wheedled: "Wonjjang, Wonjjang... we're brothers! Don't you realize that? We Koreans are of One Blood!" Wonjjang could hear the extra-big, bright-red lettering on the phrase "One Blood," though he was only half-listening. The rest of his attention was directed downward, through the smoggy air. Far below, Khao San Road was a mess, stir-fried noodle stands and racks of snide T-shirts thrashed to pieces, their scattered contents lit by the setting sun. Hastily commandeered tuk-tuks and taxis barrelled away into the dusk in every direction, and panicked Western backpackers were scattering into the neon-lit Bangkok evening, like monkeys at the sound of gunshots.

Blastman, with his American-flag cape billowing behind him in the wind, hurled balls of electricity from each hand and vomited gouts of lightning into the crowd of Kim's hirelings and desperate Thai recruits. It was amazing what a few false promises could do for recruitment in the developing world, especially under a junta: a couple of anarchist monks and a squadron of ladyboy-terrorists in glittering gold miniskirts and bustiers had blockaded one end of the street and were advancing. The ladyboys shrieked hatefully as they scattered to avoid Blastman's attack.

"Hey!" Kim hollered in irate Korean. "Are you listening to me?"

Wonjjang ploughed a fist into Kim's face as the familiar lurch kicked in and their descent began. He scanned the ground until he found Neko, his team's fearless catgirl. She was further up the street, standing in a pool of blood, her white kitty outfit and the walls all around spattered by her grisly handiwork.

Perched in her white high-heeled boots, Neko dug her claws into one of Kim's Nork — North Korean — henchtwits and lifted him above her head, flinging him into a rack of knockoff Gucci and Prada purses. Wonjjang felt a strange yet stirring blend of repulsion and attraction toward the Japanese superheroine. Watching her slash the crap out of villains was *hot*. She was working on a band of soldier-uniformed Norks. Leaping from one to the next like the cat that was her namesake, she pounced, skewering them on her long claws in a single blurred flash of steel, and tossed their shivering corpses aside. Just as she was about to slash the last one into ribbons, Kim's henchwoman Iron Monkey leaped down from a low rooftop onto her, shoving Neko to the ground.

Wonjjang winced. How he wished he was down there, near her, so that he could help her out... or, at least, beat the crap out of Iron Monkey somewhere that she could see him doing it. He hoped against hope that she'd noticed him bounding up into the sky with Kim in his clutches, fighting for the shutdown code that would disable the chicken-plague bomb. Kim was, after all, "The Madman of Pyongyang," officially — according to every trade magazine — one of Asia's Top Five Supervillains. *What could be more impressive than catching Kim Noh Wang?* Wonjjang asked himself while the two superwomen wrestled on the cracked roadway. Then a pack of shaven-headed Thai monks in saffron robes — local heroes, maybe? — piled out of a levitating tuk-tuk and converged on them, and he could see Neko no more.

"Come on!" Kim whined. "You're not even listening to me! If I tell you the passcode, will you even hear it?"

Wonjjang turned to face the psychotic dwarf and said flatly, "Fine. What is it?"

"You think I'm so foolish? That I would just *tell* you?"

"You want to live, don't you?" Wonjjang's eyes hardened, and he let go of Kim. The fall would kill him, despite his reinforced skeleton.

But Kim just laughed, his carefully coiffed curls snaking up as he fell through the air. "Fine," he shouted, shaking his head maniacally, as if in triumph. "And you will never know the..."

Wonjjang lunged and grabbed him again, plowing a fist into Kim's tubby little gut. "Shut up," he yelled against the growing din of the battle rushing up from below, and Kim obliged, bent double in pain.

As he got close to the ground, Wonjjang focused carefully on his surroundings. He had only a few moments. He swivelled his head until he found what he was looking for: his teammate Laotzu was up the street, hunched against the collapsing wall of a blown-up shop, clutching the chicken-plague bomb precariously with both hands.

Oh no, Wonjjang thought as he bounced and shot upward again into the air. Poor, simpleminded Laotzu: he looked terrified, shivers of panic rippling through his massive body of jade and uncut stone and barky wood. Laotzu was great for pounding heads and busting through reinforced steel doors, but he was not the guy you wanted stuck handling a deadly viral bomb.

But E-Gui turned up just then to help. A band of ladyboys had burst past Blastman. They rushed toward Laotzu, but E-Gui — *Ghost*, the Chinese member of

Wonjjang's shoopah-team — appeared suddenly, half-dematerialized, and swooped among them. One by one they dropped dead as his ghostly hand squeezed their beating hearts into bloody paste.

Wonjjang turned his attention back to his hostage. He slapped Kim across the face one more time, and sternly shouted, "You have a choice." His voice boomed against the rushing air around them. "Tell me the passcode, or I *feed* you the bomb and let Blastman burn you alive!"

Kim smirked and grabbed for Wonjjang's suit, but his pudgy little arms couldn't quite reach. Finally, he tucked them behind his back like a general inspecting his troops, a ridiculous bid for authority.

Kim shook his head. "Why are you supporting people who don't want to help us? We're *brothers!* If you would—" His harsh Northern accent grated.

Suddenly, Wonjjang lashed out, cursing: "E saekiya! You think *I'm* allied with enemies of the Korean people?" He changed tack, clubbing Kim's body with his fists. Real punches, this time, not interrogation strikes. He roared even louder: "You think *they're* bad for Korea? Who the hell do you think is going to get sick, you sshipsaeki? Your plague is going to kill the whole world!" They slowed through the apex of his upward final bound and began to descend toward the ground, but they were still three-quarters of a kilometre up.

"You have no pride!" Kim Noh Wang orated, raising his arms dramatically. "Your flunkyist government couldn't even make you *fly*, like the American capitalist-dog super-heroes! No, all you can do is bounce... like that stupid tiger in the *Windy Boo Bear* cartoon! Free yourself, Wonjjang! Join with your Northern brothers! Help us... instead of running around with American and Japanese bastar—"

Wonjjang had stopped listening, his eyes focused on the ground. E-Gui's ghostly form swept through the machine. Wonjjang had seen him do this before; he knew that every circuit within it was being fried, the timer and explosives rendered inert. He sighed in relief when E-Gui drifted away moments later and Laotzu placed the bomb carefully on the ground and tore into it.

Wonjjang turned his attention to the supervillain in his clutches. "Hey, Kim," he said, "looks like I don't need that passcode after all."

Kim's pleading became an inarticulate shriek as Wonjjang lifted him up over his head and flexed his muscles. The South Korean hero was well beyond feeling fed up with his Nork nemesis. How many more times could he be allowed to escape and threaten the world? Just in the past month, Kim had flooded downtown Busan with radioactive sewage, sent an army of killer robots across the DMZ, and now had nearly dropped a chicken-plague bomb that could have wiped out everyone in Southeast Asia. Enough! And if that insane Sunshine Policy passed into law Kim would become untouchable.

Wonjjang was going to kill the little prick. Now, while he still could. That stupid bouffant hairdo: he would make a fashionable corpse. He aimed at a Starbucks hidden in an alley off the main road.

In a single, almost-graceful motion, he hurled Kim downward. Hard.

"It's 'Windy the *Pooh* Bear,' by the way," he called after Kim, and then pondered which kind of a coffee to order after he landed on his enemy's tangled, mashed remains. Iced Café Mocha, he decided, hoping a reporter would snap a shot of him enjoying coffee from an *American* chain. It'd pass without comment in Seoul, but Pyongyang would be in hysterics.

Just then, a blurry streak of grey-white slammed into the little madman and bore him through the air. Wonjjang's cheer of joy at killing the evil twerp — "Aaaaassaaaaaah...!" — faded as the streak headed toward the waiting shock-cages a few blocks away. The Madman of Pyongyang would live to fight another day, Wonjjang realized with a disheartened sigh.

E-Gui. Damn him back to China! *He* had saved the malignant little dwarf's life, hairdo and all.

Wonjjang landed on his feet in front of the Starbucks and hurried out into the carnage that covered the main road. All around him, Nork thugs and minions lay scattered on the ground, groaning. Injured ladyboys and monks staggered off into the night, and the street was otherwise deserted except for a few dreadlocked Westerner hippies dressed in faux-traditional fluorescent Thai outfits, snapping pictures with their digital cameras and chatting excitedly.

A flash lit up the dark street. It came from down at the far end, where Neko had been battling Iron Monkey. Lightning blasts alternated with maniacal chittering, and the monkey woman's voice rang out: "You can't catch me, mister!" Another flash lit up the street.

Wonjjang hurried toward Laotzu and found him standing absolutely still, balancing in his hand a single perfectly round crystal sphere.

Within it swam a yellowish cloud: Kim's chicken plague. Wonjjang sighed in relief. The sphere was intact.

Neko and Blastman hurried over. As they approached, Wonjjang gave Neko a furtive once-over. Her skin-tight plush white catsuit and cute pointy-eared helmet were dripping with gore. She glanced in the direction of the shock cages, but by now Kim would be on his way to the airport, waiting to be deposited into the reinforced cargo hold of their company jet. Wonjjang wondered if she'd seen him catch Kim at all, whether she knew that *he* was the one who'd softened the monster up.

He imagined her turning to him, congratulating him on capturing Kim, giving him a nice hug and a kiss. They could retire from enforcement, get a nice apartment in Seoul, and he could spend his days at a desk, doing shoopah policy analysis and enjoying his beautiful, Japanese ex-heroine wife. Who cared if she couldn't cook Korean food? His mother would send them kimchi. It'd be perfect.

Except.

Except that it was toward Blastman that Neko turned her adoring eyes. Blastman: a blond American hero with a gigantic B insignia on his muscular chest, shining bright for all to see. Neko grabbed his hand and squeezed it, smiling broadly.

Wonjjang grumbled, "Where is Iron Monkey?"

"She got away!" Neko declared. "It's my fault, boss. If it weren't for Blastman, I'd be dead right now," she said, and, giving his hand another squeeze, she looked up into his big blue eyes. "He saved my life!"

Blastman gave Neko a peck on the cheek. "You're welcome," he said with a broad, perfect-toothed smile.

Suddenly Wonjjang wanted nothing more than a night alone, drinking in a soju tent in the alleyway warrens of downtown Seoul.

2. A HERO'S YOUR WELCOME HOME

The flight home to Seoul was short enough — it only took a couple of hours thanks to LG Corporation's private superjet — but it was tense all the way.

Wonjjang got a head start typing up his official report. Meanwhile, Laotzu gulped down as many complimentary cans of Pocari Sweat as he could hold down, his eyes riveted to the TV; he and E-Gui were watching some horrible epic kung fu flick. A few seats up, Blastman sipped some fancy Scotch whiskey mixed with Coca-Cola and made quiet conversation with Neko in highly idiomatic English. He was a country boy; when he relaxed, his speech became almost incomprehensible to anyone who wasn't fluent.

Wonjjang stopped straining to listen in after a while — it was no use, his English just wasn't good enough to understand Blastman's prattle like Neko could. But he heard enough laughter and "Totally!" out of Neko to know that she was as charmed as ever. As if to punctuate the hopelessness of understanding more than that, Wonjjang's phone chirped loudly, announcing the arrival of a text-message. He flipped his phone open.

NO PRESS CONFERENCE, read the terse order from Head Office. No explanation.

After an operation of this magnitude? That was more than strange. For the millionth time, he wondered when he'd be promoted to a position in LG where he'd be let in on anything at all. He braced himself for a moment, holding in his own mounting frustration.

"Everybody!" he said loudly, bouncing to his feet. The others looked up. "No press conference at Incheon Airport," he announced, flatly. Managerially. What else could he say?

The disappointment was palpable. No press conference, after catching Kim Noh Wang, the biggest supercriminal in Asia? Surely this was a mistake! This was the kind of operation that made a career! They'd already changed into clean uniforms! Wonjjang understood how they felt, but what could he do?

After a few moments, Blastman asked, "But can we talk to the press? Individually?"

"Okay," said Wonjjang, smiling at the idea of a workaround. No press conference, but they could *chat* with the reporters. Head office probably wouldn't like it, but this was a ridiculous directive. Better to follow it to the letter, but to give his team some slack. "Go ahead, but keep it off the record," Wonjjang said, and went to the jet's bar to mix himself a drink.

Suddenly, he felt a presence behind him. He turned to look, bottle of whiskey still in one hand and a glass in the other.

It was E-Gui. "Nice assist, today," the Chinese shoopah said ominously in fluent Korean.

"Uh, thanks," Wonjjang gave a slight, cautious nod, not so deep as to be deferential to his subordinate but enough to suggest he was more appreciative than he really was. "Do you want one?" he asked, holding up the liquor bottle.

"Thank you," E-Gui nodded, and picked up a glass, holding it out politely with his right hand. He smiled awkwardly.

Wonjjang stared tensely at him for a moment, and then said, "Why did you catch him?"

"Mmm?" E-Gui sipped his drink.

"Kim Noh Wang. Why did you catch him? Nobody would have shed any tears if he'd died back there. It would probably have been great for our careers, even. What were you thinking?"

E-Gui blinked, unmoved. "You're not very politically aware, are you?"

Wonjjang couldn't say anything then, because it was true. If he'd known his way around a meeting, he might have avoided being saddled with the job of managing a bunch of foreigners when LG had signed up for those friendly exchange-and-training deals with the Asian and North American branches of the World Superheroes' Cooperative Association. Instead, Wonjjang had found himself cursing the WSCA for years, with their silly pipe dreams of international shoopah coordination and friendship. What did it get you? Chinese shoopahs stepping in and saving Norks, that's what.

"I heard a rumour and... well, trust me, I did you a favour," E-Gui said, and leaned forward, adding softly, "And if any footage turns up you'd better say you *accidentally* dropped him." The Chinese mutant gave Wonjjang a wry smile.

Wonjjang raised his glass to his lips, ready to swallow down his resentment. But, before he could sip it, E-Gui raised his Jack and Coke in a mock toast.

"To caution," the Chinese shoopah said, and after an awkward little bow he turned and walked away.

Wonjjang shook his head but didn't say anything. Then he returned to the cabin and to the mellifluous sound of Neko laughing at another of Blastman's jokes.

Wonjjang shook his head, sat down, knocked back half his cocktail in one shot, and reclined his seat back as far as it would go.

⸎⸎⸎

"You first, Neko," Wonjjang said. Plush and white and furry, her catsuit was also fitted perfectly to her body, highlighting both the curves and the rippling muscles beneath.

"Uh, thanks... boss," she said awkwardly, and adjusted the mini-backpack that was slung over one of her shoulders. He glanced at her backside as she stepped out onto the deplaning ramp.

Blastman was right there beside her and went on ahead, saying, "Thanks!" to Wonjjang as he passed by. Beaming at Wonjjang with his dazzling white Hollywood smile, he asked, "You okay, boss?"

"Uh... no thank you..." Wonjjang mumbled. It was the first English phrase that popped into his head. Suddenly aware of the frown on his face, he gently pushed the American out onto the ramp behind Neko.

Wonjjang ended up being the last to leave the plane. Stepping out into the warm, late-autumn sun, he saw the usual mob was there to meet them: several dozen teenagers and college kids dressed up as their favourite shoopahs. Not many costumes were emblazoned with his own Sino-Korean logo, Wonjjang noted with a twinge of annoyance. His personal trademark stock was down again. Some of the teenagers were holding up a banner that read LG PAN-ASIA SUPER SQUAD: FIGHTING! He tried turning his attention to Neko's fans, but their skintight catsuits didn't compliment them as much as they did their idol: most of them were too much, well, like middle-school girls, meaning either skeletal or pear-shaped.

He spotted a small gang of middle-schoolers — pimply boys and pot-bellied girls — dressed up in Wonjjang costumes. The usuals. He almost didn't bother to acknowledge them with his usual quick salute, but, when he did, they cheered their little guts out.

Corporate crowd control was really serious that day, more than just the usual pair of gigantic almost-shoopah thugs in black suits and sunglasses. There were at least ten of them this time, arranged around the cordon. Beyond the barriers, reporters shouted out questions in Chinese, Japanese, English, and, mostly, Korean. Flashes continuously went off by the dozen.

Right outside the barrier, beside a couple of wary-looking guards, a small crowd of protesters howled. Mostly college-aged radicals, with a few middle-aged women and retirees among them, the protesters wore matching white oversized T-shirts printed with the same slogan in Korean and garbled English: DANGEROUS UNNEEDEDLY AMERICAN GO TO THE HOME! They raised their placards and fists into the air when Blastman passed near them.

But Blastman was used to this kind of thing. He sauntered closer and declared loudly against the crescendo of cusses and thrown objects, "Well, thankya, thankya verr' much!" in boisterous, weirdly accented English. He swivelled his hips and flicked off tiny flares of lightning, incinerating their flung tomatoes and eggs instantly in midair. Blastman was almost certainly making some kind of American joke with the dance and his comments, but Wonjjang really didn't get it.

Neither did the crowd. The angriest protesters continued to curse and shout while several of the rent-a-shoopahs banded together in front of them. Blastman finally shook his head with a chuckle and crossed the cordoned-off zone to where Neko was waiting, near some Western and Japanese reporters.

By the time Wonjjang was on the ground, the pair was already chatting with those reporters. E-Gui had half-dematerialized, clothing and all, and drifted down from the plane's exit hatch toward a group of recognizably Chinese newsmen, and Laotzu was chatting in awkward Korean with some of his fans, who were dressed in elaborate, awkward costumes that emulated the raw stone and uncarved wood of his body.

Wonjjang just wanted to march straight past them into the terminal. He was dying to go take a bath at his favourite public bathhouse and sit in the sauna till he'd sweated every last trace of Thailand out of his system.

But right then his handphone rang. He glanced at the caller display: UMMA. It was his mom. If he didn't answer immediately, he'd never hear the end of it. He rolled his eyes and flipped the phone open. Reporters called out to him from beyond the cordon, ignoring the fact that he was on the phone.

"Jang Won!" she hollered through the phone. *Wonjjang* was his superhero name — "Won Jjang" literally meant "Number-One Best!" — but his mother never used it. She had named him Jang Won as a baby, and that was the only name she ever called him.

"What are you thinking?" she shouted. "Why didn't you call me sooner?"

"Umma, I just—"

"Wonjjang! Can you confirm the rumours of renewed problems with your shoulder?" one newspaperwoman bellowed in Korean.

"I heard you let that awful man live," his mom said. She coughed her disappointment at him as he shook his head at the reporter. The injury hadn't troubled him in months.

"Umma, E-Gui did that. If he hadn't, Kim would've..." he lowered his voice, "...died."

"Wonjjang!" a reporter yelled. "Can you depend on your team's international members to remain faithful to our national interests in territorial disputes with their home countries?" Wonjjang cast him a nasty glare.

"Is that the Chinese one?" his mother asked.

"E-Gui? Yes. Chinese."

"I knew it," she said, despondently triumphant.

"What do you think of the warming up of relations between Pyongyang and Seoul?" This reporter, a fellow mutant, had stretched his rubbery arm out to reach his microphone close to Jang Won. As the question registered, Jang Won turned his head, the surprise obvious on his face. A flurry of camera flashes went off instantly, and someone yelled, "Will the Sunshine Policy interfere with your work?"

"Have you eaten dinner yet?" his mom demanded. It was only a couple of hours before midnight.

"I'm sorry, I'm taking an important call," Jang Won said to the reporters, and then, into the phone, said, "No, Umma." He really *was* hungry.

"As the leader of the team that captured the infamous Kim Noh Wang, the Madman of Pyongyang," a familiar female reporter called out, "how do you feel about the close inter-Korean cooperation demanded by President Kwon?"

"I'm making dwenjang jjigae. I want you to come home *right now*," his mother said.

"I'll come, Umma, but it's going to be a while. I'm in Incheon."

"Are you worried about forecasts of a dramatic rise in international shoopah-crime in East Asia as a result of the LG's intensified focus on domestic issues?" a foreign reporter asked him loudly in English.

"And who will eat my wonderful fresh jjigae? The neighbour's poodle? The President? God? Nobody who loves his mother lets her dwenjang jjigae go cold."

"Any plans for marriage, Wonjjang?" Had someone talked to his mother? He scowled, and more flashes went off in his face.

"Come on, Umma, I'll warm it up when I get home," he said in a resigned tone.

"Bring Zolaman along if you want," she added.

"He doesn't work with us anymore..." It had been three years since he'd gone freelance.

"Okay, then, that cat girl. She isn't married, is she? The Japanese one with the furry white costume?"

"*Uniform*, Umma. And I think she has plans already..." he said. He was sure she had plans. With Blastman. "Anyway, she already has a boyfriend."

"With the recent news of cuts to shoopah sponsorships, do you have any new leads on nongovernmental funding?" *Flash, flash.*

"Whatever. Force her to come. You're her boss, right?"

"Yes, Umma."

"You can do that. It's your right!"

"Yes, Umma." But, really, he couldn't.

He must have sounded dubious. His mother said, "Maybe she has a sister. I want to see my grandchildren before I die."

"Yes, Umma."

"And don't take too long. The food's going to be cold soon."

"Yes, Um..."

The connection cut before he finished saying *Umma*, which was what he'd expected: she'd said everything she wanted to, after all.

Jang Won turned to look at his teammates, all of them chatting with the friendly, loving mob of otaku, reporters, and other maniacs. Neko stood with Blastman; E-Gui stood with Laotzu. Even the lawyer in the fancy suit was chatting with the crowd. Jang Won stood alone in his sweaty slamdex uniform.

He stayed to watch Kim's shock cage being removed from the cargo hold and banged into a high-security truck before he turned his back on the cheering crowd and hurried through the terminal in search of a toilet. He could come back to talk to the reporters, he supposed, and sign a few autographs. But, first, nature called.

He found a washroom that was mostly empty and went in. The worst part about wearing a slamdex bodysuit as a uniform was that you had to pull most of it off, even just to pee. He went into a stall, shut the door, and peeled the bodysuit open slowly, so it wouldn't lock into shape. Then he lowered himself slowly down onto the toilet, vowing to himself to cut back on the Pocari Sweat ion drinks in the future, even if they were complimentary.

After relieving himself and sliding his uniform back on, he stepped out of the stall and found himself face to face with a tall, slim young woman. Her hair was cut in a neat bob, and she had big, pretty, limpid brown eyes.

"Hi-i-i!" she said excitedly, waving the way teenage girls do when they see an old friend from elementary school. She was wearing a Wonjjang uniform, same logo as his, but tightly fitted to her body. She couldn't be a day over seventeen, he guessed. Maybe less. She stepped forward, toward him, and he felt a rush of attraction to her, which he quickly suppressed. She was a high-school girl, for heaven's sake. But he felt just a little drunk being near her like that.

"You're in a men's room," he said carefully.

"I know, I just wanted *so* much to meet you."

"You can't be in here," he said, just as a man in a business suit hurried into the washroom. On the way to the urinals, the businessman stared at the two of them. Wonjjang caught a whiff of hard liquor, but he couldn't be sure whether it had come from the man... or the girl. The guy settled down to business at the urinal farthest from them.

"I just wanted to tell you how much I admire you," she said, poking a finger into his chest and then tracing soft little circles.

The businessman glanced back over his shoulder at them while he urinated, eyebrows raised.

"Thank you, but now you need to go," Wonjjang said.

"Let me give you my name card," she said. "And can I trouble you for a signature?" She pursed her lips pleadingly and leaned forward, looking him in the eye. She held out a pen.

Wonjjang forced himself to breathe, and said, "Okay." He took the pen in one hand, and the name card in the other. "Where do you want me to sign?"

"My suit, of course. On the tummy." She spread her hands out on her belly, thumbs and forefingers framing the spot she'd chosen.

Wonjjang stuffed the namecard into one of the pockets inside his cape and bent forward to scribble a signature onto her tummy. He was about to sign when he realized that the businessman was still standing there, at the urinal, but he wasn't peeing anymore. He was just watching. Wonjjang hesitated, looking at the girl suspiciously.

"What?" she said.

"How old are you?" he asked.

The businessman cleared his throat.

"How old do I look?"

"Um..." He hated that response. "Maybe... seventeen?" he lied. His first impulse had been to say sixteen.

"Ohhh," she giggled. "Thank you! I'm a college girl, a sophomore. But I'm glad to hear I look so young!"

Wonjjang relaxed and leaned forward again. He braced the suit with one hand and wrote with the other, guiltily trying to ignore the soft, smooth flesh beneath the spandex.

"Thank you," the girl said. She leaned forward and gave him a peck on the cheek, and suddenly he could smell the alcohol again. Then, after a long, very deliberate look, she turned to go. "Sorry, sir," she called in a high-pitched, well-rehearsed cute voice to the man at the urinal, and hurried out.

The guy didn't respond but simply zipped up and left, leaving Wonjjang alone, blushing, in the middle of the airport washroom with the girl's forgotten black pen in his hand.

He fished out her card. It read:

> YOU THINK YOU'VE WON?
> WE CAN GET TO YOU ANYTIME.
> WE HAVE AGENTS EVERYWHERE.
> REMEMBER THAT.

It was signed, too, in scribbly blue ink: KIM NOH WANG.

Then the pen exploded all over his clean spare uniform.

※※※※

An hour later, when Kim and his thugs had been locked up tight in an LG transport bound for the downtown headquarters, Jang Won leaped off the usual spot on the roof of a Samsung highrise a block away from his home. He aimed his body at the balcony adjoining the apartment where he lived with his mother.

He landed there with the normal, complaint-provoking thud. His mom was lucky: she'd moved the cheap new plastic balcony furniture around since he'd last been home, and he'd only barely escaped crashing right into it. The last set had been fine wicker, smashed to pieces after just such a surprise rearrangement. He sometimes suspected she'd done it as an excuse to go furniture shopping, and that the scoldings had been just to keep up appearances.

She popped her head out the kitchen window and called out, "So noisy? Come on, hurry up!" She pulled her head back inside quickly.

"Yes, Umma," he replied. He wasn't a particularly dutiful son, just hungry, and he knew better than to talk back when food was waiting on the table.

He slid open the balcony door and slipped off his shoes. Carrying them with one hand, he rushed to the apartment's front door and slid them into the shoe rack, and then hurried to the kitchen. The heady scent of fermented bean-paste stew filled the air.

Just as he reached out for the water faucet and soap, his mother said, over her shoulder, "Wash your hands, Jang Won." Her back was turned to him, and she was stirring the stew.

"Yes, Umma," he said. Suddenly he didn't want to wash his hands. He wondered whether maybe she'd developed some kind of mutant superpower when he wasn't looking, maybe telepathy? She'd been drinking the same water that had transformed him, after all. He put the soap down before lathering his hands, a little annoyed.

"Use soap," she said, without turning around at all.

"Eugh," Jang Won muttered, annoyed. He grabbed the soap and lathered his hands up, rinsing them quickly.

"Too bad you took so long. It's never so good, overcooked." The table was set out with utensils, side dishes, and ridiculously heaped individual bowls of steamed rice.

"Sorry, Umma," he said, sat down at the table, and started picking with his chopsticks at her still fridge-cold side dishes. His mother's talent for making delicious side dishes was her most attractive quality, his father had always said... until he'd passed away from stomach cancer. The kimchi was perfect: spicy and mind-numbingly sour. Around the table were laid out dishes of anchovies in red pepper sauce, silky tofu with red pepper and soy sauce, and fresh cucumber slices beside a small dish of red-pepper paste.

"Watch out, this is hot," his mother said, and turned. From the stove to the table she carried a gigantic ttukbaegi — a kiln-fired clay bowl, heated right on the stove and bubbling with soup — with a curved pair of metal kitchen-pliers, setting it down on a soft table mat. In the enormous bowl, pieces of potato and slices of green hot pepper swirled in a thick brownish broth.

As he raised his chopsticks to nab one of the hunks of potato from the broth, his mother whacked at his right hand with the hot pliers. "Put those down. Can't you see we're expecting a guest?"

He winced and looked around the table. Place settings for three. The jjigae wasn't just for him after all.

"Who's coming over, Umma?"

"Aigo," she lamented. "You know, when I was your age, I'd already had you. You don't want me to see my grandsons?"

Jang Won shook his head. "Umma! I'm too busy to get married..."

"And who will cook for my chaesa?" She was too young to worry about death-anniversary ceremonies, but Jang Won knew better than to point that out and spoil her fun.

"Look, I *promise* I'll get married someday. But now's just not a good time."

"Good time, good time," she mumbled, and switched to heavily accented English: "Have a good time."

"Um-ma!" He put his chopsticks down, ready for yet another argument. "Look, the LG Shoopah Division is going through a refocusing period, and working closely with the government now..."

"Yes, son, I read the newspaper, too. *I* think you should hurry up and get married now, while you still *have* a job. If only you'd taken government work while you could have. In *my* day, men jumped at government jobs..."

Of course, in her day, very few of those men she'd known had been mutants capable of jumping a kilometre into the air.

The doorbell rang.

"Go answer that," she commanded Jang Won. He hesitated, but before she could repeat herself, he rose and went to the front door.

There's a common saying in Korea, which is that there are three genders: male, female, and ajumma. Say that to your average country ajumma, and she might just whack you. Most younger Koreans take that as proof of the claim: ajummas — middle-aged women — somehow stop being simply women and become some kind of scary, dangerous curly-haired hybrid of the scariest traits of masculine and feminine.

What Jang Won found standing at the door when he answered it was an ugly little ajumma sporting the most mercilessly permed head of hair he'd ever seen. The ajumma-perm to end all ajumma-perms.

"Park Jang Won-*sshi*!" the little ajumma said in a deep, rasping little voice, and she coughed out a nasty-sounding, high-pitched cackle.

He nodded — politely enough for her to take it as a bow of greeting — even though her smile was perhaps the most revolting one he'd ever seen.

"Do I know you?" he blinked. He hoped not.

She shook her head vigorously, and said, "Not *yet*, but you will! I'm Mrs. Oh, your mother's newly hired matchmaker," she said with a wicked grin, rubbing her hands together as she pushed in past him. "And, my dear bouncing boy, I'm going to marry you off pronto!"

Jang Won shuddered with a dread that even the threat of a chicken-plague outbreak hadn't brought over him.

3. SOJU WANNA BE A HERO?

The day after his team caught Kim Noh Wang, the Madman of Pyongyang, and saved the world from the looming threat of a chicken-plague pandemic, Jang Won did what he did most days: he bounced his way over to the LG Diversified Central Office in downtown Seoul and spent half the day sitting at his desk, signing off on reports and wondering what the next assignment would be.

It was weird, such a normal day after such a massive success. No celebration, no party... just scattered rumours about new policies, constant congratulations, and piles of paperwork — in triplicate.

But around lunchtime Big Myoung stopped by his desk.

"Hey," Big Myoung said, and grinned. He grinned a lot, probably to show off his gold teeth. He was an old telepath from Jang Won's hometown, Gumi. He had probably been mutated, like Jang Won, by the phenol and other toxic pollutants that the Doosan Corporation had dumped "by accident" into the Nakdong River, which ran through the town. Jang Won called him "Elder Brother" though they weren't related: actually, they'd never even met back in

Gumi. Already a fixture in the office by the time Jang Won had gotten hired, Big Myoung had come on board twenty years before — in the 1970s, when LG had still just been Lucky Goldstar, a growing electronics, household goods, and superhero-services corporation. His style probably hadn't changed much since those days, from the look of his flowery shirt and his purple fake-leather jacket. The top few buttons were open, showing off his thick gold chains. He'd been dressing this way since he'd finally discovered that, unlike most men, a telepath never had to dress trendy to impress women. The pendant on the biggest of his gold chains was composed of English letters jammed together: *Cambidge Nebaska Hottyz.*

Jang Won wondered to himself what the hell that meant.

Hi Elder Brother Big Myoung, Jang Won thought at him. *What's up?*

Office party, tonight, Big Myoung replied telepathically.

Really? Jang Won tried to convey his relief mentally. *Great! My mother's got this matchmaker coming over again tonight.* He picked up an action figure, modelled on himself, from its spot beside his computer. It was a long-ago gift from one of his old co-workers, Wang "Two Blades" Ji Hyun, whose prowess with longswords and shapely behind had won her tons of sponsorships and ad deals and driven her to the peak of shoopah-stardom long ago. No more paperwork in triplicate for her. When she'd quit her job, she'd given him a goodbye present for being a nice boss: a custom-made Wonjjang action figure. Jang Won pressed down on it, and the springs in its legs compressed.

Big Myoung grinned. *Maybe it* is *time you got married, Wonjjang.*

"Not a chance," Jang Won said aloud, and released the figurine. It bounced into the air. Luckily, he caught it as he turned to see his boss strut into the huge shared office. Big Myoung followed his gaze.

Lee Dong Jae, the operations manager for the Special Talents Division of LG Seoul, had entered the room with a serious look on his face. Cupping his hands to his mouth, he hollered: "Everybody!"

Once the whole office had stopped what it was doing and turned to listen, he said, "Good afternoon! We've decided that this evening we'll host an important dinner meeting to celebrate recent successes and discuss the future of LG Superheroes Division. All food and drinks will be complimentary, of course. Everybody is expected to attend. That is all. Thank you!"

As Lee left the room, applause crescendoed and then died out, replaced by the soft, continuous murmur of voices.

"Here we go again," said Jang Won aloud.

"Mmm hmmm," replied Big Myoung. *I guess you won't have to lie your way out of the matchmaker appointment this time.*

I never lie..., Jang Won thought-mumbled.

Big Myoung pushed his sunglasses up his nose and grinned so wide you could see the gold crowns holding his molars together.

※※※

In five thousand years of culture — or so high-school teachers had always claimed — many wonderful things had been created, invented, and conceived by the genius of the Korean people: the world's first movable metal-type printing machine; the Hangeul alphabet; the miraculous dish known as *kimchi*; the most complex realization of Confucianism on Earth. But to Jang Won, none of these creations even held a candle to soju.

Soju was magical: a glue for friends, a remedy for anger, a succouring balm in times of pain and heartbreak. Soju warmed the heart on lonesome, rainy nights and dampened the fires of hopeless passions and sorrows. Jang Won had occasionally heard foreigners compare it to vodka, but it was nothing like that measly Russian stuff. It was miraculous, an almost holy liquor, made from the rice, pale sweet potatoes, and wheat of his homeland and distilled in the blessed factories of the Hite and Chamisul corporations. And it was dirt cheap.

Chilled green bottles of the stuff cluttered all the tables at which Jang Won and his co-workers were seated: soju and grilled meat, they were as inseparable as man and woman, hammer and nail, baby and mother's breast.

Soju plus meat was a tried and true formula. But Director Lee's latest discovery was a coup — a restaurant that offered the best soju, delectable pork, *and* private rooms where food and liquor could be accompanied by the other remaining joy of life: singing. A karaoke *restaurant*: this was a revelation!

"There are only a few of these in Seoul," said Lee. "It's a new kind of business... So everybody, let's enjoy! Great job, everyone, especially Park Jang Won and his team! Kombei!" he bellowed his toast, raising his tiny soju glass.

"Kombei!" the entire staff roared back joyfully, glasses raised. In unison, they knocked back their soju in a single shot and applauded.

Jang Won politely grabbed a bottle and refilled Director Lee's glass first. Lee nodded appreciatively, and declared loudly, "Let's eat!"

With that came trays of raw pork and beef to be grilled at the tables and, with the meat, more soju and, with the grilling, singing and drinking and mouthfuls of grilled pork wrapped in lettuce, the bite of garlic and hot pepper paste... and singing, and again and again the little cups of soju.

The shop-talk at the managers' table, though, bored Jang Won. He made an effort to nod at all the uninteresting observations, polite and insincere flatteries, and uptight jokes, but his eye kept straying to the foreigners' table, off to one side. They seemed to be enjoying themselves less than their Korean co-workers, who were vigorously drinking, singing, and eating. Neko especially drew his gaze. Dressed in a blue pinstripe pantsuit, she was speaking politely to Kevin — that is, Blastman, who had come to the party in typically undignified American street clothes: jeans with holes in the knees, and a T-shirt. *Real shoopahs wear suits,* Jang Won thought viciously, and noted that, in street clothes, Blastman even had a bit of a potbelly.

That was interesting. *Not so perfect after all, huh?* Jang Won thought, and shifted his attention back to his own table. He glanced at Lee, whose was talking seriously about something boring. Jang Won felt his face burning, and he knew it was bright red from the soju. He could swear he was hearing Neko sweetly calling his name.

"Jang Won! Mr. Park! Mr. Park Jang Won-sshi!"

He turned, realizing that he really *was* hearing his name being called, but not by Neko. Some of the office girls were gesturing to him, and he realized what song was coming next. It was his old standard, the song he always sang at every party, and which was considered, among his co-workers, famously *his*.

He excused himself, rose on wobbly legs, and hurried to the open space beyond the tables with moments to spare. Grabbing the microphone, he scrunched up his face and sang so hard that his throat itched inside, and his heart actually ached:

Oh Seagull! Oh Seagull!
You know the pain in my heart!
Oh Seagull! Oh Seagull!
Go and tell her, tell her ears my secret fascination!

Opening his eyes, he crooned and implored until he caught himself gazing blearily into Neko's eyes. He saw the look on her face — awkward, amused — and slammed his eyes shut again, opening them only when he heard Director Lee behind him, furiously shaking a tambourine and screaming the backing vocals at the top of his lungs.

When the next tune started, someone else — some office girls Wonjjang had never met — hurried up to take their turn at singing.

"Y'know," Director Lee said to him, "When management decided that we needed a 'Globalized Shoopah' team, I doubted we'd find anyone to run it. Not many men could deal with a bunch of foreigners like that. And I had my doubts about you. But you've done well with your team! Maybe you might be able to recover after all..."

"Recover?" Jang Won asked him, shaking his head to clear it.

"Never mind..." Lee quickly said, smiling awkwardly. "More soju?" he offered, holding up a full bottle.

Jang Won shook his head. "Excuse me, sir," he said apologetically, his stomach feeling suddenly upset.

"Yeh, yeh," Director Lee slurred, removing his arm from around Jang Won's shoulder. As Lee sat down, Jang Won made his way to the foreigners' table, where his team was seated, and plonked himself down right beside Neko. He felt everyone's eyes on him as he asked her whether she was having a good time.

"Yes, boss," she said stiffly, "but..."

"Yes?"

"Um... Where is the powder room, here?" she asked anxiously in well-spoken Korean.

"Over there..." he said, gesturing with his head, but it lolled so much that she wandered off in the wrong direction. Jang Won wondered if she was trying to escape him.

That hurt, but he said nothing as he watched her stop a waitress and get proper directions. When she was gone, Jang Won turned to Kevin, and said in English, "We're friend," pointing at himself and then sticking a finger in Kevin's chest.

"Yes, sir?"

"Friend," he repeated, slowly and emphatically. "You country, me country, it's a friend," he said, and clasped his hands together demonstratively. "USA... is a... help Korea. Many time before... I... someone is doesn't know. But I am know. *Help!* And now you and me is a special friend country. And you and me too." Claiming himself a full, abandoned little glass of soju — Neko's perhaps — he hoisted it high. The American smiled magnanimously, clinked glasses with Jang Won, and then they knocked their soju back.

Kevin made a face as if he didn't like the taste of the stuff. That troubled Jang Won, suddenly.

"You momma is... very missing?" Jang Won asked Kevin. It was another miracle of soju — it could make a man ask any question, in any language, to anyone.

"Uh, dude... Do I miss my mom, you mean? Or does my mom miss me?"

Jang Won nodded and lost track of everything else the American said in response. "Unh," Jang Won nodded affirmatively. "You missing momma is very... yes?"

More gobbledygook poured out of Kevin's mouth.

"So, you are make a love for... it's a Neko... yes?"

Kevin's expression changed. "I'm sorry, what do you mean, sir?" He looked as if he were just about to get angry, but wasn't sure whether he had understood correctly.

Jang Won's interest in the conversation waned. Suddenly everything slowed, and he was swept up by a deep, powerful clarity.

A mumbling sound to his right drew Jang Won's attention, and when he turned he saw that E-Gui was explaining something to Kevin, in English too complicated for Jang Won to follow. Jang Won really wanted to hit E-Gui, then... for saving Kim, for making him feel small, for getting in his way.

"No, no, no... you no... understand..." Jang Won slurred at Kevin. "You... love her is not, and *very!* Not trust... She Japan girl. Can't trust. You, me, friend. You no trust her, trust me, only, okay?"

"She's my teammate, sir, I need to..."

"No! You country, she country make... Boom!" he gestured dramatically, sloppily, and a few empty bottles scattered. Nothing of what he was trying to convey came across: the Japanese imperial occupation of Korea, the attack on Pearl Harbor, the Japanese shoopah-attacks on Hawaii and Seoul and Beijing and California a few years after the war... Didn't Kevin know any history?

Jang Won struggled to listen as Kevin spurted gobbledygook again. "Yes, I know. I've thought... Hiroshima... mutation... impossible... destined..." Jang Won caught only random words. He gulped down another glass of soju and chased it with some grilled pork while someone refilled the cup. The kid was *still* talking. Americans were so damned talkative. Kevin's expression was less annoyed, though, and more thoughtful.

"Kevin!" Neko's voice called from outside the room, like heavenly music. "Come on... get out... promised... ride home..."

Kevin smiled, bid Jang Won goodnight in polite, atrociously pronounced Korean, and rose to leave. Jang Won howled after him, but then he felt hands on his shoulders again and heard the intro to another of "his" songs, though he couldn't remember which one it was. The office girls were calling his name: it was time to stand.

He sang... sort of. Singing, yelling, muttering — it was a manic blend of all three, but the basic feeling must have come across, because his co-workers cheered for him enthusiastically. He swung his hips, raised his free hand dramatically, wailed his heartbreak. Someone handed him another shot of soju as the song ended, and Jang Won passed the microphone over his shoulder to the next guy, whom he assumed to be a junior employee. He drunkenly mumbled, "Here you go, kid," not bothering to look at who was next in line.

"Kid?" A blow connected with his cheek, jolting him into clarity. "When were you born, you son of a bitch? You slobbered all over the mike, too, you filthy drunken gaesaeki!" This was delivered in a voice reeking of soju, and "gaesaeki" — literally, dog-baby — was one of the worst insults there was in the Korean language. Worse, the karaoke machine was between tracks, so everyone had heard it.

Jang Won looked up to see who'd insulted him. It was Keun Dwaeji! *The* Keun Dwaeji! Now, sure, he was just a portly old pig-headed man — literally, a man with a pig's head — in a leather jacket. A washed-up desk jockey with a record tarnished by helping the Park and Chun dictatorships suppress the pro-democracy movement in Kwangju. But he'd also once been the legendary shoopah who'd led Team Hanguk against the Medvyed Mafiya in Vladivostok, who'd saved the island of Ddokdo from the Japanese back in the 1980s. Jang Won had pissed off a national hero.

Keun pulled his enormous black custom sunglasses off his snout and flexed his arms inside his huge brown cow-skin jacket. "And they call *me* a pig?" His curly pink tail trembled with rage.

Jang Won weighed his options, with all the rationality of a filthy-drunk superhero in trouble. After a moment, he simply shrugged and leaped at the pigman. He slammed his left fist, and then his right, into the pig's head. "You..." (jab) "might..." (kick to the crotch, and Keun's yellowed tusks flashed) "be..." (left hook) "older..." (a chop to the throat; the slow old hog's hoof slammed into his chest, but he couldn't feel it) "but—"

He was about to leap up and bring all of his weight down onto the pig's snout when a dozen very strong shoopah arms grabbed at him, holding him still. Dwaeji was being restrained, too, but not as vigorously.

Jang Won looked around, and saw the shock on everyone's faces. Director Lee was shouting. Keun Dwaeji had been Lee's teammate back in the 1970s; once, in a single day, they'd saved both Jeju Island and the president from a Communist attack. But Jang Won wasn't feeling apologetic. He lunged again but couldn't move at all. A string of cuss words spewed from his mouth, and then he went silent and stared the pigman in the eye.

The music had stayed off after the fight had started, and the room was utterly silent. Jang Won inhaled deeply, defiantly. Then he horked up a gob of phlegm, and spat.

The glob landed right onto the tip of Dwaeji's snout, amid shrieks of disbelief.

Jang Won snarled fiercely. "That's how old I am," he shouted, "Old enough to know washed-up when I see it! Who caught Kim Noh Wang, hmm? Me! I did!" he roared, looking around proudly. Keun Dwaeji struggled again, but Jang Won ignored him. He was looking at the faces of his team, staring in disbelief: E-Gui, and Laotzu, and... Kevin and Neko? What were *they* doing back here?

His pride deflated, punctured by shame.

Had he just claimed *sole credit* for the capture? Surely people would understand what he *meant*. He scrambled, trying aloud to piece together what he *had* meant. Their faces were so... disappointed. His head swirled with pride, anger, embarrassment, regret, and a strange, taunting lust for Neko.

That is, until he landed face-down on the sidewalk outside the karaoke diner, and the doors slammed shut behind him.

4. I'M DO IT'S MY JOB

Jang Won sat up suddenly, karaoke songs and nightmarish chittering still swirling around in his head. He was on his bedroom floor.

After his morning pee, he stumbled to the kitchen. Soju was wonderful, but the day after hurt, same as with any other liquor. Maybe worse. Jang Won's mouth tasted like a month-old soup, forgotten in the back of a bachelor's fridge.

He sat down at the kitchen table and thumbed through a catalog that the matchmaker had apparently left behind the night before. It was page after page of beautiful smiles. He had to wonder whether marriage wasn't such a bad idea.

"Rhee Ryang Hee," he read aloud, gazing admiringly at her face. It was hard to judge her body type, for she was in a traditional Korean gown that furled out from the bust, but she was probably lovely. "Hobbies: singing patriotic songs; studying our Dear Leader's speeches; performing traditional Korean music on the keomungo." *Strange*, he thought. *It's a North Korean instrument, isn't it?* A Korean proverb about who was most attractive, "Nam Nam Buk Nyeo," ran through his head: *Southern men, Northern women.* In the blur of his hangover, it had a nice ring to it. He thumbed through the book enthusiastically, until his empty stomach grumbled for breakfast.

A bowl of kimchi stew sat on the table, right at his usual place. He spooned a little into his mouth and grimaced. It was cold.

"Umma!" he called out.

No response came. Sunlight streamed through the window, onto the counter where she'd left the dishes and pots and half-chopped vegetables sitting. She'd never have done that. He called out to her again, and when no response came he rubbed his eyes and stared at the stew.

Then he saw it.

In the middle of the table sat a note written in Korean, in scribbly blue ink:

> To Wonjjang,
> The knockout drugs have worn off, finally? Your dear and darling Umma will be blown to pieces if you don't capitulate to the demands on the back of this page, all of them, in the next 48 hours. Fail in any way and your mother dies. Meet us at the top of Mount Halla at noon two days from now.
> From:
> A Friend of Kim Noh Wang

He flipped the page over, and his heart sank. The demands included money, experimental equipment from top-secret LG techlabs, and the release of a long list of Kim Noh Wang's Nork buddies and associates.

His heart raced. How was this *possible*? What about the complimentary LG alarm system and the apprentice-shoopah guard detail? He'd given up on having a secret identity, in accordance with the LG business plan, because of these safeguards. He imagined his poor umma, vicious but frail, arguing with some North Korean henchman. The Nork wouldn't stand a chance in an argument with her, of course.

But then, he wouldn't have to. One little injection would shut her up... forever.

A wave of guilt passed through him, the only son, the only one she had in the world.

Jang Won knew what his mother would say, if he rescued her: "You *see*? If only you were married, like a normal man, this wouldn't have happened!" A pang of guilt went through him: if he had come home early, sober, maybe he could have protected her. He cussed at himself and hurried to the shower.

⁂

About half an hour later, in his best black three-piece suit (and with a clean uniform stowed in his briefcase),

Jang Won finished his last officeward bound and landed on the ledge outside the window he always came in through.

It was closed. It was never closed, not even when he was late like today. He pounded on it until Big Myoung finally showed up to open it for him. The telepath had tears in his eyes.

"Oh, Little Brother," Big Myoung said, aloud for once. "What'll we do?"

"What's wrong, Elder Brother?" Jang Won looked around at all the long faces, wondering if maybe everyone had heard about his mother already. The Junior Sisters of Not-Inconsiderable Vengeance — the toughest team on staff — gazed over at him, dark runny mascara trails beneath their eyes. Men he'd worked with for years sat hunched at their desks in rumpled suits and sagging uniforms, looking broken-spirited.

"Park Jang Won! Manager Park! Come into my office now, please," a Director Lee's voice boomed from the intercom system.

Jang Won braced himself as he passed rows of desks and depressed shoopahs. On the way, he caught a glimpse of a newspaper headline:

KIM NOH WANG RELEASED FROM LG CUSTODY! NEW SUNSHINE POLICY DIRECTIVE STRAIGHT FROM PRESIDENT!

Jang Won gaped but didn't break stride. Sunshine! Wonjjang bristled. He'd never believed the policy would actually be enacted — hell, "policy" wasn't even the word for it! The strategy boggled his mind: what was the point of being nice to North Korea, whether they cooperated or threatened war? Just *hoping* that they wouldn't keep their promise to turn Seoul into a sea of fire? It made no damned sense at all. He'd laughed off the looming threat of the policy as mere rhetoric, just campaigning, but now his worst nightmare had come true. He had no idea how a shoopah was supposed to save the world by just being *nice*.

"Welcome, Team Manager Park," Director Lee greeted him mildly as he entered the office. "Please sit down." He gestured at the chair in front of his desk, and it slid back. Lee had powerful telekinetic powers, but Jang Won had never seen him use them before. It was mildly unsettling.

"Thank you, Director Lee," he said without sitting, "but I believe time is of the essence. My mother has been kidnapped and..."

Lee wasn't listening. "We're downsizing our office, and bringing in new blood to change our operational dynamics and image here at LG Shoopahs Division. I wanted to announce it last night, but it was decided that we should have one last wonderful night together before announcing it." Lee eyed him on that word, *wonderful*, and Jang Won knew he'd made the night just a little less wonderful. He remembered enough to know that much. "However, in *your* case, there is a special consideration..."

"Director Lee! My mother's been kidnapped!" Jang Won's eye strayed to a framed photo on the wall behind Lee, showing the director twenty years younger, in his famous white robes, shaking the hand of the last dictator to rule South Korea, that bastard Chun. "What happened to the security—"

"Ah, yes. Cutbacks on familial security protocols proceeded last week. You were supposed to make your own provisions. Didn't you receive that memo?"

"What memo?"

"About three weeks ago."

"I was in Thailand then. Undercover, remember?"

"Oh, how unfortunate," Lee said. "But I'm sure it was emailed to you..."

"I was tracking the world's most dangerous criminal mastermind. I was *busy*."

"Well, you really *should* check your email every day, Employee Park. In any case, I regret to inform you that due to the recent shift in direction of government policy in terms of Inter-Korean relationships..."

"How am I going to get my mother back?"

"...LG cannot afford to keep you on staff at the present. Especially since the North Korean Government has specifically demanded that you be fired."

"But they're the *North Korean Government!*" Jang Won pleaded. "Of *course* they want me fired. My team's caught half their supervillains..."

"Jang Won... please be *reasonable*. We all know these people are not nice guys. Do we have to actually *call* them 'supervillains'? Because you're the leader of the team who captured Kim Noh Wang, I have no choice. It's just... the current political climate, you understand. Besides, using local shoopahs isn't really economical anymore. Not with all the mutation experiments in China and Myanmar, and the toxic spills and nuclear waste facility accidents in Shenyang, Nepal, Tibet... Nepalese shoopahs work for wages no Korean shoopah would ever accept," Lee sighed. "It's modern economics."

"But..." Jang Won could see it clearly, again: E-Gui swooping in to save Kim Noh Wang's life. He felt sick to his stomach. "This is ridiculous! Whatever politicians say, isn't *our* job to defend the *our* people against those crazy Nork..."

"I'm sorry, Mr. Park, but that's an *old-fashioned* sentiment. I can understand that coming from some of the more senior members of the team, believe me. But you should know better. What do you think would happen to our industry, let alone our economy, if we really manage to knock the Kim regime to its knees? This isn't a political issue. It's a practical one. I realize it's not easy. And that you were hoping for a promotion, dealing with all these difficult foreigners on your team," he said with a serious, *don't you see?* nod. "For now, I suggest you think about the long term. Maybe once the storm blows over..."

"How am I going to get my umma back?" Jang Won yelped. Which, after all, was also a practical issue, as far as he was concerned.

"Shouting and screaming won't help. I can't do anything: your team members' contracts are already cancelled! They're downstairs in the HRM office right now, signing off on the cancellations and collecting their severance pay. As for me, I'm too busy dealing with the embarrassment you've caused us. Not just having to release Kim, but... by the way, you know, there was no chicken plague in the bomb in the first place. It was aerosolized chicken broth. We're done here, Mr. Park." Lee shrugged. "You have until the end of the day to clean out your desk."

Director Lee, finished, turned his attention back to his computer screen. Jang Won rose to leave, but just before exiting he turned and said, "I have to go find my mother. May I return later today to clear out my desk?"

"No problem," Lee said. "Security won't be instructed to bar you until tomorrow, when your resignation is publicly announced."

"Thank you, sir," Jang Won said politely, hurrying out.

5. SAN IS MEANS MOUNTAIN

Jang Won sat on the hard bench, waiting patiently through the understaffed lunch hour as one of the two bureaucrats behind the desk fiddled with his pen and the other argued with a white man in a suit. The official could speak English, but not very well, and the foreigner couldn't speak Korean at all. After a little urgent begging and shouting, the foreigner was dismissed with a handful of papers.

"Next," the woman behind the desk said, looking around the shoulder of the white guy in the business suit.

"But this is a matter of life and death!" he tried, but already the next person in line had surged forward, paperwork in hand. The businessman sighed returned to the benches to peer at the forms.

The Ministry of Super-Powered Justice and Social Harmony was stuffy on that hot autumn afternoon. Stacks of forms and records were piled up precariously on every available surface. Fans whirred behind the bank of public servants' desks, and with each pass the papers fluttered weakly as if threatening to revolt and scatter, if only they could throw off their paperweights. Everyone on the benches sat with stony, waiting faces, their eyes trained on their shoes, on the confusing required forms, and on the LED wall-display that showed which numbers were being served. Behind the desk, a Korean businessman was chatting with a higher-level administrator in hushed tones. A scruffy-looking, long-haired Westerner with Canadian flags sewn onto his leather jacket and his backpack was arguing with another agent at the front door — in barely understandable Korean — that bicycle theft *was* life-threatening, insisting that the Ministry dispatch a shoopah-team immediately to track his mountain bike down and retrieve it for him.

Jang Won eyed his ticket, number 56. The LED displayed, in foreboding red, 23. At this rate, Halla Mountain would be long gone by the time he even talked to anyone. But he needed help, and didn't dare ask his teammates, not after what he'd said in front of them. He sighed and leaned back in his chair. He could wait. Glancing around again, he saw the businessman consulting a pocket dictionary as he struggled through his paperwork.

"Come here," Jang Won said to the foreigner. "I'm help you."

"Me?" the man asked.

"Yes, you. My number, the 56. I'm wait. So, I am can help you. You want?" The foreigner nodded and gathered up his things to move to a seat beside Jang Won.

Here I go again..., he reproached himself silently. *Why do I always have to save the day?*

The memory of his poor mother at the kitchen table, chopping carrots and asking him that exact question, flooded his mind. She'd wanted him to get a government job, to work for this very department he was now turning to for help. *It's stable,* she'd insisted. *It's safer than working for a company! Is a desk job so bad? Is it so important that you actually beat up these crooks?* She'd thumped the table with her hand, then. *Who would marry a superhero, knowing he could die anytime?* She'd finally forbidden it, but by then it was too late. He'd already signed a contract with LG. He felt a rush of guilt: nobody ever kidnapped a government paper-pusher's mother.

The foreign businessman sat down beside Jang Won and said, "Thanks!" When they shook hands, the foreigner politely gestured with his free hand as if he were holding back the sleeve of a robe. It was the height of good Korean etiquette, the kind of thing Jang Won figured most Westerners didn't usually know enough to do.

"Very polite," Jang Won observed, taking the man's paperwork and pen. "Do you live the Korea long time?"

"No, only a few years. I've been too busy to learn the language, though. Besides, where I live, the dialect is unusual. I've been told there's no point in learning it."

"Dialect?" Jang Won asked, shrugging. "What is dialect?"

"I think the Korean word is... *saturi*," the businessman said the Korean word awkwardly, and Jang Won nodded.

"Where? Daegu City?"

"No, Jeju Island," he said. "I work for Samsung Supertronics. It's the third time I've come in here in a month, you know. Every time, they've refused to send someone. 'Increase security,' they said. That didn't help. The only remedy for supervillains is superheroes, right? This morning everyone in the lab was killed or kidnapped. I barely got away myself. And here I am again, filling out more paperwork."

"I see," Jang Won said, nodding, and took down the businessman's information. A month, he realized. This man had been waiting a month. Suddenly Jang Won wondered whether it would take them a month to do something about his mother, too. He got as far as the man's name and foreigner ID registration when something clicked in his mind.

"What's your... *moonjae*, uh... how can I say...?" Jang Won asked.

"Problem?" asked the foreigner.

"Yes, prob-lem. What's problem?"

"Well, like I said, I've been working for Samsung. There's a secret joint research lab on Jeju Island, where we've been researching a microcollider. Kind of like a small-scale, high-powered supercollider. It's very useful for researching artificial superconductive..." The foreigner noticed that Jang Won wasn't quite following. "Well, it's very dangerous. It's like, um... do you know what an atom is?" He sketched a picture of one on a scrap of paper.

Jang Won nodded.

"Imagine an atom with no nucleus." He crossed out the sphere in the middle of the atom, leaving only electrons whirling in hollow orbits. "We have artificial matter: the electrons—" he pointed at the orbiting bits in the sketch, "—but no nucleus. So we can pack these fake atoms full of... energy, or other particles. They can store pure energy. And when they blow up..." Jang Won leaned forward "...It makes a very big boom."

"They can, uh, *blowing up* the Jeju Island?"

The foreigner nodded.

"Your lab... is it maybe... in the Halla-san?"

The businessman swallowed hard. "Yes, Halla Mountain. How did *you* know that?"

"Umma," Jang Won mumbled softly, and he realized that Kim's threat might be serious. Halla Mountain?

Jang Won dug a business card out from his coat pocket and handed it to the man. "Sorry," he said, pointing at the card. "Korea language only."

"It's okay, I—"

"I'm save your lab," Jang Won said, hurrying toward the exit. He turned and added, "Maybe." No sense in getting the guy's hopes up.

The businessman rose to his feet and called out, "Hey... thanks!" He had a doubtful look on his face but tried to smile.

Jang Won bowed slightly, and then was out the door. He grabbed his phone from his back pocket. Out on the sidewalk, he quickly thumbed a message into his phone and hit send.

THIS IS SUPERVISOR PARK: DON'T GO HOME! STAY AT OFFICE! I'M COMING ~~ EMERGENCY!!

"...and that is why you're all about to lose your jobs, and why they let Kim go," Jang Won declared, his tone impassioned. He was standing on a chair in the middle of the office.

"Now wait a minute..." said Director Lee loudly, trying to interrupt him.

Jang Won ignored him. His team members were assembled around him, ready to protect him as he delivered his speech. "Earlier today, the morning after being released from custody, Kim Noh Wang and his thugs took over a secret laboratory on Jeju Island. They're going to blow it up."

Murmurs spread throughout the office. Kevin's voice was conspicuous, as he clarified with Neko what was going on.

"*That* guy?" Kevin's exasperation was obvious. "We just *caught* him, *two days ago!* Jesus, what the hell are you people *doing* here?" Kevin scowled, shaking his head in disbelief, and Neko patted him on the shoulder.

"You see, even Blastman and Neko want to help stop this — *and they're not even Korean!* How can we stand by and watch the Norks destroy our beautiful Jeju Island? Will there still be Sunshine when Jeju is gone?"

"Manager Park!" Director Kim hollered at Jang Won, and this time the interruption silenced the crowd. "Anyone who aids Mr. Park in his illegal endeavour will be fired from LG with no pension, no chance of subsequent rehiring, and no settlement package..."

"But," Jang Won added, "you'll be a *real* hero."

The silence was thick as dwenjang jjigae. Employment, or heroism? Jang Won sadly thought he knew how most people would choose. After all, he himself had chosen employment over heroism for many, many years.

Just then, Keun Dwaeji stood.

Everyone turned and watched in silence. A triumphant smile spread across Lee's face when the pigman strode across the room toward Jang Won. His hooves *clop, clop, clopped* on the tiled floor, and, as he approached, his natural pig-grin straightened out, giving him a grim appearance. He got right up close to Jang Won, crossed his arms, and leaned forward to look him in the eye.

"You really think *you* can handle this, kid?" Keun asked, stabbing a hoof sharply into Jang Won's chest. Jang Won gulped, and said, "Yes, sir." He braced himself, expecting Keun's other hoof to slam into his face. As Keun turned away from him, Jang Won sighed a little. Keun would speak against him, and nobody would join Jang Won. His umma was doomed.

"Well, well," Keun said, and Lee's face went deathly pale. Keun Dwaeji turned to the rest of the room, and said, "This unfortunately ill-mannered young fellow has woken up. Finally! I've been waiting years for someone around here to do that! After all my undercover trips to Pyongyang, after all the Norks I've captured, those gaesaeki are still running that country. And now it seems like almost nobody is willing to do anything about it. We're helping them," he indicted everyone.

The pigman cleared his throat, put his arm around Jang Won's shoulder, and looked around at everyone's shamefully lowered heads. "I'll go to Jeju Island with you, kid. But I get first dibs on Kim Noh Wang. I'm gonna clobber that ugly little bastard to death."

The tide had turned. Director Lee was admonishing the staff, but nobody was listening. Keun was a leader... others would follow.

Suddenly, Jang Won felt much more like Wonjjang again, like a real hero. "We're going to borrow the choppers," Wonjjang cried out, and a mob of them followed him up the roof, their cheers drowning out Director Lee's protests. Nobody could stop them now.

Hold on, Umma. Hold on.

6. LIKE A TWO CHOPSTICK

Ten stolen LG choppers hurtled southward across the peninsula in a scattered formation, with many more shoopahs flying alongside. They cast an imposing, mottled shadow on the ground below. Kids ran to schoolroom windows to catch a glimpse of them, and farmers looked up from their fields, waving happily, oblivious to the crisis but glad to see the shoopahs crossing the sky just the same.

Wonjjang saw his homeland below in a way he never had before. *This* was the land he was fighting to save. Not just lines on a map, or an idea. These proud mountains, these tranquil rice fields and toiling townspeople below.

"We need a plan," Keun Dwaeji said, interrupting his reveries as the southern ocean crept into sight.

"What do you suggest, sir?" Wonjjang asked politely.

"Go in hard and beat the living crap out of them," Keun Dwaeji said, without a hint of sarcasm. He caught Wonjjang's eye, and added, "After all, that's not what they're *expecting*, is it?"

"Sounds great!" said Blastman, and Neko nodded enthusiastically, flashing her claws and clapping with excitement.

E-Gui shook his head. "I don't think that's such a good plan."

"Why's that, young man?"

"Unnecessarily wasteful," E-Gui replied. "If we sacrifice too many people, we could lose out in the long run. It's not wise."

Because it might let us win? Wonjjang wondered.

"So what do you recommend, E-Gui?" Neko asked, frustrated.

"I think we ought to rely on a long-distance attack to start with. Use all the mutant powers available to us, use these choppers... *then* we can rush in. It's not like Kim's goons have many decent mutations among them. They could barely afford any proper radioactive mutations research to begin with! Less risk, better payoff."

"Assuming they haven't blown the island apart by then..." said Keun Dwaeji. He was right: timing would be *everything*.

"Then..." Wonjjang said, "Let's split up: send a major force overhead, while a small team infiltrates and catches him. Two chopsticks to squeeze Kim and pick him up. Sound good?"

"I'm in," said Blastman. Neko, Laotzu, and Keun Dwaeji agreed. Finally, even E-Gui followed suit.

"Great," Wonjjang said. "But how do we get the shoopahs who have the distance-attack powers into the air? Not all of us can fly. In fact, most of us can't..."

"Well, I've got an idea," Blastman said, and when the American explained it, Wonjjang could see Kevin, the decent-hearted kid from Iowa who was trapped inside the superhero, grinning like a farmboy who'd just discovered the biggest colony of gophers in the world and just happened to have brought his shotgun along.

❖⫶❖⫶❖⫶❖

The dimming light of sunset danced and wavered as shadows swept across the northwestern face of Halla Mountain. They were human figures, flying shoopahs and those who were borne in the arms of the fliers. Helicopters followed them, their whine breaking the silence of the heroes' approach. The shoopahs plunged through the air, steeled for the coming battle.

From the mouths and hands and bodies of these heroes rained a typhoon of destruction: electromagnetic waves, searing bolts of electricity, laser blasts, burning flame, and streams of vomited acid poured down upon Kim's assembled forces. Wonjjang saw it all through the eyes of Big Myoung, who was watching from one of the LG choppers and telepathically broadcasting the scene to the leaders of various shoopah-teams who'd joined the struggle.

"It's time," Wonjjang announced quietly to his team. They hurried down the smooth stone tunnel toward the heart of Halla Mountain. Suddenly, a deep, grinding screech halted them in their tracks, and they instinctively reached for the walls as the earth shook all around them. The shudder subsided almost immediately, but Wonjjang's team exchanged wary glances.

"Come on," Keun Dwaeji hissed impatiently. "Hurry!" He trotted down the tunnel, the others following his lead until an echoing taunt rang out from behind them: "Ah-ha!"

"Ah-ha?" Wonjjang mumbled, turning. It was Kim Noh Wang, with over a dozen henchmen. As usual, they'd seemingly come out of nowhere.

From the other direction, deeper down the hallway where the team had been headed, came a nastily familiar chittering noise. Wonjjang turned just in time to see his mother's matchmaker leap up onto Keun Dwaeji's chest and grip his head in her two hands. He struggled, slamming his hooves into her, but she twisted hard, until the pigman's neck broke. She leaped from him as he collapsed, shuddering.

"He was always an American-imperial lackey," she snapped, her eyes wild, and she began chittering again. A long tail slashed out from under the hem of her dress.

Iron Monkey! Wonjjang realized, a jolt of horror exploding in his belly when she launched herself overhead toward Kim. Blastman lashed out with a jolt of electricity, and Neko slashed at her, but she dodged their attacks and swept past them, scurrying along the wall until she leaped to Kim's side. Her gleeful chittering filled the hallway as she shed her ajumma dress, revealing a skintight army-green slamdex bodysuit beneath.

"Where's my mother?" shouted Wonjjang in Korean.

"Your mother? Oh, Jang Won," Kim taunted. "Heroes don't *have* mothers..."

"Or wives," Iron Monkey added, and clapped with vicious amusement.

"I'll kill you!" Wonjjang screamed, lunging forward. E-Gui held him back.

"Be reasonable," E-Gui said softly.

"Yes," said Kim, smiling. "Be *reasonable*. First... where are the supplies I demanded? And my friends?"

Wonjjang struggled against E-Gui, and shouted, "Dead. I'll kill them all, every one of them, with my own two hands, if anything happens to my mother. *Where is she?*"

Kim sneered. Blastman watched, a perplexed look on his face. "What's going on?" he asked. He couldn't understand a word they were saying, but electricity crackled around his two fists. He was on the verge of attacking Kim and his underlings.

"What, you too?" grumbled E-Gui in English, and he dematerialized his free hand, plunging it into Blastman's chest.

"Bukkoroshite yaru zo," Neko growled at E-Gui. *I'm gonna beat you to death*, it meant. Though he couldn't speak Japanese, Wonjjang had heard her say it enough times to know what it meant.

Kim and Iron Monkey revelled in the heroes' discord, cackling. Kim's other henchmen cautiously joined in a few moments later.

Blastman looked at E-Gui in shock. "You're my teammate. Are you going to...?"

"No!" E-Gui yelled. "Just... calm... down. What will happen if we kill Kim before we get the information we need?" Blastman nodded, and E-Gui extracted his hand from the American's chest. "Now, help me with Wonjjang." Blastman reluctantly grasped Wonjjang's arms, restraining his onetime supervisor. Wonjjang struggled, his head full of images transmitted by Big Myoung: heroic fliers being shot down from the sky, descending broken with battle cries and farewells on their lips.

"Where's his mother?" E-Gui demanded in Korean.

"Down there," Kim gestured, further down the tunnel, where Iron Monkey had appeared. "Hurry, maybe you can grab her before the island gets blasted apart."

"How do we shut down the machine?"

"Give me your choppers' startup and override codes, and I'll tell you..."

"Aie, sshiballoma!" Wonjjang roared, struggling again. "I'm gonna beat you till you cry, you baby-dog!" Blastman held him firmly but didn't try to shut him up. "What do we need him for? He doesn't know anything. Let me at him!"

E-Gui switched to Chinese, speaking to Kim but eyeing Wonjjang carefully. But he was soon silenced by a loud sob.

It was Laotzu. Wonjjang struggled against Blastman's grip to turn and look at the Chinese-Korean shoopah, who was hunched over the body of Keun Dwaeji.

"When I was young," Laotzu said, sobbing, "my mother would give me comic books about real-life Korean shoopahs. She said it didn't matter how ugly I was... that I could be a hero like Keun Dwaeji someday. Now," Laotzu rose up, tearful. "He's... dead." He turned and began shouting at E-Gui in Chinese.

They argued, their incomprehensible exchange crescendoing quickly and then falling apart. Wonjjang could feel Blastman's attention wandering, his grip loosening by degrees while all those strange words flooded his mind. Wonjjang waited until Blastman was completely lulled into distraction, and then he tore himself free. Crouching quickly, he launched himself up and rebounded off the tunnel wall toward Kim, who was already making a move.

Quick as an ajumma nabbing a seat on the subway, Wonjjang became a lethal weapon. Bouncing from wall to wall, Wonjjang spun himself round the axis of his hips, so that his feet were facing the Nork, and compressed himself like a spring. At the last moment, he slammed one foot outward. It connected with Kim's face with a crack, and the Nork madman sailed up through the air above his henchmen, tumbling in silent shock up the tunnel, back the way he'd come. Before any of the goons had time to grab him, Wonjjang rebounded and streaked past them. He bounced once more off the tunnel wall and landed on his feet behind Kim's thugs, blocking the space between them and their leader.

"Yaaa, yi saekideul! Deombyeo!" he said, and assumed a taekwondo fighting stance.

Deombyeo — "Bring it on!" — was an invitation that Kim's henchmen couldn't pass up, but they would have done better to think about the crowd of shoopahs behind them. Most of the henchmen stupidly rushed at Wonjjang, but moments later a wave of mutilation crashed upon them from behind. Neko's claws flashed, her screams echoed amid the splattering of a dogman's guts. Blastman puked globules of ball lightning at a pair of deformed monks. Laotzu dove into the crowd of soldiers and mutants, threshing them like wheat with his uncarved-stone-and-wood arms.

The few Norks who made it to Wonjjang didn't last long. He was a blur of fists and kicks, rebounding from walls and flinging stunned soldiers in every direction. But more Norks came... they flooded down the tunnel from outside, howling mad, and Wonjjang had to keep moving if he was to avoid being caught. He bounced and kicked and punched, entranced by the movement of bodies, the steady beat of punches and kicks, the music of snapping bones, so that at first he failed to notice the walls of the tunnel shuddering again. When he did notice, his heart sank.

Umma—

Wonjjang abandoned the battle, bouncing over the brawling mob and down the hallway.

After a few hundred metres, the din of the battle gave way to a roar so immense that Wonjjang could hardly think in its presence. He bounced on, around a couple of sharp turns, until he reached an enormous laboratory.

There sat his mother, at a computer console, fiddling with the keyboard and mouse. Behind the computer, a glass barrier sealed off a bare-walled white room with a small glowing red box at its centre.

"Umma!" he called out, and bounced straight to her.

She shrieked and tucked her hands behind her back immediately, pretending they were still bound, until a look of recognition came across her face.

"Oh, it's just *you*," she said loudly, relaxing.

"What are you *doing*?"

"What, this? Oh, aigo, aigo," she lamented. "I can't seem to get this silly thing to shut down. It's in English. I heard him thinking... er, *saying* the password," she said, with a sly little smile, "But, you know, I haven't studied English in years."

"It's in English?" Wonjjang yelped, crestfallen. *Heard him thinking?* he repeated to himself. Suddenly, a lot of his childhood made sense.

"Yes," she shouted, and smacked him in the belly, hard. "Now you see! After all the times I told you to study English harder, and you kept going swimming in the Nakdong instead..."

Jang Won frowned. His mother never missed a chance to scold him about how he'd brought mutation on himself by swimming instead of studying, and he usually just let her, but there wasn't time now. "Umma, let me try," he interrupted her, hopeful. He was good with computers. Maybe he could figure it out.

"What? No!" she shouted over the growing din. "We have only fourteen minutes! You go catch that Kim boy. What a nuisance! He smells like foreign liquor! He's such a dreadful brat, no wonder he's still unmarried. Now, send your American friend here to help me. He speaks English, right?"

Wonjjang bristled, but his mother was a real, old-school ajumma — there was no telling her what to do. "Yes, Umma," he said, nodding dutifully, and bounced away in a flash. If he didn't catch that blasted midget shoopah-criminal, his mother would never stop nagging him.

He returned to a scene of carnage in the hallway. Blood, bits of fried flesh, and slivers of shattered bone clung to the walls, the floor, and everyone's uniforms. Only disembodied E-Gui was free of gore. Panting and exhausted, they were just finishing off the last of Kim's relentless henchmen, who were gleefully sacrificing themselves for nothing.

An image flashed in Wonjjang's mind then, transmitted by Big Myoung: Kim Noh Wang, scurrying down the mountainside as fast as his pudgy legs could carry him.

"Kim's getting away!" Wonjjang hollered, as the last Nork thudded to the floor. He grabbed Blastman by the arm, and said, haltingly, "Mom... my mommy is... stop machine. She say... you help she..." he said, pointing at Blastman.

"Me?" Blastman asked.

Wonjjang nodded, and explained, "The computer... Englishie computer. Thirteen minutes left... Boom!" He pointed down the hallway, mimicked an explosion with his hands, and ordered, "Blastman, *go!*"

Blastman took off, and Wonjjang turned to face E-Gui. In Korean, he said. "I know your government doesn't want you to fight Kim. If you can't help us, get out of our way. Kim's insane. He's going to destroy this island, and it won't be long before Shanghai, or Beijing, is next. Stop protecting him. Go help Blastman, if you won't fight with us."

E-Gui frowned grimly and closed his eyes for a moment. Then, without so much as a second look or a single word, he stepped out of Wonjjang's way and drifted off after Blastman.

To Neko and Laotzu, Wonjjang yelped, "Let's go!"

Laotzu gently hoisted Keun Dwaeji's broken body onto his gigantic, barky shoulder, and they set off toward the exit.

→•I•·I•·I•←

Laotzu's stone-and-jade fist smashed open the locked steel exit doors to reveal a hellscape. The slopes of Mount Halla were littered with the tangled bodies of Norks and some of LG's finest shoopahs, and the air was full of their moans and screams.

Still, a few airborne heroes had managed to stay aloft, swarming around a helicopter. *That's where Kim is*, Wonjjang realized, and it occurred to him that the stream of images Big Myoung had been transmitting had cut out sometime earlier.

He ignored a pang of worry for his friend and said, "Let's go!"

Neko and Laotzu — with Keun Dwaeji's body still on his shoulder — ran after Wonjjang toward the spot beneath the swarm of shoopahs. As they got closer, they could see more clearly what was happening: the strong hands of a few dozen heroes desperately gripped the landing supports on the bottom of the chopper, holding it in place. But slowly, surely, the chopper was tugging its way free. A gunshot rang out above, and an airborne shoopah plummeted from the swarm, blood spurting from her chest.

Laotzu roared in anger — there was no way he'd even get close to the chopper — but Wonjjang seized him by his rocky arm and said, "It's alright. Bounce me!"

Laotzu brightened. Without dropping Keun Dwaeji's corpse, he grabbed Wonjjang around the waist, lifting him overhead.

"I'll grab you after one bounce," Wonjjang yelled to Neko, and then, to Laotzu, "After this..."

"After this, I'm going to go find Iron Monkey," Laotzu told him.

"You can do it," Wonjjang shouted, ignoring his suspicion that Iron Monkey was with Kim.

Laotzu smiled ferociously as he held his boss over his head. "Ready?"

"Now!" Wonjjang bellowed, and Laotzu slammed him into the ground as hard as he could, so that Wonjjang rebounded high. As he passed the chopper, he yelled his encouragement to all the shoopahs clinging to it. When Wonjjang began to fall again, Laotzu lifted Neko up in a single enormous hand and lobbed her up toward him.

Still descending, Wonjjang caught her with both hands, around the waist, and lifted her above his head. As he connected with the ground, he absorbed the energy of the impact into his legs, and then he pushed up with all his might, sending himself rebounding toward the chopper with Neko still overhead. When they got close, he flung Neko through the open side-door. Her bloodcurdling battle-shriek filled the air, and Wonjjang caught a glimpse of flashing claws and spraying blood before he began falling once again. With any luck, one more bounce would get him into the chopper, too.

He slammed into the ground so forcefully that the stone cracked beneath his feet. He used his muscles to rebound as hard as he could, sending himself straight toward the bottom of the chopper. It wobbled overhead, and all he could do was hope that it wouldn't move so much that he'd fly straight into the helicopter's blades. On his way up, he saw a figure forced out the door, falling toward him. It was one of Kim's poor nobodies, dressed in cheap fake slamdex. The man wouldn't survive the fall, unless he was a mutant — and the chances of that were slim — but what sent a chill through Wonjjang was the look on the Nork henchman's face. The plummeting Northerner stared dully through him, betraying no hint of fear or sorrow. It was as if he were already dead. Wonjjang glanced down to where Laotzu had been, but the big lummox was already running up the mountainside, so Wonjjang turned his attention back to the chopper.

It had climbed higher into the sky. The shoopahs anchoring it were tiring out, though a number of them had noticed Wonjjang's approach and were hauling one side of the helicopter down to angle the door for him to bounce through. Wonjjang's aim was true: he passed through the doorway with stunning precision.

The inside of the chopper was a mess. The floor was slick with blood and goop, and the air stank of fresh wounds and hard liquor. Neko was clinging for her life, with one set of her claws sunk into the cushions of a seat in the rear of the cabin. She slashed her other set of claws at a nimble, evasive figure that Wonjjang recognized immediately as Iron Monkey, but Neko missed as the Nork sprang into the air and spun behind her, chittering wickedly. Wonjjang cursed at Iron Monkey as she wrapped her tail around Neko's throat. The catwoman struggled desperately, stabbing her vicious claws blindly over her own shoulder. The Nork continued to chitter with glee, dodging Neko's slashes and crushing the Japanese shoopah's neck.

"No!" Wonjjang howled, and slammed himself against the wall behind him, launching into the air toward the struggling pair. Neko's eyes widened when he sped toward her, but suddenly a hand flashed before him and fluid sprayed onto his face. His eyes reflexively shut against the sudden, searing pain, and he raised his hands to his face.

Someone or something ploughed into him, and Wonjjang yelped in shock. Just then, the floor of the chopper's cabin righted itself. Wonjjang felt a weight on his chest and the blows of small, iron-hard fists pounding into his face. He fought to open his eyes, but they were watering and everything was blurred. His arms flailed, until something cold and hard and very tight closed around one wrist, and then the other, binding them together.

A maniacal laughter filled Wonjjang's ears, and he forced his eyes open and stared at the blurry form astride him.

He could make out enough — beady little eyes, the green slamdex Mao suit, and that stupid bouffant hairdo — to know that it was Kim Noh Wang. He slammed his head back against the floor and it rebounded hard, thumping Kim in the face. But the little psychopath held on, shrieking in rage as he began slapping Wonjjang across the face and screaming, "I warned you! You had your chance to serve the Dear Leader! You could have been a Hero of the People!" In the background, Neko and Iron Monkey's struggle became frantic, and then Iron Monkey shrieked in pain.

"Ryun Ja!" Kim shouted, his voice high-pitched above the whine of the helicopter, and Wonjjang's vision cleared a little. "Now!" More of the burning fluid splashed through the air from behind Kim, where a blurry figure now stood, and Wonjjang's eyes began burning again. Kim clung to him like a kid on a bucking pony, while Wonjjang kicked and struggled. When moments later his ankles, too, were bound in cold metal, Wonjjang shivered in panic. Not far from him, Neko and Iron Monkey's desperate screams filled the air as their fight intensified. Suddenly he could feel a face close to his, and the garlic-and-cognac reek of Kim's breath wafted into his nostrils.

"We're going to take you home with us, Jang Won, and re-educate you. You're going to be a great asset to the People's Republic... and I'm going to train you personally." The little monster laughed, and the stink made gorge rise in Wonjjang's throat.

"Never!" Wonjjang shouted.

"Fine, have it your way," Kim said, and the weight shifted on his chest. Wonjjang struggled to break his bonds, but he wasn't strong enough to snap steel. He never had been. Suddenly, he was struck by a vision of the future that awaited him, should Kim succeed: he'd seen pencil-sketches of the "freak gulags," the concentration camps where dangerously powerful mutants were brainwashed into serving Kim's government. He could see himself sleeping on the filthy floor of a tiny hut, hundred-pound weights on each ankle to keep him from bouncing away. Trudging through his life, until maybe someday he became crazy enough to actually accept a mission. Blow up some subway station in Tokyo, or bounce into downtown Seoul with a knapsack nuke on his back. His body stiffened, as if trying to die in order to avoid such horror, and he forced his eyes open again. He wanted to see Kim, so he could remember how he'd been captured, what he'd been fighting for so long. So he would not give in and become a Nork agent.

"Ryun Ja," Kim called out again, his head turned. "Inject him, now!"

Over Kim's shoulder, Wonjjang made out a blurry figure struggling to advance as the helicopter floor began slowly to tilt again. Everything — Wonjjang, the blood all around him, Kim on his chest, the hazy figure beyond — slid suddenly toward the peril of the open doorway.

The figure got close to him, and he caught the unmistakable scent of...

...*hard liquor?*

Ryun Ja? It was a girl, Wonjjang realized. She was dressed in Nork slamdex, with her long dark hair dangling around her shoulders. He couldn't see her face clearly, but he saw her hesitate. Then Neko screamed, "No!"

He blinked his eyes hard, willing himself to see, and opened them again.

The Nork girl was still there, blurry, clutching something in her hand. Kim was shouting something at her, his voice inaudible because his head was turned away from Wonjjang. She was not looking at Kim, though: she was staring over his shoulder, at Wonjjang himself. Despite the blurriness, he could see the hesitation on her face.

This was his chance, his last moment to escape the prospect of permanent bondage. He carefully raised his head up as high as it would go, and then with all his strength he slammed it back against the floor of the chopper and let his spine go completely rubbery. His head swung up into the air and spun like a tetherball, clobbering Kim in the back and sending him sailing through the air.

Kim landed in a slippery puddle of blood just as the helicopter tilted sharply, and he slid straight for the doorway. In a flash, Iron Monkey was streaking through the air toward him, with Neko right behind her. Iron Monkey caught Kim by the arm and hauled him back into the chopper.

Wonjjang sat up, flung his back against the ground, and bounced himself to his feet, landing right in front of the Nork girl. Suddenly, he was drowning in the scent of cognac, and in her dark eyes, and in the nearness of her, even while Neko and Iron Monkey struggled over Kim on the floor nearby, their battle having devolved into a kind of blood-spattered tug-of-war.

"Why?" he said, his voice hard but quiet, and then, instantly, he realized that he *knew* her face. He recognized her lips, her long black hair, those beautiful, determined brown eyes, and that scent of cognac that hung all around her. This girl who smelled like French liquor, she was... the college girl from the airport washroom — the agent who'd given him the exploding pen! So beautiful — how could she be a Nork? How could he fight her? He wanted to *kiss* her, to swing an arm around her body, but his hands were bound together with tight metal handcuffs. He raised them up toward her.

"I just... I—" she said, fumbling in her pockets, and Wonjjang's heart sank. If she drew out a weapon, he'd have to hurt her. But a moment later she had a key between her fingers, and she grabbed at Wonjjang's cuffs. While she unlocked them, he stared at her and read the history of pain clearly written on her face. She had suffered. The lines around her eyes spoke of living as a mutant under a government of psychopaths. She had the face of an angel who'd been trapped in a nation-sized prison camp.

And now she was setting him free, this strange Ryun Ja girl. The handcuffs snapped open, and she knelt to unlock the leg irons when Kim suddenly wriggled free from the grip of the battling women and pounced at her.

"What are you doing?" Kim shouted, bowling her over. "Betrayer! Defector!" he roared, clubbing her in the head with his balled fists. Before Wonjjang could bend forward and strike Kim down she calmly flicked her fingers at the Nork leader, sending droplets of fluid into his face, and then quickly jabbed him in the leg with a syringe. Kim cursed and howled in pain, his hands on his eyes, and tried to stumble away, but Wonjjang was too quick: he grabbed Kim by the back of his uniform and hoisted the struggling dwarf off the floor. From the corner of his eye, Wonjjang saw Iron Monkey shove Neko out the chopper door and then bolt toward them.

A moment later, Wonjjang's leg irons came loose, and he spun and hurled Kim outside after Neko, hoping she might catch him on the way down. He knew from experience that she would land on her feet no matter what. She wasn't called Neko — "cat" — for nothing. His attention was focused almost completely on Kim's vile henchwoman, who had invaded his home and kidnapped his mother.

"You!" Iron Monkey screamed, and Wonjjang had just enough time to reach out his arms to grab a handle on the wall and a passenger seat for support and then go completely rubbery as she slammed into him. His body rebounded violently from the blow, and Iron Monkey was flung out through the doorway in a flash.

Suddenly, Wonjjang and Ryun Ja were alone in the chopper. The pilot's seat was empty. But it was an LG chopper, so he supposed it was flying on autopilot.

"Why did you...?" he asked, moving closer to her.

Suddenly, the chopper spun out of control. Maybe there wasn't an autopilot function after all? Without a word, Wonjjang rushed the girl to the doorway and, hand in hand, they leaped from it. On the way down, he wrapped his arms around her, and said, "Whatever you do, don't let go of me."

"Never," she said, and squeezed him tightly to herself, her face so close to his that he could almost feel her lips. He barely noticed the abandoned helicopter spin off towards the ocean.

As they fell, Wonjjang was entranced by how her hair flapped wild and beautiful around her face, with those dark eyes staring at him, so hard and at the same time so lovely. When they drew close to the ground, Wonjjang gripped her around the waist and lifted her up, to shield her from the coming impact. He caught a glimpse of the chopper far above, still spinning out of control, abandoned by the swarm of weary shoopahs who'd anchored it for so long. When his feet slammed into the ground with an enormous thud, his legs absorbed not only the shock his own fall but also that of the girl's. He then set her down carefully.

Only a couple of feet away, Neko was perched on top of Kim Noh Wang. She skewered one of his arms with a claw, screaming, "...and that's for the Japanese girls you kidnapped!"

The Madman of Pyongyang shrieked in pain.

"And this," she dragged the claw through the flesh of his arm, "is for attacking Tokyo. And *this*..." she slipped another claw into his belly as he shrieked some more, "...is for being a complete *bastard!*" She drew the claw out slowly, drawing out a loop of bloody intestine hooked on its curved end.

Wonjjang looked on in shock, wondering why he'd ever been so attracted to her.

"Neko," he said. "Don't. He deserves worse than death. Let's make him *really* suffer."

Kim laughed wickedly, coughed up a little blood, and narrowed his eyes, scowling at the girl who'd betrayed him. He opened his mouth, but Wonjjang knelt quickly and slapped his hand over it.

"No more slogans, Kim," he said. "You're finished. Maybe the government won't touch you, but I know someone who'll teach you a lesson you'll never..."

But only a moment later Wonjjang yanked his hand away from the Madman of Pyongyang's mouth. The little twerp had bitten him! He scowled at the leering Nork, bracing himself for a torrent of maniacal, nonsensical slogans and nationalist prattle, but instead Kim's eyes went bleary and he slumped back, slipping into unconsciousness.

"Knockout drugs," Ryun Ja said, holding up the syringe she'd used on Kim, which had been meant for Wonjjang. The others nodded, and then, with Neko still eyeing the Nork girl warily, Wonjjang dragged Kim's body up the wreckage-strewn mountainside to where the surviving shoopahs had begun to gather. Some were dripping blood, while others were merely bruised and weary-eyed, but they all smiled proudly.

"Gotcha!" Wonjjang proclaimed loudly, lifting the unconscious criminal above his head. They cheered.

As the cheers petered out, Wonjjang heard a familiar voice: "Let me through," it said.

"Umma? Gwenchana?"

"Of *course* I'm okay," his mother snapped, shoving her way through the crowd. "My, how *ugly*! Why'd you knock him out? I was gonna tell him off!"

Blastman stood close behind Jang Won's mother. "E-Gui shut the microcollider down. He said to say it was good working with you. And to say... goodbye."

Wonjjang nodded, then heaved Kim's limp body over his shoulder. "Let's get out of here!"

"Aren't you forgetting something?" the Nork girl said, looking from Wonjjang to his mother. She bowed firmly and smiled at Wonjjang's umma, and Wonjjang was sure he'd never seen his mind-reading mother smile so widely in all his life.

7. ALL'S WELL THAT ENDING

"Tell me, tell me... why does your beautiful wife smell like yangju?" It was the third time in twenty minutes that Jang Won had been asked why his wife smelled like Western liquor.

He glanced over at his bride, Ryun Ja. Soft afternoon sunlight streamed through the picture windows of the reception room at the Gumi City Big Love Royal Wedding Hall, lighting up her face and the intricately embroidered traditional Korean wedding gown she wore. Jang Won was struck by a pang of joy. She retained her firm Northern features, but her stoniness had softened in the past months, and the fear in her eyes had all drained away. She would never forget life in the North — the hell of the mutant camps, the lies and brainwashing — but she had moved beyond it all, finally.

Yet she still had that same fiery beauty about her, gesturing as she spoke to Jang Won's mother. Her lustrous long black hair trailed down her back — he'd asked her not to put it up for the wedding, since it was so beautiful hanging loose like that — and he watched her place her hand over her mouth gracefully when she laughed at her mother-in-law's response. If only his teammates were still in Korea to see him now.

"She's a *special* mutant," he said, quietly, with an air of mystery. Beside him, Big Myoung chortled. "Modified to secrete cognac. Kim Noh Wang brought her along everywhere."

"Jinjja?" Jang Won's younger cousins exclaimed in disbelief.

"Yes, *really*," he said. "After making love, I can sip it from her armpits. I asked her to grow out her armpit hair, so it collects better."

"Liar!" one of his cousins said, shaking his head.

Another cousin laughed, and said, "Me, I want a wife who sweats *soju*!"

"Ahhhh, that would be *delicious*," his cousins all said, their eyes suddenly dreamy.

Laughing, Jang Won raised his glass and commanded, "One-shot!" Everyone followed suit, clinking glasses, and they gulped down their shots of soju in unison. As the ritual of refilling glasses resumed, Jang Won excused himself and crossed the room to his wife's side.

"Hey!" he said to his wife with a grin. "Carefully buttering up your mother-in-law?"

"I was just asking Ryun Ja when the grandchildren will be coming," his mother said with a half-smile. "I hope a baby is coming soon, Jang Won?"

Jang Won fought the urge to argue with her. It was his wedding day; it was supposed to be a happy occasion. "If she's asking me, she must not have liked your answer, right, honey? What did you tell her, Ryun Ja-sshi?"

"We have so many things to do," his bride answered. "Freeing the North won't be easy, and I'm not ready to give up or retire from our paying work, either," she said, smiling. The small business she, Jang Won, and a few other ex-LG shoopahs had started was thriving, and more and more people were beginning to listen to their message about the North, too. The Sunshine Policy was on hold, and alternatives were being debated in Congress with a vigour few had imagined possible. The Great Leader up North had agreed to compensation: a thousand cases of Hennessy Paradis cognac and an undisclosed amount of taxpayer's money — but crowds of protestors had made it clear to the Southern government that any more cooperation, including Kim's release to the North, would result in the defenestration of every member of the Lee Administration. Perhaps big changes were finally afoot, and Ryun Ja and Jang Won had decided to make sure they were a part of it all. "Maybe we'll have time for children after all that. I'm still young."

"*You're* young," Jang Won's mother said, "But I'm not. Jang Won here took so long to find you... I thought I'd die before he found a girl..."

"And yet, here we all are," Ryun Ja interjected with a smile. "It's wonderful, isn't it? Impossible things *can* happen."

"Impossible?" Jang Won feigned outrage. He felt a tap on the back of one of his legs and turned to see Kim Noh Wang standing behind him, in a tiny custom-tailored suit, one hand grasping the hem of Ryun Ja's gown. One of his fat little wrists was bound in a thick metal tracker-bracelet rimmed with blinking lights.

"Yes, Noh Wang?"

"You think this is over?" Noh Wang sneered, an evil look in his beady little eye. Jang Won just looked at him with pity as he threatened him: "I've got plans for you, kid, things you can't even imagine. You're going to wish you were never..."

"Kim Noh Wang!" Jang Won's mother shrieked, and she sprang to her feet. "You said you'd be a good boy. Do I have to teach you your lesson again?" She turned to Jang Won and said, "I'm sorry, son, he promised he would behave. He's been acting up lately, talking about Iron Monkey sending him secret messages. I'm starting to think it's impossible to change his heart..."

His mother set off after Kim, who had fled under a table surrounded by retired shoopahs knocking back shots of soju and chowing down on barbecued pork. She dove under the table and caught Kim by his pudgy little legs, and he shrieked in distress.

"It's okay," Ryun Ja said, and, daringly, kissed her husband right there in front of everyone, not caring who might see. The boozy fumes clung to his lips as she pulled back from him, winking. "Don't give up on him, mother-in-law!" she called out, and then, to Jang Won, she added, "Sure, we have to keep him chained up for now, but, who knows, he might give up his evil ways someday, right? Even impossible things happen sometimes..."

Jang Won leaned forward and kissed his lovely, cognac-flavoured wife.

Wylde's Kingdom
David Nickle

PILOT:
LOOK OUT FOR JIM!

Max first spied the two fanboys through the mosquito netting surrounding the bed in his nearly submerged Brazilian apartment. He was sure he had them pegged: just another couple of bottom-feeders churned up from the silt by Atlantica, who'd tracked down their hero Jim to his dank retirement here at Serra Do Mar Bay. They'd kicked in the door, true. But Jim fans had done far weirder things in Max's experience.

One fanboy had an acoustic-guitar case slung over his shoulder. "Either of you know 'Girl from Ipanema'?" Max asked. Although it wasn't what he was going for, they both laughed appreciatively.

The two introduced themselves as Dan and James, and, as James pointed out, *James* was another name for *Jim*. James was the one carrying the guitar case, and he set it down on the floor and opened it while Dan explained in detail just how much Max's work as Jim on *Wylde's Kingdom* had meant to him. Trying to be polite, Max noted he had put on a little weight since then and didn't think he could do the stuff Jim had done anymore. Just as politely, James pointed out that was one of the reasons they were here. "You have put on a few pounds there, Jim," agreed Dan.

Then Max heard a click, followed by a whine that sounded like a vacuum cleaner cycling up. James stuck his head up. He was holding a narrow plastic hose that ended in a gleaming steel needle. A hissing whistle came from its tip, and Max realized what his dormant survival instinct had been trying to tell him since they showed: these guys weren't fanboys at all — or, at least, not just fanboys. They were professionals: barrio cosmetic surgeons, the very worst kind.

Max stirred, trembling toward thoughts of escape.

Years ago, back when he was a regular on *Wylde's Kingdom*, and his day consisted of garrotting gorillas and chainsawing rampaging elephants, that instinct would have seen him clear. It would have thrown Max out of bed and had him halfway to the door before the fanboy-surgeons had a chance to react. If one of them had managed to grab him, he probably could have wrestled the needle of the AbSucker 2020 away from him and jammed it into one fannish orifice or another to break the hold, made it to the door, and dived off the balcony into the bay in the span of a dozen heartbeats.

But not these days. Max *had* put on a lot of weight — two-fifty sounded about right, and three hundred wouldn't really have surprised him — and he hadn't exactly been physically active during his voluntary convalescence here. So when he grabbed at the needle, the fan pulled it out of the way easily, and speckles of dizziness darkened Max's vision before he could do anything about it.

"Don't stress yourself," said Dan, who was holding the second hose-and-needle assembly from the AbSucker in one hand. It was hissing, too. Before Max could do anything more, he felt a sharp pain on his left side, and he realized James had managed to skewer him in the love handle. Max felt another prick on his right handle. The AbSucker's motor whined as it started to work on both sides of him, siphoning off eight months of accumulated lipids like they were a milkshake.

James tried to be apologetic. He explained that, usually, they'd have him onto their boat in Rio, and if he wanted he could even have had a general anaesthetic and in just under an hour woken up eight months younger, with none of this painful and clearly disturbing fuss. They would have given him a mint.

"But we were under instructions," said Dan.

"Just doing what our boss tells us," said James.

"Your boss?" gasped Max.

James looked down at his own T-shirt, which was emblazoned with a scan of Jerry Wylde, ubiquitous pith-helmet covering his hairless scalp and his antique Sharps hunting rifle slung over one narrow shoulder. Dan looked over at it, too, then back at Max. Dan nodded, his open-mouthed grin an eerie parody of the one Wylde sported on the shirt.

"Our boss and yours," said Dan.

The AbSucker made an ugly *whup!* sound as something thick passed through the orifice. The way Max was feeling, he thought it might be a testicle.

"Mr. Wylde wanted everything to be just right," explained James. "He wanted you to 'recontextualize.'"

"And he said you needed to have an 'adequate sense of danger,'" said Dan.

"Yeah," agreed James. "Those were his exact words. 'Recontextualize.' 'An adequate sense of danger.' Mr. Wylde says that's when you're at your best."

The three of them were quiet for a moment — James and Dan contemplating the words of the master, Max contemplating the sagging flesh below his ribcage. The noise from the guitar case shifted from suck to slurp, like the milkshake was finished, and James snapped out of it.

"Shit!" he yelled, and reached down and flipped off the machine. "Almost got your liver," he said as the sucker cycled down. When Max didn't laugh, Dan patted him on the shoulder.

"Joke, Jim," he said.

The wind picked up then, and the broken door swung open. Dan hurried to close the door against the returning rage of Atlantica, and Max shut his eyes.

"I'm not Jim," he whispered.

⇥∗⇤∗⇥∗⇤∗⇥

But that wasn't entirely true. Max was Jim — and Jerry Wylde had made him that way.

Jerry Wylde and Max had hooked up the year the first hurricane cluster of Atlantica had been tracked. Jerry Wylde was still with Disney, exec-producing a now-defunct celebrity arena show called *Let the Games Begin*. Max had been working in a string of middling-successful Bollywood sitcoms, the latest of which was an extended-family urban musical actioner called *Look Out for Shoorsen!*

With *Shoorsen!*, Max had managed to achieve just the level of celebrity *Let the Games Begin* liked best: sufficiently known to pull in a few ratings points, but not so famous their agent could alter even a semi-colon on the standard Disney contract.

Legend had it Jerry had been the one to pick Max, over the objections of some of the execs who were worried about how Max's recent, well-publicized bout in rehab would play. But that was crap — Jerry didn't have anything to do with the decision to make Max a centre-forward in the East-versus-West Five-Ball Sudden-Death Australian-Rules Soccer match. In those days, Jerry Wylde didn't soil his hands with booking decisions. When the two met in the dressing room, Jerry mistook Max for a member of the camera crew, then, once corrected, faked his way through an embarrassingly inaccurate appreciation of this season's *Shoorsen!* and got Max's name wrong.

Even in those early days, the one thing Jerry Wylde was not was a detail man: he spent his days pushing the envelope, articulating vision, and that day he had such immense envelope-pushing, vision-articulating plans that he was more preoccupied than usual.

In his ghostwritten autobiography, Jerry would take an entire chapter to carefully explain how Disney was poised to drop the metaphorical ball on *Games*, that after just three years in circulation, it was headed for a ratings nosedive, and that what would later become known as the Five-Ball Bloodbath was his honest attempt to inject some life into the ailing property.

From Jerry's ghostwritten autobiography, I, Jerry:

Disney's problem with Games was the same problem they'd been having since "Steamboat Willie." They settled into a safe spot that only *seemed* dangerous, and their Five-Ball Sudden-Death Australian-Rules Soccer spot was a perfect example: divide a pack of mid-level television actors into teams, throw down five balls instead of one, and tell them they can do anything they want to get as many of those balls between the goalposts as they can before the commercial. Ooh, they do sound extreme, those rules: *Do anything you want.*

Well, I'll tell you something: to an actor, doing anything he wants means driving his convertible to his beach house where he'll screw his actor girlfriend while his agent is signing him for a movie deal that'll let him take a different actor girlfriend to the Oscars and screw her in a different way when he wins, all of which he regards as nothing more than his God-given *due*. Kicking a ball into a net in Five-Ball Sudden-Death Australian-Rules Soccer? I don't care how good actors these guys are; there's no motivation, and the audience can smell that.

I could sure smell it — and that's why I made sure their uniforms were scented a little differently: with what I like to call *Eau de Jerry*.

Eau de Jerry was Wylde's affectionate name for a pheromone soup tailored to drive the five African rhinos Jerry had managed to hide on-set into a mating frenzy.

None of the actors, of course, had any idea. Billy Kaye, the surgically stunted 26-year-old who'd been playing the same precocious eight-year-old on *Ungrateful Bastard* for the past eighteen years, did complain in the dressing room that the uniforms had a funny smell to them. But the rest of the team wrote the observation off as more of the overpaid dwarf's well-documented backstage whining. It was ironic: when the balls dropped and the rhinos charged out,

Kaye was one of the first to go down — or up, rather, gored on one of the great beasts' horns and tossed into the air like a discarded action figure. The Man-Boy Who Cried Rhino, Jerry later dubbed him.

Seven other celebrities died in the televised bloodbath that followed. Another eleven were maimed, and the rest suffered more minor injuries. Or most of the rest did.

Live on television, Max Fiddler — and only Max Fiddler — came through the ordeal unscathed.

Emerging from his Serra Do Mar Bay apartment and struggling through the rain toward his psychopathic fans' limousine, Max still wasn't sure how he'd survived that bloodbath. He'd seen the tapes enough times: watched himself leap out of the path of a charging rhino, bolt across the pitch to the opposing team's goalposts, and shimmy up to the top, then jump again when a couple of smitten rhinos rammed into the posts hard enough to knock them down. He saw himself grab onto the bottom of the camera crane that was even then pulling in for the closeup on what could have, should have been his death scene. Max watched as he swung overtop and wrestled the camera operator like he was the last Nazi guard on the truck with the Ark of the Covenant in the back. Max did remember that fight, or at least the feelings it had brought out in him — a strange mix of terror, elation, and vestigial guilt as he finally managed to unstrap the operator from his seat and knock him 25 feet down to the astroturf below. The feelings were there, but the particulars were lost forever. Something within him had taken over and guided him to safety. Max chose to simply call it his survival instinct, but in Wylde's autobiography the ghostwriter found a better name: "Max Fiddler's Inner Jim."

The ghostwriter hadn't needed to embellish the events that followed. Jerry had indeed been the first one onto the pitch, before the rhinos were subdued, and he had stood directly underneath the crane smoking a locally banned cigarette, gazing wordlessly up at Max for almost a minute before the floor director, surrounded by three terrified PAs brandishing cattleprods and cellphones, came out to take Wylde off-set and bundle up the camera operator.

✢•I•I•I•✢

Transcript of the subsequent meeting between Jerry and Max in the Disney World Trauma Center, from I, Jerry *(pretty much how Max remembered it, too):*
JERRY: Hello, there. I'm Jerry Wylde.
JIM: Yes, I believe we have met. Just this afternoon.
JERRY: And I'm sorry — you are...?
JIM: Max Fiddler. *Look Out for Shoorsen!?* Didn't we have this conversation?
JERRY: Max Fiddler. Ah, no. You're Jim. Right?
JIM: Max Fiddler. I am an actor.
JERRY: An actor. Listen, Jim — I don't want you to take this the wrong way, but the one thing you are *not* is an actor. You have more *cojones* 'tween those gams than half of those bozos on the pitch showed today.
JIM: That is only because your triceratops spread their cojones across the pitch, Mr. Wylde.
JERRY: You exaggerate. And they are rhinos. Triceratops are dinosaurs, and dinosaurs are extinct. Rhinos are alive and kicking. Where'd you go to school, Jim?
JIM: Idaho. Why are you calling me Jim? I keep telling you my name is Max Fiddler, that is the name on the contract I signed, which by the way I also read all the way through, and I did not see any mention of rhinos in the—
JERRY: Whoa, Jim. Settle down. I don't handle the contracts, and we don't have a lot of time for me to look into it for you anyway. But listen — let's cut to the chase. I've got some new projects on the horizon — big projects. Stuff that's going to turn Disney and Fox and the whole goddamn planet on its ear. Hey, riddle me this, Jim: what do you get when you cross a nature show with a fishing show?
JIM: That would be...
JERRY: A hunting show! Ex-actly! Do you remember the last time you went hunting — sat in the scrub for hours with your dad's old M16 and a box of hand grenades, waiting until the moment — the precious, perfect *moment* that deer shows up in your sights?
JIM: I've never been—

JERRY: Never been hunting! Of course you haven't! Who hunts deer these days? *I* can't afford the price of a license, and I'm loaded! Okay, how about this: you ever shove firecrackers up a frog's asshole? Watch that little bastard *hop*? No? Stick an aerosol can and a cigarette lighter under a wasp's nest? Hold a magnifying glass over an anthill on a sunny day?

JIM: Actually, not—

JERRY: Gahh, you're shitting me, Jim. I saw you out on that pitch today. That was not a prissy little rhino-hugging second banana from the subcontinent I saw climbing that goalpost. Oh, no. You're one cold-blooded survivor Jim. You're a survivor, and you're more.

JIM: You tried to kill me.

JERRY: Yeah, Jim. I guess I did. (Pausing sheepishly) And you know what? I think I succeeded.

JIM: Huh?

JERRY: Yeah. I look at you, and I don't see any trace of that Max Fiddlehead—

JIM: Fiddler. Max *Fiddler*.

JERRY: —Fiddle. Whoever. I don't see any trace of that guy in you. You're Jim — the guy that faces five sex-starved African bull rhinos, scales a sheer goal post then leaps — *leaps* through the air and knocks the camera op out of his seat to dominate the whole show! Forget *Look Out for Shoorsen!* — from now on, it's Look Out for Jim, world! *Look Out for Fuckin' Jim!*

※•✧•✧•※

At that point, a phalanx of Disney cast members had burst into the room, fired off a taser into Jerry's ass, and, with nothing but that and a commandeered restraining wheelchair, effectively ended the meeting.

But the meeting had lasted long enough for Jerry Wylde to leave his mark. As Max lay alone in the dark room, halfway down the biggest adrenaline crash of his life until then, he played Jerry's words over and over in his head: *Look out for Jim.* Jerry Wylde was a lunatic, thought Max, and not a particularly unique one either. *Look out for Jim,* he'd said. The trouble with guys like Jerry Wylde, thought Max, was they figured they could motivate you with nothing more than some meaningless catchphrase — *Look out for Jim*, for Christ's sake — and make you dive off a cliff with it. Like that was all it took.

Max got out of bed. The linoleum floor of the room was cold under his bare feet. They kept these rooms too cool — after three years in New Delhi, Max was used to the heat and he could have stood a little Florida sunshine. Right now, the only light came through the drawn blinds of a single window, and it cast only the faintest, greenish glow over everything.

"Look out for Jim," whispered Max. He shuffled over to the window, put his hand on the blind.

As he did so, there was a terrible *crunch!* sound, as of breaking glass, followed by the escalating moan of spreading cracks. There was another sound as well, somewhat more distant, and for Max the room got even cooler.

It was the sound of wind. Big wind. Max inched the curtain back, looked out through the spider-web cracks of the window, and saw just how big a wind could get.

Three thick-waisted tornadoes were dancing across the Magic Kingdom under a sky green as a frog's ass. The infirmary was second-storey, and most of his view was blocked by a grass-covered berm, but Max could see the top spires of Sleeping Beauty's Castle as one of the tornadoes brushed against it. For an instant, it seemed as though the wind was working like a lathe on the fantasy parapet, sending bits of it flying off like woodchips, but then the funnel shifted maybe three dozen feet the wrong way, and the tower disappeared inside it.

"Look out for Jim," said Max, as one of the other tornadoes began to grow and moved away, the castle now erased from the skyline. Then something else slammed into the window, shattering it — and once again Max was running, slamming open the door to the hallway, which was already filling up with patients and orderlies and security guards. No-one seemed to notice him as the adrenaline started pumping and his survival instinct — his "inner Jim" — took over.

"Look out for Jim!" he yelled, and pushed his way into the first stairwell he saw. In no time at all, he was safe in the tunnels under the studio theme park. He would be stuck there for seven and a half days, while Atlantica's first-ever foray onto the mainland United States reduced eighty percent of Walt Disney World to the swamp and scrub and mud from which it had sprung.

By the time the job was done on Disney, Max's agent had done pretty much the same thing to his contract with *Shoorsen*'s producers in New Delhi. Against his agent's advice, Max handled the talks with Jerry Wylde himself.

EPISODE 1:
THE PASSION OF THE VOLE

Max took advantage of the screen and mini-bar in the wide seating in back as the two fan-surgeons up front found some dry highway and hauled inland to Rio. The weather was the shits, and Max didn't want to know about it. So rum cooler in hand, he shut the Weath-Net scribe — which was tracking a tentacular offshoot of Atlantica scraping its way down the coast — and settled on one of the Argentinian sitcom feeds. They were showing the first season of *Happy Days*, when Joanie was a kid, Fonzie was still a greaser more threatening than lovable, and Ron Howard at least superficially resembled the mid-twentieth-century teenager he was supposed to be playing. It was the only season of the show with any artistic integrity as far as Max was concerned. Although it had been dubbed in Portuguese, he watched it raptly as Dan steered the amphibian over and around the remains of the highway into Rio. He suspected both of the fans were glad he'd found something on the screen. Like most fans Max had encountered through his career, these two ran out of conversation after the first hello.

Max was glad for the distraction of the screen himself. He hadn't seen Jerry Wylde — even onscreen — for something like three years. *Wylde's Kingdom* had enjoyed a good seven years at the top of the ratings, but now it was faltering and most networks had shunted it to the bottom of the schedule. "I'll show you an endangered species," Wylde had said in one of the early promos, in front of a loop of Jim lobbing hand grenades into what Wylde's team of researchers believed was the last African mountain-gorilla nest in existence. "Now *that's* endangered!"

⇢⊹⇠⊹⇢⊹⇠

The limousine crawled up the highway into the suburbs of Rio and finally stopped behind the ruins of a shopping mall. There was a sleek yellow VTOL executive shuttle waiting for them when they arrived. The flight crew were huddled in the lee of a little quonset shelter, arguing in Italian.

James and Dan jumped out of the limo, opened the door, and hauled Max out. The rain was coming down so hard now that, when Max turned his face toward it, he felt like he was drowning. He was only able to make it across the dozen feet to the hatch of the shuttle because his two abductors-fans-surgeons-whatever-the-hell-they-were helped him.

"This is where we get off," said James.

"Take it easy, Jim," said Dan, smiling through the downpour. Max thought both fans looked relieved to be rid of him, and he didn't blame them. Max sighed and turned to climb into the relative dark of the cabin.

"Max Fiddler."

Max recognized that voice instantly. "Mimi?"

The shuttle's cabin was a reinforced bubble affair, with round windows spread polka-dot across the walls and ceiling. The woman who was sitting inside was just a shadow against a rainy circle of slate-dark sky. "None other," she said. "You look great."

"Thank you," said Max. "I feel like a drowned vole whose balls were cut off with rusty nail-clippers."

"From what I hear about you lately, that's got to be an improvement." Although her face was still obscured in silhouette, there was a familiar smile in Mimi's voice. It was a familiarity that chilled Max; he should never have gotten to know this woman so well. She patted the seat beside her. "Come sit by me," she said.

Max hesitated.

"Oh Christ, Max, get some self-esteem. We're going to be working together — the least you can do is sit beside me on the way out."

"Alright." Max sat down beside her as the hatch behind him swiveled shut and the sounds of the storm stepped back a few yards. With the storm farther and Mimi nearer, Max's eyes adjusted and he got a good look at the woman behind the voice. The years had been far kinder to her than to him: the line of her jaw and cheek was as smooth, her wide brown eyes as intelligent, her mouth as wide and generous as ever; and her jet-black hair, although tied back in a thick pony tail, showed none of the grey that had begun to fleck Max's thinning mane over the past few months. No, Dr. Mimi Coover looked every bit the innocent woman-child she had been when, as a young Canadian marine biologist, she first signed with *Wylde's Kingdom* as technical consultant on the televised slaughter of the last three living St. Lawrence beluga whales.

"Prison seems to have agreed with you," said Max.

"Careful, Maxie," she said. "There but for the grace of God..."

"I meant it kindly," said Max.

Mimi shrugged. "Doesn't matter. I didn't actually serve much of my sentence; my skill set's in short supply these days, and GET snapped me up pretty quickly for their oceanographics lab. Serving my sentence saving the environment I was so bent on destroying. And with only a little social engineering..." Max grimaced ("social engineering" was Mimi's euphemism for "alcohol-assisted seduction") "...gaining access to an otherwise classified library of abstracts and raw data you would not believe."

"Lucky you," said Max.

"You don't know how lucky," said Mimi. She flashed a wide, white-toothed smile with a larcenous glint that erased any illusion of innocence. "I'm putting us back on the map, Maxie. The things I've found..."

"I do not want to know," said Max.

"Think," said Mimi, "*Nautilus.*"

"What does an exercise machine have to do with anything?"

"*Nautilus.* You know — Captain Nemo? *Twenty Thousand Leagues under the Sea*? The giant—"

Max couldn't hear what Mimi said next — the turbines had begun to cycle up for takeoff, and it took a second for the noise-dampers to kick in.

"—Well, I've found a nest of them!" finished Mimi. "A nest! Filled with *hundreds* of them! *Hundreds*, Max! Nobody's been able to find more than one in nature, and here we've got a nest! Jerry is positively thrilled. That's why he wanted you back — this is going to put *Wylde's Kingdom* back on the charts."

"Whatever," said Max. "I'm tired."

"Tired, hmm? We'll see about that." Mimi sidled closer as the VTOL lifted off the pad and started its queasy ascent over the storm. She rested her head on Max's shoulder, and her hand fell on Max's thigh. He could feel her fingernails through the cloth of his jeans. "You weren't being literal about being a castrated rodent? Were you, *Jim*?"

"Actually," said Max, "yes. Pretty literal."

Max settled back in his seat as Mimi's hand withdrew and she sighed. The old survival instinct, Max thought, was finally kicking in. It was about time.

→•I••I••I•←

The world looked better at ten thousand feet.

For one thing, Max could see the sun — and some uninterrupted blue sky. He couldn't remember the last time he'd seen blue sky and taken it for granted. Atlantica and its bastard offspring had darkened the planet's surface pretty effectively, and every time the clouds moved you went out and basked in it, melanoma be damned. It was tough to get worked up about something as trivial as skin cancer under the too-rare brightness of direct sunlight.

From up here, even Atlantica didn't look so bad — clean white cotton-balls marching off forever, mixing into a vortex so wide you needed to be in orbit to see it for what it was: the beast that had wiped out close to half the Earth's population over the past decade and set the other half on the fast track to a soggy and wind-ravaged stone age.

It was no wonder, thought Max, that Jerry Wylde's star was waning under such a cloud: Atlantica had made the so-called Last Great White Hunter redundant.

In Jerry's first season, Atlantica wasn't charted as anything more than a grouping of hurricanes in the mid-Atlantic: Hurricane Colin, Hurricane Donald, Hurricane Elroy; then Freddy and Gerhardt and Helmut; Irving and Kenneth and Lothar; Marvin and Noel and Otto. Only when it persisted past the usual hurricane season, crested the alphabet at Zoe and survived past Christmas, did Weath-Net name it for what it was — Atlantica, Earth's answer to Jupiter's spot — the world's first persistent superstorm.

Then, Jerry Wylde was already halfway through the 26-episode first season of *Wylde's Kingdom*, building his studio on the *S.S. Minnow*, a loaded-down oil tanker anchored off British Columbia, and fending off subpoenas from a dozen different governments. With the help of Max and a team of zoologists, he had identified and exterminated eight species of animals that were headed that way anyway.

The first season was a good one for Max. He didn't even mind being addressed only as Jim by everyone he saw: hell, in half a season he'd become more famous as Jerry Wylde's athletic animal troubleshooter than he'd become in six seasons as Shoorsen's pink-bellied second banana.

Jim did everything: jumped from helicopters into alligator-infested swamps, staged commando raids on lion prides, reprised his debut with the rhinos on an African veldt in the two-part special *Rhino Revenge* — this time armed with a Russian-built hammergun and benefiting from some heavy-duty air support. He even had his own line of action figures — which sold like hotcakes — and a prime spot in the *Wylde's Kingdom* console game, which, although less successful than the show, still made Jerry Wylde a mint.

By the end of the show's first season, Atlantica had taken a sizable chunk out of the Eastern Seaboard of the United States and reduced the islands of the Caribbean to little more than a few depopulated atolls.

As Jerry and his crew were preparing for the second season with a trip to the fragile, still-icy regions of the Antarctic, the Global Ecological Trust was beginning to mobilize. It probably shouldn't have surprised anyone that the multinational force sworn to restabilize the planetary ecosystem by persuasion or force should target Jerry Wylde and his nose-thumbing television program as public enemy number one.

One person it didn't surprise was Jerry himself. It turned out he had good reason for locating his studios on board an oil tanker: when the GET gunboat pulled up alongside the *S.S. Minnow*, demanding Wylde surrender to the justice of the world court, Jerry asked hypothetically how many years they thought he'd get if he were to blow the stopcocks on the tanker's two million barrels of crude oil and spread it all across the West Coast salmon beds — which he said would be easy to do before, as he put it, "you get a single one of your Greenpeace-surplus zodiacs into the water, you tree-hugging candy-ass dupes."

Predictably, GET ordered the gunboat's withdrawal, and the second season of *Wylde's Kingdom* kicked off without further harassment — although Jerry was effectively Polanskied from GET-signatory nations ever after.

And so it went. Tidal waves exfoliated Hawaii and the Philippines after California made good on its century-old promise to slide into the ocean. Waters continued to rise, with the ever-swelling Atlantica egging them on. Meanwhile, Jerry and Jim slogged their way through season 2, then season 3, and then half of season 4.

Jim probably could have stayed on for longer quite comfortably. The nice thing about working with Jerry was it didn't require you to think much: Jerry had it all worked out. On Jerry's advice, Jim fired his agent and lawyer, and let the *Wylde's Kingdom* accountants look after him so he could concentrate on the work.

Max had been used to keeping himself in shape, but only as the camera demanded. Jim, on the other hand, had to not only look good, but *be* good. Sit-ups and weight-training with a Hollywood-refugee personal trainer wouldn't cut mustard — so Jim spent his every waking moment not in the infirmary in the *Minnow*'s training maze with the former SAS team that made up Jerry's personal guard.

So, yes, Jim probably would have continued in such a way indefinitely, a willing lapdog to the *Wylde's Kingdom* entertainment machine, were it not for the arrival, in the middle of the fourth season, of the new crew of naturalist consultants led by Dr. Mimi Coover.

In *I, Jerry*, the ghostwriter professed not to have a clue about what drove the wedge between Jim and Jerry Wylde. A third of chapter 12 was devoted to a maudlin and accusatory meditation on the falling out: "Did I neglect Jim in some horrible, horrible way? Did I miss a single feeding, fail to exercise him, neglect his entertainments for even a second? Was I such an irritating seatmate on the trans-Atlantic flight of life that there was no other way?"

Ah, if only Jerry had known. Sitting on the shuttle, Max studiously avoided looking at Mimi — although he was hotly aware of her gaze on him. On board the *Minnow* he had fallen in love with her, and he had to admit he was deathly afraid of repeating the mistake here in the stratosphere.

As Jim, Max had lived the life of an aesthete. Between training and performance, there wasn't much time remaining in his day for anything but sleep. Although Max later learned his inbox was overflowing with every imaginable kind of sexual offer, Jerry never gave Jim a chance to read a word of it.

So when one night Mimi stole down to Jim's dressing room, dressed in nothing but a pair of retro-porn cutoff jeans and a lumberjack shirt with several of the buttons strategically removed, Jim was defenseless. And when she breathlessly informed him she had watched him in action since she was a child — spotting his heroic potential in the very first season of *Look Out for Shoorsen!*, then seeing it realized past even her pubescent dreams in *Wylde's Kingdom* — Jim was lost to her.

Yet if it were as simple as that — a beautiful groupie, a secret rendezvous in the dressing room, followed by a few more secret rendezvous in the training room, on the bridge, in three of the *Minnow*'s lifeboats... just that, and Jim would have been fine. But Dr. Mimi Coover was more than a groupie. She was a marine biologist; the kind of marine biologist who would sign on board the *Minnow* to work for Jerry Wylde. And she had... ideas.

"Do you ever wonder," she said one rainy night as they lay sweating underneath the tarpaulin of Lifeboat 6, "why Atlantica?"

"Yes," said Jim immediately.

"And California? Why now?"

"They'd been predicting a quake like that for years," said Jim, then, when he felt the sweat-damp skin of her thigh peel disappointedly from his own, added hastily: "But, yes, I do wonder why now."

Mimi rolled over onto her stomach, propped up on her elbows so she looked down at Jim. "It's true what you say, though. We have been predicting a massive, continent-splitting earthquake along the San Andreas fault — and for *decades*, not just years. Just like we've been anticipating a superstorm like Atlantica for years, and we've been warning about the rising of the oceans, and we've been worrying about mutant viruses like the ones vectoring across North America and Asia right now. So I guess I shouldn't be surprised?"

"Guess not," said Jim.

"I shouldn't be surprised," she continued, "that half the Earth's population is drowned or starved or dead from disease; that the United Nations is gone, replaced by an ecologically overcompensating military machine that throws you in jail if your car doesn't pass emission standards and shoots you without trial if you cut down a tree in your backyard. And I guess I shouldn't be surprised Jerry Wylde and his throwback hunting show, which seems to be doing nothing but hastening the process of planetary death, is the ratings hit that it is."

Mimi got up and pulled the tarpaulin back. Cool, sharp rain pummelled down on their naked bodies, and Mimi swivelled her long legs over the gunwale and jumped onto the *Minnow*'s deck. No slouch in the jumping department himself, Jim followed easily. But Mimi was still halfway to the nearest hatch.

"I'm sorry!" he shouted, feet slapping the metal deck plates as he hurried to catch up with her. Mimi stopped and turned.

"For what?" she demanded.

"For—" Jim paused, searching for some kind of culpability "—for hastening the planetary death!"

Mimi laughed, and threw her arms around him. "Hastening the *process* of planetary death, is what I said. God, Jim, you are so malleable. You're like the soft top of a little baby's skull — I could draw a happy face there with my finger, and it would stay that way until the day you died."

Jim's mouth opened and closed, but no words came out — his mind was filled then with the horrifying image of Mimi's thin finger digging happy-face furrows on newborns' heads. Her flesh suddenly felt as cold and clammy as the fish she studied. But she only held him tighter when he tried to pulled away.

"Here's the secret," she whispered. "The world *is* dying, Jim. It's a terminal case — the life that's infested it, become it, has run its course, and the world is reverting to its older, more natural geological state — joining its stately brethren of rocks and ice and gas-balls circling the sun. The world's dying, and the world knows it. It's obvious, and we should welcome it."

Jim reached up and pulled Mimi's arm from his shoulder. He stepped back. Mimi was grinning at him through black strands of hair washed over her face like seaweed in the storm.

"No way," said Jim.

"Oh, don't be stupid, Jim," she shouted. "The world is ending — Jerry Wylde is finishing it off, and you're right there with him! And now so am I! Centre stage!" She threw her head back so the rain ran into her eyes, her mouth. Lightning flashed paparazzi-silver across her naked body, made an apparition of her — ribs standing out in sharp relief, eyes shadowed into black and unknowable pits, mouth wide and streaming water as her head came back down to look at him.

"Centre stage," said Jim.

"Centre stage," repeated Mimi. "Good, Jim. You're catching on."

She took two more steps forward, and her hand came to rest on Jim's bare buttock. The tips of her fingers pressed furrows into the muscle there. "Let's make a baby," she hissed through bared teeth.

Jim thought about that for a minute; and thinking about procreating made him think about too many other things he'd never, ever considered. The inevitability of the end of the world. Jerry Wylde's complicity in that end. His own complicity. Mimi Coover's sharp fingertips digging drawings into their baby's skull. Jerry Wylde filming it for season 5.

A sudden wave of conscience and self-loathing flooded him, like a tsunami over a Thai whorehouse.

Jim reached around, grabbed Mimi's wrist, and pulled her hand off his behind. "Forget it," he said. "I'm out of here."

→•⁑•⁑•←

Within a week, Jim was indeed out of there — gone without a trace, in fact — and Max Fiddler was alone in Lifeboat 6, firing off the last of his signal flares calling for someone — anyone, in the thinning population of the dying planet — to rescue him from the storm-swollen waves of the rising sea.

EPISODE 2:
A NIGHT AT THE ZOO

The shuttle dropped from the stratosphere and lanced back through the cloudy flesh of Atlantica. The cabin pitched and went dark for a second before the lights came up.

"Where are we going?" said Max.

Mimi clapped. "A question! The eunuch vole wonders after its fate!"

Max shrugged. "The world is ending, and we might as well welcome it. That doesn't rule out curiosity."

"Fair enough." Mimi grinned. "We're going to the top of a mountain."

He raised his eyebrows. "That's interesting," said Max. "Jerry finally sold his tanker?"

Mimi's smile broke into a laugh. She mimed a firing handgun with her forefinger. "Gotcha," she said. "It's a sea mountain. On the Eastern Scotian Shelf."

Max blinked.

"Near Nova Scotia?"

"So we are going to the *Minnow*?"

"Where else?" said Mimi. "Oh, you are going to *love* this, Maxie."

The shuttle banked on its descent, and Max thought he could see lights below them in a tanker-shaped oval, shining through the thinning cloud and thick sheet of rain.

"I cannot wait," he said, and looked away.

⊱┈┈┈┈┈⊰

They were greeted on the deck pad by a couple of raincoated production assistants and a video crew. The PAs were shouting non-sequiturs into headsets hidden under their hoods as they led Max and Mimi through a Stonehenge of crates and equipment across the broad plateau of the tanker's mid-deck, under a wide, corrugated-steel awning. Max was still wiping the rainwater from his eyes when the studio lights kicked in and the video crew pulled back for a wide shot.

Mimi elbowed him: "Stand up straight," she hissed. "You're live."

Max didn't have to be told twice. He'd spent the better part of three decades in the business, and his instinct in this area was even more deeply ingrained than his survival instinct. Max's spine straightened like a zipper pulling closed, and he felt his lips slide back like covers off a missile silo, to launch a white-toothed grin he thought he'd shelved for good the day they stopped booking him on *The Tonight Show.*

Max bounded across the floor of Jerry Wylde's soundstage, up the three shallow steps to the set, and landed perfectly on the sofa beside Jerry's desk, which had been faced with a single word, sea-green lettering on a midnight-black screen: KRAKEN! Nuremberg banners reading the same hung behind the set, illuminated from below with white-hot spots.

Somewhere deep within himself, Max Fiddler screamed.

But he was in character now, deep in character, and the scream was a quiet thing. Jim certainly didn't hear it. He reached across the desk and clasped the thin, hairless hand that belonged to Jerry Wylde. Jerry was wearing a hot-pink double breasted Armani and his pith helmet. Without a thought, Jim told him how sharp he was looking tonight. Outside the still-open hatchway, lightning flashed close. But the lights in here were bright enough that Jim could ignore the flash. The neo-primitive cargo cult tribe who made up Jerry Wylde's studio audience were loud enough that Jim didn't have to ignore the thunder that followed. He couldn't even hear it. They were chanting something he couldn't quite make out and twirling their arms around their heads in tightly choreographed mayhem, and they looked quite terrifying with their frisbee-stretched lips and sponsor-scarified foreheads. Jim waved.

"Ahoy there, Jim!" yelled Jerry as the audience began to settle down.

"Ahoy yourself, Bwana Jerry," said Jim. He'd started calling Jerry *Bwana* at the start of the second season but hadn't used the word since the beginning of the third. The audience let out a nostalgic cheer. Jim crossed one lipo-weakened leg over the other and threw his head back in a near-perfect execution of the talk-show laugh.

On cue, the audience started to chant again. This time Jim understood what they were saying: "Kra-ken! Kra-ken! Kra-ken!"

"Right," said Jim.

Jerry put his hand over the mike. "Ah, it's time," he said into his lapel. "Let's go to clip, Jeffrey."

Jeffrey, whoever he was, didn't take even a heartbeat to shift gears. The studio went dark for barely a instant, and then the CGI projectors fired up and everything became a mottled green. The studio audience went into a panic with the unscripted change, but the projectors faded them to shadowy ghosts, and the dampers made their shouts into distant gurgles. Shit, thought Jim, his survival instinct grumbling. This was too real: every sense but smell told him they were under water.

"The deep blue sea," said Jerry, standing up and beckoning Jim to do the same. "You ain't seen nothing like this recently, have you, Jim?"

A heads-up prompter appeared in glowing red letters a few inches from Jim's eyes. Marks the same colour bled up through the floor. As with the prompter, these glowed like brand tips to Jim but wouldn't be picked up at all on camera.

"I haven't seen anything *but* this, Jerry," read Jim, moving to mark 1 and facing the direction of the arrow. "The whole world's sinking, in case you haven't noticed."

Jerry shrugged expansively. "Why Jim," he said, "I'm not talking about the water. I'm talking about..." and Jim moved to mark 2, just a step away and facing the opposite direction "...this!" finished Jerry, his face obscured behind a silvery tumult of virtual bubbles.

This time Jim screamed along with Max.

He was facing a giant, glowing mass of tentacles — some of them must have been a dozen or more feet long — and staring into what seemed to be an immense eyeball, as big as a soccer ball. And then it was gone, jetting past him, and Jim could see the creature's full cigar-shaped body, the tentacles at one end, a wide fin as big as a ship rudder at the other. The behemoth had snuck up behind him while he was reading his prompter. *Jee-sus*, thought Max. It must have been sixty feet long, glowing like a motel road sign from end to end; the suckers on its tentacles were each big enough to wrap a baseball.

"Captain Nemo," whispered Max, momentarily shocked out of character and into recollection. "A kraken. *Twenty Thousand Leagues*..." The welds on Max's vault of suppressed Disney memories slipped open, and Max peeked inside long enough to remember the movie: *Twenty Thousand Leagues under the Sea*... James Mason and Kirk Douglas and a submarine, and, yes, a great big rubber squid.

Jerry elbowed him in the ribs. "Line," he hissed.

"What the hell was that?" read Jim, a little too quickly. "Some kind of sea monster?"

Then Mimi stepped out of the murk, eyes focused on her own cue cards. She had changed into a form-fitting yellow wet suit and was carrying a drum-loading spear gun over her shoulder.

"In a way," she read, once the audience had applauded her entrance. "That's a giant squid, Jim."

"Aww, Doctor Mimi," said Jerry, aping disappointment with his usual brazen subtlety, "I wanted to see a *kraken*."

The muted audience went back at the chant with a renewed vigour.

"Well, Jerry," read Mimi, "that may be just what you're looking at — there's every reason to believe the legendary kraken, which were supposed to have plagued shipping routes for hundreds of years, were actually foraging giant squid, who..."

Jerry's eyes shifted their focus to some point beyond the horizon.

"...mistook early sailing vessels..."

Jerry wandered after the squid, leaving Jim and Mimi alone on-set.

Mimi, ever the trouper, finished her line: "...for food."

"Boy," read Jim, "I can't wait until I take on one of these things for real, in a battle broadcast live around the world—" he swallowed, his throat incongruously dry given the illusion of ocean around them, before he read the next set of words "—just three days from now."

"*One* of them?" Jerry shouted from the murk — probably behind the A camera. "Just *one*? You know what they say, Jim: you can't have just one!"

The air around Jerry was disrupted by a burst of bubbles and motion. Max stumbled and almost fell as the image of the squid came back for a second pass — something he should have anticipated. But it wasn't the one giant squid that freaked him out — it was the seven others, as big or bigger, that followed in the first one's wake.

"Jee-sus!" he yelled. "What the hell's that?"

He'd missed his cue again — the prompter flashed angry red and white — so he read: "Are my eyes deceiving me? Or are there eight giant squid down there?"

"At least," read Mimi. "What you saw was an image-enhanced holo we took just yesterday afternoon, from a divebot array just eight hundred feet below this ship. There could be more down there. *Far* more, in my professional opinion."

The audience *ooh*ed.

"Far more," said Jerry, rubbing his hands together with a sandpaper sound that gave the lie to the illusion of water around them. "Like the sound of that, don't you, Jim?"

Can't have just one, thought Max/Jim crazily before the dark, frothing sea went darker behind his eyes, and he fell to the studio floor in a dead faint.

EPISODE 3:
THE CABINET OF DOCTOR JERRY

They gave him a shot of something to wake him up for the welcome-back party, and whatever it was it certainly did the trick — Max was so alert that he felt like he could kill every one of the 37 houseflies crawling in and out of his ears if he wanted to, with nothing more deadly than the rock-hard tip of his newly rigidified tongue. He walked into the retrofitted mess hall unaided and sidled up to the bar.

Max looked around the room for some conversation, but he was a little dismayed to realize he recognized almost no-one. Max sighed and took careful sips from the drink the barkeep placed in front of him. It could have been anything from mineral water to goat's urine to his drug-benumbed taste buds.

It was actually okay not knowing anybody to talk to; Max was in no mood for conversation anyway. All he would get would be some armchair-producer critiques of Jim's last season on *Wylde's Kingdom*; or, worse, some liposucking fanboy gushing over just how dangerous a giant squid really was, reeling off statistics and little-known facts about how big their beaks were and how long their tentacles could reach, and marvelling at how much balls Jim — they would call him Jim, not Max, always Jim, because Max was a nobody and in their formative years Jim had been the next best thing to a positive role model — just exactly how much balls Jim had going up against the kraken, and not just one, but seven... ten... a hundred — Christ, who knew how many? *Did he have a plan?*, they'd ask. *Would this be Jim's last hurrah?*

"Sure'y no'," said Max to himself, his tongue about as agile as an ice-splintered tree stump. He must have said it louder than he'd intended; he drew uncomfortable stares from nearby conversations. Max took another sip of his drink.

He began to wonder what he was doing here in the first place. It was true, there wasn't really much he could have done to resist the AbSucker attack, and he could be excused for a certain amount of lassitude in its aftermath, as they ferried his sagging skin to the shuttle pad. Once on board the shuttle, it would have been tricky for him to do anything, really, but wait until they landed. And, on board the *Minnow*, Jerry had tricked him with lights and cameras, so, even had he wanted to, there wasn't anything to be done then either.

But now — was he going to wait until Jerry dropped him into a nest of giant squid, or whatever it was he was planning for him, before he took some kind of decisive action?

Action.

Max spotted two exits: the one he'd come in from, which led to the dressing rooms and studio after a few turns and ladders; and the washrooms, which Max recalled had a second exit leading through to an old barracks room, which after some doing led to the main deck and the lifeboats.

Max made up his mind. He swallowed the last of his mysteriously flavoured drink, got up, and headed for the washrooms, trying his best to look nonchalant. It must have worked — not a soul even looked up as he left his party. Once out of the room, Max hurried along the narrow corridor, past the doors with the stick-figure sign and through to the barracks room. It was being used as a storeroom for the bar and was filled with crates of whiskey and beer and Pepsi. Max stepped gingerly around them and hurried down the hall. Max took a deep, optimistic breath. Things were going smoothly — just up a ladder, down this corridor, through a galley — or maybe a studio — and there he was: right next to the exit.

Once on deck, it would be a simple repetition of his last escape: into a lifeboat, row like the devil's behind you and, after a couple of hours, make with the flare gun and hope for the best.

Max's optimism flagged for an instant at that thought. The last time he'd tried this stunt, it hadn't actually gone that well. A Japanese fishing trawler had picked him up after two days at sea, and the crew had recognized him instantly. Initially, Max had thought that was a good thing — Jerry had always led him to believe that *Wylde's Kingdom* was universally revered: the only real critics were the fanatics at GET, said Jerry. But the truth was more complicated. The crew of this trawler were indeed regular viewers of the show, but as it turned out there were sharp divisions of opinion on just what kind of contribution Jerry and Jim were making to the world of televised entertainment and, following from that, the world in general. The long and the short of it saw Max barricaded on the bridge with a half-dozen rabidly loyal fans while the majority of the crew gathered mutinously below decks. The more reasonable of their number merely demanded the captain conduct a trial-at-sea for crimes against the planet. Others were ready to go so far as scuttling the ship, if it meant ridding the world of even a portion of the evil *Wylde's Kingdom* franchise.

Max was better off with the fans, but only marginally. The captain had damn near shattered Max's elbow in a marathon arm-wrestling match, and the cook had been agitating for a karate tournament — the *Wylde's Kingdom* website apparently claimed that yellow-belt Jim was a black-belt world champion, and the triple-black-belt cook wanted to try him out.

Max had been lucky: the trawler was part of a Sony-owned fleet, and *Wylde's Kingdom* still had enough cachet that Max was more valuable to the company's media division alive than dead. So the Sony security forces squashed the mutiny, rescued Max from his fanboy-allies, and moved him to a Tokyo hotel suite, all within a few hours.

Max found the ladder that led up to kitchen or studio and paused.

The ratings of *Wylde's Kingdom* being what they were these days, Sony would not be as quick to pull Max's fat from the fire a second time.

"Fug i'," said Max. He scurried up the ladder and came out in one of the galleys. It was busy, all steam and sizzle and shouting, as Jerry's craft services team prepared tray upon tray of the particularly bland cheese and fish canapés that Jerry favoured. One of the chefs there did notice Max, and for a moment he feared he was discovered. But the woman took Max's arm, led him to one of the doors, and kindly explained that Jerry had declared craft services off limits to him until after the show.

"Sorry, Jim," she said. "I'll make you up a nice fish broth later if you like."

"'Kay," said Max, relieved. He stepped out the door, and then opened another door, and then he was on deck. Lightning flashed at him in greeting, and the hard rainwater drenched him immediately. He walked stiffly out into the dark storm.

There were no lights in which to hide here, no trickery to bring about his transformation into Jim. Max was alone with his thoughts. A bank of lifeboats swung in the wind, and he thought about lowering himself in one of those. He thought about the two days or more he would spend in his stolen lifeboat. He thought about the Grand Banks fishermen who plied these parts, and the *60 Minutes* segment he'd seen on them last year. He thought about the prospects of being rescued by one of their boats and just what they'd do to him when they found out who he was. And he thought about giant squids, and what they'd do to him by comparison.

"Fug i'," said Max.

He stepped back through the hatch and shut it behind him.

Max took a deep breath and headed for the *Minnow*'s aft decks — where last he remembered they kept the gymnasium, the infirmary, and his old training maze.

⇢•⇥•⇤•⇠

Max had been working out for barely an hour before Jerry showed up with the med team and the video crew. The intrusion pissed him off: three days was a hopelessly short time to train to begin with. He couldn't afford to be doing live segments with Jerry today if he were supposed to be doing live segments with giant squid in three days. When the unit producer sidled up to the thigh-sculptor machine to tell him he was on in five, that was what he told her.

"Don't worry," said the producer, a woman with a horse-long face and thinning red hair. "Just keep doing what you're doing. You with me, Jim?"

Max sighed and mentally stepped back.

"I'm with you," Jim said.

Jerry was standing slack-faced in the arch of the entryway sipping from a bottle of vintage spring water. He nodded when the producer signalled him, then came over by Jim's side. The videographer followed him. Max could tell that they'd started rolling: Jerry's slack features came alive, with the same demon-jester grin that adorned all his merchandise.

"Jim," he said. "Jim Jim Jim Jim Jim."

Jim started another set of extensions, wincing at the pain of tearing muscle and stretching ligament as the hydraulics hissed in the bowels of the machine. "Hey, Jerry," he said.

"Just keep doing what you're doing," said Jerry, and turned to the camera. "Jim is preparing for the fight of his life. So he doesn't have time for idle chit-chat — isn't that right, Jim?"

"Right," said Jim.

"Shh! Every extension, every contraction of those atrophied muscles of yours puts you one tiny step closer to being a match for the kraken, and I don't want to stand in your way — so shh!" Jerry put his finger to his mouth. "Shh! Remember, Jim, the giant squid is probably the fastest animal on the planet — it's got nerves as big around as your little finger, and that's a bandwidth to beat. And its suckers? They have little ridges of chitin around them that work like drill bits on your skin." Jerry made his hand into a claw and turned it back and forth like he was unscrewing the lid of a jar. "Let one get ahold of you, and it'll bore a hole into your flesh. So be strong, Jim! Be strong!"

Jim nodded. "You got it, Jerry."

"Okay," said the producer, "cut it. How was that, Mr. Wylde?"

Jerry's face sagged. "Fine," he muttered. "Send the team over. Time to juice him up."

※※※※

Max barely felt the injection when it pricked his arm. Jerry and the TV crew walked out as the steroidal spasmodics kicked in. The med team stayed behind, putting a roll of padding between Max's teeth and helping him onto a restraining stretcher so he wouldn't injure himself in the early stages of the muscle-building phase.

"You rock, Jim," said one of the medics. "I just wanted to say that before your hearing goes."

"Temporarily," added the one who'd administered the injection.

Max's back arched in hyper-orgasmic fervor, as the spasmodics went to work on the weakened muscles in his lower back. He made happy death-throe noises through his clenched teeth as the ringing started in his ears.

⁕⁖⁕

The spasmodics worked and kneaded Max's musculature for about six hours before they let him go, and at the end of it Max felt exhausted but good: the AbSucker had overdepleted him, but the spasmodics set the balance right. This cocktail was better than anything he'd used before; Jerry had obviously found a better supplier. These new drugs left his face and back smooth and acne-free, while strong, telegenic muscles rippled and twitched along his arms and legs and abdomen.

"I'm ready for anything," said Max. "Even your ridiculous squid, with their finger-thick nerves and their suckers that remove chunks of flesh like a drill bore."

Mimi ran a razor-nailed finger appreciatively along Max's left pectoral.

"That's the spirit," she said. Mimi had shown up about an hour earlier, on the spasmodics' down curve, as his hearing was beginning to return, to talk about the shooting schedule and go over the equipment that Max would have at his disposal. Max hadn't been able to ask questions during the briefing, but there wasn't any need to: aside from the military-issue dive armour, everything on the list was gear that Jim had used many times before. The explosive-tipped spearguns; the razor-wire net pellets; the hum-knives and trank-spears and suit-mounted mini-torpedoes.

He might have asked more questions when Mimi started talking about the squid themselves — but they wouldn't have been any more in-depth than "Is there some point to telling me all this?" Or "Who cares?" But the questions wouldn't have been any more effective than the grunts and moans that were all Max could manage: Mimi had developed a theory, and the only way that Max could stop her from explaining it to him would be to escape in a lifeboat again.

Mimi's theory was that they were sitting on top of an ancient hatchery — and that a shift in ocean currents had raised the temperature in that hatchery by the few degrees it would take to inflate the birth rate and, combined with the Wylde-hastened extinction of their natural enemies the sperm whales, had the effect of unlocking the gate on the kraken population explosion. What she wasn't so sure about was how so many of the squid had managed to grow to maturity and remain in such a small area. These creatures were giants, after all, with giant-sized food requirements, and the biomass oughtn't to be able to sustain them in such a large population.

"The GET researchers had apparently found some evidence of cannibalism," she had said. "Squid-bits in the bellies of a few captured adolescents. But cannibalism is a population limitation as well as a sustainer: an adult squid would have to eat a lot of babies to keep himself going, and on a daily basis."

There, Max had thought between spasms, with the babies again.

Now, he sat up on his cot and took Mimi's hand from his chest.

"Why are you back here?" he said. "Aren't you violating your parole or something?"

Mimi laughed — a surprisingly harsh noise, sharper than her nails. It made Max wince.

"I have my reasons," she said. "The money being only one."

Perhaps it was the familiarity brought on by his new sheath of muscles, combined with his proximity to Mimi — but he was filled with the sudden recollection of his last sight of her those years past, naked and demonic on the deck of the *Minnow*, selling him on the beauty of emptiness.

"Those squid are an affront to you, aren't they?" he said.

Mimi raised her eyebrows but didn't say anything.

"You can't understand why they're thriving — and you can't abide by their thriving either. They're one more stopgap against the sterilization of this planet." When she didn't object or disagree, Max stepped back from her.

"Are you going to bolt again?" said Mimi. "Jump in a lifeboat and row back to the mainland? I should warn you, don't think about going home. That little Brazilian hideout of yours is under water now — according to

Weath-Net, Atlantica is on the move, Maxie, redrawing the South American coastline as we speak."

Max felt something stretch and snap in his throat as a final spasm shuddered up his spine.

"No joke," said Mimi. "South America is *shrinking*."

Christ, he'd *lived* there, and he'd have been dead there if the liposucking-fans hadn't shown up. Come to think of it, if the liposucking-fans hadn't shown up, Max would have welcomed dying. In more than an abstract sense, that had been precisely what he'd been doing there: waiting to die, killing himself by lassitude.

And the fact was that nowhere he turned did Max find anyone with an even slightly more optimistic view. What was the point in living past the moment when the future held nothing but Atlantica? A giant storm and rising oceans and earthquakes and plagues? Hundreds of millions of people wiped out by Antlantica and its after-effects? For the first time since the bubonic plague decimated Europe in the middle ages, the global human population was in actual decline.

And so Max had taken a boat down the Amazon — a trip that less than a hundred years earlier would have been a trip of a lifetime, a jungle adventure with piranhas and anacondas and tapirs — but now followed a muddy shoreline washed clean of human habitation by a combination of clearcutting and the river's constant flooding. He had ended up in Brazil, squatting in the upper storeys of a sunken apartment house on the edge of Serra Do Mar Bay, eating and sleeping and drinking away the last of his so-appropriately named kill fee, waiting for the end.

Even Max's unbeatable survival instinct, his "inner Jim," could only take him so far. It had required Jerry — or Jerry's employees, anyway — to bring Max back from the brink of death.

"We're all you've got," said Mimi, closing the gap between them. Her hands grasped the back of his neck and pulled his face down to her half-open mouth.

Although the spasmodics had made him more than strong enough to fend her off, this time Max couldn't summon the will.

EPISODE 4:
KRAKEN!

The sky over the *Minnow* was incongruously clear the morning of Jim's dive into kraken waters. Jerry had prepped Jim with a full hour of on-air pre-show interviews, so by the time they led him out to the dive armour Max was so submerged as to be nonexistent.

It wasn't the same for Jerry. His shoulders slumped as they went single-file along the catwalk to the dive crane at the ship's aft section, and by the time they were climbing the stairs to the dive crane platform he seemed positively dejected.

"What is it, Jerry?" said Jim.

"Goddamn Atlantica," he said. "It's back in the Caribbean, and that means, before too long, it's going to hit Texas and Florida and the whole Eastern Seaboard."

Jim slapped Jerry's shoulder — a gesture that was one of the first character tics in Jim's repertoire of stock responses to Jerry's antics. "Take it easy, big guy," said Jerry automatically.

"It seems pretty nice here," said Jim. In fact, it was gorgeous — the sky was a clear robin's-egg blue, and the morning sun drew colour from even the drab and ungainly *Minnow*. The small part of Jim that was Max basked in it and regretted that, in a few moments, that brightness would be left behind for a dive eight hundred feet under the ocean.

"Oh yeah, great for your suntan. But think about our audience," said Jerry. "If you even have a thought in that pin-shaped head of yours."

Jim slapped Jerry on the shoulder again.

"Who the hell's going to be watching us with Atlantica running that far inland?" continued Jerry. "Everybody on one half of the continental US is going to be busy nailing up plywood on their windows if we're lucky, and sucking seawater if we're not. The one thing they are not going to be doing is watching us hunt squid."

"You can't generalize," said Jim.

"Ah, screw you," said Jerry irritably.

He might have said more, but they emerged onto the dive crane platform and into the view of three cameras and the studio audience, who were seated on bleachers to either side of the equipment. Jerry lifted his hands in the air and led the chant: "KRA-KEN! KRA-KEN! KRA-KEN!" Jim hollered along gamely, then slapped Jerry on the back one more time, and climbed up the few steps to the place where the dive armour hung, open at the back and resembling nothing so much as a giant cockroach, cut open and disembowelled, so only the exoskeleton remained. As they'd rehearsed, Jim raised his arms above his head, rose onto his toes and fell forward into the thing's belly. The servo-motors did the rest, closing the suit behind him and clicking the seals, making the carapace complete. Jim wiggled his arms and legs until the flesh fell against the biofeedback contacts properly. The suit's arms extended with his own, and the HUD flashed up test forms a few inches in front of his eyes. These were meaningless to him, but Jerry had assured him that the controls had been dumbed down and the HUD wasn't really more than a special effect. The important part was the cues, green on the red of the HUD, that told him what to say and when to say it.

"All systems are green," read Jim.

"And green means—" started Jerry.

"—Go!" finished the audience. The crane swung out over the gunwale of the ship, and then Jim felt a sharp jolt and fell. He hit the water with a spine-wrenching smack, and the suit took over.

When Max came to, the HUD told him he was already at four hundred feet — just halfway down to his rendezvous with the video crew and the deep-sea studio with its cable commlink to the surface.

Until he reached that studio, he would be utterly alone: just Max, the ocean, and the recorder in his suit. He took a breath of suit air and watched through the darkness for the star-cluster glow of the studio lighting rig that would eventually rise on its tether to meet him.

"Hey Jim," said Mimi. "You okay in there?"

Mimi was one of the five crew members in the studio sub. There would be a camera on her, and if Max had wanted to he could have watched her on the head's-up display. But he didn't want to see Mimi right now. He read his lines. "Just fine, Doctor Coover — but I'm getting a mite peckish. Got anything to eat in there?"

"Maybe we'll have some calamari later on — together." She silkily adlibbed that last word.

The studio was quite near now. It was a bubble sub, suspended in the middle of a geodesic titanium cage rimmed with lights and cameras. From the briefings, Max knew it was immense — something like a hundred fifty feet in diameter, with a cable of steel and polymer and fiberoptics a dozen feet thick extending up to the *Minnow* — but as close as he got, it resembled nothing more than a particularly garish Christmas-tree decoration to Max.

The whole massive bauble twisted slightly on its tether, sending spears of light sweeping through the dark water. The HUD flickered in Max's suit with a rejoinder to Mimi's adlib. But Max minimized it and peered out into the shifting gloom. Adrenaline sluiced through his arteries like quicksilver, as the light spears panned and flickered over the bellies of giants.

"Do you see that?" he whispered.

The bauble shifted again, and several of the lights winked out.

"Mimi — Doctor Coover?" said Max.

Mimi didn't answer him directly. But her microphone picked up enough of the frantic chatter of her crewmates — "Shit, we've lost the feed!" "—Forget the feed, Hank, we're—" "—pressure! We'll implo—" — to give her an excuse. The bauble was swinging erratically. The lights were winking out in a now familiar expanding pattern. Max had more than a clue as to what the problem was.

They'd hit paydirt: the squid had arrived, apparently in force. At least one of them had a grip on the submarine and was yanking on its moorings — and one of them was heading straight toward Max.

"Jim." Max whispered it like an invocation, as his own suit lights winked on, the servo-cameras fired up and the HUD came back in deep crimson combat mode. The numbers and bar-graph displays blurred in front of his eyes, however, as he got his first good look the creature in front of him.

It was impossible to tell scale exactly, but this thing looked far larger than the sixty-foot glow-monsters they'd used for the infomercials. From Max's perspective, it was a nebula of tentacles that filled the ocean, lined with suckers as big as dinner plates and centered around a beak that gleamed like sharpened mahogany.

Max flailed backward, the jets at his waist instantaneously translating the impulse into a rearward thrust that should have taken him far from harm's way.

It should have — but as fast as the biofeedback chips were in the suit, the kraken's thigh-thick nerves were that much faster. A long tentacle lashed behind Max and wrapped around him like a boa crushing a muskrat. There was a sickening sound of tooth-on-metal as the suckers tried to bore into Max's armour.

Max watched in horror as the image of the beak grew larger in his faceplate, opening and closing, and then as a cloud of black — emerging from the squid's ink sac, no doubt — began to billow toward him like a steroidal blackout. And then there was just the HUD, deep red on black, and the sound of more suckers going to work on his suit, and a terrible clicking sound coming up through his ribs, as the beak made contact with his armour. Max felt his eyes heat up with tears of despair.

His commlink crackled. "Okay!" shouted Mimi. "We've got the feed back! Jim — you alright?"

Jim was too busy to answer — and the power draw for the EelSkin jolt he'd activated wouldn't have let him transmit for a few seconds anyway. The HUD dimmed for a second while it powered to send its 150,000 volts through the suit's skin, and then went black for what seemed like an eternity for the discharge. When the display came up again, the beak-scraping and sucker-drilling sounds were gone, but the world was still black out there and Jim wasn't fooled into thinking the kraken was gone, too. He made a fist, raised his right hand in front of him, and sent a torpedo speeding into the darkness. It made contact almost instantly, and, giving it another second to burrow a little deeper, Jim raised his thumb against the detonator pad.

This time it wasn't his jets that sent him backward. He tumbled head over heels through the darkness for what the suit said was 83 feet before he escaped the giant ink cloud. It hung above him in a black thunderhead, the dim glow of the burning phosphorous at its core flickering like lightning.

"Scratch one kraken," Jim improvised.

The commlink was silent. Jim tongued the cue-card HUD. <STANDBY>, it blinked back in green letters.

"Hey," said Jim. "Anybody read me? Mimi? Jerry?"

Still nothing. He minimized the cue card and called up the commlink status bar. The words <SIGNAL LOSS> blinked amber across his view, even as his depth gauge rolled higher.

"Ah," said Max Fiddler, "shit."

⇢•⇤•⇤•⇢

From I, Jerry:

Danger is a media-induced state.

Alright — I'll grant you there was a time that this wasn't so. Back in the days when a bad weather forecast meant you should bring your umbrella to work and not a submarine, when ocean-view property was actually a selling point, when catching the flu meant taking a few days off work and not updating your will, yeah, alright, danger meant something. That's because danger is a study in contrast — it's the threat of something worse around the corner, a catastrophic disruption of your delicate equilibrium. And if you're going to disrupt that equilibrium, it goes without saying it must exist in the first place. No equilibrium, and people have nothing to worry about — nothing to disrupt. Shit just happens.

Except, that is, here by the screen. I'm constantly amazed at you zombies — drop my pal Jim on a savannah with a pack of pissed-off white rhinos, give him a box of hand grenades and a shoulder-cam and suddenly you're all squirmy and alive again. You start thinking and worrying and fretting — "Holy crow, Ethel, you think old Jim's met his match this time?" "Oh Jeb, I don' know, I jes' don' know. Them rhinos nearly finished him the first time, and this here's in their natural en-vi-ron-ment." For those fleeting moments in front of your screen, you morons actually start to give at least a vicarious fuck about someone's survival, if not your own.

I tell you — if Jim and I had come along thirty years earlier, that spark we're igniting every week might actually have given me some hope for this dying wreck of a planet.

※·I·※·I·※

Max stabilized himself at six hundred feet and switched on his armour's sonar to sweep the ocean above him. It wouldn't show him squid — they were too close to the ocean's density to register — but, with the ink-clouded water intervening, sonar was the only way he could find the studio and the commlink to the surface. He hung still and quiet, listening for the ping that would point him in the right direction.

Listening — and watching for another kraken.

Except Max didn't hear anything but the rasping sound of his own breath, and he didn't see anything but the dark of the deep waters, the dying star of phosphor in the dissipating ink cloud. The sonar quacked as it finished its first hemispheric sweep of the motionless waters around him, adding final confirmation:

The kraken were gone — and so were the studio and his link to *Wylde's Kingdom.*

Christ, thought Max, *Jerry must be shitting himself.*

It was possible that the *Minnow* had managed to pick up a small portion of his battle with the squid — but even if the crew had managed to fire the whole thing up the cable, the fight had lasted barely a few seconds, and most of that would have taken place in the midnight cloud of ink. And the script hadn't anticipated a battle this early in the show anyway; Max had seven hours of air in his suit, and Mimi and the team of oceanographers had expected that a few hours would be spent on scripted chit-chat and a guided tour of the installation before any squid came up to investigate.

And now, just twenty minutes into Jerry's big ratings comeback — "Kraken!" — was all but over.

Max started to chortle at Jerry's unhappy misfortune — but at a soft ping from his headset, he stopped himself, listening for it to repeat.

The sonar pinged a second time, and then a third, and the dive computer flashed confirmation: it had located the studio sub, two hundred feet to the north of Max and below him by about four hundred feet. On the third ping, the computer announced that the studio sub was descending, and quite rapidly.

Max checked the dive armour's help file. The structure and the life-support and propulsion system were all rated for a mile and a half, but the harpoon gun was only good for half that, and the cameras weren't rated any deeper than a thousand feet. So as far as Jerry and the show were concerned, the studio and its inhabitants were already casualties.

Of course, by now *Wylde's Kingdom* would be a ratings casualty in and of itself. Max had been around long enough to know that people didn't tune in to Jerry Wylde to watch him get creamed.

Max hit the dive sequencer with his chin and told the suit to lock onto the studio's signature and follow it down. Strictly speaking, Max knew the decision was counter-survival, but that was fine with him: off the air in the depths of the Atlantic, Max's inner Jim really had no say in the matter.

⇢⊹⇠⊹⇢⊹⇠

The pings multiplied as Max and the studio descended further: they were approaching bottom, or more accurately, side — moving in a neat diagonal toward the southern slope of the sea mountain. The dive computer correlated the pings with its oceanographics database and came up with a three-dimensional map of the mountainside, which it displayed in a small window at the top of the HUD. Max and the studio were represented by little red triangles. The graphic was gorgeous — it reminded Max of the time he and Jerry had made a tiger-bombing trek to the southern Himalayas — and Max became so engrossed in the memory that he nearly gave himself a concussion against the back of the helmet when the one of the cameras popped with a crack like a gunshot at 1,287 feet.

Head throbbing, Max wondered just what he expected to do when he got down there. If he were serious about rescuing Mimi and the rest of the crew, he would have done better to surface and report on the situation to Jerry. If he were halfway responsible, never mind just survival-oriented, Max supposed, that's what he'd do.

The second camera imploded at 1,315 feet, but this time Max was braced for it and just winced.

The thing was, Max wasn't halfway responsible. What he was, apparently, was more than halfway suicidal. And no amount of AbSucker treatments or spasmodics or steroids or anything else could mask that.

But what he also was, he realized, was damn curious.

Because from the look of the graphic on his HUD, the sub studio had just come to a landing on a high ledge of the mountain Mimi believed to be a giant-squid breeding ground.

Max accelerated downward, toward the now-motionless sub. Once again, the lights emerged from the murk — not as many as before, but enough to see by — and Max made sure to film it, in the seconds before the suit's third and final camera cracked under the pressure.

⇝⋅Ⅰ⋅⋅Ⅰ⋅⋅Ⅰ⋅⇜

"Mimi," said Max as he grew nearer. "Do you read me?"

"Jim?" Her voice sounded woozy, like she'd been drinking.

"Max," said Max.

"Max," said Mimi. "What the hell are you doing here? You should have broken for surface right away. Jesus, you should do that now... It's trouble down here."

There was a lot of silt stirred up around the studio; all Max could make out was about a dozen shafts of light, tangled in an opening-night criss-cross. The shafts didn't move, but they flickered now again, as though occluded by something very large passing above. Something the shape of a squid.

Max thought about it: if the sub had only fallen, it should have fallen straight down, not on a diagonal — from what Max had gathered, it was essentially a diving bell, with no locomotive power of its own. Something had pushed it.

"Trouble," Max repeated. "How many squid?"

"Three," said Mimi. Her voice was trembling, and he could hear the ugly chuffing sound of a man's tears in the background. "One's about thirty feet, another one's just a baby — fifteen, seventeen feet. And a big one — I can't tell how big, but from the parts of it we've seen, I'd say it tops a hundred."

"Feet?" said Max.

"Feet," confirmed Mimi.

As if on cue, Max saw an immense tentacle pull itself out of the cloud and wave a moment in the water, trailing silt in gossamer threads. It was wrapped around an object — a metal triangle, very tiny in the huge tentacle. It was a piece, Max realized, of the squid cage.

"It's got a piece of the cage," observed Max.

"Yeah," said Mimi. "It's got quite a few pieces of the cage. They all do. The bastards are cooperating... This makes no sense, Jim... Max... Ah, shit. Squid shouldn't be smart enough for this. They're opening us. Listen."

The commlink went silent for a moment — and sure enough, Max could hear an echoing sound of rending metal: both over his headphones and vibrating through the walls of his armour.

"Wow," said Max.

"Yeah," said Mimi, her voice taking on a weary affection. "*Wow*. God, Jim. You are *so* malleable."

Max nudged on the jets and inched forward. His heart was thundering, and his mouth was dry as a desert. What the hell *was* he going to do here? Three squids, and one of them big as Godzilla. The monster tentacle let go of the metal and descended back into the silt cloud, which itself immediately expanded away from a mysterious crash-and-scrape of metal on rock within it. One of the lights winked out, and then another, and one more.

Max hit the jets again, and now he shot down toward the cloud of muck. "Mimi!" he shouted into his commlink. "What's going on in there?"

Mimi was speaking quickly, shouting herself over various alarms that were sounding in the background. "Shit! Shit! They've stripped away the cage! Ah, shit! It's gotten in! Jesus, Jim, *it's inside the cage!*"

Max entered the cloud, and his view filled instantly with dancing motes of dirt. Fearful of hitting the mountainside, he reversed the jets. "Jim, Jim, Jim," he muttered desperately. "You would know what to do." But there was no Jim: Jim was just a character Max played on television.

And, this deep down, there was no such thing as television.

There was another crash, nearer this time, but it somehow sounded softer. It took Max an instant to realize why: he wasn't hearing it over the commlink.

"Mimi!" he shouted. The familiar amber <SIGNAL LOSS> was his only answer. It was followed shortly by a *crack!* and a monstrous belch.

The silt cleared for an instant, and Max could see the wreckage: a twist of geodesic titanium, two or three lights dangling from wire, surrounding a shattered tangle of metal and plastics, all beneath a galaxy of air bubbles shooting toward the surface.

And he could see the squids. The smallest of them was indeed inside the cage, tail sticking out of the wreckage as its tentacles rummaged greedily inside. A larger squid hung above, tentacles spread like a spider's web over the wreckage. And the third squid — the giant one, the hundred-footer — lay supine on the rock, its tree-thick tentacles lazily gripping torn pieces of the cage like they were toys. Its eye was as big as a manhole pit, and as black.

Max called up the heads-up display for the harpoon targeting system, and centered on the giant. It wouldn't be a difficult shot by any means. His thumb hovered below the trigger, and he was about to fire, when the small squid emerged from the wreckage. It had something in its tentacles. Max couldn't help but watch.

It was one of the bodies, or most of one. Mimi? It was hard to tell — the body was not in good shape. It trailed blood like ink from its torn abdomen, and Max thought about babies — about the one Mimi had wanted to make with him. Maybe she had furtively conceived already. If it was Mimi's body, their little zygote would be mingled in with the cloud. Max shuddered.

The squid dragged the body behind it, wrapped in three long tentacles, over to the giant's head. The giant's tentacles rippled and spread apart, and the smaller squid disappeared within them, dragging the body behind it. There was a flurry as the tentacles shifted, and a tremor went along the length of the kraken's body.

Max swore softly. The little squid was *feeding* the giant. These creatures were cooperating, to pillage the wreck and eat the TV oceanographers. God, he thought: if only we were live now...

Of course, if they were live, it would have been Jim and not Max, and he would have pressed the trigger the second the targeting system showed a lock, and the whole thing would have gone up in a brilliant phosphorous explosion. Then, before the fires had even dimmed, Jim would be off looking for the hatcheries and planting some shaped charges there, and moving off just far enough to escape the blast, but not so far he'd lose the shot. Jim would not feel a pang of regret about the deaths of the people in the studio sub, particularly Mimi, who might have been pregnant with his child. Jim would be so caught up in the moment that he probably wouldn't have realized it had happened. And Jim would certainly not pause to wonder at the significance of giant squids cooperatively cracking open a studio submarine and sharing the meal, what that meant about the way squids' brains worked, and just what kind of a hierarchy they'd managed to build for themselves down here in the aftermath of their unlikely population explosion.

And, thought Max as he heard the *click!* of chitinous squid-sucker boring against his armour and felt himself being drawn backward and up and then fast around, Jim would not have let a fourth squid get the jump on him from behind. Not as easily as Max just had.

The side of the mountain filled Max's view for only an instant before the impact came. It wasn't hard enough to rupture the suit, but it was surely enough to twitch his thumb. The ocean around him caught fire as the phosphorous harpoon tips burst and ignited in the deep-sea water.

SERIES FINALE:
I, MAX

The GET team found him in the evening, a coal-black knob at the edge of the *Minnow*'s spill. They were using hovercraft too small to haul the armour on board, so Max didn't actually see a doctor until one of the craft had hooked up a chain and hauled him back to the base at Sable Island and a team of GET engineers cut him out of the damaged suit.

Max was a mess. The hard-shell suit had protected him from nitrogen narcosis, but at some point Jerry's three-day regimen of spasmodics and steroids and liposuction had caught up with Max. When the med team cracked open the suit, they found him in full spasmodic flashback.

He'd already shattered his left elbow, cracked his collarbone, and nearly bit his tongue off. Apparently he'd been hallucinating as well.

Max's delicate condition led to a spirited but inconclusive debate among the command staff as to whether to press the same charges against Max as they planned to lay against Jerry Wylde, and ship them both back for trial immediately. Because there were far too many unanswered questions, and Max Fiddler might be persuaded to answer them if there was a chance that charges could be stayed.

Where, for instance, was enviroterrorist Mimi Coover? Was she alive or dead? Where were the files she'd stolen from GET when she took flight? And, of prime concern, why did Jerry Wylde, mid-broadcast, pull the stopcocks on the *Minnow*'s oil tanks and unleash the largest oil spill the planet had seen in three decades? All Wylde would say on the matter was the oil spill was the only way he could save his ship, but that didn't make sense; the threat of an oil spill was the only thing that had saved him from arrest for the better part of a decade. He'd done the equivalent of shooting all his hostages when he opened his tanks.

The only explanation they had to go on was the story that everyone in the world who wasn't battened down against Atlantica saw on their screens. And that, the staff agreed, was not an acceptable answer. Wylde's CGI squid-monster was more convincing than the one in the old Disney movie, but it was still pathetic: a desperate attempt to inject some life into a questionable property that should have been killed a long time ago. There was something else going on — and Jerry Wylde and what crew they'd managed to round up so far weren't saying what that thing was.

So they determined to wait for Max Fiddler to regain his senses and tell them what had really happened. Then, and only then, would they take him and Wylde outside, skip the trial, and shoot them both.

Waiting, as it turned out, carried its own risks.

Two days after they arrived, the sky over the GET base was a Jovian bruise, purples and golds and reds that swirled above them and mingled into a malevolent blackness in the east. The oil-dappled waters in the Sable Island shallows — where the complex's hadrosauric buildings perched on thick alloy legs — reflected the rare beauty of that sky like the mirror on a cokehead's coffee table.

No-one stopped to appreciate that beauty. The sky told them all what the satellite ring would confirm once they reached the command polyp, at the low-lying island's highest point. Atlantica was back on the move.

⇥•⌖•⌖•⇤

Max awoke to the roar of wind, the *crack!* of breaking glass, and a nail-tip pain in his elbow. Someone was tugging on his cast.

"Christ, Jim, get up. I can't do this by myself."

Max's eyes slurped open. "Ow," he said. "Jerry?"

"Fuckin' A, Jim-bo." Jerry pulled at Max's arm again. "I got a wheelchair here. Now come on, get up. The shit's hitting the fan here, and we gotta move."

Max winced and sat up. He blinked in the dim light of an infirmary room. Jerry was wearing orderlies' greens, and, sure enough, he was leaning against a gleaming chrome wheelchair. Max grimaced and swung his feet onto the floor, then swung his behind around and into the wheelchair. Jerry turned it around and pushed it out the door and into a darkened hallway. Behind them, there was another crack of breaking glass, then a howling, and Max felt an icy wind cross the back of his neck. Jerry hurried along the corridor.

"You saw something down there, didn't you?" said Jerry.

"Mimi's dead. So's the rest of the crew on the studio. They were eaten by squids. How do you like that?" Max took a deep breath as Jerry pushed him into a pair of swinging doors. Beyond was a waiting room, rimmed with high frosted windows and a thick metal door marked EXIT on the opposite side. There was a candy machine in one corner, the front of which had been smashed with the fire axe that now lay propped against it. Max and Jerry were the only people in the room.

"A lot of people are dead," said Jerry. "A lot of people are going to be eaten by squids. Squids won, we lost. Next!"

Max noticed water seeping under the exit door. The puddle grew as he watched, like a bloodstain.

"Atlantica," said Max. Last time they'd spoken, Jerry had mentioned the storm had moved to the Caribbean and was getting ready to take on the Eastern Seaboard. "It's here now?"

"Here," said Jerry, "there. Everywhere. But particularly here. The GET bastards evacuated this morning, before their harbour swamped."

"And they just left us here?"

"Just left us here."

Max thought about that. He leaned back in the wheelchair.

"Where's here?"

"Sable Island," said Jerry. "GET's got a base here."

"So they just left us here," said Max.

"The guard said I wasn't worth the bullet it'd take to shoot me," said Jerry. "Asshole. We gotta get out of here, Jim-bo. We're going down."

"You shouldn't have pulled the stopcocks on the *Minnow*," said Max.

Jerry shrugged. "What can I say? I freaked out. You didn't see all those squid — all grabbing at the hull, *scraping* it like fingernails on a blackboard. Like they knew I was the one. Like they were smart. And that big one... Jesus, he could have torn the *Minnow* up the middle, and he was getting ready to. I could tell, Jimmy, and I freaked, alright? Sue me." Jerry's eyes went wide. "I freaked."

"I see," said Max.

Jerry nodded, and smiled in a panicky way. "You would have handled it different, right, Jim-bo? Big survivor guy. You would have had a better plan. Shit, buddy, I wish I'd had you on the deck. I may know television — but you... You got an instinct for this stuff."

"I'm not Jim," said Max. "My name is Max Fiddler. I am an actor."

Jerry squinted at him. "We're not back to this, are we? Alright, Max, Jim, whatever you say. Tell me what you saw down there. See where those smart bastards lived? Anything we can use?"

Max looked around him. The entire floor was covered in water now and more was coming. He thought about the mountain and the giant squid — and the glimpses he'd had of the rest of it: the quivering walls of eggs that clung to the upper slopes of the sea mountain and the adult squids that circled them, guarding against the hungry smaller ones; the spectacle of a thousand squid, diving back to their homes in the trench, in sensible retreat from the spreading oil slick around the *Minnow*; and the behemoth, large beyond scale, that fell past him in the sun-dappled waters near the surface, trailing black strands of the same oil slick that would coat Max's own armour just a second later; its great black eye as large as Max, with a depth to it that, at first, Max mistook for intellect.

Maybe it was partly intellect he saw in the squid's eye, but he also recognized something more intimately familiar — and ultimately far more dangerous.

Max wheeled himself over to the exit door. He braced the wheels with his hands and opened the door with his foot.

"Is this a plan?" Jerry asked hopefully. "Because we could sure use a survival plan right now, Jim."

Rain hit him in a sheet. Max squinted through it, at the raging Atlantica outside. The ocean had indeed come up to the doorstep — if it were clearer outside, he would no doubt be able to see to a flat watery horizon, interrupted by nothing but the tops of a few buildings, and perhaps the semi-circle of a radar dish, poking above the waves.

Behind him, Jerry Wylde shouted something, but it could have been a dog barking at his heel; the roar and thunder of Atlantica was all.

AFTERWORD

They say it's not the length that counts, it's how good you are with what you've got — regardless, this time around, *Tesseracts* went for the long ones.

Seven long ones, to be exact — offering a variety of shapes, tastes, textures, colours, and thrills.

Long stories, too short to be called novels but lengthier than a *short* story... novellas. Now, there's some disagreement as to the exact length of a novella. Some people have invented subdivisions to further confuse matters: novelettes for the shorter novellas, short novels for the longer ones... whatever. At one point, it all becomes too jargony to matter.

Some novellas are long enough to be a book all on their own, so we went for the shorter end of the spectrum, in order to showcase a diversity of stories and writers, in keeping with the spirit of the *Tesseracts* anthologies. When we sent out the call for submissions, we asked for stories that fell between ten and twenty thousand words: short enough to be able to include a lively selection, but long enough to let writers really inhabit and explore the worlds of their creation... and long enough for readers to come along for the ride and be armchair travellers on these fantastic voyages.

Canadian, global, mythological... fantasy, fable, science fiction... humour, drama, adventure... superheroes, monsters, lovers... past, present, future. Seven worlds of entertainment and wonder; seven fantastic visions by authors with distinctive voices and startling imaginations.

We received close to two hundred submissions — and, among those, more than enough to fill at least three books with top-notch novellas of speculative fiction from Canadian writers.

These seven stories are the very best of the fiction that was sent to us — state-of-the-art 21st-century Canadian speculative fiction.

True to the *Tesseracts* tradition, the authors here strike a balance between established writers on the Canadian SF scene and new storytellers whose bold, striking voices are only starting to be heard; between veterans of the *Tesseracts* anthologies and authors appearing in this series for the first time.

Canadian writers have few venues for novellas, and readers of Canadian fiction few opportunities to enjoy them.

Who knows? Maybe the idea behind this *Tesseracts* volume will catch on, and we'll soon get to read more Canadian novellas of the fantastic.

Claude Lalumière
Montreal, March 2008

Biographies

Toronto writer **E.L. Chen**'s stories have appeared in publications such as *Tesseracts Nine*, *Strange Horizons*, and *On Spec*.

Claude Lalumière has edited seven previous anthologies, including *Open Space: New Canadian Fantastic Fiction* and *Island Dreams: Montreal Writers of the Fantastic*. His fiction has appeared in *Year's Best SF 12*, *Year's Best Fantasy 6*, two previous *Tesseracts* volumes, and many other publications. His work has been translated into French, Italian, Polish, Russian, and Spanish. He writes the Fantastic Fiction column for *The Montreal Gazette*.

Jill Snider Lum, a native Torontonian, is the author of the adult-literacy SF/fantasy reader *Maggie's Luck and Other Stories*. In 2007, her story "The Sweet Realm" appeared in the special Pirate issue of *Shimmer*.

Randy McCharles is a software developer and a fantasy and science fiction enthusiast from Calgary, Alberta. His fiction has previously been published in the *Robyn Herrington Memorial Short Story Contest* (1997, 1998, 1999, 2000, 2001, 2006), *Okal Rel Anthology II* (2007), and *Tesseracts Eleven* (2007). He is chairman of the 34th World Fantasy Convention (Calgary, autumn 2008).

Derryl Murphy's first book was his collection *Wasps at the Speed of Sound*, and in 2009 *Cast a Cold Eye*, co-written with William Shunn, will be released. "Ancients of the Earth" is the fourth in his Magic Canada series to see print, and hopefully enough will eventually be out and about to justify a whole book.

David Nickle's stories have been published in anthology series such as *The Year's Best Fantasy and Horror*, *Tesseracts*, *Northern Frights*, and *Queer Fear*, as well as in magazines such as *On Spec* and *Cemetery Dance*. His work has been adapted for television and audiobook. His novel *The Claus Effect* (with Karl Schroeder) is available from Edge Science Fiction and Fantasy Publishing. He has won the Bram Stoker Award (with Edo van Belkom) and the Aurora Award (with Karl Schroeder). He lives and works in Toronto.

Brett Alexander Savory is the Bram Stoker Award-winning editor-in-chief of *ChiZine: Treatments of Light and Shade in Words*. He has had nearly fifty short stories published and has written two novels, *The Distance Travelled* (2006) and *In and Down* (2007). His first short-story collection, *No Further Messages*, appeared in 2007. When he's not writing, reading, or editing, he plays drums for the hard-rock band Diablo Red. He lives in Toronto with his wife, writer/editor Sandra Kasturi.

Gord Sellar was born in Malawi, then emigrated to Canada with his family as a small child. He grew up in Nova Scotia and Saskatchewan and studied at the University of Saskatchewan and Concordia University in Montreal. He's been living as an expatriate in South Korea since 2002. Since attending Clarion West in 2006, his work has appeared in such venues as *Asimov's*, *Nature*'s Futures, Rudy Rucker's webzine *Flurb*, and *Fantasy Magazine*.

Grace Seybold has lived in Montreal since 2001. She graduated from McGill University in East Asian Studies. "Intersections" is her second piece of fiction to see print. She has written nonfiction for *The Montreal Gazette*, the *Westmount Examiner*, and *Polymancer Magazine*.

Michael Skeet is a two-time Aurora Award winner who is in his third decade of writing fantasy and science fiction. He lives in Toronto. His work has appeared in three previous *Tesseracts* anthologies, and he coedited *Tesseracts 4* with Lorna Toolis.

Our titles are available at major book stores and local independent resellers who support Science Fiction and Fantasy readers like you.

EDGE Science Fiction and Fantasy Publishing

Tesseract Books

Dragon Moon Press

www.edgewebsite.com
www.dragonmoonpress.com

Our titles are available at major book stores and local independent resellers who support Science Fiction and Fantasy readers like you.

Alien Deception by Tony Ruggiero -(tp) - ISBN: 978-1-896944-34-0
Alien Revelation by Tony Ruggiero (tp) - ISBN: 978-1-896944-34-8
Alphanauts by J. Brian Clarke (tp) - ISBN: 978-1-894063-14-2
Apparition Trail, The by Lisa Smedman (tp) - ISBN: 978-1-894063-22-7
As Fate Decrees by Denysé Bridger (tp) - ISBN: 978-1-894063-41-8

Black Chalice, The by Marie Jakober (hb) - ISBN: 978-1-894063-00-7
Blue Apes by Phyllis Gotlieb (pb) - ISBN: 978-1-895836-13-4
Blue Apes by Phyllis Gotlieb (hb) - ISBN: 978-1-895836-14-1

Case of the Pitcher's Pendant, The: A Billybub Baddings Mystery
    by Tee Morris (tp) - ISBN: 978-1-896944-77-7
Case of the Singing Sword, The: A Billybub Baddings Mystery
    by Tee Morris (tp) - ISBN: 978-1-896944-18-0
Chalice of Life, The by Anne Webb (tp) - ISBN: 978-1-896944-33-3
Chasing The Bard by Philippa Ballantine (tp) - ISBN: 978-1-896944-08-1
Children of Atwar, The by Heather Spears (pb) - ISBN: 978-0-88878-335-6
Clan of the Dung-Sniffers by Lee Danielle Hubbard (pb) - ISBN: 978-1-894063-05-0
Claus Effect, The by David Nickle & Karl Schroeder (pb) - ISBN: 978-1-895836-34-9
Claus Effect, The by David Nickle & Karl Schroeder (hb) - ISBN: 978-1-895836-35-6
Complete Guide to Writing Fantasy, The - Volume 1: Alchemy with Words
    - edited by Darin Park and Tom Dullemond (tp)
    - ISBN: 978-1-896944-09-8
Complete Guide to Writing Fantasy, The - Volume 2: Opus Magus
    - edited by Tee Morris and Valerie Griswold-Ford (tp)
    - ISBN: 978-1-896944-15-9
Complete Guide to Writing Fantasy, The - Volume 3: The Author's Grimoire
    - edited by Valerie Griswold-Ford & Lai Zhao (tp)
    - ISBN: 978-1-896944-38-8
Complete Guide to Writing Science Fiction, The - Volume 1: First Contact
    - edited by Dave A. Law & Darin Park (tp)
    - ISBN: 978-1-896944-39-5
Courtesan Prince, The by Lynda Williams (tp) - ISBN: 978-1-894063-28-9

Dark Earth Dreams by Candas Dorsey & Roger Deegan (comes with a CD)
    - ISBN: 978-1-895836-05-9
Darkling Band, The by Jason Henderson (tp) - ISBN: 978-1-896944-36-4
Darkness of the God by Amber Hayward (tp) - ISBN: 978-1-894063-44-9
Darwin's Paradox by Nina Munteanu (tp) - ISBN: 978-1-896944-68-5
Daughter of Dragons by Kathleen Nelson - (tp) - ISBN: 978-1-896944-00-5
Digital Magic by Philippa Ballantine (tp) - ISBN: 978-1-896944-88-3
Distant Signals by Andrew Weiner (tp) - ISBN: 978-0-88878-284-7
Dominion by J. Y. T. Kennedy (tp) - ISBN: 978-1-896944-28-9
Dragon Reborn, The by Kathleen H. Nelson - (tp) - ISBN: 978-1-896944-05-0
Dragon's Fire, Wizard's Flame by Michael R. Mennenga (tp)
    - ISBN: 978-1-896944-13-5
Dreams of an Unseen Planet by Teresa Plowright (tp) - ISBN: 978-0-88878-282-3

Dreams of the Sea by Élisabeth Vonarburg (tp) - ISBN: 978-1-895836-96-7
Dreams of the Sea by Élisabeth Vonarburg (hb) - ISBN: 978-1-895836-98-1

Eclipse by K. A. Bedford (tp) - ISBN: 978-1-894063-30-2
Elements of Fantasy: Magic edited by Dave A. Law
& Valerie Griswold-Ford (tp) - ISBN: 978-1-8964063-96-8
Even The Stones by Marie Jakober (tp) - ISBN: 978-1-894063-18-0

Fires of the Kindred by Robin Skelton (tp) - ISBN: 978-0-88878-271-7
Firestorm of Dragons edited by Michele Acker & Kirk Dougal (tp)
- ISBN: 978-1-896944-80-7
Forbidden Cargo by Rebecca Rowe (tp) - ISBN: 978-1-894063-16-6

Game of Perfection, A by Élisabeth Vonarburg (tp)
- ISBN: 978-1-894063-32-6
Gaslight Grimoire: Fantastic Tales of Sherlock Holmes
edited by Jeff Campbell & Charles Prepolec (pb)
- ISBN: 978-1-8964063-17-3
Green Music by Ursula Pflug (tp) - ISBN: 978-1-895836-75-2
Green Music by Ursula Pflug (hb) - ISBN: 978-1-895836-77-6
Gryphon Highlord, The by Connie Ward (tp) - ISBN: 978-1-896944-38-8

Healer, The by Amber Hayward (tp) - ISBN: 978-1-895836-89-9
Healer, The by Amber Hayward (hb) - ISBN: 978-1-895836-91-2
Hounds of Ash and other tales of Fool Wolf, The by Greg Keyes (pb)
- ISBN: 978-1-894063-09-8
Human Thing, The by Kathleen H. Nelson - (hb) - ISBN: 978-1-896944-03-6
Hydrogen Steel by K. A. Bedford (tp) - ISBN: 978-1-894063-20-3

i-ROBOT Poetry by Jason Christie (tp) - ISBN: 978-1-894063-24-1

Jackal Bird by Michael Barley (pb) - ISBN: 978-1-895836-07-3
Jackal Bird by Michael Barley (hb) - ISBN: 978-1-895836-11-0
JEMMA7729 by Phoebe Wray (tp) - ISBN: 978-1-894063-40-1

Keaen by Till Noever (tp) - ISBN: 978-1-894063-08-1
Keeper's Child by Leslie Davis (tp) - ISBN: 978-1-894063-01-2

Lachlei by M. H. Bonham (tp) - ISBN: 978-1-896944-69-2
Land/Space edited by Candas Jane Dorsey and Judy McCrosky (tp)
- ISBN: 978-1-895836-90-5
Land/Space edited by Candas Jane Dorsey and Judy McCrosky (hb)
- ISBN: 978-1-895836-92-9
Legacy of Morevi by Tee Morris (tp) - ISBN: 978-1-896944-29-6
Legends of the Serai by J.C. Hall - (tp) - ISBN: 978-1-896944-04-3
Longevity Thesis by Jennifer Rahn (tp) - ISBN: 978-1-896944-37-1
Lyskarion: The Song of the Wind by J.A. Cullum (tp)
- ISBN: 978-1-894063-02-9

Machine Sex and other stories by Candas Jane Dorsey (tp)
- ISBN: 978-0-88878-278-6
Maërlande Chronicles, The by Élisabeth Vonarburg (pb)
- ISBN: 978-0-88878-294-6

Madman's Dance by Jana G.Oliver (pb) - ISBN: 978-1-896944-84-5
Magister's Mask, The by Deby Fredericks (tp) - ISBN: 978-1-896944-16-6
Moonfall by Heather Spears (pb) - ISBN: 978-0-88878-306-6
Morevi: The Chronicles of Rafe and Askana by Lisa Lee & Tee Morris
  - (tp) - ISBN: 978-1-896944-07-4

Not Your Father's Horseman by Valorie Griswold-Ford (tp)
  - ISBN: 978-1-896944-27-2

Of Wind and Sand by Sylvie Bérard (translated by Sheryl Curtis) (pb)
  - ISBN: 978-1-894063-19-7
On Spec: The First Five Years edited by On Spec (pb)
  - ISBN: 978-1-895836-08-0
On Spec: The First Five Years edited by On Spec (hb)
  - ISBN: 978-1-895836-12-7
Operation: Immortal Servitude by Tony Ruggerio (tp)
  - ISBN: 978-1-896944-56-2
Operation: Save the Innocent by Tony Ruggerio (tp)
  - ISBN: 978-1-896944-60-9
Orbital Burn by K. A. Bedford (tp) - ISBN: 978-1-894063-10-4
Orbital Burn by K. A. Bedford (hb) - ISBN: 978-1-894063-12-8

Pallahaxi Tide by Michael Coney (pb) - ISBN: 978-0-88878-293-9
Passion Play by Sean Stewart (pb) - ISBN: 978-0-88878-314-1
Petrified World (Determine Your Destiny #1) by Piotr Brynczka (pb)
  - ISBN: 978-1-894063-11-1
Plague Saint by Rita Donovan, The (tp) - ISBN: 978-1-895836-28-8
Plague Saint by Rita Donovan, The (hb) - ISBN: 978-1-895836-29-5
Pretenders by Lynda Williams (pb) - ISBN: 978-1-894063-13-5

Reluctant Voyagers by Élisabeth Vonarburg (pb) - ISBN: 978-1-895836-09-7
Reluctant Voyagers by Élisabeth Vonarburg (hb) - ISBN: 978-1-895836-15-8
Resisting Adonis by Timothy J. Anderson (tp) - ISBN: 978-1-895836-84-4
Resisting Adonis by Timothy J. Anderson (hb) - ISBN: 978-1-895836-83-7
Righteous Anger by Lynda Williams (tp) - ISBN: 897-1-894063-38-8

Shadebinder's Oath by Jeanette Cottrell - (tp) - ISBN: 978-1-896944-31-9
Silent City, The by Élisabeth Vonarburg (tp) - ISBN: 978-1-894063-07-4
Slow Engines of Time, The by Élisabeth Vonarburg (tp) - ISBN: 978-1-895836-30-1
Slow Engines of Time, The by Élisabeth Vonarburg (hb) - ISBN: 978-1-895836-31-8
Small Magics by Erik Buchanan (tp) - ISBN: 978-1-896944-38-8
Sojourn by Jana Oliver - (pb) - ISBN: 978-1-896944-30-2
Sorcerers of War by Kristan Proudman (pb) - ISBN: 978-1-896944-64-7
Stealing Magic by Tanya Huff (tp) - ISBN: 978-1-894063-34-0
Strange Attractors by Tom Henighan (pb) - ISBN: 978-0-88878-312-7
Sword Masters by Selina Rosen (tp) - ISBN: 978-1-896944-65-4

Taming, The by Heather Spears (pb) - ISBN: 978-1-895836-23-3
Taming, The by Heather Spears (hb) - ISBN: 978-1-895836-24-0
Teacher's Guide to Dragon's Fire, Wizard's Flame by Unwin & Mennenga - (pb)
  - ISBN: 978-1-896944-19-7
Ten Monkeys, Ten Minutes by Peter Watts (tp) - ISBN: 978-1-895836-74-5
Ten Monkeys, Ten Minutes by Peter Watts (hb) - ISBN: 978-1-895836-76-9

Tesseracts 1 edited by Judith Merril (pb) - ISBN: 978-0-88878-279-3
Tesseracts 2 edited by Phyllis Gotlieb & Douglas Barbour (pb)
- ISBN: 978-0-88878-270-0
Tesseracts 3 edited by Candas Jane Dorsey & Gerry Truscott (pb)
- ISBN: 978-0-88878-290-8
Tesseracts 4 edited by Lorna Toolis & Michael Skeet (pb)
- ISBN: 978-0-88878-322-6
Tesseracts 5 edited by Robert Runté & Yves Maynard (pb)
- ISBN: 978-1-895836-25-7
Tesseracts 5 edited by Robert Runté & Yves Maynard (hb)
- ISBN: 978-1-895836-26-4
Tesseracts 6 edited by Robert J. Sawyer & Carolyn Clink (pb)
- ISBN: 978-1-895836-32-5
Tesseracts 6 edited by Robert J. Sawyer & Carolyn Clink (hb)
- ISBN: 978-1-895836-33-2
Tesseracts 7 edited by Paula Johanson & Jean-Louis Trudel (tp)
- ISBN: 978-1-895836-58-5
Tesseracts 7 edited by Paula Johanson & Jean-Louis Trudel (hb)
- ISBN: 978-1-895836-59-2
Tesseracts 8 edited by John Clute & Candas Jane Dorsey (tp)
- ISBN: 978-1-895836-61-5
Tesseracts 8 edited by John Clute & Candas Jane Dorsey (hb)
- ISBN: 978-1-895836-62-2
Tesseracts Nine edited by Nalo Hopkinson and Geoff Ryman (tp)
- ISBN: 978-1-894063-26-5
Tesseracts Ten edited by Robert Charles Wilson and Edo van Belkom (tp)
- ISBN: 978-1-894063-36-4
Tesseracts Eleven edited by Cory Doctorow and Holly Phillips (tp)
- ISBN: 978-1-894063-03-6
Tesseracts Twelve edited by Claude Lalumière (pb) - ISBN: 978-1-894063-15-9
Tesseracts Q edited by Élisabeth Vonarburg & Jane Brierley (pb)
- ISBN: 978-1-895836-21-9
Tesseracts Q edited by Élisabeth Vonarburg & Jane Brierley (hb)
- ISBN: 978-1-895836-22-6
Throne Price by Lynda Williams and Alison Sinclair (tp)
- ISBN: 978-1-894063-06-7
Time Machines Repaired Whie-U-Wait by K. A. Bedford (tp)
- ISBN: 978-1-894063-42-5
Too Many Princes by Deby Fredricks (tp) - ISBN: 978-1-896944-36-4
Twilight of the Fifth Sun by David Sakmyster (tp)
- ISBN: 978-1-896944-01-02

Virtual Evil by Jana Oliver (tp) - ISBN: 978-1-896944-76-0

Writers For Relief: An Anthology to Benefit the Bay Area Food Bank
edited by Davey Beauchamp (pb) - ISBN: 978-1-896944-92-0